PILLARS

Pat Cronin

PublishAmerica
Baltimore

First printing

ISBN: 1-4137-1395-5
PUBLISHED BY PUBLISHAMERICA, LLLP
www.publishamerica.com
Baltimore

Printed in the United States of America

Dedication

Je me souviens

October, 2005

Donna -

Congratulations on Waiting Wives!

I hope you enjoy Pillars -

Pat Cronin

Acknowledgements

Getting a book to publication is no easy task for a first time novelist. Thanks to Candi Donaldson, for formatting the manuscript to a presentable stage, and Sandra Curci, who found a diamond in the rough in author Charles Edward Blazek. Charles, thank you for putting me in touch with PublishAmerica.

Special thanks goes to my editor, Carol Givner. "Literature is, as Hemingway called Paris, a 'moveable feast'."

A representative from PublishAmerica mentioned that first time novels can inadvertently be up to 80% autobiographical by the author, whether intended or not. Rest assured, PILLARS is a work of fiction. Any similarity of events, or characters to persons living or dead is purely coincidental. The inspiration for PILLARS stemmed from the works of three authors recommended for future reading – Dr. Brian Weiss, "Only Love is Real", Sylvia Browne, "The Other Side & Back: A Psychic's Guide to Our World Beyond", and "Life on the Other Side: A Psychic's Tour of the Afterlife", along with the Neale Donald Walsch trilogy, "Conversations with God". The folks who put me onto these works have influenced my outlook forever. You know who you are. Thank you for the enlightenment.

To my wife and children, thank you for putting up with the days and nights of house echoes – "Dad's still writing in his chair."

Author photograph taken by John Gallagher.

BOOK I

"What did the Royal Cluster say?"
"What it always says."
"Did it mention your yellow hue?"
"It did. The hue will change to blue at enlightenment."
"So this past life did not teach the Lesson?"
"Perhaps. Upon reflection."
"What was it like?"
"Forgettable."
"Isn't it always?"

I

The orange bunting was too short.

The pleated cloth lay in a heap at the foot of the long folding table, abandoned next to its cellophane package with the label "8 Feet" printed upside down.

The slight woman responsible retreated from the draping material in the cavernous lobby and entered the confines of her office. She left the door slightly ajar.

"Maintenance?" she beckoned in shadow into a two-way radio.

"The requisition was for a twelve foot table bunting. Can you bring a replacement over when you deliver the course materials?"

The order ended as abruptly as it began with a precision stab to the hand held console. The woman turned and exited the cinderblock office. A ray of lobby light illumed the nouveau mauve paint covering the interior of the glorified coat closet. The color contrasted with the gray metal desk and chair, the only furniture in the room.

The door locked instantly, as soon as she kicked the foot stopper off the institutional carpet. It was a backward soccer style heel sweep, really, a move mastered by those dogged with the experience of habit and monotony. She tested its security and smiled at the efficiency of her domain known as Administration.

The appearance of a young girl with penny loafers standing at the table caught the woman off her usually unbreakable guard. They appraised each other for a brief moment.

The Administrator quickly adjusted her navy blue business suit, unusual wear for a Sunday afternoon, to assume a stern posture of crispness. She brushed her glossed nails across the clear plastic tag pinned to her right lapel, making sure the computer lettering accented graciously, "Hello, My name is Ruth Meyer".

The girl stood on the opposite side of the folding table. Clad in tan farmer's overalls, she struck the pose of most recent college graduates. Her shoulders sagged in front of apparent authority revealing the naivete of entering a business environment. Her frame was relaxed and supple, eons away from that aged hunch that burdened the corporate oppressed. A tight, sleeveless, rainbow-striped tee shirt cut low from her neckline. The overall bibs covered the area where cleavage would show. The Administrator quickly surmised from the tall slenderness that it would not be much.

The girl's cheekbones were set high on her face, accentuating a rich complexion deepened by her heritage and set in purpose more by way of birth than life experience. Long brown hair flowed straight off each of her shoulders. The angle of manmade light brought out the sparkle of green in her light brown eyes. She wore no makeup.

"May I help you?" Ruth asked.

"Is this where we register?" the girl responded meekly.

"I am sorry, my dear." Ruth checked the time on her watch and tapped her wrist as if it was to blame. "You are four hours early. Registration is not until six o'clock this evening."

The girl looked down at her fingers. She grasped their tips to hide the trembling anxiety that seemed to vibrate through her body.

"I was afraid you might say that. My flight came in early."

"I wish I could offer you some accommodation, but Maintenance will not have any supplies or room keys here for another couple of hours. I suppose you can make yourself comfortable here in the lobby until then."

The girl backed up a step. She peered around the gray concrete column towards the side door where she'd entered. Three matching black suitcases sat between the entry foyer doors. Two navy blue garment bags draped their top.

"Have a seat on the couches," Ruth said begrudgingly. "I can call someone to carry your things inside while you wait."

The girl cast a thin smile. She slowly turned to see three couches shaped horseshoe-style around an oak coffee table. It was a relief to finally get some offer of help. A five dollar tip at the airport to a Jamaican cab driver—or at least she thought he was Jamaican—was apparently not enough to comprehend the English phrase "Could you please help me with my bags?"

The girl chose to sit on the middle couch and loosened the leather cord string on her handbag that resembled a medieval type of satchel. She extracted the remaining cigarette from its box. Between the four-hour plane flight, chaos at the baggage terminal, and a language barrier with the taxi cab driver, it seemed ages since she'd last inhaled the sweet taste of nicotine.

Damn, my last one, she thought. A thin blue stream of smoke blew through her pursed lips. It formed a hanging cloud in the dark, sterile air.

"I am sorry, my dear," Ruth said, scrunching her face as if she'd bit a lemon. "There is no smoking allowed in the Brigadier Conference Center."

II

The Administrator disappeared down a hallway towards an exit labeled "South Entrance". She had not offered an option on where to extinguish cigarettes. There were no receptacles in the massive lobby area.

The girl stood. She started towards the familiar side entrance and saw a uniformed guard with a white arm patch marked "Security" carrying the garment bags to the couches.

"Excuse me," she said as they passed each other between the inner entry doors. He didn't stop. She continued through the outer glass doors and snuffed the cigarette out on the concrete sidewalk. The door clicked to a lock in the same manner as the Administration door had moments before.

She panicked and throttled the door handle back and forth. Within a second that lost it's meaning, the Security guard was at the door. He released the metal latch bar.

"Security here is tight, ma'am," the guard smiled, obviously amused by her fluster.

"I can tell. The taxi cab driver and I tried to get in through every entrance of this building when we first came in from the airport. Every door was locked. I was about to give up hope, when by chance we found this side entry open."

"Shouldn't have been open," the guard said, pausing to study the door before finishing the stowing of her luggage near the couches and then meandering towards the front end of the unlit lobby.

The girl sat alone on the unyielding cushions. The arms of the divan were framed with wood, evoking no invitation to rest one's head as a living room sofa. Refuge was meant to be temporary.

The odyssey of her day had been exhausting. She put her feet up on the coffee table and stretched her jet-lagged legs. From atop the lobby ceiling, television screens were mounted kitty-corner at each concrete support column.

"Do the TVs work," she asked once the guard reappeared.

"Those are not regular TVs," reported the guard. "They are internal electronic mail screens. You will see company information and chat-rooms of sorts on them during the workweek. They are used by all the Brigadier employees."

With the prospect of no television, she rose again from the couch. She strolled around her luggage like a drug-sniffing dog.

"Is there a place around here that sells cigarettes?"

"On the other side of Farmington Avenue." The guard pointed to the glass front entrance. "Carlos Market is on the corner next to the Laundromat."

"Will I be locked out if I go that way?"

"Oh the door will lock on you, ma'am, but I will keep an eye out to let you back in."

The afternoon air was no better than the temperature controlled sterility within the building. A city bus departed away from the Brigadier Conference Center. It spewed a puff of gray smelly exhaust towards the walkway.

The front area of the Center was manicured with blooming flowers and spotless curbs. The other side of Farmington Avenue bordering East Hartford resembled a ghetto war zone. Road debris of crushed coffee cups, cigarette butts and losing lottery tickets all seemed to instinctively know to blow away from the Conference Center side of the street.

She had to wait for a traffic light change in order to cross the busy street before entering an urban under-society that she never before had encountered. Two black men stood back from the curb. Their backs leaned against grates of rod-iron protecting the windows of Carlos Market. A grocery cart with a front wheel missing blocked the store's entrance. It was filled with bottles, cans and clothing – looking as if they were probably someone's worldly possessions.

She walked quickly past the two black men. They held no qualms openly gazing her up and down. Nodding with approval, they whispered something between them. Immediately they burst out laughing. The girl with penny loafers worked her way around the cart and into the store.

A dark-skinned man under a turban stood behind the service counter on the register floor, which was concocted two feet above the customer queue. A young black boy no more than fourteen was at the counter trying to buy a pack of cigarettes. Without legal identification, he was having no luck.

"Hey lady, buy me some butts?" It was more of a command than a request.

"Sorry, I don't think so," she replied—raising her eyebrows on the word "think" for effect.

"Ultra Light 100s please," she directed at the turban.

"Bitch!" the boy shouted and shoved his way out of the store.

The transaction was quick. She was back on the street corner in an instant.

The owner of the grocery cart had returned, and now stepped in front of her. The girl found herself staring at a homeless woman—looking to be in her forties, but probably a lot less. Wearing a heavy woolen winter coat and soiled kerchief atop her head, she made a point of showing off the gap between her front teeth.

"Honey, do you have five dollars for me?" the hag said with a gasp.

Five dollars, the girl with penny loafers thought, what happened to "brother-can-you-spare-a-dime?" The body odor emanating from the wool coat made her purse her nose and mouth. She tried to hurry past.

"Sorry!"

"My, what pretty buttons," the homeless woman noticed cutting into her path. She reached towards the brass colored hitches on the overall bibs. The girl expected the grubby fingers to fondle her buttons. Instead, the woman grabbed one of her breasts. With her thumb and forefinger, she gave it a hard twist.

The boy from inside the store had joined his two buddies against the rod-iron grate. All three witnessed the accost and howled with laughter—high-fiving each other. They jeered for more.

The girl jolted in shock. Feeling a strong hand grab the pant's strap on her shoulder, she was pulled backward off of her feet. She let out a scream.

"Come quickly this way ma'am."

It was the Security guard from the Brigadier Conference Center.

Ruth Meyer held the front glass door open as the guard escorted the girl with penny loafers across Farmington Avenue and back up the manicured walkway. The Administrator no longer looked like a stern governess. Rather, her face was ashen-white with fear.

"Come back in," Ruth Meyer fretted. "I think we can find a room for you right away."

The guard scurried down the corridor. He returned in less than a minute with a can of diet ginger ale. The girl sat and cried on the horseshoe-shaped couches while Ruth Meyer next to the coffee table rubbing the quivering hands. What had happened shocked and frightened the pair beyond what was real. Neither had bargained for the dregs of society to violate their haven.

"I am not supposed to do this, dear," Ruth consoled. She dug into her jacket pocket. "Here is the key for Room 810. It is the top floor of the Conference Center—the only suite where smoking is permitted. We use it only when one of our outside regional management execs is in town. In this case, I think we can make an exception."

With murmured gratitude, the girl rode the elevator car to the eighth floor with Ruth and the guard standing silently at each side. The Brigadier staff carried her luggage to the numbered suite. They departed only after she insisted she needed no help unpacking.

Alone, she walked weakly to the windows of the suite and viewed the panorama that was downtown Hartford, Connecticut. Directly across the street sat the gargantuan brick headquarters of the Brigadier Insurance Company.

Hartford, Connecticut – insurance capital of the world, and not a thing to eat, she thought. She lay down across the queen bed closest to the window. Fidgeting inside her handbag, she retrieved a foil pack of airplane pretzels. She chewed on a couple and managed to swallow. The sustenance gave her the wherewithal to drum up the courage to phone home to her Mom to let her know she arrived safely.

"Hello, Mom?" The greeting could not be masqueraded, and she immediately broke down again into tears. She cried for almost an hour into the phone receiver—telling her Mom she wanted to go home.

III

Sunday night registration for the Brigadier Insurance Home Sales School was scheduled from six o'clock pm until nine o'clock sharp. The pre-admission package mailed out to the twenty-six student candidates clearly instructed that the Conference Center would be locked for the evening after nine o'clock. Stragglers would have to find lodging elsewhere for the night if they were late.

Peter Collins from Worcester, Massachusetts ambled through the South underground parking lot entrance and into the lobby at precisely 8:55PM. No need to waste time lolling around if you do not have to.

"Hello my name is Ruth Meyer," Peter Collins recited from the plastic lapel card. "Do you always look so happy meeting somebody new?"

He watched as she looked down the crisply bunted orange tablecloth. One Welcome Package envelope remained. It personalized his belated arrival in calligraphy.

"The only thing keeping me from an early night's sleep is checking you in, Mr. Collins."

He smiled and apologized for pushing the time limit.

"Room 415?" He confirmed taking the key from her.

"The elevators are to your right, Mr. Collins. Good night."

Peter Collins entered his assigned suite. Immediately he was impressed with the quality of accommodations. He opened the wall-length curtains to garner a view of the city. The brick wall of the neighboring building stared blankly across a narrow alley.

"Well 'Hello my name is Ruth Meyer'," Peter Collins laughed. "I guess the early bird gets the worm around this place, huh?"

IV

Corporate activity was in full operational gear when Peter Collins arrived back to the lobby at promptly seven o'clock the following morning. In accordance with the admissions instructions, he wore the obligatory conservative suit with white dress shirt and tie—the perfunctory dress code during business hours at the Brigadier Conference Center.

Across from the elevators hung a large orange wall banner emblazoned with the black Brigadier corporate logo. Beneath it, a computer printed-paper banner read, "Welcome—Spring Semester—Home Sales School".

A string of orange clothed buffet tables lined the banner walls. Coffee, tea and juices with all the complements sat at one station. Cut fruits, bagels and fixings accompanied the second station.

A small group of student candidates milled around the buffet—some strolling in and out of the classroom amphitheater entranced between the two tables. Besides the cursory nod or short hello, there was not much conversation going on at such an early hour.

Peter passed on visiting the breakfast tables. He greeted Ruth Meyer as he crossed the amphitheater threshold.

"Welcome, Mr. Collins," Ruth smiled. "Did you find yourself a good night's sleep?"

"Actually Ruth, I could not help but stay up until the wee hours of the morning," Peter responded. "The view outside Room 415 is so magnificent. I cannot wait until I tell my colleagues at my agency back home how accommodating the Brig has been to me."

Her face furrowed as if she had eaten a lemon. She realized Peter Collins was aware of company protocol as it applied to satisfying the whims of its strongest national agents.

"There is a claims management group departing the center today," Ruth backpedaled. She touched Peter's elbow in assurance. "If you drop by my office after today's program, I am sure we may be able to facilitate an upgrade."

The Brigadier Conference Center amphitheater was a state-of-the-art technological marvel. Four rows of spacious tiers accommodated movie theater style chairs with individual writing tables and matching rear credenzas for material storage. The lecture area at the floor level of the oval room contained a wall-to-wall whiteboard. Flip chart easels were spaced at each corner. A myriad of wall switches controlled projection screens housed in ceiling tubes, a variety of spot and track lighting, along with room air and temperature controls. The floor was jacked with outlets for microphone sound systems, standard electrical outlets and personal computer networking. Large sound control panels were suspended in the rear of the room at odd angles to maximize acoustical efficiency.

"Your place is there to the right, Mr. Collins," Ruth pointed. She turned away to greet another candidate.

At the second seat along the right aisle of row two rested an official looking placard with the computer-printed name "Peter Collins". In smaller block letters beneath the name "Worcester, Massachusetts".

He entered the seating area he would call home for the next four weeks. Atop the movie seat was a large plastic briefcase box with a large "Brigadier" molded into its front side. Peter opened the box. A plastic card reading "Hello, my name is Peter Collins – Worcester, Massachusetts" laid on a series of labeled workbook manuals and other papers.

No wonder no one is talking to each other in the lobby, Peter thought. They do not have their name tags yet.

Student candidates filled the amphitheater in a steady stream. Many gave lost looks—staring at the name placards as they strode across the lecture area. An awakening sense of consciousness surfaced when they spotted their name. There would be a subtle quickening of pace to the assigned spot. Everyone had complied with the required conservative business dress code.

Peter leaned forward across his desk to read the placard on the seat to his right. The aisle seats to his left had no placards. Peter assumed he would have only one neighbor.

The placards were angled in such a way that they were difficult to read directly from any of the desk seats. They were definitely set for the benefit of the lecturers at the front of the room.

"James Stankos—Oxford, Massachusetts", the right placard stated.

Great, Peter thought, I got someone from Mass. Stankos showed up within the minute.

"Oxford, Mass," Collins greeted. Stankos returned the firm handshake.

"You do not happen to know the Coughlin family do you? I was roommates with Mark Coughlin in college."

"Mark Coughlin? I sure do," Stankos smiled. "I was the quarterback Mark's junior year at Oxford High."

Collins knew immediately that he and Jim would hit it off. Funny though, Peter thought. It seems so many washed up jocks assimilate to the insurance industry. The art of closing an insurance deal is in many cases nothing more than winning a game—the thrill of victory and the will to overcome the agony of defeat.

Jim revealed that he worked at the Barton Insurance Agency. It happened to be owned by his brother-in-law. Collins smiled. The Barton Agency was well known in the Worcester area. The owner of Barton was an ex-fullback at Holy Cross College.

"I don't know," Stankos confessed. "I was pretty up in the air on what I was going to do when I got out of college. I married Gill's sister and he offered me a respectable job where you get to wear a shirt and a tie. I have been there ever since."

Peter and Jim both learned they each had a lot in common. They were within months of turning thirty-five years old. They had been married to local sweethearts for over a decade. Each had two children—all boys.

They also shared one additional trait. They were two of the oldest student candidates in the Home Sales School program. Aside from a couple pairs of gray sideburns in row four, the rest of the group looked like they could be no more than a few years over the legal drinking age.

Peter gazed over Jim's talking head. He spotted a pair of cordovan penny loafers resting under the writing table on the other side of the room in row three. Sleek white tights rose from the loafers. The legs were blocked at mid-shin by the facing of the writing table. Collins followed the outline of the desk to the long brown hair. A face soaked with tears was resting in the girl's hands. Peter bobbed his chin to gain Stankos' attention.

"Did you see that girl over there," Peter said under his breath. "She looks like the daughter of a Cherokee chief."

Jim turned over his left shoulder for all of two seconds. He turned right back.

"Oh yeah," Stankos acknowledged. "I saw her."

"Why do you think she is crying?" Peter tried to avoid staring.

"One of the guys out front told me," Stankos illumined. "She is from somewhere out in the Midwest. First time away from home. I guess she has this boyfriend who she is homesick for in a big way."

V

“Ladies and gentlemen—let us get started, shall we,” the voice heralded from the lectern. “As you know, my name is Ruth Meyer. I can truly say I have enjoyed meeting each and every one of you since you have arrived here to the Brigadier Conference Center. Welcome to Hartford, Connecticut—the insurance capital of the world.”

Ruth paced the lecture area without the need of a microphone. She carried the posture and polish of a fine finishing school, and she knew it.

“You—ladies and gentlemen, have been carefully selected by Brigadier’s strongest agents countrywide to attend the most prestigious of all schools specializing in property and casualty insurance—the Brigadier Insurance Home Sales School. In a cooperative effort to develop the best of the best of professionals committed to our industry, both Brigadier Insurance and your agency have invested its time, energies and dollars to acquaint you to this intensive course of study. When you leave here in four weeks and return to your agencies, we are confident that you will be poised to be a leader in the field of commercial insurance. You will become a productive asset not only to your agency, but to our Brigadier Insurance products. Not only that—we guarantee you will make a lot of money.”

A unified laugh emerged from the tiered oval accompanied by a smattering of hands clapping. “Yeah!” a solo shout erupted.

“Before I introduce our distinguished faculty, let me first go over some of the important aspects of the Home Sales School program. First, thank you all for adhering to our dress code. It is important to convey to the over three thousand Brigadier headquarters’ employees the professionalism and commitment of our agents. The air temperature here in the Conference Center is regulated at all times. You will not feel the need to remove your suit jackets in the lobby or classroom areas.”

“Second,” Ruth continued. “Please remember that cigarette smoking is not permitted in the Conference Center building. If you must seek the relief of a cigarette, we ask that you smoke outside of the building.”

Peter detected a slight glance from Meyer once finished her statement.

Does she know that I am a smoker, he thought. His suspicion quickly evaporated when Ruth's eye darted to the left side of the room. Collins tried to zero in on the target of the second glance. Who was she looking at?

"By pressing the elevator buttons marked "B", you can access our cash-only cafeteria," Meyer continued within a heartbeat. "Breakfast is served prior to your seven o'clock start—beginning each morning at 5:30AM. You will share the benefit of dining each lunch hour in the company of many of our Brigadier employees. I do hope you will take the opportunity to meet and mingle. Dinner at night will be on your own time. Your portfolio boxes contain a list of area restaurants and diners we recommend. Many are within walking distance for you folks from out-of-state who do not have automobiles."

A number of student candidates opened their plastic boxes. Only about half had discovered the "Hello, my name is" cellophane cards.

"Now please, no need to examine your portfolio boxes right now," Meyer reacted to the ad hoc pinning of name cards to right lapels. "Believe me, you will have a full knowledge of those contents within a very short period of time."

Flustered—a number of candidates discreetly nudged their boxes under the writing tables. Peter gawked at the behavior of some of his peers. Christ, he observed, some of these turkeys were actually taking notes on this stuff.

"There are a host of safety issues that are a concern for everyone here at the Aetna Conference Center," Ruth deadpanned. "We may be in the insurance capital of the world, but we are also located in the part of the city known as East Hartford. East Hartford, ladies and gentlemen, happens to be a very economical and socially depressed area. Unfortunately, we have a very high crime rate here. We insist that you never travel on foot beyond the routes recommended in your portfolio guide. Never travel alone and always make an effort to be part of a group. Our security measures are extremely tight throughout the Brigadier campus, but from time to time, incidents do happen."

Meyer's eye again darted to the left side of the amphitheater. God damn it, Peter scolded as he failed a second time to find her target. Who is she looking at?

"Prior to today's ten o'clock break, we will be convening in the garden area of the lobby for our special class photograph," Ruth concluded. "As many of you know depending upon your agency, the class photograph is a special tradition at the Brigadier Home Sales School. Our previous graduating classes are all prominently displayed in the Hall of Honor outside the lobby area. Your photo will be featured in the Brigadier Agent newsletter published monthly to all fifteen thousand Brigadier agent offices throughout the United States. In addition, you will each receive a complementary copy to hang in your offices for when you return home. I ask that you remember to remove your plastic name cards from your lapel and leave them here in the amphitheater before we break. We try to attain the utmost of professionalism in every class photograph."

Some of the candidates, including the ones taking notes, began removing their cards. What dolts, Peter thought.

Ruth proceeded to introduce the most anxious of faculty professionals seated patiently in the orange chairs behind her. Tracey Benison was the Head of the Brigadier Conference Center and, no doubt, Meyer's boss. She was about twenty-three years old. Three times within a half minute span, Ruth mentioned to the class that Tracey Benison was a graduate of Yale University. At each instance, Benison would cut a compromising smirk. A doting nod was granted to the handful of "oohs" and "aahs" embellishing the pedigree.

VI

Break time could not come soon enough. Those candidates adroit enough to hit the continental breakfast early were darting to the restrooms. The later risers scurried to their first injection of caffeine and sustenance.

The group soon assembled in the garden area of the Conference Center lobby for the class photograph. The garden area scaled three stories in height. A large deciduous tree prospered within the middle glass solarium.

Ruth had taken position at the top of the second story mezzanine that encircled the garden. A professional photographer stood at the ready on Meyer's right side. His telescopic lens sat expertly on a large aluminum tripod.

"Shorter folks to the front please," Meyer called down. "Our taller candidates to the rear. Let us form three equal lines, ladies and gentlemen."

The group sized each other with short glances. Three columns of relative proportion slowly developed.

Standing a mere five foot eight, Peter did not need a prod to realize he was a front row candidate. He assembled in the middle of the front row next to a fellow of equal stature—or lack thereof. The professional photographer spied through the camera lens at the initial set up.

"You—right there—yes, you," the photographer startled the assemblage with his pointed commands. "Please move to the other side of that person next to you. Yes—that is it—good. And you, sir, in the back left...."

There were roughly half a dozen positional changes. Ruth and the photographer affirmed they had the group just right.

"Okay everyone," the photographer exclaimed. "Smile and look at me—the count of three."

Twenty-six student candidates and the Brigadier faculty present mugged for the camera. Ruth Meyer had a difficult time maintaining her daintiness running down the steps. The photographer jumped back from the tripod just as she assumed her trademark left flank position.

"Hold it!"

The candidates appeared startled at the photographer's panic. They looked side to side at one another. The photographer descended the wrap around steps at a hurried pace to the garden floor. He abruptly stopped next to the person standing sixth from the right in the back row. The photographer was totally captivated by her looks.

"You—you need to be our centerpiece," the photographer exulted. "I want you to move up to the front row."

"But I am five foot nine," the centerpiece responded.

"My dear, you are wearing flats," the photographer noticed the cordovan penny loafers. He chuckled. "Believe me, you are perfect for our centerpiece."

The girl with the penny loafers followed the photographer to the front of the candidate group. He positioned her in between Peter Collins and the guy of somewhat equal stature—or lack thereof.

Peter felt a twinge of squeamishness. He chalked it up to another stroke of good fortune.

The photographer resumed his position at the tripod. Ruth made a cursory review of the change.

"Okay people, let us try this again," the photographer glistened with a triumphant sense of accomplishment. "On the count of three."

The candidates grinned to the mezzanine concourse.

"Wait!"

The shout this time was from Ruth Meyer.

"My dear," she directed to the girl next to him. Ruth was hesitant to touch. "Did you forget? I asked that you remove your name cards from your lapels."

The girl who looked like the daughter of a Cherokee chief sheepishly reached for the inner pinning. Peter seized the chance to sneak a peek at the computer-printed tag.

"Hello, my name is Lynn Cloud—Duluth, Minnesota. My name is Peter Collins."

VII

The candidate group dispersed in varied directions at the close of the picture session. Many went to the elevators—perhaps to seek greater privacy than the relief provided by the lobby restrooms. Others went to call on the telephone to either their home or office.

Lynn Cloud disappeared within the elevator herd. Peter wanted to say something beyond his "you-used-it-once-too-often" name card line, but the time had passed. He had not had a cigarette since arriving in Hartford the night before. His body craved that first hit of morning nicotine. He headed out the side entrance. The flick of his lighter harmonized with the click of the lock.

As 10:15 approached the dial, Peter returned to the door to discover his travail. He knocked on the glass and peered through cupped hands for help within. The amphitheater door was closed. The late morning session had started.

"Shoot!" Peter shouted. He rapped on the glass a second time.

Lynn exited the elevator and proceeded across the lobby. The incessant banging caused her to stop. Peter waved. He hoped she would recognize her picture partner.

"What forever are you doing out there," Lynn asked as she pushed on the horizontal metal latch bar.

"Sneaking out for a butt," Peter lamented. He stepped inside the building. "Christ, I think I am the only one at the Brigadier Home Sales School burdened with the vice of cigarette smoking."

For the first time in over twenty-four hours, Lynn Cloud laughed.

"No, you are not the only one."

Peter paused. For a brief instant he looked directly into the light brown eyes with a green sparkle. The twinge of squeamishness returned to his belly.

" I smoke too, that is where I came from," Lynn revealed. She sensed the same connection when she looked at Peter. There was something deep inside his blue eyes, but she ignored it. Must be just one more harangue this trip is playing with my mind, she surmised.

"But where," Peter asked. He hoped she did not perceive the hesitancy before he spoke. "You did not light up inside the Conference Center, did you?"

"I have a smoking-allowed suite."

"A smoking-allowed suite," Peter furrowed his eyebrows. The gesture prompted Lynn to look closer into the blue eyes. "But Ruth Meyer said...."

"She arranged it for me," Lynn interrupted.

"Ruth Meyer?"

"I will tell you about it later," Lynn giggled. Something inside told her to stop staring. She motioned that they should join the class. "God, you make me laugh."

VIII

Tracey Benison opened the late morning session with her spin on the program overview.

"Ruth is always kind enough to leave the extracurricular events to me," Tracey grinned. "This stuff you will not find in your portfolio boxes."

Peter and Lynn entered on opposite ends of the amphitheater. No one seemed to pay any attention to the coincidental tardiness. Peter caught himself looking over to the third row of the oval's left side as he sat.

"If you have not heard by now, the stomping ground for business after-hours at the Brig is Teapots," Benison gleamed. "I will play tour guide for you tonight after dinner. You can all make your acquaintance to the local watering hole. Before we go, gentlemen, I have one word of advice. Do not wear your necktie into Teapots. When you go in, look up at the ceiling. There are hundreds of neckties tacked to it. The bartenders are instructed to snip off the tie from anyone silly enough not to realize it is R&R."

A few chuckles came from the oval. Candidates from large agencies with Home Sales School alumni nodded to their neighbor with an "I told you so" grin.

Peter attempted to discretely pan his view to the left side of row three. He was overwhelmed with the fear of Lynn catching his peek. He gave his head a double shake. What is that magnetism, he thought.

"Many of you come from agency offices with a proud tradition of Home Sales School recognition awards," Tracey continued. "Yes, when you complete our program in four weeks, you will all receive diplomas at our commencement dinner at the Cromwell Country Club. When you return home, I am sure you will notice how proudly our alumni display their diplomas in their offices. I must say, Brig underwriters and representatives are particularly impressed when they see the Home Sales School diploma in an agent's office. Many have a blue ribbon sealed to the bottom corner of the diploma. A select few may even have a red ribbon. It does not happen often, but from time to time you may even stumble upon that graduate with both the blue ribbon and the red ribbon embossed on that same diploma."

"Now I know how competitive 'bringing home a ribbon' means to some of your agencies," Tracey gestured her fingers as quotation marks for effect. "Some of you from the national brokerage houses have special compensation bonuses tied to the ribbons."

A couple of heads nodded acknowledgement. One fell down to the desk.

"The blue ribbon is for academic excellence," Tracey informed. "It is measured off of one criteria—scoring ninety percent or above on your final examination. It is not unusual that someone can miss the blue ribbon by as little as a point or even a half point. Keep this in mind when you receive your graduation packet at Cromwell. Your final exam test results will be included to show how you scored in each test section."

"The red ribbon is the championship award—the one everyone comes to the Brigadier Home Sales School to win," Benison glowed. "It goes to the one team who wins our sales contest. In week two, you will be arbitrarily broken up into five teams of five students. Each team will represent a separate insurance agency. During weeks two and three, a series of meetings will be scheduled with a panel of Brigadier executives. They will be posing as one client seeking insurance for this very facility—the Brigadier Conference Center. Every interview will be conducted here in the amphitheater in full view of the other competing teams. The buying panel has been carefully scripted with an outline of special needs they are looking for from an insurance agent. Your challenge will be to uncover those needs. In week four, your team will present an insurance proposal to best address those uncovered needs. For those of you with alumni in your home office, you should know now that the panel script changes with each Home Sales School. No two scripts are ever alike. Ultimately, there will be one special unique need that if properly discovered and addressed will win the red ribbon."

"Only five of you in this class will bring that red ribbon home," Tracey paced the floor. "The key to this challenge is teamwork. With arbitrary picking of the teams, you will need to quickly identify the strengths each person in your group brings to the table. It is just like your agency back home. The players were already on the field the first day you arrived at work. Learn to take maximum advantage of those players around you."

"You will recall in your pre-admission package you were asked to bring a supply of business cards with you to distribute to each of your classmates. This is a fun way to kick off our introductions. The exercise is simple. Each of you will have three minutes to distribute your cards to everyone. At the same time, telling us a little bit about you. Three minutes may be an eternity for some. It will not be enough for others. This exercise is intended to be fun. Talk about anything you like—your personal background, what you do at your agency, your family, your hobbies."

Tracey moved to the far-left side of the amphitheater. Heads in the oval followed her movement like fans at a tennis match. Peter conveniently peered back once again to row three.

"Why don't we start with you, Chris," Benison motioned to the first person in row one. She waved her hand like an orchestra conductor. "We can proceed up and down each row from left to right."

"Well awright!" the light gray suit responded. The oval smiled at the start-up exuberance of the first candidate selected. Chris jumped up from his movie chair. He pulled the rubber band wrapped business cards from his right jacket pocket. "My name is Chris Tripoli. I hail from the Huntley Wright Insurance Agency in New Orleans, Louisiana."

Tripoli darted left to right across the front row. He adeptly handed a card to each recipient with his left hand. At the same time, shaking hands with his right.

"Hi, my name is Chris Tripoli," he repeated in front of each desk.. He looked hard into the eyes of the person. Each student responded by identifying his or her own name. Chris would end each greeting with a different wrap-up.

"Certainly privileged to make your acquaintance," he said to one.

"If you ever get down to New Orleans, be sure to look me up," to another.

"It is God's country in New Orleans," to a third.

He finished his sequence in precisely three minutes. A tall black suit rose behind him as soon as he resumed his seat. Bespectacled, the black suit stepped down to the lecture area. He called for Ruth Meyer to assist in handing out his business cards for him. Meyer's sudden movement in the room forced the roost of Peter's head perched towards row three.

"Good morning, my name is Ken First of Levigne and First Agency of Syracuse, New York. It may appear somewhat trite to have someone pass out promotional material for me. There is a reason for that," the black suit raised his finger. "For three generations of family ownership at Levigne and First, our motto is that insurance is a people business. Business cards do not sell insurance. People do."

Peter and Jim smiled to each other. Less than five minutes into the introductions, and already different personality styles were emerging. Peter looked back over Stankos' shoulder to Lynn Cloud. Any green sparkle in her eyes seemed to be gone. The golden brown eyes were focused on the speaker. She was smiling. More secure in the setting.

Ken First returned to his chair in a little less than the permitted three minutes.

"Um, my name is Brad Heller from the Island Insurance Agency of Belmont, California," the heavyset balding gray templed suit clumsily rose beside Lynn in row three. He gestured with his hands close to his pockets. "I did not realize I had to bring business cards with me. Sorry."

"That is okay," Tracey reacted to the introversion. "We can hand write one for you on an index card after class and photocopy it for the class. Please—go on."

Heller swallowed. He told the group about his up and down career in a variety of service-oriented businesses. He was forty-five years old and admitted that he was "catching up" in the business world for lack of a college education.

"I just finished up a Dale Carnegie sales course my boss made me take," Heller miscued. Standing for less than a minute and a half made involuntarily sway on his feet. He stretched to find a close to his presentation. "Hopefully this Home Sales School will help me too."

Tracey nodded her approval at Brad Heller's effort. She ignored the "that guy is on his last leg" and "I hope he is not on my team" glances from the consensus of the oval.

The introductions continued. Peter figured it would be close to an hour before it would be his turn. He absently listened to the blend of rising suits—taking partial note of who exhibited the strongest communication skills and confidence. He mentally calculated how long it would take for one certain person from Duluth, Minnesota to speak.

Lynn rose from her movie chair. She did not wander from her desk. Rather, she stood at attention. Her business cards were centered on her desk. She picked them up and quickly glanced to her left and right. Two suits from row four immediately jumped from their seats and stepped down the far-left aisle to offer assistance in passing out the cards. Most of the oval's attention shifted to watch the suits intermingle between rows. Peter stayed his focus on the tall brunette.

She wore a red and orange plaid skirt with a large yellow safety pin clasping on the front. The skirt had not been visible when Peter first noticed the penny loafers beneath the desk. It confirmed the presence of long, thin shapely legs. A blue suit jacket covered a wooly blouse that had a wide turtleneck.

Her head was slender with a sharp cut nose that may have been somewhat too large for the face.

Peter was most captivated by her brown eyes. They reminded him of the reindeer eyes in those children's animated television specials during Christmas.

Besides a small gold chain over the top of the turtleneck, the only other jewelry Lynn wore was a couple of rings on her fingers. Each ring was colored. Peter apprised that she indeed was not married.

He did not hear much of what she had to say. He was too focused on the presence before him.

"Hi, my name is Lynn Cloud from Duluth, Minnesota," he picked up from the sheepish grin at the outset. He heard her say she was twenty-one years old and that she had been with the Boylston Agency, "her first real job", for almost two years. Her area of expertise was personal lines insurance—automobiles and homeowners.

"I have avoided getting into commercial insurance," Peter picked up on Lynn's closing words. "It seems too cut-throat and competitive, but my boss was urged by Brigadier to send someone to the school. So here I am.

Peter smiled and leaned back in his chair as Lynn sat down. He was surprised how candid someone could be in such a forum. No one else in the group that may have had reservations about the program had been honest enough to say they were reluctant to be there. Instead, the introductions following Lynn's seemed to be a hodgepodge tooting of invisible horns. It was a good half an hour before Jim Stankos stood up.

"Hi, I am Jim Stankos from the Barton Insurance Agency in Oxford, Mass."

Jim spoke about the hometown Americana he relished in Oxford. His brief four- year stint at his brother-in-law's insurance agency was described more as a salve to be able to earn a living in a small New England town. The alternative he acknowledged would be to join the other worker bees that commute the highways each morning to Worcester or Boston in order to afford living in suburbia. The commitment to be close to his family created a backdrop for Jim to describe his objectives in the insurance business. The direction caught Peter totally off guard.

"The Barton Agency is a really small one," Stankos seemed happy to say. "Not like the one Peter Collins works at." As he gestured towards Collins, the eyes in the oval focused on Peter. "My goal in life is to be with my wife and two boys. I have a nice book of business clients that keep me going—and that is just fine with me."

"Everyone in our part of Massachusetts knows about the success of business people like Peter Collins," Stankos continued. "He may be the one selling the million dollar deals in our region, but that arena is not for me. I hope to learn a lot and become friendly with all of you. In the end though, you can be sure my goal will not be in the lion pit with the heavy hitters like Peter Collins."

Jim returned to his movie chair. His smile seemed to certify the fortitude to his life goals. He slapped Peter on the back. Peter was flattered by the unexpected attention. He absorbed the "who is that guy" look from the student candidates in the oval. "Million Dollar Man" was overheard amongst the whispers. Folks were noticeably counting with their fingers the number of speakers remaining before the turn would come to Peter Collins.

When Peter did stand up, he casually handed a small set of business cards to his neighbors in the tiers above and below. He kindly asked if they could pass them down each row. He did not travel to the lecture floor to speak. There were too many bells and whistles on the lecture floor. Peter surmised that the technological gizmos drew away the attention of an audience. So he backed up a few steps. He centered himself in the right aisle stairway of row two. The angle was such that it would take an effort for a disinterested eye to wander.

The class interest resurrected after the soliloquies of bland suits that followed Jim Stankos. The wonder was there. Who is this guy that a competitor would refer as a Million-Dollar Man?

"Good morning everyone," Peter smiled. "I must admit Peter Collins has been referred to by a lot of names over the years, but it is the first time he can recall hearing 'Million Dollar Man'. Despite a reputation that may precede me let me take a moment to give you a little of my background. I live and work in the same city where I was raised—Worcester, Massachusetts. I graduated from college some years ago and got my MBA at night."

The mention of an MBA created Peter's desired effect. A number of heads nodded in the oval. Most had not reached the age to have an MBA. The ones that were seemed to show no ambition.

"For the first thirteen years of my business career, I was a banker," Peter relayed. "I started out dialing for dollars collecting delinquent car loans. I rose to the position of Vice President at the bank's regional office in Worcester. My specialty is large corporate accounts—concentrating on leveraged buyouts. Perhaps this is where my friend Jim here has come to know me as the Million-Dollar Man. One of the controlling directors of the bank happens to own the insurance agency I started at three months ago. I guess you could say Peter Collins was given the proverbial 'offer you cannot refuse'. My business plan is to seek out the same opportunities in insurance that I had in banking. Instead of closing loans, hopefully it will be Brigadier Insurance products."

A high foreheaded dark gray pinstriped suit seated in the row in front of Peter was the last speaker of the exercise. He rose with abruptness and faced his audience from the front of his writing table.

"Good afternoon everyone," the suit said coyly. "The face on the clock indicates it is now afternoon. From the look on some of you, the fact that we are beyond our lunch break is quite disconcerting. Let me first start off by congratulating Mr. Tripoli and Mr. Collins. My colleagues at Miles and Mason's Providence, Rhode Island office have told me you win the sales contest by first assessing your competition with exercise number one. Who in the room can succinctly present their introduction in precisely three minutes flat? I took the liberty of timing each of you during your remarks. Mr. Tripoli and Mr. Collins—perhaps in spite of yourselves, you were the only two here who hit three minutes on the dot."

Tracey and Ruth flinched at the front of the lectern. Aside from the breach of their secret measuring tool, the brashness was no way to warm the crowd.

"My name, ladies and gentlemen, is Craig Hinson. I have brokered insurance at M&M for the past four years. Yes, everything you have heard about M&M is probably accurate. We are the largest brokerage firm in the United States for one reason and one reason only. We demand excellence in all our client endeavors. My office in Providence holds the record for graduating three consecutive double ribbon winners at each of the last Home Sales Schools. It would have been four in a row, but the last guy only came back with the blue. That promptly shifted him out to our satellite office in Knoxville, Tennessee."

Hinson laughed at his own inside joke. A couple of heads turned to a blue suit frowning in row four. Didn't that fellow a few speakers earlier say that he was from Knoxville?

"M&M pays handsomely for the Brigadier ribbons," Hinson composed himself. "I will receive a ten thousand dollar bonus for each ribbon I bring home—doubled for both. For those of you fortunate enough to be assigned to my team—let me say in advance, 'you are welcome'."

"And Mr. Collins," Hinson turned to face Peter directly. "Million dollar deals may be something big in—where did you say you were from?

'Wooster'?"

Both Peter and Jim conveyed poker faces. People from Providence loved to mispronounce Worcester.

"Let me just shake your hand in advance and say 'bring it on'."

All eyes captured the clock tick to exactly the one hundred and eightieth second when Craig Hinson sat down.

IX

Opening lunch was not scheduled in the cafeteria. Instead, the class was hosted to Brigadier's senior management executive dining room on the top floor of the Conference Center.

Six round tables were set to seat five. It allowed student groups of four to have an interactive opportunity to meet one of the top brass of the nation's predominant property and casualty insurer. A tuxedoed maitre'd greeted the groups ascending the elevator cars.

"Welcome ladies and gentlemen," the maitre'd recited. "We have no assigned seating this afternoon. Make yourself comfortable wherever you wish."

The tables were set with fine white linen. Orange napkins crested each spot encircling centerpieces of fresh flowers. The glass corner walls exposed a panoramic view of downtown Hartford.

The half dozen senior executives stood against the entrance wall greeting the student candidates with warm "How do you do's".

There was a certain way, Peter determined, that the executives would select which table to sit at. He appraised the table arrangements and walked to where he ascertained would be the most visible spot in the room. He chose the front table closest to a narrow oak podium.

Jim joined Peter to his right. Within a couple of seconds, two other suits completed the front table. One of the two was Chris Tripoli from New Orleans. The second was a light blue pinstriped suit. His name card labeled "Hello, my name is Brian Fitzgerald—Buffalo, New York." Tripoli and Fitzgerald landed concurrently at the same airline terminal the night before. They shared a taxi to the Conference Center. Though their acquaintance was less that twelve hours old, the coincidence of their flights landing at the same time created a mutual camaraderie.

"What was with that guy Hinson," Tripoli asked as they introduced themselves more formally.

"That guy certainly caught my attention," Brian Fitzgerald chimed.

Peter shrugged his shoulders. The incident in his mind was not worthy of a reply. He scoped the room once again. It was interesting how the student candidates attracted after a cursory "let's get to know each other" exercise. Craig Hinson had taken possession of the adjoining front table. The suits with the most serious demeanors agglomerated to him.

"Looks like that bunch sucked on lemons as appetizers," Fitzgerald side-mouthed.

Lynn sat prominently at the center-most table. She was companioned with the other female student candidates. The rear tables were occupied with the bland suits. They seemed content with their topic of choice - risqué one-liners. Guffaws of laughter erupted at sporadic intervals from the back of the room.

Peter Collins watched as the Home Sales School faculty greeted the senior management representatives. The senior managers intermittently spread out to the various empty seats at each clothed table.

"Ralph Heffling—Head of East Coast Operations," the manager addressed to Peter's table. He circled the quartet with warm handshakes.

The conversation was courteous. Heffling asking about each candidate's travel to Hartford and subsequent accommodations.

Peter glanced over to the Hinson table. The forehead from Miles and Mason was quizzing the executive guest on the travails of Elizabeth Sanderson—the Brigadier legal counsel nominated for the U.S. Supreme Court only to be rejected because she employed an illegal alien as a housekeeper. The forehead was openly outspoken on his take of the episode. He had no problem expressing his views in a loud voice about the liberal Democrats who squashed the nomination.

A penguin uniformed server within earshot of a diner's beckon call stood sentry to each table. White wine was offered as an accompaniment to the courses of garden salad and chicken cordon bleu with asparagus.

Peter's classmates at the table dutifully declined the wine offering. It was an implied protocol not to accept alcohol at lunch—particularly mid-session of day one.

"Fellows, I suggest to take advantage of this unique opportunity," Ralph Heffling nodded for the penguin to pour. " You will not see the Brig springing for liquor again until you make it to Cromwell Country Club."

Queries to senior management relating to the strategic direction of Brigadier met noncommittal one-word answers at each table. Either the manager was not at liberty to discuss matters of policy and procedure, or they just plain did not want to talk about it. It was the candidates from out of state who were able to eventually find a common discussion ground. Where to make weekend road excursions. Conversation bubbled between tables. Destinations were described—New York City or Boston, the coastline of Long Island, Cape Cod, or even spring skiing in Vermont.

Craig Hinson loudly pronounced the existence of his parents' summer home in Newport, Rhode Island. He made certain everyone heard of the family's forty-eight foot yacht moored in Jamestown Harbor.

"Isn't he a piece of work," Brian retorted. "Loves to brag, but God forbid he will ever even think of inviting anyone there."

The second glass of Chardonnay prompted Ralph Heffling to abort his earlier intention to make a few welcome remarks at the oak podium. He asked the penguin to inform his colleagues that the luncheon was meant to be informal. They could direct their candidates to excuse themselves at any time should private time be desired before the afternoon session. The reprieve created a number of emptying tables. Peter noticed Lynn was gone too—obviously not a big fan of raspberry and crème.

Peter pressed the hallway elevator button. A familiar voice sounded from across the corridor as he waited for a car to arrive.

"Hey, want to sneak a quick smoke?'

It was Lynn Cloud. Peter smiled and walked down to the door where she stood. He followed her into the room. The pair of queen-sized beds, desk and chair, and matching dressers with TV matched his suite identically. The only difference was the window view of the city. And the ashtray sitting on the windowsill.

Peter sat on the end of the front bed. Lynn pulled an Ultra Light from its box on the desk. She lit it with her lighter. Peter gratefully accepted the offering.

"I could not help but notice you were crying this morning," Peter opened. He pulled a deep drag from the cigarette. Lynn watched as a couple of smoke rings blew through the air.

"Jeez," Lynn chuckled. "You are not much for mixing words, are you?"

"Well no, I guess I am not," Peter stared. "Are you okay?

Lynn gathered the ashtray from the windowsill. She carried it across the room and handed it to Peter.

"I did not have the best of travel days yesterday," Lynn said quietly. She sat facing Peter from the end of the opposite bed.

She recited her tale. Saying goodbye to the boyfriend she had been seeing on a steady basis for the past four months. Arriving in Hartford four hours ahead of registration. The similar experience of being locked out of the side door. She was steady and firm when she finished with the homeless cart lady incident.

Peter sat quietly. He did not interrupt, nor move from his position. He snuffed the cigarette in the ashtray.

"Okay, I am finished now," Lynn declared. She slapped her palms to her lap.

"Like I asked you," Peter asked. "Are you okay?"

"Yes, I am better now," Lynn smiled. "You know, I think you and I are the only two in the class who smoke. We may end up spending more time together. So you better get yourself okay."

"Get myself okay?" Peter was surprised.

"Yeah," Lynn chided. "What is with you and this 'Million Dollar Man' ego? Christ, you sound even worse than that Hinson dude referring to yourself in the third person."

"What?" Peter exclaimed.

"I must admit Peter Collins has been referred to by a lot of names over the years, but it is the first time he can recall 'Million Dollar Man'," Lynn mimicked. "Let me give you one piece of advise Mr. Third Person—lose it!"

X

"A good crop of blue-chippers," Ralph Heffling announced. He laid his third glass of Chardonnay on the rear table.

Ruth and Tracey were the only remaining faculty representatives at the table. The others had cut out early as soon as the last student candidate left the executive dining room. Proper protocol was not to leave until after all of the student candidates finished their dessert and departed.

A couple of senior managers meandered towards the group.

"Do you have the floor plan," they chimed in unison. Ruth reached into the briefcase lying by her feet. She produced the vinyl chart with green backing. Tracey pushed the untouched raspberries and crème from the place settings. The chart was set on the table linen.

There was a stillness of silence as the amphitheater floor plan was analyzed. Assembled on the chart was a replica of the oval design with four rows of transparent windows. Small name cards indicating each desk's occupant and hometown had been inserted in each slot.

Ruth had taken special care to note which student candidate had been seated with each senior manager. The opening Home Sales School luncheon had become a ritual for the senior managers. They would size up the chemistry of the student candidates' characteristics and give their opinions on team formations for the red ribbon contest. As in the case of previous Home Sales Schools, Meyer was prepared to answer a plethora of bullet questions. "Who was that sitting across from me with the red tie?" or "What was the name of that fellow who looked like a basketball player sitting over at Armstrong's table?"

The basic vision was to break up the friendship cliques that may have formed early amongst the candidates. It made for a diverse team makeup. It was also intended to broaden the candidates' ability to mix with an array of others.

The primary mission was to distinguish the five most prominent class leaders—the future so-called "Captains of Industry". These leaders would be divided into separate teams to hopefully captain a balanced group.

The morning introduction exercise provided a handy thumbnail sketch to complement the opinions of the senior managers. In addition to Meyer's floor plan, Tracey offered her notes from the morning exercise. It contained a pre-printed grid of criteria. The top of the paper listed six general categories—Communication Skills—Confidence Level—Time Management—Experience—Technical Ability—Other. Vertical boxes emanated below each category matching up with the candidates' names listed down the left margin. Benison had rated each person on a scale of one through five—five being outstanding.

The first three criteria were easiest to judge. Experience and technical ability were not always so clear cut. It depended in large part to the substance presented by the candidate during their three minutes. "Other" was to some extent "the wild card" factor. That chutzpah, or lack thereof, indistinguishable in definition, but worthy in the formation of teams.

"Ralph, there were three candidates I scored with perfect fives on the first three criteria," Benison reported. "Peter Collins and Chris Tripoli who were seated at your table, and Craig Hinson, who sat across from you at Janet Armstrong's table."

"Those fellows at my table were a good bunch," Heffling nodded. "As I have told you before, if you run into a bunch you would feel comfortable with on a weekend golf getaway—then split them up."

Benison and Meyer nodded. Neither played golf. As a matter of fact, they had missed their noontime aerobics workout next door at the headquarters' fitness center. They planned to make it up at the class scheduled for six o'clock. Nevertheless, they understood the point made by the head of East Coast operations.

"Hinson is the one from Miles and Mason, isn't he," Janet Armstrong ascertained. "Boy, he is one abrasive sonuvabitch."

"Do you know he had the audacity to bring up his bonus incentive at M&M during the exercise," Benison added.

Ralph frowned and twisted the stem of his wineglass. The Miles and Mason bonus incentive had become a bone of contention at Brigadier. It was too exorbitant. The smaller agencies sending representatives to the Home Sales School were in no position to offer their upstarts financial rewards of that size. It was a thorn in Ralph Heffling's side whenever he made agency visits in the field. "Hey Ralph," agency owners would lament, "can't you get John Wellington to tone it down a bit over at M&M? It sends the wrong message to our graduates. They all come back with their hands out."

John Wellington was Heffling's equivalent at Miles and Mason—Head of East Coast operations. Heffling had diplomatically approached the bonus plan with Wellington on two different occasions. He had gotten nowhere. M&M was a worldwide player for Brigadier, and Wellington knew it. He would even allude to the fact that the Brig was no bigger than M&M.

"Well, Ralph, old boy," Wellington responded at their last meeting. "Sounds like you are having trouble cutting winning agents from a different cloth."

Wellington stabbed the dagger even deeper. He mandated Brigadier to display a color photograph on the Brigadier Agent newsletter cover whenever a double ribbon winner returned home to M&M. Until the Knoxville exile, three consecutive School editions had the growing countenance of M&M alumni gloating with the framed double ribbons. John Wellington was seated in the middle of each shot in his high-backed leather chair.

"Hinson told me he was offended that Plimpton McAllister did not attend the luncheon," Janet Armstrong informed the table. McAllister was the Chairman and Chief Executive Officer of Brigadier Insurance. "He said his friends at Miles and Mason mentioned meeting Mr. McAllister when they attended the Home Sales School in the past. He asked me where Mr. McAllister's office is in the headquarters building. He also wanted to know the name of his executive secretary. He plans on going over there to set a dinner appointment. I believe his parting words were 'if Plimpton cannot make the time to have lunch with us, then it will cost him a dinner'."

This was the last straw, Heffling determined. No one referred to the Chairman of Brigadier Insurance by his birth name, Plimpton, which was actually the maiden name of his mother, donned on the chief when women of privilege had yet to learn that hyphened surnames could preserve prominence in a family fortune. Insiders knew the only suitable substitute for "Mr. McAllister" was "Mack".

"Tracey," Heffling sneered. He focused on the floor plan. "Who are these people you marked with one's and two's?"

"A lot of them were the quieter ones," Tracey replied. "Snorting at their one-liner jokes at the back table."

"Didn't one of them forget to bring business cards," Armstrong smiled. "A Dale Carnegie castaway from California?"

"As a matter of fact, yes," Benison laughed.

"Then stick those guys with Hinson," Ralph ordered. "Let us see how he floats his boat with that crew."

"Mr. Heffling," Ruth interrupted. "Craig Hinson is more perceptive than you give him credit. He will see right through an ambush."

"I suppose you are right, Ruth," Heffling mused. The East Coast head took a gulp of Chardonnay and placed the goblet on the table. "We cannot set up a total pitfall."

There was a discreet sigh of relief at the table. Only Ruth had the fortitude to question Ralph's decision-making. Perhaps it was because of her seniority. The table remained hushed while Heffling stared at the floor plan and grid.

"I know," Heffling suggested. "Put that fellow Brian Fitzgerald who was at my table in Hinson's group. He is a pretty affable guy. Hinson will have some respect for him."

The group nodded at the skeleton formation Ralph had planned.

"This is interesting," Janet Armstrong pointed to the grid. "Tracey, you rated only one five in the "Other" column. Who is it?"

Tracey scanned the grid. "Lynn Cloud," she announced.

"Why the five," Armstrong asked.

"I do not really know," Benison reflected. "There is something unique about her beyond good looks. She was the only one in the group who seemed content with the way her job is set up at home. She was brave enough to admit she is totally happy selling personal lines insurance. She has absolutely no interest in dealing with commercial accounts."

Ruth informed the group about Lynn's unenviable welcome to the city of Hartford. She admitted her leniency in assigning the top floor smoker's suite reserved for out-of-town senior managers. Janet Armstrong cringed at the mention of the smoking suite. She was an outspoken proponent of Brigadier's new smoking ban. She asked Ruth if she suspected any other student candidates would take issue with the anti-smoking policy.

"The only other smoker I suspect is Peter Collins," Meyer tattled. "I overheard Lynn Cloud invite him into her room a short time ago for a cigarette."

Janet threw her hands to the air.

"Duluth, Minnesota," Ralph ignored the bickering. He mulled over the floor plan. "I have never met with any agencies out there...."

Tracey and Ruth focused their attention on the East Coast head. Janet Armstrong realized that while Ralph Heffling may be an ally of the smoke free campaign, it was not the issue of the moment. She shut her trap.

"I will tell you what," Ralph furrowed his brows like a chess master at the board. "Assign Lynn Cloud to Peter Collins' team. I have a hunch."

XI

Tracey Benison called the afternoon class session to order.

"Ladies and gentlemen, let me introduce Sam Carvellas, your sales coach for the next four weeks."

The sales coach was left with his players.

Sam Carvellas looked to be about fifty years old. Though twenty pounds overweight, he struck the image of being a jock in his day. He explained his twenty-year background in a variety of sales roles that included insurance. He had been at the Brigadier Home Sales School for the past six.

"Each afternoon we will concentrate solely on sales techniques," the coach opened his lesson. "We will practice techniques through small group role plays. You will have the benefit of speaking out loud in front of others. You will also get constructive feedback from your peers."

Carvellas began to count sequentially across the rows. "One-two-three, one-two-three...." He then divided the ones to the back left section of the amphitheater. The two's were centered in the middle of the room. The three's to the front right.

Peter was a three. So was Lynn. Peter did not have to leave his movie chair. He cavalierly sat with his face pointing to Sam Carvellas as Lynn picked up her belongings. She moved to Jim Stankos' spot—vacated when he joined the two's.

"Do you mind if I sit here?" Lynn propositioned.

The seating arrangement did not change for the rest of the four weeks.

XII

Teapot's Café was located three blocks walking distance from the Brigadier Conference Center. Its rundown wood frame sat in one of the most depressed spots in East Hartford. The assortment of tenement houses across the street appeared never to have been able to hold a coat of paint.

Each dwelling in the neighborhood was protected by chain link fencing long since rusted by age. The only colors beyond the drab greens and grays radiated from the billboards spanning the breadth of the expressway arched above the blight.

The Home Sales School initiation to Teapot's in prior years had been an enjoyable fringe benefit in Tracey Benison's duties. The establishment was the landmark of Brigadier Insurance. Visitors returning from the Brig were always asked by their colleagues "Did you make it to Teapot's?"

Economic uncertainty at Brigadier Insurance had taken its toll on the taps at Teapot's bar. For decades, the unwritten rule was that if someone at the office did not claim some barstools by five o'clock sharp, you would be cast somewhere deep in the Brigadier herd. Crowds would stand as long as five deep at the bar on weeknights until nine o'clock. That was usually when spouses began calling their breadwinners home.

Tracey noticed the transformation as soon as the Home Sales School concluded its group march down to the watering hole. It had been weeks, perhaps months, since the Conference Center director could recall anyone from the office saying "Hey! Who wants to go for a drink?"

The barstools were vacant save for a couple of locals who were seated in the corner near side the entrance. A half a dozen or so local kids in their early twenties assembled at one of the back area pool tables. They absently stared at the mish-mash of pool balls scattered in an amateurish way across the green felt. A couple of the kids moved to the neighboring foos-ball table—digging into their denims for quarters.

Each class member immediately stared to the ceiling as they entered the bar—pointing at the reward. The clippings of necktie fronts covered the entire bar area as advertised.

The bartender stood sentry at the taps as the flock meandered across the bar. Smaller groups of male students were forming. They scoped the bottles lining the rear mirrored wall and mulled their favorite forms of libation. Drinks were not ordered until the women in the group situated at their stool of choice. The groups stepped in closer to the bar once the layout was established.

Two of the bland groups gathered around Lynn's stool. The hee-hawing began about the prospect of having too much to drink. Peter found himself encircled by Jim and Brian Fitzgerald. He knew he would be shut off from any conversation this evening with Lynn. Elbowing through the blands would make him look like a dolt.

Craig Hinson was mixed between the group of blands. Peter did not pick him out at first. The candidates were a little tougher to distinguish—the dark suits replaced by casual wear. Hinson unzipped his leather jacket. He placed it on the back of Lynn's stool.

"Hinson has a necktie on," one of the blands blurted. The semi-circle burst out laughing to Hinson's high-foreheaded glee.

"Cut it off! Cut it off," the blands chanted.

The bartender ambled to the side of the bar. He produced a foot-long pair of shears. As the chant continued, the bartender walked around the bar. His face beamed down on the soon-to-be-victim.

"Sir, your wardrobe is a disgrace," the bartender announced in a high octave. "In the honor of my bottled brethren, I hereby declare you stripped of your dignity."

The bartender ceremoniously took hold of the bottom wedge of paisley silk. He lifted it high between the sacrificial lamb's eyes. The shears were extended. A sudden snip at the base of the collar left Hinson with a mere inner stub of slain cloth - hanging as an orphan from the tattered knot.

The blands went crazy with applause, while the bartender scurried back with his booty to locate some thumb tacks.

"Folks," Hinson announced. "Call me superstitious. You have all been privileged to witness the rite of Miles and Mason double ribbon champions. No M&Mer has ever been denied victory once they have been de-flowered at Teapot's orientation night."

Hinson high-fived his followers as the sound system speakers erupted.

"Hey folks—it is karaoke time!"

The group turned in unison to the pony-tailed deejay in the far corner of the room. He was clad in a black tee shirt with the pink emblem "Teapot's" across the chest. His black cowboy hat was an appropriate match.

A couple of pool-game observers clapped and hurriedly paced to the deejay table. They grabbed the pencil stubs and jotted song request numbers on paper slips. Their favorites were memorized. No need to resort to the three ring reference binders.

The cowboy accepted the first completed slip from a heavyset black girl. He knew her selection without having to look at the scribbling.

"Aw-right Marcia," the cowboy waved. "You are up!"

A cassette was popped into the black console. The television screens mounted throughout Teapot's corner ceilings sprang to life. The title "I Honestly Love You" appeared in block letters across the terminals. "Artist: Olivia Newton John" was in lower case letters along the bottom.

Karaoke was a new phenomenon to the Home Sales School group. A few tried to sing along with the words scrolling over the sets. After a set of ill-fated bars, they quickly realized the song selection was not conducive to getting a party going. The audience was mute as the black girl passionately bellowed off key into the hand held microphone.

The second selection was not much better. A boyfriend-girlfriend duet tried their hand at Meatloaf's "Paradise by the Dashboard Lights". They started the piece with sporadic laughter—elbowing each other and ribbing "You go", "No—you go". The muffled sound of Meatloaf's background voice accompaniment could be heard faintly. The unsung words scrolled in a fast pace along the screens.

"Come on—sing," a few shouts sprung from the pool table area.

The pair composed themselves. They focused on the screens. Instead of carrying the tune, the duo more or less screamed noise into the microphones.

The cowboy escaped the charade. He hand-carried a couple of the three ring song binders to the Home Sales School clusters at the bar. The pages were enveloped in vinyl sleeves protecting them from spillage.

"Come on folks," the cowboy coerced. "Have yourself a hand at karaoke."

The duet was finishing Meatloaf's last stanza. "I am praying for the end of time—so I can end my time with you." They did not make it to the end. The girlfriend was fed up with her partner's playful antics. She dropped the microphone back on the deejay table and headed back to the pool table. She shouted "You suck!"

"Yeah, well up yours," the boyfriend countered. He stormed out of the door.

A less than comfortable boredom blanketed the Home Sales Group once the boyfriend hit the street. One cluster slowly flipped through the vinyl song sheets. No one showed much interest or zeal in being the first candidate to expose why insurance was chosen as a career rather than singing.

"Peter," Tracey whispered from behind Collins' shoulder. "This crowd is dying a slow death. Will you do me a favor and sing a song?"

Peter did not turn to acknowledge the voice. He took a long pull on his bottle of beer. Focusing straight ahead at the lonesome cowboy, Collins raised an eyebrow.

"Why me, Ms. Benison," he side-mouthed.

"Because this school group is quickly taking on the personality of that Craig Hinson," Tracey confessed. "Spark some life into them for me."

Benison paused and looked down.

"Please?"

Peter furrowed his brows at the downtrodden Conference Center director. Craig Hinson did have a sobering effect on his prey.

Peter walked to the cowboy. He flipped open the remaining binder on the deejay's table. He did not need to peruse the offerings. Instead, he pointed to his choice.

"This one," Peter said. He did not fill out a slip. Rather, he kept his eyes on the cowboy as the ponytail bobbed to seek the fingered option. The cowboy smiled. The Sales School group hooted and howled as Peter took hold of the microphone.

"Sugar Sugar" flashed on the screen. "Artist: The Archies". A few of the older candidates whistled between their fingers.

A broad grin formed on Tracey's face as Peter sang the beginning of the song. Her intuition on the five star grid chart proved more than correct. Not only did Peter exhibit that "life of the party" personality, he could sing too. As a matter of fact, Benison thought, his voice sounds better than the original artist.

The cowboy was gratified too. Karaoke deejays, particularly the experienced ones, know which songs in their books can get a nightclub rocking.

"No doubt this dude has done this before," the cowboy shouted.

Peter could see his audience wake. The chattering had stopped. Even the cue sticks silenced. The patrons began clapping and singing along. The energy enthused Peter to get deeper and deeper into the heart of the song.

"Ah sugar… ah honey honey… You are my candy girl—and you've got me watching you!"

Peter glimpsed to Lynn at the bar. She held a radiant smile from ear to ear—resting her hands on her propped up knees.

The gathering roared as the song came to its end. Peter simply shrugged his shoulders. He gave a courteous bow, and handed the microphone back to the cowboy.

"One more song! One more song," the gathering chanted.

"You can't stop now, Man," the cowboy grinned.

Peter laughed. He returned to the bound songbook. The cowboy's grin widened upon eyeing the second fingered selection.

"Build Me Up, Buttercup" —"Artist: The Foundations."

A few heads turned from the monitors after reading the encore title. "What an odd song to pick," Peter overheard. He smiled. In the karaoke world, Peter strategically chose perhaps the easiest homesick crowd sing-a-long tune ever written.

"Hey, I remember this song," the audience buzzed as the words filled the screen.

"I know the words to this one!"

Peter sang the first verse with the deftness of a professional. Groups usually start swaying together, he thought, by the second round of "I need you—I need you—more than anyone darling, you knew that I had from the start."

Sure enough, it happened as if on cue. Tracey beamed as the class swayed arm in arm.

Peter handed back the microphone at song's end. An appreciative cowboy shook his hand.

The women at the bar rose from the stools. They zipped their jackets. Lynn joined the first group's trek back to the Conference Center.

XIII

The contest sales teams gathered in the second floor Conference Center meeting rooms. Being the initial evening strategy session, the teams had been uncertain of any specific room assignments.

Peter Collins walked directly to the first accessible room he saw. His team followed, prompting Hinson to eye the action.

"Come on, fellows," the M&Mer calculated. "Let's try a meeting room at the end of the hall."

The meeting rooms were sparsely adorned—containing only the necessary educational supplies. Four white meeting tables formed a large rectangle in the middle of each room. An array of institutional metal chairs was neatly spaced in the surroundings. The interior wall fronting the hallway contained an erasable white board. A flip chart easel sat in the corner of the back wall.

Collins' team scattered around the table. They organized their respective file notes. The initial session was designed to strategize a format for the next week's opening sales interview. As Sam Carvellas advised for any first time introduction to a new business prospect, the exercise was a "break the ice" get-together.

"This is a rapport building opportunity," the coach instructed earlier that afternoon. "Remember some key elements to the sales process. Be mindful of the "fish on the wall" mentality. Do not sit before a new business prospect and dive right into the topic of business. Observe personal items in a buyer's office—like the proverbial fish on the wall. Get the buyer talking. People love to talk about themselves—particularly about off work time activities. Start out with an open-ended question, like 'where did you come to find such an interesting fish'."

"Remember, too, that you will be meeting with a three person buying panel," Carvellas counseled. "You are a team of five. It is your option how many of you actually participate in the interview dialogue. Sellers outnumbering buyers at a meeting can lead to a subtle intimidation you may not even be aware of."

Collins' team's first course of business was to select a scribe to record notes on the white board. The seated men in the group peered down to the end of the table at the sole female representative. Lynn looked down for a second. Typical, she thought, the girl is always the designated secretary. Peter caught the momentary hesitation. He jumped from his chair.

"I will be the scribe," Peter ceded. He moved toward the white board. Lynn exhaled.

Peter searched the board's tray. It was barren of any erasable writing instruments. The only resources were a couple of plastic backed foam rubber erasers. Peter scanned the periphery of the room. There they are, he discovered, on the back easel.

"Lynn," he pointed matter-of-factly. "Could you please pass me that Magic Marker?"

Lynn's eyes opened as if they were going to pop from her head. Her mouth was agape.

"What did you say," she amazed.

Oh my goodness, Peter conjectured. Did I offend her for fetching something?

"I said," Peter swallowed. "Could you please pass me that Magic Marker."

"That is what I thought you said," Lynn roared. She threw her hands in the air—slapping them heavily on the table.

"What is so funny," he puzzled. Lynn grabbed her sides. She fell back in her seat laughing hysterically.

"Did you just hear yourself," Lynn rolled. "Magic Maa-kaa! Magic Maa-kaa? You know, I have been meaning to mention that 'Baa-ston' accent to you—but I have kept it in—until I heard that one!"

"Say it again, will you," Lynn giggled. "Say 'Magic Maa-kaa'."

The three men seated at the table did not seem particularly tickled by the jest. They chuckled briefly at their counterpart's amusement. Their attention turned quickly back to their notes.

Peter looked across the room at Lynn. They laughed together for a moment—Lynn staring at Peter with that typical "gotcha" look. They made eye contact. It was the first time Peter had ever really looked into the light brown eyes with green sparkle. Lynn was surprised too. She never remembered noticing how blue Peter's eyes were. *What was happening*? The smiles disappeared from their faces.

Time—at that exact instant—ceased to exist. The others in the room appeared statuesque—staring at their empty notepads. Their movements were suspended like mannequins in a storefront window. They were oblivious to the mystery. Peter froze his stare to the being cast before him. There is something in that face—in that look.

The warp was over in a snapshot second. Peter shook the cobweb from his head.

"*Have we met before*?"

XIV

Monday morning of week two welcomed a buzzing of early morning activity at the Brigadier Home Sales School. Student candidates were no longer strangers in the oval amphitheater. Uncertain "hello's" no longer existed. Friendships had been formed. Personalities bloomed.

A dozen of the out-of-state candidates commandeered two minivans and ferried to Martha's Vineyard for the weekend. The impromptu excursion was originally contrived more to rattle Craig Hinson's nerves than anything else. Chris Tripoli and Brian Fitzgerald each billeted a van on their own credit cards. It was their treat.

"If Hinson wants to lure us to Newport, Rhode Island only to let us watch him toot around the harbor in his boat and give us a cursory wave on shore," Fitzgerald mused, " then screw him!"

The aura of an unseasonably warm spring weekend on the Cape Cod island was more than the group anticipated. For some of the Mid-western candidates, it was the first time they experienced the blue magnificence of the Atlantic Ocean.

The Vineyard groupies were gathered on the rear platform of row four when Peter arrived. The tail-end comments about Gay's Head and souvenir clothing were just dying down.

"So—how did you like Martha's Vineyard," Peter greeted as he sat down next to Lynn.

"We celebrated my birthday," Lynn smiled.

"Your birthday," Peter remarked. "I did not know you had a birthday. Had I known, I would have got you a little something."

"I am not much into presents," Lynn said.

"So are you at that point in your life where your age is a secret?"

"No," Lynn smiled confidently. "I am twenty-two."

The youthfulness was sobering. Peter changed the subject.

"I bet the Atlantic Ocean was quite a surprise to see, huh," Peter boasted. "Pretty big body of water, don't you think?"

Lynn shook her head. A typical East Coast comment, she mused. She had heard it so many times before.

"Let me remind you from your grammar school social studies," Lynn smirked. "We do have Lake Superior in Duluth, Minnesota."

"Yeah, but that is just a lake."

Lynn shook her head a second time—surrendering to the ignorance. She dug into her black portfolio box for the morning lesson.

XV

A nervous excitement filled the air in the oval. It had been seven days of intense morning lectures on insurance policy forms and conditions. Afternoons were devoted to Sam Carvellas' role-play simulations.

"The order of interviews will be drawn from a hat," Tracey Benison announced. The teams were ready to show their stuff. Sam introduced two underwriting managers from Brigadier headquarters. They would join Tracey to form the buying panel. The pair sat before a barren open table on the lecture floor. Tracey stood in front of the table. She reminded the teams of the contest parameters.

"The three of us have memorized a scripted scenario. We have some unique requirements that must be addressed for insuring this Conference Center facility. Tomorrow's diagnostic interview session is intended to give you the opportunity to survey the grounds and delve into some specific risk management exposures. Suffice to say, this afternoon's session is merely a way to warm up to your buying group. In the end, the ultimate decision of selecting our agent will come down to the best recommendation that meets our unique need, or needs; however, a lot of subjectivity can come into play. Remember, people like to do business with people they like."

The first couple of interviews were uniform and casual. The buying panel was polite to their suitors. The underwriters were versed to be pleasant. No confrontation was planned for this initial exercise.

Chris Tripoli's team interview was the third of the day. Peter and Craig Hinson inadvertently made eye contact when the Tripoli team was announced from the hat. Their thoughts were identical. They were saving the best for last.

As with the first twenty-minute interviews, the Tripoli team selected three representatives to meet with the buying panel. The remaining two team members sat housed in the oval to make observational notes. Chris had a warm, laid back style. His personality hit it off particularly well with the two headquarter underwriters. With the hospitable manner of a Southern gentleman, Chris digressed from the business of insurance. He demonstratively detailed the joys of trolling for catfish in the Louisiana bayou. The buying team loved it.

The oval resumed its courteous applause when Tripoli's team concluded. They accomplished the end goals of an initial meeting. There was a buyer's commitment to meet again. Any necessary information will be provided. And the contacts were authorized to purchase.

Craig Hinson's team was selected fourth. Good, Peter thought when the name was announced. There is an old adage with insurance sales. Last one in gets the deal.

All five members of the Hinson team approached the floor. In a preconceived fashion, Hinson and one of his serious demeanored dark suit cronies placed their chairs directly in front of the panel's table. The remaining three formed a straight line of seating directly behind them.

Following the perfunctory "hello's" and "why don't we sit down's", Tracey could not help but ask, "why are you three sitting in the back?"

"Ms. Benison," Craig raised his hand to address the anticipated question. "These individuals represent a sample of our junior agency associates. We ask them to accompany us to all of our meetings—primarily to act as note-takers. It enables them to benefit from having the opportunity to witness first hand how trained professionals like me and my colleague here conduct our business."

What a pompous ass, Tracey thought. Her lips soured. Typical big brokerage firm mentality.

Hinson realized Tracey was disenchanted with his explanation. He decided to avoid any further confrontation. He directed his sole attention to his male counterparts on the panel. Though Hinson and his crony hit on all the formula objectives, the conversation was strained. Tracey had been ostracized from the discussion. She sat with her arms folded. Hinson became fidgety. It would be difficult to re-establish any rapport with her. Less than five minutes remained in the awkward interview.

Brad Heller, the Dale Carnegie grad from California, was relegated to junior agency associate duty behind Hinson and his crony. Even he could sense the conversation was dying on the vine.

"Gee, where did you come across such a fine fish on the wall," Heller piped.

There was a smattering of chuckles from the oval. The buying panel looked at each other. As if rehearsed, they turned to the empty white board behind them.

"Excuse me," one of the headquarter underwriters asked. He was unaware of Sam Carvellas' coaching technique. "There is no fish on the wall."

The oval competitors began to howl in laughter. Craig turned around and glowered at Heller. His anger projected from the reddened high forehead. How could you be so stupid to think up an imaginary fish on the wall?

Tracey did not appreciate the rudeness of the oval's interruption. More so, she took offense to Hinson's volatile reaction to a student candidate she felt was being totally boxed out of the exercise process.

"Why Mr. Hinson," Tracey remarked. "Is there a problem?"

Hinson snapped back around and cut a seething smile to his questioner. He had not been prepared for the perilous tailspin of the past several minutes.

"Ms. Benison," Hinson attempted to regain some semblance of composure. "I appreciate the commitment your company gave our agency a few minutes ago to move forward in pursuing a risk management proposal for the Conference Center. We look forward to our appointed time tomorrow. We promise that you will be quite impressed with the thoroughness of our diagnostic evaluation."

Peter's team quietly made their way down to the lecture floor. The oval's attention, however, was devoted to Hinson and his team as they gathered themselves. The events of the prior interview set a somber air over the amphitheater. Several student candidates avoided the potential of catching Hinson's suspicion of who was laughing during his interview. They busily recorded observation notes. There was no need for Tracey to announce the final team of the day. It was implied.

Peter's team also strategized to opt for a five person selling team rather than three. The Collins' seats however were uniformly spaced. A single row of chairs was arranged in front of the buying panel.

Tracey posed a similar line of open questioning to the group.

"My, I am surprised to greet five representatives from your agency this afternoon," she lured. "For some reason I assumed when we set our appointment only three folks were coming from your office."

Tracey was accustomed to breaches in the body count formula from previous Home Sales School contests. Teams deciding to include all five persons were usually prepared to account for such an opening inquiry. What she did not anticipate was the choice of designated spokesperson.

"I am glad you asked us that question," Lynn responded. "Our agency is a full service provider of risk management products and financial services."

Peter sat back in his chair to interpret the actions of the male participants in the buying panel. Like them, he smiled at the rapport building interchange Lynn was developing with Tracey. Peter had guessed correctly. One of the members of the panel did turn out to be a female.

"All of those other teams have too much testosterone to even think of using a female team member as their lead spokesperson," Peter strategized in the nights leading up to the event. "Having Lynn as our Opening Day pitcher will differentiate us from the rest."

Lynn Cloud described each of her four colleagues as experts in a certain insurance field. She limited her remarks about each team person to just a sentence.

"We are really here today to learn more about you," Lynn's smile was captivating. "Please, tell us more about the Brigadier Conference Center."

The team committed to employ the 80:20 rule. Let the buyers speak eighty percent of the time. If you find yourself pontificating for more than twenty seconds, then you have probably made whatever point you were trying to convey. If so, then stifle!

The members of the team took turns asking open-ended questions. They made sure to hit on all the formula objectives.

One of Sam Carvellas' tips was mirror imaging. The art was to select an individual on the other side of the table and mirror their motions in a subtle way.

"If a buyer scratches his nose, wait a few seconds and scratch your nose," Carvellas advised. "If they put their elbows on the table to 'get down to business', then you do too. People subconsciously do business with people that are like them. So put yourself aside. You become them."

The mirror imaging role-plays at the end of week one were difficult for many of the student candidates to grasp. The tendency for most salespeople is to worry too much about what they are going to ask next. Many times they do not even listen to what a buyer is saying. They are too fearful of that dreaded "hole in the conversation". Mirror imaging in Sam Carvellas' opinion was a tactful way to relax the environment. Regardless, casually crossing one's legs, or setting a hand on the chin the first time you meet someone was a new phenomenon.

Peter had observed some of the early teams practicing the art during their interviews. The Headquarter underwriters were unaware of Sam Carvellas' coaching technique. On a couple of occasions an underwriter would catch a mimicker. There would be an inquisitive "are you copying me" gaze. The imagers would quickly abort their mission. No one attempted mirror imaging during the last few interviews.

Peter relaxed in an upright position in his chair. His team was performing ably. Out of the corner of his eye, he glimpsed at Lynn. Well, I'll be darned, he amazed. Lynn was mirror imaging Tracey Benison. The earlier imagers were trying their hand with the male buyers. Lynn was the first one to pick out Tracey.

Tracey's return to good spirits was obvious after the Hinson debacle. The more Lynn mirrored her image, the higher the spirit of the interview rose.

Lynn was the first to rise from her seat to close the interview.

"Remember fellows," Peter had warned the night before. "Do not sit until the women are seated—rising is likewise."

The Headquarter underwriters rose on cue to meet Lynn's handshake. Lynn crossed to shake the seated Ms. Benison hand. Peter and his selling brethren did not move from their laps.

"Gentlemen," the underwriters queried with extended hands.

"Ma'am?" Peter Collins requested.

Tracey smiled and rose to her Ivy League feet. Collins and his seated colleagues rose with a military crispness. They shook hands goodbye.

Chris Tripoli stood at his movie chair and began to clap.

"Bravo y'all," he complemented in true New Orleans fashion. "Bravo!"

XVI

The screech of the hallway horns woke Peter from a deep slumber. He rubbed his eyes and rolled over in the queen size bed. He tried to squint at the clock radio positioned on the nightstand. The neon numerals on the face glistened 3:23. He dropped his head back into the pillow.

It was after one o'clock in the morning when he arrived back to the Conference Center. He had been asleep for less than two hours. Sunday evenings at home had dragged out longer and longer as the weeks at the Brigadier Home Sales School elapsed. The first weekend home, Peter left shortly after Sunday dinner to take advantage of the remaining daylight. Drive time is an hour and a half drive from Worcester to Hartford. Week two's departure time was pushed back after eight o'clock. That way it would be easier on Mommy to have Daddy tuck the boys in bed for the night. In week three, Peter departed just after the eleven o'clock news. His wife Marianne felt more comfortable falling asleep in an empty bed knowing Peter set the thirty-minute sleep timer after the newscast.

The horn continued its rhythmic pulse.

"What is that? The fire alarm?" Peter could hear from outside his door. A couple of student candidates must have been investigating the source of the commotion. He pulled a second pillow over his head. It hardly muffled the nuisance. Pranksters tripping fire alarms was an age-old annoyance in student dormitories. Why does it have to happen when you are in your thirties? Peter squeezed his eyes shut. He tried to resurrect an art developed in college days—falling back asleep despite a blaring siren.

The Brigadier Conference Center could not be compared to a college dormitory. Fire prevention and loss control safety evacuation plans were a mandated priority. It did not take long for Peter to come to this realization. Within a couple of minutes the hallway was teeming with security guards. With a choreographed regimen probably rehearsed one hundred times over, the guards methodically initiated fire evacuation procedures. Peter could not disregard the flashlight baton's rap on his door.

"Please make passage immediately out of the building," the guard recited when Peter inched open the door.

"Isn't it just a false alarm?"

"We cannot be certain, sir," the guard replied politely. "We received a report over the radios of possible smoke on the top floor."

Peter closed his door. He dug out a pair of sweat pants from his dresser drawers. He pulled them on and stepped into a pair of sneakers. The guard remained patiently in the hallway until Peter emerged from his room with a draped jacket over his shoulders. They headed towards the elevators.

"I am sorry, sir," the guard instructed. "The elevators cannot be used during an evacuation. Security is posted in the center stairwell. If you could go through that door on the left, they can assure your safe exit."

Peter assumed his failure to react at the first instance of hearing the fire alarm would mean he would be one of the last student candidates to leave the building. He was wrong. Only a half dozen quivering bodies occupied the designated evacuation gathering area on the other side of the street. Security was having a difficult time convincing the weary visitors. No, this was not a practice drill.

Peter joined up with Jim on the street curb.

"What time did you get in," Stankos greeted.

"Little after one," Collins replied.

"Me too," Stankos shrugged. It was Jim who planted the seed in Peter's head about leaving home Sunday nights only after the wife was ready for bed. Jim squeezed every possible minute out of being with his family.

Student candidates streamed from the Conference Center at a steady pace. The wardrobes for evacuation were the focus of some amusing chatter. Jim heeded the voice of emergency. He stood barefoot on the cold cement sidewalk—wearing a tee shirt and gym shorts. Some had the presence to grab a bathrobe and slippers on their way out of their suites. Others like Peter had on a hodgepodge of mismatched outerwear.

"I did not know you wore eyeglasses," Jim observed.

"I wear contacts most of the time," Peter confessed. "I was trying to give my eyes a rest before popping them back in the morning."

Peter Collins fingered the smears off of the lens. The evacuees examined the Conference Center roofline from street side. The rumor of smoke reported on the upper floor seemed to spread faster than the alleged fire. Sirens of fire trucks were heard approaching in the distance.

"Ladies and gentlemen, we need to perform a roll call. Please respond 'here' when your name is called."

The uniformed guard had already performed a headcount. It was two people short. The roll call was a procedural means of identifying the missing—without calling attention to the absences.

The guard confirmed the first three names when he got to "Cloud". A tingle of grief crawled up Peter's spine when the second "Cloud" went unanswered.

"She is in Room 810," Peter called out to the guard.

"We know," the guard responded lifting his radio handset to his mouth. Two large hook and ladder trucks arrived at the scene. Fully equipped firefighters jumped from the trucks and ran into the building. Peter could see two security guards re-ascending the glass faced center stairwell. What if she was smoking in bed, Peter feared.

The ensuing ten minutes seemed like an eternity. The street guard appeared somewhat agitated with Peter's "Is she okay?" inquiry at every two minute interval. Another security guard accompanied by a Fire Department Lieutenant approached the evacuation group.

"Everything is safe to re-enter the building," they announced. No explanation was offered about the source of the alarm. Peter resisted the security guard's agitation.

"Excuse me, but I do not see Lynn Cloud out here. Please tell me, were you able to find her?"

The security guard aimed to put the situation at ease.

"Yes sir, we located Ms. Cloud. She was safely removed from the building."

"Then why was she not here," Peter insisted.

"Sir, we had a second evacuation gathering spot on the other side of the Conference Center.

The events of the evening abbreviated the start of Peter's normal morning routine. By the time he showered and dressed, time permitted only a quick coffee-to-go from the Cafeteria before the scheduled class session.

Jim apparently faced the same dilemma. He was stirring the powdered contents in a Styrofoam cup when Peter arrived.

"Did you hear we have a little romance here at the Brigadier Home Sales School," Stankos remarked. He handed Peter a plastic cover. "Seems your friends Brian Fitzgerald and Lynn Cloud fell in love during the road trip to Boston over the weekend."

Peter attempted to contain his surprise. He fumbled at ripping a hole on the coffee top.

"Lynn did not respond to the security guards rapping on the door during the fire alarm last night because she had Fitzy in her room," Stankos continued. "When they missed roll call Security entered her room with a pass key. That's when they found them."

"So, the story about another evacuation spot on the other side of the building was a bunch of bullshit."

XVII

Peter and Jim entered the amphitheater together. Lynn had a beaming smile on her face as Peter approached his movie chair.

"Hi, Peter," Lynn glistened. "How was your weekend?"

"Fine," Peter mouthed. He placed his coffee on the writing table. Preferring not to sit down, he glared over to the left side of the oval to row three. Brian Fitzgerald was sitting at his desk with a serious look on his face. He pensively listened to a couple of blands chatting in row two. Isn't he trite, Peter fumed. He slumped into his chair. Lynn did not take her eyes off of Peter Collins.

"We went to your beloved city of Boston this weekend," Lynn said excitedly. "We went to Cheers and I got a sweatshirt! We were going to go to the Red Sox game. We got to Fenway Park and saw the Green Monster and everything. It was such a riot! We went to this 'baa' right next to the Green Monster, what was it called, oh what the heck, I forget! The 'baa-tenda's' had accents just like yours! We asked them if they knew you. It was so funny! Unfortunately, the game got rained out."

"That is too bad," Peter deadpanned. He could not even look at her.

"So you know what we did? Lynn bubbled.

"No, what," Peter sneered. God, she did not miss a beat.

"We decided to go to Salem, you know? Where the witch trials were?"

"Yeah. I know."

"Well it was all rainy and creepy, so we did not stay too long," Lynn laughed. "So we drove up the coastline to New Hampshire! Do you know what is legal in New Hampshire?"

"No. What?"

"Tattoos! Tattoos are legal in New Hampshire!"

"I think I know that."

"So you will never believe what happened."

"Try me."

"Brian Fitzgerald and I got matching tattoos!"

Peter turned and faced Lynn for the first time.

"You what?"

"That's right," Lynn laughed out loud. "Matching tattoos! I always wanted one, and I guess Brian did too. We got an identical long-stemmed pink rose on the right side of our front hips. Kind of close to the belt buckle."

"I think I am going to be sick," Peter looked away from the branded giddy one.

"Hey, what is wrong?" Lynn placed her hand on Peter's sleeve. "Didn't you have a nice weekend with your wife?"

Peter glowered back at the branded voice. Was she breaking my stones? He moved his sleeve from her hand and glared back up towards Brian Fitzgerald. Fitzy always knew of Peter's friendship with Lynn. Now, he was totally ignoring the right side of row two. It was like he could care less whatever conversation was transpiring.

"My weekend was fine."

Lynn sensed Peter was hurt. Maybe she crossed the line.

"Hey, Peter," Lynn whispered softly. "Let's go to my room for a cigarette at break, okay?"

"I don't know, Lynn."

"Peter—look at me," Lynn requested. Peter turned. She nodded.

"Let's go to my room for a cigarette at break."

XVIII

Peter felt strange going back into Lynn's suite. He had enjoyed cigarette breaks there countless times before. Now, all he could do in the alien environment was envision a fireman's passkey turning in the door. He did not want to sit down on either end of the beds. Which one were they caught in? Instead, he leaned against the side of the desk. God, he thought, I am in such an ugly mood.

Lynn sat and leaned back to lay down at the head of the window side bed. She pulled a cigarette from the box on the night stand.

"Want one," she offered.

"No, I don't think so," Peter replied. He crossed his arms and looked down to the floor.

Lynn lit her cigarette. She inhaled deeply and leaned her head against the back bed board. Her exhale was a narrow stream.

"Peter, what do you want from me," Lynn demanded.

"You know what, Lynn," Peter's eyes expanded. Peter did not realize that his feelings for Lynn were so strong as they were until now. "I guess it is silly for me to want anything. You and Brian—are you serious?" Peter threw his hands in the air. "And matching tattoos? My God, Lynn, why?"

"Peter, you are married to a wife with two young boys at home," Lynn said softly. "What difference should it make to you?"

Peter shook his head. His focus remained on the floor. Lynn got off of the bed and walked over to her friend. She sat at the end of the bed so she could look up to his face.

"Answer me, Peter," Lynn whispered. "What difference should what I do make to a married man?"

Peter paused to assemble his thoughts. A conversation to this degree was not what he expected when he got up in the morning.

"Lynn, I thought what we had was something special," Peter confided. "You know how deeply I feel about you."

"Well, I care for you deeply, too," Lynn admitted. Her thoughts shifted briefly to the number of times she said that to people. The hypocrisy of past relationships created a lump in her throat.

"Then why did you sleep with Brian Fitzgerald?"

"If it makes any difference," Lynn grabbed a hold of Peter's palms. "We slept under the covers together, but that was it. Nothing happened. I have my boyfriend at home and he has a girlfriend. We got talking while we were up in Boston. After a couple of beers we were feeling kind of sad. You were nowhere around. You were back home with your family. It has been two weeks since we have been away. It was just kind of nice for each of us to have someone to hold while we slept. That was all."

Peter took a deep breath. He did not realize his sigh was audible.

"Peter, you are a thirty-four year old married man with a lovely family."

The reality was like a cold slap in the face. Peter walked away to the window with his hands in his suit pockets. He stared at the skyline of Hartford.

"Peter, I love you," Lynn revealed. "But I love you like a father—nothing more, nothing less."

"Great," said Peter. He walked out the door.

Peter headed to the lobby restrooms. He entered the men's room and approached one of the urinals. A familiar voice called out.

"Peter, I was wondering if you could do me a huge favor?"

It was Brian Fitzgerald. He was finishing his business at the sinks. His arms were spanned like wings. He reiterated. "Huge!"

"I was wondering if I could borrow your car tonight? Lynn and I wanted to go out on a little dinner date."

Peter caved to the irony and chuckled.

"Sure, son."

XIX

The Interoffice Memorandum sat in isolation on her office desk. Tracey ran her fingers over the orange colored officer title embossed on the official corporate letterhead. From the desk of Ralph P. Heffling, Executive Vice President—East Coast Operations. It was unusual to receive such a memorandum directly from the East Coast chief—particularly first thing on a Monday morning. There had to be at least four levels of command on the Brigadier organizational chart between Ralph Heffling and Tracey Benison. Why was this not first cleared through proper corporate channels?

Benison analyzed the memorandum. It was "cc-ed" to Ruth Meyer also. A senior manager forwarding correspondence to an underling without first touching base with the supervisor? Something was up. The message was short and succinct.

"Please report to my office at your first session break this morning. Ralph."

Ruth met Tracey Benison at her office door as soon as class was dismissed at ten o'clock.

"Do you know what this is all about," Benison asked her loyal aide.

"Ms. Benison, I have no idea."

"Well, let's be off to see what happens," Benison shrugged. "At least we are not being summoned at three thirty on a Friday afternoon." That was when victims normally receive pink slips.

Tracey and Ruth managed to negotiate the traffic and cross the street to the side brick entrance of Brigadier Headquarters. The pair traversed the three hundred foot marbled hallway that spanned the right side wing of the historic structure. Upon reaching the center foyer, they gazed up the magnificent rose marble walls to the cathedral ceiling four stories above. No matter how long an employee worked for the Brigadier Insurance Company, the aura of the entrance foyer was still breathtaking.

The main corporate elevators were operated manually. Brass plates engraved "this car up" were mounted above each transport bay. Matching number plates were affixed at the side of each shaft. A light system pioneered with the advent of electricity indicated through the plates the floor of each car as the elevator moved.

Visitors were required to sign in with Security in order to access the executive suites. Tracey and Ruth checked in at the main counter. They reported the scheduled appointment with Ralph Heffling. Security telephoned the sixth floor.

"Ms. Tracey Benison and Ms. Ruth Meyer are here to see Mr. Heffling," the guard informed. He paused for a moment and hung up the phone.

"Mr. Heffling is awaiting your arrival," the guard confirmed. He handed them each an official Visitor badge.

Benison and Meyer pinned the badges to their right lapels.

"Mr. Heffling's office," they announced as they moved toward the elevator. There was no need to specify the floor to the uniformed bell hop.

The bell hop acknowledged the nod from the security guard. He released the accordion-style brass cage. The women entered the car to begin their ascent.

Eleanor Gilmartin, Mr. Heffling's executive secretary was waiting at the receiving area when the elevator doors opened. A curt nod welcomed the guests. They were requested to have a seat in the waiting room. Gilmartin made a light knock on the massive mahogany doors. She inched into the executive office as if she were an intruder. Mr. Heffling was informed that his appointments had arrived. No sound was heard in response. Gilmartin returned to her desk and sat down. Upon the precision of one-minute passing, she returned to the mahogany doors. Without further instruction, the secretary opened the doors widely.

"Mr. Heffling will see you now," Gilmartin invited the guests to enter.

Tracey and Ruth had been to Ralph's office in the past. The bureaucratic means of entrance had not wavered. Eleanor relished the formality of protocol.

The luxury of the surroundings was no less impressive. Ralph was seated in a red leather armchair diagonal from his desk area. He looked tired and drawn since the last time the Conference Center staff saw him at the Home Sales School luncheon.

"Come in Ladies, sit down," Heffling motioned to the matching armchairs across from the oriental carpet where is feet rested. Tracey and Ruth took their seats. They remained motionless.

"John Wellington from Miles and Mason had the gall to call me at my home at ten o'clock last night," Heffling informed. "Seems your boy Craig Hinson has been complaining to his office back home that he was assigned a bunch of idiots on his sales contest team." Benison and Meyer glanced to each other.

"The contest process so far seems to be progressing very nicely," Tracey reported.

"Nevertheless," Heffling countered. He lifted his hand to interrupt the explanation. "Those stooges at Miles and Mason may be on to the fact that we may have stacked the deck against their ringer. Ladies, I am afraid we may have to shuffle the cards a little bit."

"What do you mean," asked Benison.

"You know what I mean, Tracey," Ralph exhaled. "We have to subtly re-assign a player or two."

"But Mr. Heffling," Ruth protested. Her seniority allowed her to voice what Tracey was reluctant to state. "We have never permitted player changes once the interview and strategy sessions have started."

"In this case, Ruth, we are going to have to make an exception," Ralph surrendered. "Believe me when I tell you. John Wellington can make our lives very miserable. It is not worth the hassle."

"What do you have in mind Ralph," Tracey acquiesced.

"Hinson's biggest gripe is a fellow on his team from California," Heffling shared. "He claims the guy is completely worthless."

"Brad Heller," Ruth informed.

"Who?" Ralph leaned forward.

"Brad Heller," confirmed Tracey. "You remember him, Ralph. The Dale Carnegie guy who forgot his business cards."

"That must be the one," Heffling nodded. "We need to move that gentleman to another team."

"Are we going to have to rig the contest for Hinson to win too," Ruth interjected.

"Absolutely not," Ralph shouted. Ruth's impertinence bordered on insubordination. He rose from his armchair and paced to the front of his desk.

"I may have bowed to Wellington's one request, but the line is drawn there. John Wellington was told explicitly last night that the integrity of the Home Sales School contest will be compromised no further."

Neither Tracey nor Ruth dared flinch from their spot. Heffling demanded obedience.

"Who is Hinson's strongest foe?" he asked.

"Peter Collins," Benison and Meyer's replied without hesitation.

"Collins," Heffling mulled. "The fellow I had lunch with, right?"

"Yes, he is the one."

Ralph stared at the ceiling and pondered.

"Didn't we put a last-second assignee on his team," Heffling recalled. "Someone who rated high in the 'Other' column of your grid, Tracey?"

"We did Ralph," Tracey affirmed. "Lynn Cloud—Duluth, Minnesota."

"Has she contributed to the team so far?" Heffling inquired.

"Well, we have gotten through the initial interviews and strategy meetings," Benison reported. "Nothing too substantive to this point, but she seems to be very well-liked by Mr. Collins."

"Oh," said Heffling raising an eyebrow.

"It is nothing like that Mr. Heffling," Ruth discounted. She decided to err on the side of caution with the East Coast chief. "Mr. Collins is a married man. Lynn Cloud may be an attractive young lady, but they are merely friends."

"Very attractive indeed," Ralph responded. He sat on the high-backed desk chair. "Okay, Ladies, this is what I would like you to arrange. Move Heller to Peter Collins' team and Lynn Cloud to Hinson's. Maybe if Hinson reports home that he has something worthwhile to look at in his meetings some of this heat will subside."

Tracey caught sight of Peter exiting the lobby restrooms with Brian Fitzgerald. He was handing Fitzgerald a set of car keys.

"Peter, may I have a word with you for a moment," Benison asked.

The request was short and to the point. The faculty was concerned that the teams were not balanced. The contest results could be skewed.

"I was hopeful to plant a seed in your mind, Peter," Tracey suggested. "You can think about it and get back to me. The concept would be for Brad Heller to join the agency team that you are on, and Lynn Cloud will switch over to the agency team that Craig Hinson happens to be on."

Peter furrowed his brow again at what was the second request Tracey made of him.

"Tracey," Peter answered. "I do not have to think on anything. Consider it done."

XX

Lynn emerged from the back meeting room. As she made her way down the hallway of the second floor Conference Center hive, she spotted Peter. He was standing at the door of her old team's strategy quarters—greeting Brad Heller with a hearty handshake.

"Well put a ring on her finger and kill the fattened calf," Peter exclaimed. "The Prodigal Daughter has returned."

"Thanks, Dad," Lynn smiled.

Heller did not understand the inside joke. He excused himself to shake hands with his new teammates already seated in the meeting room. Dale Carnegie would have been impressed.

It was Brian who told Lynn about the player shuffle during lunch in the Cafeteria. They had developed an odd early relationship. More than half of the class knew of their bedfellow sleeping arrangement. While the number grew, Fitzy preferred to act like nothing existed. He intentionally avoided contact with his evening roommate during the day. She could kibitz with Peter, and her girlfriends all she wanted as far as he was concerned. Aside from the dinner date planned for later that evening, Brian consciously declined sitting with Lynn at lunchtime too. That was why Lynn was so gratified when Brian unexpectedly approached her at the Cafeteria salad bar. He was bubbly and animated with his news announcement. Lynn was actually excited about joining Fitzy's contest team. Perhaps a little more daily contact would blossom the functionality of their relationship.

"So what brings you to this part of town," Peter continued. To a certain extent, he was relieved with Lynn's departure from the team. Cooling off the amount of constant daily togetherness could be the right tonic to relax his increasingly confusing feelings.

Lynn replied matter-of-factly that she was heading to the sixth floor lounge to gather a flip chart. Her new team mistakenly left the tool behind following an afternoon of filling out ACORD insurance applications. Actual Brigadier underwriters were scheduled to peruse the applications that night to rate premium pricing for the contest proposals.

"Team chemistry can be funny," Lynn bemused. "Craig asked Brian to have the Minnesota 'Go-for' the flip chart. He thinks his new nickname for me is quite hilarious. What is irritating is that he directs his orders to Brian instead of me."

Peter's mind flashed back to the mystical moment with the Magic Marker. Now she was the Minnesota 'Go-for'—a sad play on words for the state university mascot—the Gophers. He said nothing as he watched Lynn walk down the hall.

The contest teams adjourned for the night after a fifty-minute interchange with their respective underwriters. Peter returned to his fourth floor suite. As he inserted his room key into its knob, he surprisingly eyed Lynn striding down the hallway. She was lugging the bulky flip chart.

"Are you lost," Peter joked. "I thought you had a date tonight?"

"I am looking for my team," Lynn exasperated. "They were not in the meeting room when I got back. I figure Craig decided to have a more private meeting with the underwriter."

Lynn dropped the flip chart to the floor. She checked the time on her wristwatch and peered to the far end of the corridor.

"I am sick of carrying this thing," Lynn bemoaned. "I have searched the common lounges on every floor. Beats me if I can find them."

"What time are you and Brian heading out to dinner," Peter changed the subject.

"In a half an hour," Lynn looked off. "Do you think they wrapped up by now?"

Lynn retrieved the paper chart. She stood still for a moment.

"You know, I was really looking forward to meeting with that underwriter," Lynn confessed. "I was the one who filled out every box of those darn ACORDS."

"You knew how to fill out all of your applications," Peter marveled.

"Actually Craig designated me as official secretary," Lynn shrugged. "He said he wanted no chicken scratch on our submission."

"Matters like these require 'women's penmanship'," Lynn mimicked. "I am surprised that creep did not ask me to sit on his lap to take dictation."

"I am impressed that you were able to figure out how to fill out all of the stuff in all those application sections," Peter replied.

"That is what is such a kick in the pants," Lynn criticized. "Hinson already had a full set of ACORDS completely filled out when we sat down this afternoon. He recited to me what to put down on each form. Brian asked him why we could not just use the package he already had? But he was so headstrong to get my pen on a different set. He would not even let us see what he had written. He would hold them in his folder like he was reading a restaurant menu and dictate."

XXI

Peter returned early to the Brigadier Conference Center. It was the homestretch week of the Home Sales School. Marianne and the kids were going to his mother-in-law's for Sunday night dinner. He excused himself from the obligation.

"I need to get a jump start on the lesson reading for the final exam," he said.

The cavernous lobby appeared empty when he arrived. He carried his garment bag with a replenished supply of dry-cleaned business suits. A roll-along suitcase coasted at his side. It contained a fresh ration of underwear and socks.

Peter pressed the elevator button marked "up". He turned around to wait for the car. His wristwatch told him it was nine o'clock.

He found Lynn sitting on a bench across from the doors—watching him.

"Lynn." Peter withheld his surprise. "I didn't expect to see you."

Lynn responded with a narrow grin. She looked down to her fiddling fingers. Peter set his bags on the ground. He strolled up to the bench with his hands in his pockets.

"So what brings you to be sitting all by yourself like this on a Sunday night?" Peter questioned. Peter knew the out-of-state crew had planned a trip to Long Island Sound as their weekend get-away. Brian and Lynn announced that they planned on laying low for the weekend. They were content sticking around the Conference Center.

She did not respond to Peter's inquiry. The hesitation prompted Peter to scope the left and right sides of the lobby.

"So, where's Fitzy?" he asked.

"He is over at Teapot's with a couple of the guys," Lynn stated.

"Why aren't you over there too," Peter asked.

"I was earlier," Lynn informed. "Brian wanted to stay and play a few games of pool. I decided to come back to do some laundry."

"So, you are waiting here for Fitzy to come back?" Peter hypothesized.

"Actually," Lynn glimpsed to the South Side Entrance. "I was hopeful to catch him so he could escort me across the street to the Laundromat. I have a load of clothes over there in the dryer."

"Well, shoot Lynn," Peter quipped. "I can escort you over to the Laundromat." The elevator car opened.

"Let me run these bags up to my room. I will be right back in a jiffy."

The lobby was vacant when Peter returned. He dialed Lynn's room number from the lobby wall phone. There was no answer. Peter meandered in the lobby for a couple of minutes. Slowly he strolled to the Front Entrance. He peered through the front lobby doors. Across the street in the Laundromat he could see her. She had found a suitable escort. Brian was at her side.

Peter watched through the glass doors. Brian was reaching into the dryer and pulling out Lynn's personal items one piece at a time. He would hold each prize high in the air. Teasingly, he would play keep away. Lynn bashfully grabbed the garments from him. As she turned to fold the recovery into a large white pillowcase, Fitzy would produce another secret possession. The game seemed endless.

Peter shrugged his shoulders. He began his journey back to his room. He treated himself to a diet soda at the lobby vending machine.

At ten o'clock, there was a knock at Peter's door. It was Lynn.

"May I come in?" Lynn asked.

"Sure," Peter said. He wanted to cavalierly hold the door open with his hand high on the door—like they do in the movies. When the girl obediently crosses the threshold underneath the arm. Lynn was a smidgen taller than Peter though. He had to keep the door open with his back instead.

"Peter, I am sorry I did not wait for you to come back," Lynn apologized. She sat on the end of the door-side bed. "Brian showed up right after you left. I felt obliged to go over with him. I did not feel quite right telling him you were coming back to escort me."

"Why?" Peter challenged. "Since when do you fell not quite right about saying anything to anyone?"

Lynn offered a sheepish smile. She looked down to the floor. Her fingers were fiddling again.

"I called Minnesota Friday night," Lynn revealed. "I broke up with my boyfriend."

Peter closed the door. He walked across the room to the neighboring bed and sat down.

"For Brian?"

"Yeah," Lynn looked up. "For Brian."

"I thought you were head over heels for your boyfriend back home?"

"I thought I was, too," Lynn confessed. "Things have changed a lot over the past three weeks, Peter. My boyfriend is a twenty-six year old egocentric. He was cool to be with. Letting me tool around in his Nissan convertible. From a materialistic perspective, it was fun—the jewelry, the trips. I have come to realize, though, that there was not a whole lot of substance. He is not exactly what I would call a real man."

Peter stared at the institutional reproduction framed on the wall. He reflected for a moment—summoning the courage to ask the question burning inside.

"What about Brian's girlfriend in Buffalo?"

"He called on Friday night, too."

"Are you sure he did?"

XXII

Craig Hinson's team had been drawn to go second in the second set of contest meetings. His style and presence improved substantially from the first date with the buyer's panel. Hinson selected only one team member to sit with him at the interview survey. Brian and Lynn were among the spectators in the amphitheater. Tracey diplomatically backed off from asking why the early back row junior associates were missing. Ralph's message in restructuring the teams was reverberating. "Do not give Craig Hinson a hard time."

Hinson's clipboard contained an exhaustive list of detailed questions. Peter had to marvel at the obvious technical ability of the high forehead. He was venturing into areas, Collins mulled, that were not even touched upon in class.

Hinson closed his interview with a line of questions relating to the Conference Center Cafeteria operation, asking about workers compensation classifications for kitchen employees.

"We are not required to provide workers compensation insurance for the kitchen staff," one of the headquarter underwriters on the buying panel flatly responded. "The Cafeteria operation is leased out under contract to an outside third party.

Hinson smiled curtly and closed his interview.

Craig Hinson courteously declined a pair of crony offers to grab a light supper that evening at the Hog River Grill Diner. He wanted to retire early to his room. The alibi was acceptable. It was precisely six o'clock when Hinson dialed the Providence, Rhode Island toll free number from his desk side telephone. After a cursory greeting and line transfer, the echo of a speakerphone receiver popped into his ear. The cherry wood walls of the Miles and Mason conference room walls appeared in his mind. Imagining the assemblage of the worldwide firm's top production underwriters awaiting his call was intoxicating.

"Go ahead, Craig," John Wellington instructed. "Tell us what you have got."

The underwriters sat at the ready—penned to analyze the results of their previously prepared checklist.

XXIII

Craig fulfilled his promise. He followed John Wellington's lead and made a dinner date with Plimpton McAllister, Chairman of the Board and Chief Executive Officer of the Brigadier Insurance Company. Hinson requisitioned a dinner party for four guests. The uncertainty of not knowing whether Brad would be replaced on the team was a convenient excuse for not requesting a party for five. Brian was the one designated to tell Lynn she could not attend.

Craig was not bashful invoking the Miles and Mason privilege at the dinner. At Wellington's suggestion, he baited Mr. McAllister to admit to a Brigadier corporate membership at Cromwell Country Club. Hinson promptly weaseled a complimentary weekend golf foursome. Towards dinners end, Hinson learned of Brigadier's heavy financial support of the city's beleaguered entry in the National Hockey League—the Hartford Whalers.

"I will tell you what," McAllister anticipated the second request for a freebie from the M&M protege. "There are only two tickets remaining in our corporate luxury box for next Wednesday night's Whalers game. You are welcome to those as my guest. I will let Ms. Gilmartin in my office know that you may be calling for more tickets. We can arrange for group seating along the glass if you would like to invite anyone from the Home Sales School."

"I know it is not exactly the Bruins and the Sabres, but you certainly should reconsider and join us," Brian justified Craig's chutzpah after the fact to Peter Collins. "You know, he really is not that bad of a guy."

"I can see you can be bought off with a golf round, huh, Fitzy," Peter retorted. Peter held to his principle. He would not allow Craig Hinson the benefit of sitting in the throne of the luxury box so that he could condescendingly wave down to his worthless subjects in the arena below.

Lynn agreed to accompany Brian to the game. Out-of-staters like Chris Tripoli were quite excited by the invitation. They had never witnessed live professional hockey.

Peter compromised to meet the hockey fans for a post-game nightcap.

The party was planned at Player's Sports Bar & Grill—close by to the Hartford Civic Center.

Face off was scheduled for seven o'clock. Rendezvous at Players's would be around ten thirty. Jim committed to a post-dinner pickup basketball game in the Conference Center gymnasium. He told Peter he would meet him in the lobby after his game to go down to Player's around ten.

Peter was grateful that Jim Stankos was available. They could walk into Player's together. It would camouflage Peter's real desire to perhaps spend some quality time with Lynn. He hoped Brian would get caught up in an honorific conversation with Craig and his cronies.

Finding a parking spot in the Capital district was more difficult than Peter and Jim expected. Player's parking lots around Union Place were blocked with orange traffic cones. A banner waved at the attendant booth – "HOCKEY GAME – LOTS FULL."

Peter maneuvered his car back up Farmington Avenue. Stankos fingered an unoccupied street meter three blocks up on Garden Street. The duo parked the car and walked down to the bar.

The ambiance of Player's Bar & Grill was different from what Jim and Peter were accustomed to in Massachusetts. A large New York Yankees emblem adorned the top of the bar.

"I do not think we are going to like this place," Stankos cringed at the hated logo.

The revelers at Player's were crammed into the building like a can of sardines. The Home Sales School group was fortunate enough to set up camp along the right side of the restaurant. Peter was able to make out Lynn wedged into the far corner of a six-person booth. Brian was seated next to her. Why is it every time I see her in a bar I cannot get near her, Peter wondered with a cursory wave.

"Sorry guys—all the booths are spoken for," a referee-shirted waitress shouted. She elbowed by with a loaded tray raised over her head. "You are going to have to clear this area. Standing room is over on the other side of the bar."

Lynn viewed Peter's helplessness. The occupants of her booth were busy digging into a large basket of onion rings smothered in ketchup centered on the middle of the table. She shrugged her shoulders and smiled in reply to Peter's subconscious plea for her to move out of the booth. Brian extended an oversized ring in front of her face.

"Let's head over to the other side," Jim shouted in Peter's ear as Lynn bit into the onion ring. He could barely decipher the message. Was it the noise level, or Brian swabbing ketchup off the corner of Lynn's mouth?

"Pick your poison, Peter," Stankos exclaimed as they negotiated the line standing on the other side of the bar. "My treat."

"Give me a shot of tequila and a beer," Peter deadpanned. He could make out Lynn wedged in the booth amid the crowd frenzy. It was a weird aura. Patrons buzzed around the establishment like fireflies. It was a controlled chaos. People flitted about their business—yelling their conversations as if it was natural to scream in order to be heard. The agglomeration of noise created a drone of garble. And there alone in the corner sat the presence of Lynn Cloud. Peter heaped a glob of salt between his thumb and forefinger. It was like she was the only person existing within the havoc, Peter sensed. God, he felt low.

Jim watched as his friend licked the wad of salt. He downed the shot in one gulp and sucked hard on a slice of lemon. The violating sensation of the alcohol deadened Peter's awareness. He shook his head in reaction. His view of Lynn inside the booth became blocked with crowding bodies.

Craig and one of his cronies arrived next to Jim. They attributed their tardiness to the post-game condiments afforded to the luxury box. Peter was disgusted. Jim was actually asking Hinson to describe the amenities.

"Bartender, another tequila."

"Collins, Stankos," Craig glowed. Why couldn't he refer to us by our first names Peter begrudgingly thought? "There are some fellows here I would like you to meet." Peter Collins absently shook the hands of the two names he did not feel compelled to remember.

"They are reinsurance specialists who negotiate large cap accounts," Hinson bragged about his new found acquaintances. "You guys never deal in large caps, do you?"

In less than two minutes, Peter surmised that the two reinsurance suits were as pompous as Hinson himself. They chided the measly income of independent insurance agents. Each one joined Craig in a salute to those who made in excess of six figures a year.

Peter ignored the boasting. He ordered a third tequila. He could not see if Lynn was still wedged in her stationary position. This is going to be a long night, he thought and frowned.

One hour and three tequilas later, Player's started to empty. The booths began to rouse. Its occupants shimmying out of their coops. Lynn traversed to Peter's side of the bar. Brian made a quick turn to the Men's Room.

"Jeez, Peter," Lynn gawked when she saw her friend's face. "How much have you had to drink?"

"I dunno," Peter quipped.

"Well, you are not driving in this condition," Lynn determined. "Give me your keys."

Peter rode shotgun back to the Brigadier Conference Center while Lynn drove. Jim and Brian sat in the back seat.

"Hey, Million Dollar Man," Lynn joked. She got a kick out of Peter owning a family styled sedan. "How about you surrender your humility and give me and Brian this car as a wedding gift when we get married?"

"How did you enjoy the hockey game," Peter ignored the jab. The alcohol's effect had kicked in. Peter placed his hand on Lynn's leg. Brian was so animated describing the hockey game to Jim that he did not pick up on the liberty.

Lynn looked down at Peter's hand. She made no motion to return the wedding banded appendage to its owner.

"I am not much of a hockey fan," Lynn volunteered.

"You aren't," Peter asked incredulously. "A Minnesota girl like you?"

Jim and Brian exited the car as soon as it reached its berth in the underground parking garage. Lynn remained behind the wheel. Peter summoned a deep breath.

"I have a confession to make," Peter exhaled. "I was really hoping to talk to you tonight."

Lynn breathed a slight exhale. The direction of the conversation deepened beyond her comfort. She ventured for a subject change. Her eyes glistened.

"How would you like to see my tattoo?"

Lynn helped Peter from the passenger side of the vehicle. Jim and Brian were puzzled by his wide grin. Lynn ably guided him towards the garage elevators. Fitzy refused to acknowledge his girl's arm under Peter's shoulder—not in front of Jim Stankos.

Jim was as blind to the inebriation. He pressed the elevator button "L" for the lobby. Upon arrival, he challenged Brian to race him to the gymnasium, challenging the first one to hit a shot from half court would win five dollars a man.

The diversion was a coup. Lynn and Peter stood under the near side basket, retrieving Jim and Brian's macho air ball heaves. Lynn soon became bored with the charade.

"Come on, Peter," Jim shouted after another round of misses. "Let's see your old athletic prowess."

Peter shagged an errant ball and slowly walked to center court. Throwing baseball style, he hurled a line drive towards the hoop. The ball's arc was minimal, hitting the back end of the rim, and ricocheting through the net. Peter raised one arm to the air and grinned as he loped off of the court.

The aimless chance of good fortune invigorated the contestants for five dollars. Both Brian and Jim ran to the ball racks to garner more ammunition.

"Wait! Watch this one, watch this one," they each shouted.

"I am going to help Peter to his room," Lynn waved to join Peter's stride to the lobby. Neither Brian, nor Jim noticed how she wrapped her arm around stumbling victor, or was he?

Basketballs continued to careen off the ends of the gymnasium as Peter and Lynn boarded the elevator for the fourth floor. Peter smiled at Lynn as the doors closed. He leaned his head forward and rested it upon her shoulder.

They did not utter a word as the elevator car rose. Lynn wrapped her arms around him. It was bliss. He kept his arms to his side as she held him.

Lynn stood at the side of the bed next to his outstretched body. With the smile of a vixen, she unbuttoned the top of her dungarees. She slowly unzipped her pants. Her eyes never left those of her host. She erotically revealed a pair of soft-laced pink panties. She extended her thumb into the lace and proceeded to move the panties down.

The rose appeared in the area Peter had envisioned in his dreams. He expected the tattoo would be of a large rose bloom—but it was not. Rather, it was a small pink bud with a long-thorn stem.

As he gazed at the coloration, Lynn continued her smile and thumb. She did not cease the hand movement until the top of her pubic hair was clearly visible.

She stood at attention before her friend.

"So what do you think?" she asked in a sexual tone.

Peter reached and touched the rose. With two fingers he stroked softly around its borders.

"I think you are beautiful," Peter whispered.

"I thought you would like it," Lynn teased. She popped into the air zipping and re-buttoning her pants in one quick movement.

"Lynn, please," Peter sat up onto the side of the bed. He grabbed Lynn's hands.

Lynn removed the smile from her face. She sat across from Peter on the adjoining bed.

"What is it, Peter?" Lynn whispered.

"There is something I have been meaning to tell you," Peter whispered back. He leaned his face closer to Lynn. She responded. The teasing foreplay was gone. Their mouths were inches apart. Peter could feel Lynn's breath on his lips. Her eyes were closed. Her breath had become shorter—more passionate.

"Lynn, I … I," Peter stammered.

"Yes, Peter?"

Peter closed his eyes. He leaned to kiss Lynn—but there was nothing there. Lynn leaned back to a perpendicular position.

"Peter, I think I better be going."

XXIV

"The final examination consists of two hundred multiple choice questions," Tracey Benison reminded the anxiously awaiting oval. " The test evaluates your general understanding of the ten policy forms we have covered along with applying those aptitudes to some select case studies. There are twenty questions interspersed throughout the test concentrating on each of the ten sections. Each question is worth two and a half points."

"To earn the blue ribbon you cannot answer more than four questions incorrectly in a given section," Tracey counseled. She broke the cellophane seal packaging the exam packages and handed a stack to Ruth. They split to each end of the amphitheater to begin passing out the questions. "You will have the opportunity to review your results a week from Friday at the graduation dinner. The results will show how you fared in each section."

Peter looked to the movie chair to his right. Lynn returned a small grin. The stapled test packets laid face down on their writing tables.

"It is now 9:02," Ruth confirmed from the overhead Simplex clock mounted above the lecture whiteboard. "You will have until twelve o'clock noon to complete the exam. You may now turn your packets over and begin. Good luck."

The opening case study dealt with general liability insurance.

"I hate general liability," Peter recalled Lynn's lamentation at the prior night's study session. He smiled at the first question and thought to himself that Lynn must be cursing in her head. "I will never deal with general liability insurance again after I get back to Duluth."

"That is how I feel about personal automobile insurance," Peter remembered shrugging. A light tap of a pen stub on the writing table to his right broke his tangent thinking.

Peter kept his head stationary. He adroitly shifted his line of sight to the origin of the tap. The source of the sound pointed at question four. Peter consulted the choices on his answer key. In a purposeful manner, he resorted to the scratch pad reserved for mathematical calculations cornered at each table. He scrawled the letter "C". The original signal was returned with a single tap. The message was quickly wiped out after a hesitating moment.

The first question about personal automobile insurance greeted the candidates about twenty minutes into the exam. Peter was pretty certain of the correct response. Rather than react to instinct, he tapped his pen. The earlier interlude was intriguing.

The letter "A" appeared on the neighboring pad. The message scratched out seconds after the light responding tap. It confirmed his planned choice.

The monotony of boiler and machinery cases and inland marine questions dragged into the second hour. The sporadic tap became a welcomed escape from the systematic brain frying.

Lynn surrendered her will to general liability. Any pertinent question was addressed with a tap. Peter acquiesced to the ploy. If an automobile related question arose, he would not bother reading the question. A single tap was all that was necessary.

XXV

The noose had dropped from the gallows frame. The construction appeared makeshift from its cubed pedestal to the squared arch above. The one armed good guy enveloped by the noose was perilously close to his demise. There was only one last chance for his savior to make rescue.

The decision was made. It would be an all or nothing attempt at saving the victim. Solve the puzzle of the circumstance that created this ill-fated doom. Letters written to the ultimate authority were having no success.

The savior leaned towards the gallows. In a swift move, the last two spaces filled the pedestal above. "I-N-F-L-E-C-T-I-O-N," the savior conjured.

The second arm appeared from the victim's side. The effort had been fatal.

"HANGMAN," Lynn scribbled in the left margin of her workbook.

Peter leaned against his writing table. He drew the symbol "?".

Lynn crossed over the "F" and the "L". She replaced the spots overhead with an "S" and a "P".

The hangman first surfaced during a discourse on business income coverage under a boiler and machinery policy. The scheduled guest speaker from the Hartford Steam Boiler Insurance Company had a conflict develop last minute at his office. A substitute was delivered in his stead. The ill preparedness of reading from another person's notes made for a long morning.

Lynn offered the puzzle to Peter as a peace-making gesture. The night before at Teapot's had been embarrassing for both of them.

It was Lynn who mentioned that her agency team planned to visit Teapot's after their nightly strategy session. Peter's group had made the trek part of their nightly routine. Perhaps we can relax and have a drink together, they had conjectured.

Jim and his team were already at Teapot's when Peter and his group arrived. Collins joined Stankos at the bar to watch the tail end of the television broadcast of the Boston Bruins and Montreal Canadiens at the Boston Garden. A Bruins win would solidify a top spot heading into the Stanley Cup playoffs.

An attractive young local girl approached Peter at the bar. He could tell she had been drinking heavily.

"The cowboy told me, my friends and I should ask you to sing Karaoke," the girl pawed at Peter's shirt cuff.

"I am only on my first beer," Peter toyed. He was somewhat flattered by the young girl's attention. "Maybe in a few minutes."

"You promise," the girl placed her finger on Peter's chin. He nodded. She turned and strolled back to her friends giggling at the back pool tables.

"Peter," Jim called, mesmerized by the final game seconds ticking off in the corner of the muted television screen. "What is that song the Canadien fans chant at the Forum when they beat the Bruins?"

"The song?" Peter asked.

"You know," Stankos gleamed waving his hand. "Na – na – na- na, Na- na –na –na, Hey – hey – hey, Kiss Him Goodbye! You should sing that song!"

"Yeah," Peter laughed. The girls huddled giggling in the back corner flooded him with a rush of energy. The cowboy injected the requested Steam cassette into the Karaoke machine. The night crowd seemed awakened by the sudden yells coming from the back of the room.

"Ladies and gentlemen, my friend over there at the bar and I are from Massachusetts," Peter shouted into the microphone. A couple of whistles and claps came from the girls. "We just watched our Boston Bruins beat those no good Canadiens. If you are a Whalers fan, you know how good it feels to beat Montreal. As our way of saying thank you for treating us so nice while we have been in Hartford, I have a little song I want to sing—but I am going to need some of your help."

Peter waved for the girls at the pool tables to join him. They came running en masse to his side. The Montreal farewell song was an obvious thorn in Whalers fans' sides too, Peter observed. The crowd began hooting and hollering as soon as they recognized the tune.

The crowd was singing at the top of their lungs when Craig Hinson's team entered the bar. In order to avoid being bumped from the unison sway of the singers, Hinson along with Brian and Lynn moved to some empty stools at the front of the bar. They watched the spectacle that was Peter Collins.

"Come back to the pool tables," the attractive girl slurred as she pulled at Peter's cuff when the song ended. "I want you to meet the rest of my friends."

Lynn noticed how close the girl's ear was to Peter's in order to be heard above the applause. She spun her stool around. Peter looked back to the bar before accepting the girl's invitation. Once again, Lynn's attention was elsewhere. She was surrounded on all sides.

"Sure," Peter took the girl's hand. "Show me the way."

The conversation at the stools bored Lynn to death. She ignored the continuous contest strategy discussion and scoped the room for Peter. She spotted him at the back pool tables. The young girl had warmed up to hugging him. Lynn sat silently as she watched Peter's reaction. At first, he stood frozen—somewhat taken aback by the forwardness. Lynn's shoulders sunk as Peter wrapped his arms around the girl—hugging her back. The girl teetered in Peter's arms. Lynn could not tell if the girl wanted to dance, or fall on her face. The movement caused Peter to twist to regain the admirer's balance. The motion positioned Peter to look directly back towards the bar. His eyes met Lynn's directly.

The noise static in the room seemed to evaporate. How awkward was this, Peter face read. The girl in his arms felt like dead weight. Lynn raised her head to regain Peter's attention. She began to mouth a message across the room. Peter squinted through the smoky air to decipher her plea. "Get over he…."

The transmission was cut off before it finished. Brian leaned over and cut off Lynn's view. He planted a wet kiss on her mouth. The suddenness caught the recipient totally off her guard. Lynn seemed paralyzed as Brian wrapped his arms around her. He repeated his kiss. The noise static in the room returned to full volume.

Peter became flustered. The young girl hanging from his front torso had begun kissing his mouth. At first he was unaware of the inebriated advance. Then, he looked like he began to welcome it.

"Stop it, Brian," Lynn scolded. She convulsed her body to get the arms off of her as if she had an ice cube thrown down the back of her shirt. Brian's public acknowledgement of her existence was one thing. Craig's disdainful leer at the display another. But the view back across the room was the most alarming. Peter was kissing his draped companion.

"Come on Brian," Lynn quivered. "I am ready to go back."

Lynn knew Peter was having a difficult time coming to terms with his feelings for her. Between the tattoo exhibition and now Teapot's, she could tell he was out of sorts. She diagrammed a four by four grid of dots on her workbook's left margin. Peter furrowed his eyes at the odd sight.

"DOT GAME," she scribbled. Peter's eyes remained furrowed. He shrugged his shoulder.

Lynn animated the game. She connected the dots into squares. A player's initials were drawn into the completed square.

"Alternate turns like tic-tac-toe," she wrote. "Most squares win."

XXVI

The amphitheater emptied quickly at the ten o'clock break. The inhabitants confined to the two-hour lecture on flood insurance sought the outside refuge of the bright springtime morning.

A plethora of business suits milled the sidewalks. Many of the employees at Brigadier headquarters shared the same intent to bask a few minutes in the Hartford sunshine. A number of the student candidates joined the queue lined at a curbside vending truck seeking their next injection of caffeine.

Peter and Lynn walked quietly side by side down the sidewalk to the rear South Entrance of the Conference Center.

Their morning cigarette ritual had become a routine. The habit of exiting the side lobby doors at each break and sitting on the secluded bench reminded the couple of what it must be like for partners sharing a lifetime. No longer would one have to ask "Do you want to have a cigarette with me?" Their being was implied. They savored the moments together.

They knew the final days at the Home Sales School were winding down. Peter instinctively drew the disposable lighter from his pocket. He silently lit his companion's Ultra light. The brown mane would tilt forward to the glowing cupped hand and lean back gracefully. Peter would bob in response to his own cigarette. They would take their seat together.

The early weeks of cigarette breaks were initially discussions of personal backgrounds and getting to know one another. As time went on the conversations evolved into spirited conversations about religion, politics and current events.

The final days delved deeper into their hearts. They confided their personal feelings—their individual dreams and ambitions for life after the Brigadier School.

Lynn focused on independence, and the ability to be self-reliant. Accepting a position in an insurance agency, initially, was an answer to "getting something full-time", but now it meant a lot more than that. She had experienced the opportunity to face clients who had a problem, and to resolve their ordeal without the assistance of others. It gave her not only the motivation to move onto the next level as a business professional, but also made her realize she could do things for which others depended, on her own.

Peter's ambitions were altruistically different. The satisfaction of serving clients in need had been delegated to others at his insurance agency. Instead, his ladder of success supported the pockets of those who worked at lower levels in his office, coming to depend on his new business generation as a way of "keeping things going". It was not only a weekly payroll that had come to rely on his efforts, but a wife, children, and community. Continuous ego stroking was needed to keep his pump primed.

Five minutes passed without a word spoken. Lynn snuffed out her stub in dainty fashion at the foot of the bench. She produced two sticks of chewing gum from her shoulder bag. As the couple peered to the rolling expressway on the horizon, Lynn extended a stick to Peter in their usual practice. He received the offer without as much as a glance. Lynn popped the gum into her mouth and began to chew. As was custom she wrapped her cigarette stub in the tin foil wrapper. She neatly stored the refuse in her bag for later disposal.

Peter flicked his butt into the evergreen bushes. Lynn could see the collection of his discards accumulated at the mulched base of the bush that safeguarded their haven of solitude. Peter glimpsed at the bush. It affirmed why Lynn meant so much to him. She did not scold, nor did she pick up after him. Lynn smiled at the sense of tranquil security.

"What are you thinking about," Peter broke the silence. Lynn had been unusually quiet. Lynn looked down to her feet for a moment. She returned her stare to the expressway.

"I don't know," Lynn breathed. "I guess I was thinking about how I wish I was still on your agency team."

Peter's team had performed marvelously at each stage of the contest. A couple of the bland teams had already given up any hope of winning the red ribbon. There was no mistaking the sense in the amphitheater. Peter was the odd-on favorite to be declared the winner that Friday night.

Peter regretted that he condoned Tracey's request to change players so abruptly. A lot of water had passed over the dam since Lynn referred to Peter as a father figure that day.

"Why do you say that?" Peter asked. He willed himself never to admit to Lynn that he sanctioned the shuffle.

"I felt like I was important when I was on your team Peter," Lynn frowned. "I cannot begin to tell you how demeaning Craig has been to me. He is without a doubt the biggest chauvinist pig I have ever met. If I so much as utter a word at one of his precious strategy meetings, he bites my head off."

Lynn stood up. She attempted to shake off her somberness by pacing in front of the bench.

"His little barbs at me are nothing short of sexual harassment. He always has that 'why don't you sit down, Cutie' comment. It infuriates me!"

"What does Brian do when Hinson treats you like that," Peter asked after a momentary pause. If it were me, Peter thought, I would nip that attitude real fast.

Lynn looked down at Peter. He always seemed to have a knack of asking that hard, thought provoking question.

"Brian?"

"Yeah, Brian," Peter nodded. "He was the one so excited about having you on the team. I would think he would have made sure you were not the glorified team secretary—fetching charts and stuff. Which reminds me—did he ever explain where they took off to meet that underwriter without so much as waiting for you?"

"Peter, I like Brian," Lynn stated. "I like him a lot. I do not want to ask him to fight my battles."

Peter stood up and began to walk back to class. Lynn instinctively matched the stride to his side.

"You know what Lynn," Peter conjectured. "Maybe there is a reason for all of this. Here you are starting your career in a male dominated industry. It is chock full of Craig Hinsons. Maybe you are going to have to learn to deal with it."

XXVII

She was back sitting on the South Entrance bench. She did not react to the bang of the latch as the glass door locked into the secure station behind her. She had come to sense his presence.

"You were magnificent today," Lynn stared at the overhead expressway. "I am so happy for you. That red ribbon is yours, and I was so happy for what you did for Brad Heller during your final sales presentation."

Peter had Brad perform the final portion of the morning sales close. He asked the Dale Carnegie disciple beforehand what area of insurance provided him the most comfort.

"I guess I tend to fall back on life insurance and group benefit plans," Heller admitted. "Just the way you fall back on your banking background."

"In that case," Peter Collins planned. "let us play to your strongest suit."

In the post contest wrap up Sam Carvellas announced that Brad's final transition into cross selling a life insurance and group benefit plan was the best example of effective account rounding he ever witnessed at the Home Sales School. He wished he had videotaped Heller's words. Future classes would benefit from such training.

"I thought Brian did a good job," Peter observed. Deep down inside he knew how well he did. He figured a little humility would not hurt.

"That bastard," Lynn announced. The damnation startled Peter.

"Fitzy?"

"No," Lynn said softly. "Craig." She sniffled at her nose with a tight wad of tissue. Her clenched fist hid how soaked the wad became before Peter's arrival. Peter sat down on the bench.

"He told me I was not allowed to last night's final rehearsal meeting. He even told me he changed his mind about having me collate and bind copies of the final proposal," Lynn stopped and looked at Peter. "Said it was 'shark repellent to any Peter Collins pillow talk.' He is a total bastard."

Peter looked out at the expressway. Lynn returned to the tissue wad.

"I was surprised he was so technical," Peter reflected on Craig's earlier presentation. Hinson was a total bastard, but the thought of Lynn brooding about "pillow talk" was not the worst thing in the world. "I have a hard time envisioning an everyday insurance buyer understanding all that insurance form mumbo jumbo."

"That was all his doing," Lynn stated. "It was either his way or the highway."

Lynn exhaled a deep breath. She stuffed the hardened wad in her pocket.

"Peter," Lynn resolved to rise above the adversity. "I would like you to do me a favor. There is no way I can stomach sitting with Craig at the team table tomorrow night at graduation. I am sure Brian will be sitting next to me. I sure would appreciate it if you will sit at my other side."

"Besides," she added and smiled ruefully. "If tomorrow is our last night together, I want to be damn sure you are sitting at the stool next to me as soon as we walk into Teapot's post-graduation party."

XXVIII

Cromwell Country Club was a Tournament Players Course. It played host to Sammy Davis Jr.'s Greater Hartford Open, its private membership a list of the world's top insurance executives and Hartford society elite.

Peter emulated a lot of the student candidates. He drove his own car to the conferment at Cromwell. Many planned to cut an early exit after dinner. For most, they wished to return home as soon as possible. Being with their families for the weekend was the most pressing desire.

Peter promised Lynn he would stay for the party afterwards at Teapot's. He had called home and told his wife he would see her and their two boys early Saturday afternoon.

A string of automobiles followed the courtesy vans that shuttled the out-of-state candidates to the Cromwell grounds. Peter met up with Lynn and Brian in the parking lot as the group was escorted to the clubhouse banquet room.

Ralph Heffling's promise held true. Graduation night was only the second occasion where the Brigadier Insurance Company provided complimentary liquor to the Home Sales School agents. The soon-to-be graduates did not shirk this opportunity for free libation. The standard fare of draft beer at Teapots's had been replaced. The open bar requests changed to dry martinis and manhattans.

Lynn looked radiant. Peter wanted to tell her so, but it was tough to do with another at her arm. Her bubbling merriment reflected on all the agents' faces. The examinations and competitive contests were over. In twenty-four hours time they would all be home.

Brigadier Insurance provided a price-was-no-object five star dinner. Consommé was served followed by an eye-appealing salad of unique garden lettuces and sprouts. An appetizer of fresh salmon topped with a lemon cream sauce was followed by a minted sherbet to cleanse the palate. The main entrée was surf and turf. Two baked stuffed shrimp paired with filet mignon and green beans almondine.

The wait staff hovered over the tables throughout the evening. Their charge was to make sure no goblet emptied of the red and white table wines of choice. A dessert cart was wheeled to each table offering an array of sweets and cordials.

Tracey served as MC for the evening. She and Ruth Meyer stood at a wall-side table to the rear of the elevated podium. The pair manned the station of graduation certificates awaiting their owners.

"Our first course of business this evening is to announce the winner of the red ribbon sales contest," Tracey informed the group. In past years the blue ribbon winners for academic excellence were announced ahead of the sales contest. Recipients opened their graduation packets once they returned to the tables. Having a blue ribbon winner stick their certificate in the air shouting "Hey I won the red ribbon too!" waxed the anticipated sales contest results melodramatic.

Tracey pulled a white sheet of paper from the concealed podium shelf. She placed it on the pen-lit tilted top.

"I suspect that tonight's winners were unaware that they were the only one to stumble upon the existence of the Cafeteria lease during their line of questioning at the diagnostic interviews. Our buying panel was keenly tuned into looking for the recommendation of business income coverage on tenant betterment and improvements at the final sales presentation. None of you specifically cited our special dominant buying need."

Purdy signaled to Ruth to turn up the banquet room lights. All eyes squinted back towards the illuminated podium.

"Our buying panel recessed after your presentations to examine your written sales proposals in greater detail," Susan Tracey explained. "We needed to put your sales process abilities on a back burner. Our final determination was made under our primary criteria. Who addressed our single unique need most effectively?"

"Only one group identified the required endorsement by form number in their written proposal," Tracey motioned a finger to the air. "Ironically, I am not too sure if the presenter knew exactly how the form responds; however, it was specifically defined in the recommendation's Glossary."

"YES!" erupted from the silent crowd. The source was confident of the upcoming victory announcement.

"The winners of the Brigadier Home Sales School red ribbon contest are Craig Hinson, Brian Fitzgerald, Bill Connelly, Brad First and Lynn Cloud!"

Peter was sandwiched between the winners' seats at the table. The team collectively jumped from their chairs.

"I don't believe it! I don't believe it," Lynn gushed. The screams between the fingers at her mouth emulated the chosen queen at a beauty contest.

Peter slid in his chair back from the table. Lynn and Brian grabbed a hold of one another. They jointly hugged the mentor of their team. The tribal group embrace created a unison howl.

"We did it Craig! We did it," Lynn bubbled. Peter watched as she kissed Craig Hinson on the cheek.

There is one critical element to any successful insurance agent. The ability to hide the disappointment of defeat. Show some class and recover quickly. Peter tried to display his good wishes—joining the applause of the banquet room. This one was tough though.

The courteous applause strengthened as the team winners ambled arm-in-arm to the podium. Peter cast a lone silhouette at the vacated table.

"Smile for the Brigadier Agent newsletter," Ruth shouted as she took spontaneous snapshots of the winning group.

Lynn led the revelers back to their seats. Each carried an envelope with blue and gold foil diagonally wrapped around its corners.

"My office is going to be so thrilled to see I won the red ribbon," Lynn announced to no one in particular. She was ecstatic over the unexpected turn of events. Peter reached and shook Lynn's hand. Acknowledgement of any congratulations was nonexistent. Lynn's sole focus was to join her comrades' preoccupation. Ripping open their foil packages.

"Double bonus," Craig yelled. The blue and red ribbons intertwined the certificate in his waving fist. The abruptness caught his teammates off guard. None of the others had the blue intertwined embossing. Craig was the only double ribbon winner.

The commotion surrounding Hinson's high fives delayed Lynn's attention to her packet. She was not even looking at her papers as she extracted them from their sleeve. Her certificate was sealed with both the blue and red intertwined ribbon.

Lynn gasped at the sight—but said nothing. No one was watching her. She flipped to the remaining contents of the envelope. A final grade report showed a chart reflecting gray bars in each of the examination sections. Each bar exceeded the ninetieth percentile. Behind the report was the opening day color class photograph.

"Look, Peter," Lynn voiced her first reaction to the contents. "You are standing next to me in the picture."

Peter eyed the centerpiece of the photo. His mind drifted. He could see Lynn crying in row three that first morning, and her later day rescue of him from the locked side entrance.

"Peter, do you know what this means," Lynn startled him from his daze. "I got the blue ribbon. That means you did too." She winked.

"Peter Collins," the amplified noise interrupted from the rostrum. They must be giving out the blue ribbon awards, Peter surmised. He marched to the front of the room. The tables clapped loudly for the just-missed sales contestant. A few "Peter-Peter" chants bulleted the room. Peter accepted his blue and gold foil package.

Peter returned to the table. He did not bother to open the envelope. Instead, he casually laid it on the clothed table surface. He clapped loudly for each successive blue ribbon winner. Rise above the anguish of defeat, he resolved. He joined in the same first name chants.

The wave of nausea swelled when the fifth consecutive bland returned to a neighboring table. Everyone was receiving blue and gold foil wraps on the graduation packets. Didn't Tracey Benison say the award winners receive foil envelopes?

Peter could not remember what Tracey said. Was the foil significant or not? As a matter of fact, Peter thought, I do not remember anything after she said Craig Hinson won.

Peter glimpsed over to Lynn. She was chatting excitedly with Brian. The diversion allowed Peter to discreetly slide his package under the tablecloth at his lap. He quietly sliced the package open with his butter knife.

He gulped when the contents emerged.

The blue ribbon was absent from the certificate. Peter pulled on the sides of the envelope. He pirated a deeper look into the package. Could the ribbon have fallen off?

The jail cell patterned bars of the final exam grade report sneered back at Peter's inquisitive eye. One bar was markedly shorter than the others.

Peter paused to check the activity at the table. Lynn was still in deep conversation with Brian. Peter dug his forefinger and thumb into the chasm of the envelope. He pulled out the striped sheet.

Nine of the ten bars exceeded the ninetieth percentile. One bar fell below the threshold for honors recognition. It reflected the eightieth percent range.

There were six wrong answers on the blue ribbon barring section—two more than allowed to meet ninety percent.

Peter swallowed. He scanned the bottom of the chart to scrutinize the label on the stunted appendage.

Personal Automobile.

XIX

The Brigadier Conference Center was empty when Peter returned from Cromwell Country Club. Even the security counter was vacant. The dress shoe heel click echoed through the lobby as he walked to the elevators.

While the shuttle vans emptied their cargo at Teapot's, Peter neatly stacked his luggage in the back seat of his car.

The barstool at Lynn's right hip remained the rest of the evening. The intended occupant journeyed instead on the ninety-minute trek back to Worcester, Massachusetts.

The automatic garage doors at the Collins' residence began to rise. They welcomed the returning traveler as Brian, and one of the ex-basketball player blands, carried the intoxicated Lynn Cloud into the Conference Center lobby.

Peter abandoned his luggage in the entry foyer. He made his way up to the master bedroom. The light on the nightstand clock radio showed it was 2:02 in the morning.

Marianne Collins stirred to see who interrupted her slumber. She smiled at the intruder and peered at the clock. At the same time, in a place called Hartford, Connecticut, a man named Brian Fitzgerald began making love for the first time to a woman named Lynn Cloud.

Peter mumbled that he wanted to come home early. He climbed into bed. Marianne returned to her steady sleep.

Peter lay on his back for several minutes. He stared blankly at the ceiling. *I wonder what she is doing right now*, Peter wondered.

Brian rolled back on top of his lover for a second intercourse.

BOOK II

"Want to discuss it before the teacher comes?"

"Mankind is at war. The killing is violent."

"That must account for the steady stream of incoming light. So many blue spirits mixed with the others."

"The enlightened decided to incarnate. They must have known there were important life lessons to leave behind."

"Did the cluster show the fate of your body before you decided to go?"

"No—not at this level. It would have been a hard life to choose had it been known."

"How did death come?"

"A bullet in my back. I was running away. My commandant picked up the rifle I left on the ground. He shot me with my own gun for leaving my post."

"You chose this exit point?"

"The cluster said there were earlier points I elected to avoid."

"Did it foretell a greater lesson had you decided not to run?"

"It said that does not matter. I chose to run."

I

There is an old adage in the business world. Bankers never display diplomas in the office. Doctors, lawyers and dentists always hang sheepskin. Perhaps it reassures the patients or clients in the waiting room. Thank goodness this guy looks like he knows his stuff. Perhaps it avoids the urge to vomit when the bill for service is rendered.

Insurance people like to assimilate to the health and legal professions. Wall frames can be diverse in an insurance office. An insurance designation certificate from a mail order school catalogue can appear just as dubious as an Ivy League bachelor's degree. Insurance buyers seem to connect with the strange series of letters that follow an agent's name. Who knows what the initials mean? But they must be important.

Twenty-four newly coveted Brigadier Home Sales School diplomas were framed and mounted on agency walls interspersed throughout the country. The chances of anyone asking about the absence of a blue or red ribbon on the majority of the certificates were slim. Only actual Home Sales School grads, or an Brigadier employee exposed to the Hartford headquarters, even knew of the existence of the ribbons. And unless you had one, who even cared?

Unless of course, you are a ribbon holder. That is a different story entirely. Co-workers and customers are treated for years to come to the highlights of a battle won.

Peter took a cue from his banking days. His certificate and class photograph were condemned to the duty of lint collection. The night he returned from Cromwell Country Club, the envelope was shelved face down on top of the wall bureau in his master bedroom. It would not see the light of day.

Peter hoped five weeks of backlogged paperwork would greet his return to the agency. Filtering through the first day of pink telephone messages and mail alone could hopefully take his mind off of Brigadier Insurance.

Insurance however can be drastically different from banking. Loan applications can sit unattended while lenders are out of the office. Insurance paperwork cannot linger. Mail is opened and processed immediately.

The inability for Peter to pick through a mountain of mail was frustrating. I could be run over by a bus and this agency would operate just fine without me, he lamented to himself. It was the Wednesday after Cromwell when the ring of the telephone broke the silence in his office.

"Peter, I have a serious matter to speak about with you. Do you have a few minutes?"

Peter sat silently as Ruth Meyer tactfully rattled her tale.

The cobwebs of jet lag had evaporated. Lynn walked proudly into the Boylston Agency's headquarters in Cloquet, Minnesota. Trips to the home office were normally confined to a Personal Lines staff meeting the third Thursday of every month. Returning with the spoils of the double ribbons was a special occasion. It was too significant to wait for the late month meeting. The President of Boylston Agency invited the distinguished alumnae to morning coffee at the corner office.

"Tell me the details Lynn of how you pulled off a double ribbon."

The broad grin of the doting President slowly dissolved as Lynn recited her story. The red ribbon was a team accomplishment, but his prized winner had been shut out of competing.

II

"Wellington, you son of a bitch," Ralph screamed. "That pompous fool you sent over here compromised the integrity of our Home Sales School."

Heffling was reeling. The earlier telephone call from the Brigadier Midwest regional chief was totally unexpected. The caller was a rising star on the corporation's organizational chart. Heffling knew to keep liberties at arm's length with his geographic peer. Her good looks and presence could make the Midwest chief Heffling's boss one day.

Heffling was dumbfounded by the report. The Midwest chief had first contacted Tracey Benison. The slight of not touching base with Ralph first created a Pandora's box. The Midwest chief's initial intention was to corroborate the events of the sales contest with those of Lynn Cloud's irate President. Whether consciously or not, Tracey let it slip. Ralph switched Lynn to Craig Hinson's group halfway through the contest.

"The move was very harmless at the outset," Benison had commented. "Ralph Heffling originally thought Lynn Cloud might bring a sparkle to the team."

The Midwest chief did not take the "sparkle" comment well. She had experienced the chauvinistic leers and side remarks all too often during her mid-management days at the Hartford headquarters. Perhaps Lynn's agency president was right, the Midwest chief concluded. Lynn was sent to the Brigadier Home Sales School as a representative of the Great Lakes region. She got there and she was harassed by a pion from Miles and Mason. Far worse was Ralph's involvement. He could be construed as a consenting party to a lewd set up.

Legal suits alleging sexual harassment and discrimination were erupting across corporate America. Case precedent on forms of physical touching or verbal abuse was varied. Court outcomes were often severe.

There was one common element of any harassment claim. Legal costs to investigate a case were exorbitant. And Lynn's President demanded a full and thorough investigation. The matter was taken quite seriously by the Midwest chief. Heffling redirected the scourge to his perceived source.

“Your days of bullying the Brigadier are through, Wellington,” Ralph continued his tirade. The telephone shook in his hand. “Do not even bother to send in your trophy picture of Miles and Mason double ribbon winners. I will be damned before that picture is ever printed in the Brigadier Agent newsletter.”

III

Ruth Meyer had the privilege of knowing the tepid background of Brigadier's senior management's concern. She tactfully tempered her remarks to Peter.

"Peter, you and Lynn became somewhat friendly while you were here at the school, didn't you," Meyer pried. "Did any issues regarding Craig Hinson ever arise in your conversations?"

"Craig Hinson shut Lynn Cloud out of the closing strategy sessions," Peter conveyed. It was the first time he said Lynn's name aloud since returning from Hartford. The words "Lynn" and "Cloud" felt foreign slipping off of his tongue. Was it taboo to use those syllables together? What's so wrong about saying her name, Peter wrestled in his mind. It was almost like he was using an obscenity. His frustration translated to the situation he was trying to remember. Lynn was beset with a lot of adversity the final couple of weeks in Hartford. And my response to her plea for guidance, Peter thought to himself, was to tell her to rise above it.

"Lynn mentioned more than once the liberties that Hinson took with her," Peter refocused his attention back to Meyer. It was soothing to repeat Lynn's name. "Hinson seemed to take particular pleasure in constantly ordering Lynn to 'sit her cute little butt down and be quiet'."

"Peter, Brigadier legal counsel has initiated a full investigation into what happened to Lynn at the Home Sales School," Ruth masked her reaction. "I hope you do not mind, but they will be calling you regarding a deposition."

The Brigadier phone bank opened an incoming call as the Meyer-Collins line disconnected.

"Plimpton McAllister," the voice announced. "John Wellington here from Miles and Mason. Do you have a minute to chat?"

IV

The emotional high of the double ribbon victory rippled into all aspects of Lynn's day-to-day life.

Prior to the Home Sales School, Lynn possessed the drive to address only the most critical necessities of life. Her natural cautiousness was perhaps an adjunct of her parents' persistent hesitation in life to spend money. Matters as trivial as having a tooth fixed became major crises. Lynn learned to schedule her own dental appointments and pay cash.

The confidence created by the Home Sales School experience however swung Lynn to higher aspirations.

Within the week of her return to Duluth, she confidently marched into Krenzen Honda on Mall Drive, and drove off the lot in a brand new black Accord. No down payment was required. The prospect of negotiating the acceptance of a rust bucket trade in was simpler imagined. Sixty monthly payments weeks ago would also have been daunting. There was a new catalyst now motivating Lynn beyond zero percent financing.

Financial commitments of things like car loans were no longer imposing. Neither was rent payments. Lynn contacted a girlfriend from Duluth East High School. Together they leased a small downtown apartment.

The prospect of affluence prospered. Boylston Agency was encouraging Lynn to elevate to a stronger position within the organization—to switch to commercial account sales.

The bond with Brian Fitzgerald was just as promising. Had she found Mr. Right?

Fitzy held true to the promise he made the last night at the Brigadier Conference Center. He flew to Duluth for Lynn's house-warming party at the new apartment. The long Memorial Day weekend was full-spirited. Lynn basked in the concept of a permanent lifetime commitment.

Transacting a round trip ticket to see Brian in Buffalo, New York in mid-July was even easier than Lynn expected. It also gave the opportunity to break in a new credit card.

Everything was falling into place—until the disturbing telephone call arrived.

"Management has had a change of heart," Lynn's Personal Lines Manager reported from the Cloquet office. "Why don't we stick to the personal lines end of things in Duluth? Commercial account sales may be a little of a reach."

V

Attorney Martin Swedberg was a man of polish. The Brigadier counsel specializing in employment practices called Peter as if he were looking up an old buddy. Coach Sam Carvellas would have admired Swedberg's ability to build rapport.

"Teapot's Karaoke cowboy has not been the same since you left Hartford," Swedberg chuckled. The comment made Peter wonder if he ever met the attorney or not. Swedberg was smooth. Peter kept his guard.

"You are the last Brigadier Home Sales School grad to be contacted," Swedberg reported. "Aside from the red ribbon winners, not too many of your classmates had much to offer as far as Lynn Cloud's experience in Hartford was concerned. If there was one constant in my interviews, it was to 'contact Peter Collins'. Ironic, huh? Seems your class is of the opinion you were friendliest with Miss Cloud."

"Mr. Swedberg, I am more than happy to help you out here," Peter deflected the jab. "Please do not feel compelled to browbeat me."

"From everything I have gathered you can probably shed a lot of light on the subject," Swedberg volunteered. "I must say the testimony I have so far is quite contradictory."

"Craig gave Lynn a real tough time at the school," Peter offered. "If you like I can cite several specific instances."

Martin Swedberg remained quiet as Peter recollected the final days of the sales contest. Obviously this guy is taking furious notes, Peter assumed from the silence.

"I am sorry to hear of these episodes Mr. Collins," Swedberg interjected. "It certainly appears to be a very unfortunate misunderstanding."

"Misunderstanding," Peter puzzled. Swedberg abruptly changed his course of questioning.

"Tell me Mr. Collins, did you have any contact with a fellow student named Brian Fitzgerald?"

"Yes, I know Brian," Peter responded.

"Were you friends?" Swedberg asked.

"I would say Brian Fitzgerald and I have a mutual respect for each other," Peter admitted. "We share a lot of similar interests. Yes, I guess you could say Brian Fitzgerald and I are friends."

"Was Lynn one of your similar interests?" Swedberg suavely asked with the tone of a life-long confidante.

"I beg your pardon?" Peter replied.

Swedberg knew he was coming on perhaps a bit too strong. Peter could detect an audible breath on the other end of the telephone.

"Peter," Swedberg flatly continued. "A few of your classmates speculated to me that they suspected Brian Fitzgerald and Lynn Cloud may have had a relationship beyond mere friendship. A couple of them were a little more certain that their relationship was an intimate one."

Martin Swedberg paused for dramatic effect.

"Peter, were you aware that Mr. Fitzgerald spent almost every night at the Conference Center in Lynn Cloud's room?"

"Yes. I was aware."

"Peter, did your friendship with Lynn Cloud ever deviate to intimacy," the lawyer stung.

"Not that it is anyone's business," Peter realized the direction the attorney was developing with the pattern of conversation. "But the answer to your question is no."

"Thank you for speaking with me, Mr. Collins," Martin Swedberg concluded. "I will let you get back to work."

"Wait a minute, Mr. Swedberg," Peter interrupted. "What about Craig Hinson? You have asked me virtually no questions about him."

Peter was unable to finish his second sentence. The phone line had gone dead.

VI

The Midwest regional chief greeted the arrival of the Lear jet at the airport. Employment law specialist Martin Swedberg was the lone passenger to disembark the craft.

The chief made no diverting stops. The Brigadier company sedan traveled directly to the Cloquet corner office. The meeting would not last longer than fifteen minutes.

Swedberg's report summarized the key points of the exhaustive six-week investigation. Every student candidate and faculty member including Sam Carvellas had been interviewed.

"There is strong evidence of improprieties taken by Craig Hinson," Martin Swedberg stated upon opening his briefcase. "Mr. Hinson indicated that he did not hold Lynn Cloud's insurance abilities in very high regard. He regrets that some of his remarks may have been taken disparagingly. For that he is very apologetic."

"Miles and Mason Agency had their own legal counsel attend our direct deposition of Craig Hinson," Swedberg continued. He read from a bound report folder. Copies were not made available. "We have subsequently been informed that Miles and Mason has documented Mr. Hinson's personnel file with a written disciplinary warning in response to his behavior."

The President of Boylston Agency's head produced a single nod from the corner desk. The gesture affirmed to Martin Swedberg that his plan was falling into place.

"Miles and Mason counsel also informed us at the deposition that they held an internal hearing with Mr. Hinson prior to our arrival that day," Martin Swedberg continued. "Mr. Hinson told his office the primary difficulty he had with Lynn Cloud was one of character. Mr. Hinson disclosed that out of the entire co-ed group, a student named Brian Fitzgerald and Ms. Cloud were the only ones who blatantly conducted a sexually illicit relationship. Hinson said the pair being assigned to his sales contest team had a very negative impact on their strategies and effectiveness. In addition, Lynn Cloud maintained close contact with Hinson's main competitor throughout the contest—a fellow named Peter Collins. Craig Hinson did not trust Lynn Cloud's relationship with Peter Collins, which may I add he also suspected was illicit."

A frown surfaced from the corner desk. Martin Swedberg was not a specialist in his field out of sheer folly.

"Miles and Mason has notified us that the Hinson matter has been addressed internally. They consider the matter closed," Swedberg pointed his head to the text of his narrative. The delivery of his ultimatum did not require eye contact with his host.

"Should Ms. Cloud decide to seek relief through the courts," Martin Swedberg read," Miles and Mason is prepared to challenge any allegation through the strong arm of the law."

Maintenance of positive relations with all Brigadier agents countrywide is imperative; however, there is strength in size. The Boylston Agency President knew it would be foolhardy to challenge both Brigadier and Miles and Mason. The behemoths could squash any challenger if they so desired. It would not be unusual if ire was raised for M&M to spend a blue-chip team of brokers anywhere in the nation to pirate the largest client of a smaller competitor agency. And if that client did not happen to be written by the Brigadier Insurance Company, Miles and Mason would have a more than cooperative insurance carrier to execute the deed.

"Thank you for all your diligent efforts," the Boylston Agency President stood and shook the Brigadier representatives' hands. "This matter will indeed be closed. Please pass along my gratitude to Ralph for sending you out here Mr. Swedberg."

"You are entirely welcome, sir," Martin Swedberg snapped his briefcase shut. "Unfortunately, I will not be able to extend your message to Mr. Heffling."

"No?"

"Mr. Heffling has tendered his resignation."

VII

In the weeks that followed the ceremonial closing at Cromwell, memories of the Brigadier Home Sales School became blurred and unpleasant. An unexpected letter changed the dimness of the experience. Chris Tripoli had mailed a group letter to his classmates. Each agency letterhead had been word-processed to personalize the salutation.

> Dear Peter:
>
> The time we all spent together in Connecticut earlier this year was most enjoyable. Thank you very much for your support and insight in the fine industry of insurance.
>
> I hope that we all share some great experiences and friendships for many years to come.
>
> The City of New Orleans has a lot to offer, so should any of you get close to this area please call so we can get together and "catch up" with each others lives.
>
> Again, best of luck with your success and please let me know if I can ever help.
>
> Sincerely,
>
> Christopher M. Tripoli, C.I.C.

Peter reflected on the words atop the mid-day mail stack. Chris was a true gentleman, Peter surmised. Who else would have thought to send an expression of thanks from the stack of business cards distributed on day one?

Peter neatly folded the letter back into its envelope. He tucked it into the plastic Brigadier portfolio box of archived workbooks. He then wandered to the office kitchen. Perhaps I can salvage one last cup out of the muddied coffeepot, he thought. He poured the thick sludge and turned off the four-hour old warmer. After doubling the normal dose of powdered cream to soften the blackened caffeine, Peter returned to his desk.

He circular filed the remaining stack of direct mail pieces. Insurance journals and newsletters were shelved for Friday afternoon perusal.

The baby blue colored agency envelope postmarked Duluth, Minnesota sat isolated on the month-at-a-glance paper ink blotter. The loopy letters of the hand-written address was like seeing an old friend.

Lynn Cloud.

Peter stared at the address for a moment. The not-so-pleasant memories began swelling back.

Rather than ripping at the back of the envelope in the manner reserved for Chris Tripoli, Peter dug into his desk drawer for a formal letter opener. No matter what it says, Peter thought, I do not want to mar this keepsake. He extracted the baby blue matching letterhead from its sliced conveyance.

Dear Peter (Dad),

How are you doing? I really missed not seeing you after the banquet. You should have been there. I flashed my tattoo to everyone at Piggy's!I have talked to Brian almost every day since I've been home. He is coming to Duluth next week and I am going to Buffalo over the Fourth of July. Start car shopping! You may loose your Sundance!

I keep looking at our class picture. It is amazing that I was standing right next to you and, at the time, you were an absolute stranger. And now that I know you, I can honestly say that you are really strange! No, I wanted to write you a letter because I kinda miss you.

Brigadier's lawyers called me the other day. They want me to give a deposition on what happened with Craig. They probably just have to go through this procedure to save themselves from a lawsuit, because I didn't try to pursue anything.

Well, I better get back to selling those million dollar insurance policies! I would really like to hear how you are doing occasionally! And someday I would really like to meet your wife. I want to meet the saint that has to put up with you every day! I barely made it! Maybe we can meet for "dinna" someday. You owe me after all the cigarettes you scammed out me! Take it easy!

Sincerely,

Lynn A. Cloud

Peter placed the open sheet next to his telephone. Throughout the day, co-workers drifted into the office delivering faxes and memos. Peter took solace in the apparent disregard for the typewritten note. Insurance letterhead documents blend into the scenery. Between an occasional telephone call, Peter resorted back to re-read the message.

Following the five o'clock ritual of customer service representatives and colleagues herding for the office exits, Peter returned to his desk to search for some personalized stationary. The top couple of navy blue cards emblazoned Peter F. Collins had yellowed from age. Peter sifted through the stationary packet to locate the best candidate worthy of a one way trip to Minnesota.

"Lynn Dear" Peter scripted in his best penmanship. "Dear Lynn" was too ordinary, Peter figured. Brian Fitzgerald probably writes "Dear Lynn".

Lynn Dear,

It was so nice hearing from you. Too bad things could not come together for the last night at Teapot's. Guess I was not quite up to hearing Craig Hinson's tribute to the sacred Miles and Mason crypt of clipped neckties.

The Brig lawyer called me too. I sensed after answering his questions that the branch that Hinson will hang from will be pretty low to the ground.

Things for me are going pretty good on the work front. The Brig underwriters are bending over backwards to report back to Hartford that we are writing new business. The owner of our agency received an offer to sell out to a San Francisco based outfit. A handful of us here have counteroffered to keep internal ownership. Brigadier Insurance has offered practically full financing to support our bid. Looks like it could go through. Went to Hartford to meet with their financial bigwigs. Guess What? No more Ralph Heffling! Sense he got canned. You can cut the tension in the air at that place with a knife.

Good luck with the trip to Buffalo. Keep in Touch.

Peter

VII

Lynn had never been inside Victoria's Secret. She passed the Mall of America window front many times during previous excursions to Minneapolis. Midwestern girls never stand face front to peer at the half-torso mannequins. A style is developed to tactically vision the laced lures out of the corner of one's eye.

She noticed the male-dominated patronage inside the store as soon as she got off the escalator to the Mezzanine Level. Such an intimidation would have veered the daughter of a Cherokee chief in past months to the neighboring Orange Julius stand. Things were different now for the double ribbon winner. She marched into the lingerie boutique—ready to break into the first of her American Express Travelers Checks.

"May I help you?" the powder-caked blonde offered.

"Yes, you may," Lynn nodded confidently. "I would like to see what you have in laced bras and panties."

"Do you prefer any particular color?" the perky blonde asked.

"Most certainly. I would like something in silver and something in black."

"Nothing in red?" the blonde inquired. "Red is a gentleman's first choice."

"No," Lynn retorted. "I hate red."

"Size?"

"34C".

Monica Chambers was dumbfounded. Since childhood Lynn kept her vital statistics top secret. Monica now found herself ambling over to the underwear section with her closest friend and the perky blonde.

My Gosh, Monica thought. Half a dozen men's heads turned at the "34C" revelation. Lynn did not even blink!

Monica and Lynn had maintained a lifelong friendship since growing up in Duluth. They conversed as pen pals while Lynn was at the Brigadier Home Sales School. Monica was able to keep a close tab on the budding love affair with Brian Fitzgerald.

Since Lynn's return from Hartford, Monica had witnessed a remarkable transformation in her friend. Lynn had always been somewhat introverted. A few months prior, Lynn was impressed with the notion of hobnobbing with an older man whose only apparent quality was providing unlimited access to a convertible sports car. Personalities sure change Monica noticed when one falls head over heels in love.

Monica was happy to see Lynn so animated. Their visits had become few and too far between since Monica took a job and an apartment in Minneapolis. Having Lynn as a roommate even for a night promised to be eventful—but journeying to Victoria's Secret was unexpected. Monica assumed the day before transporting Lynn to the airport for the flight to Buffalo would be limited only to a gossip-filled dinner at a local restaurant. Lynn however exhibited a new energy that would undoubtedly carry over to the early morning flight departure.

"I want everything to be just right," Lynn smiled as she checked her purchases from the store.

"Isn't it funny," Lynn remarked once they returned to Monica's apartment. "I just realized I have never called Brian's house at night. I either call him at the office or he always picks up the long distance charge and phones me at my place."

Lynn fumbled through the bowels of her pull-strapped leather satchel.

"Ah, here it is," she exclaimed. She produced the dog-eared business card. The 716 area coded number was pencil-scratched on its backside.

Lynn picked up the telephone to report her safe arrival to Minneapolis. In less than twenty-four hours time she would be back in her lover's arms.

"I wonder if his parents will like me," Lynn speculated as she dialed the number.

"Hi Brian! It's me," Lynn bubbled at the sound of the answering voice.

"Brian?" the woman's voice queried. "Who is this?"

"This is Lynn. I am looking for Brian. Who is this?"

Lynn detected a shuffling of the Buffalo phone. Muffled voices could be over heard through the hand-covered mouthpiece.

"Lynn, what number are you at? I will call you right back."

It was Brian.

"Brian, what is the matter," Lynn pleaded. "Who was that woman? Is everything all right?"

"I left those papers at my office," Brian tactfully responded. "I guess I will have to run back over there and try to get back to you."

"Papers at the office," Lynn chortled. "Honey, what are you talking about?"

"I will call you right back."

Monica sat glumly on the sofa. Lynn sat beside her. The double ribbon winner ached for a cigarette, but knew better than offend her non-smoking friend. She settled for ringing her hands.

"Monica something is wrong," Lynn frowned. "Brian never sounded like that before."

Monica could not offer a reason for the confusion. She sat silently and watched as Lynn scuttled through a final check of her plane tickets, photo identification and travelers checks. The ring of the telephone fifteen minutes later made the girls jump from their seats.

"Brian," Lynn answered before the second ring.

"Hi, Lynn?" Brian whispered. Lynn could hear traffic in the background. Was he at a pay phone?

"Brian," Lynn bawled. "Is everything okay? You scared me half to death."

"We need to talk Lynn," Brian said slowly. "I do not think it will be such a good idea for you to come to Buffalo."

Lynn's knees began to quiver. She pawed to confirm the kitchen seat behind her before collapsing.

"Lynn a lot of things have changed since I came back from Duluth after Memorial Day weekend," Brian continued. "You know I was keeping in touch with my girlfriend here. I have to make a choice."

"What are you telling me, Brian," Lynn wept.

"Do not come to Buffalo."

Lynn sat with her face in her hands for thirty minutes afterwards at the kitchen table.

What a fool I am, Lynn felt. How can I raise my eyes in front of Monica—with this silly Victoria's Secret bag hanging on the back of my chair?

Lynn straightened to reveal her green bloodshot eyes.

"He is married," Monica stated flatly. "My tarot cards told me so."

IX

It was coming up on Peter's first year anniversary in the insurance business. The eleven-month span since he decided to leave banking saw a host of successes. Thanks to the Brigadier Insurance Company, Peter was now a full partner in the largest insurance agency in central Massachusetts. He had convinced enough of his former banking clients to buy their insurance from him. His self-generated book of renewals ratified the first year salary laid out by his peers who took a shot with their investment. Despite the spring sabbatical to the Brigadier Home Sales School, Collins was the second highest producing salesperson in his office.

Peter had been married to his hometown high school sweetheart Marianne for fourteen years. Their Irish-Catholic families were well known in the Worcester community. Peter and Marianne Collins' social standing was also rising. Peter served on the volunteer boards of the Rotary Club and Chamber of Commerce. Marianne focused on their two boys' local soccer program and the hospital guild. Once their income hit the leadership benefactor level, the Collins would no doubt be slated for presidential positions in all their endeavors.

As the sole income earner of the family, Peter used the burden of mortgage payments and parochial school tuitions as a tonic of motivation. The pressure to generate more commission dollars was relieved whenever the bimonthly baby blue stationary arrived.

The handwritten notes began on Peter's birthday at the end of September. Marianne would religiously send a card to Peter's office the prior day—assured of prompt next day delivery by the local postman. Lynn mailed her own card a few days earlier—calculating three-day delivery around weekends.

The birthday cards lay side by side on Peter's ink blotter.

Peter sliced open Lynn's card first. It was scripted in customary fashion.

"Dear Dad".

Lynn mentioned the last minute break up with Brian.

"He did not want me to come to Buffalo. Figured a better life with his old girlfriend. His loss!"

Peter read the message with mixed emotion. He was glad Fitzgerald was out of Lynn's life. It must have been one hell of an emotional roller coaster ride though.

The bottom of Lynn's birthday card included a homemade present. It was a Dot Game. Three rows of dots traversed below Lynn's loopy signature squared by three down.

"I will give you the first move," Lynn noted.

Peter took a pair of scissors and clipped the Dot Game from the bottom section of the card. There was no need to keep the top portion's reference to Fitzy in their correspondence.

The Dot Game could reach each office in a week's time. The twelve moves necessary on the nine-dot grid were complete by Christmas. As at the Brigadier School, Lynn won the game three squares to one.

Most commercial insurance accounts renew on January 1st. While April 15th is a dreaded date for accountants, the holiday season is traditionally a frantic time for insurance agents. Lynn's baby blue stationary became a welcomed break in the lull following the usual post-renewal chaos.

Lynn manufactured a new Dot Game. The updated version was centered on a single baby blue sheet. It contained an even square of carefully spread dots—fifteen by fifteen. She had taken the liberty of making the first move. Peter mentally calculated the number of necessary moves to complete such a grandiose grid.

"Lynn Dear," Peter wrote back with the counteroffensive second move. "Are you aware that assuming no change in the price of stamps it will cost each of us $43 to finish this thing?"

Peter was elated as he dropped his response in the street mailbox outside his office. He did not know what was more satisfying—the massive Dot Game's implication that Lynn wanted to stay in touch for a very long time?

Or perhaps it was the "XO" scribbled next to her name.

X

The emotional pain of life without Brian was masked. The once a week Worcester, Massachusetts postmark recessed an otherwise melancholy existence.

Peter was always long-winded in his "Lynn Dear" epistles. In every instance, his messages were upbeat and positive. He was conquering life. It was not hard for Lynn's mood to rebound after reading the notes accompanying each Dot Game move. Invariably though, the doldrums existence of Duluth, Minnesota would rear its ugly head.

A strung out homeless man tried one night to break into Lynn and her girlfriend's Third Street downtown apartment. The kicking to the door intensified despite the audible screams of the terrorized tenants. Lynn panicked. Instead of going to the back bedroom to call 9-1-1 as urged, her roommate disappeared. There was no phone call for help. The roommate decided to flee down the rear fire escape on her own.

The roommate returned the next morning to learn Lynn contacted the police in time to nab the invader. He was caught entering the apartment through the rear door that was left ajar. The police found Lynn huddled at the front door barricade. She was neither aware of the roommate's abandonment, nor the open rear door.

Lynn told the roommate she was moving out. She would not return home to her parents. As difficult as the financial difficulty would be, Lynn entered into a lease at the Mount Royal Pines Apartments. The complex was much more residential and secure.

None of these travails would be mentioned in the Dot Game letters.

More distressing was the attitude Lynn developed towards members of the opposite sex. Her younger brother Adam had a motto devoted for dating—"Burn or be burned".

Brian's burn was still sensitive to the touch.

Lynn adopted the thick-skinned motto. Her weekend jaunts around the Duluth singles scene were loose and noncommittal. In the year following the aborted plane trip to Buffalo, Lynn took advantage of nine one-night stands.

It was implied at every pick-up that the night would end in bed. A couple of interludes were with old classmates from Duluth East High School. The best exercise being with the ex-quarterback who captained the football team.

Most of the intercourse was with complete strangers. Lynn knew the majority of the suitors just wanted to get in her pants one time. Hopefully they would never see each other again. Occasionally, she would spot an attractive man who would remind her of someone. She would make her own direct proposition for a good time. No strings attached.

Her preference was to screw in the guy's bed or backseat. That way, they would not know how to contact her later. Lynn would rather risk a companion's apartment neighbor catching sight of her toting her bra and fagged out panties in her hand escaping at three thirty in the morning than face a one-timer at sunrise.

One night, Lynn met an incredibly attractive young man at the lounge of the Hawthorn Suites at Waterfront Plaza. The fellow was new to the Duluth area. He cut a nice figure in his tailored business suit. His conversation was courteous and respectful.

It was Lynn who commandeered the situation. She fluttered her fingers over the middle of his trousers.

"How about we find someplace a little more private?" Lynn recited.

The young businessman did not expect such a direct invitation in a reserved place like Duluth. He was not about to squander the opportunity. His vehicle obediently followed the Accord's path to the Skyline Court Motel. It did not appear to be the first time the Accord cut this particular path.

Lynn stood in the center of the roadside motel room. She requested her visitor to stand still. She methodically unclothed the gentleman—never looking into his eyes. He stood erect at the bedside. Lynn returned the favored foreplay. She removed her clothing—stitch by stitch. Each piece was indiscriminately tossed atop the business suit pile.

Lynn attacked. She leaped on top of the man. The lovers synchronized their fall on top of the bed. Lynn could feel the man's passion as he held her tightly. His kiss was deep and emotional.

Lynn opened her eyes to glimpse at her soon-to-be-oneness. His eyelids were closed. She could sense the lover's feeling for his new found partner.

An internal spirit waved through Lynn's being.

"What am I doing?" Lynn jumped sideways off of the man.

"I am sorry," the naked man flustered. "Did I do something wrong?"

Lynn began to cry uncontrollably.

"Don't you see what is going on here," Lynn bawled. "I cannot even remember what you said your name was. I want nothing from you. Can't you see I am going to use you, and never speak to you again?"

Lynn fumbled to reassemble her clothing.

"Never again," she exclaimed as she exited the room. "Never again!"

XI

The lightning passed Lake Superior and flashed upon Wisconsin. A slow rain fell steady on the parking lot of the Skyline Court Motel. Lynn ran out of the motel room into the wetness of the night.

It was an eerie space of silence.

Puddles reflected the spotted glow of the perimeter light poles. It was as if dozens of circled lights—eyes of the past—were watching.

She bumped into the front hood of the young man's car parked so neatly between the newly painted lot lines in front of Room 3. There would be a bruise above the right knee.

Lynn was oblivious to the pain. Her mind was spinning in a trance-like void.

She tripped off of the sidewalk curb in front of the room onto the pavement. Driveway sealer had recently been applied to the surface. Lynn could feel the tackiness of the seal on her bare feet as she stepped on a filled-in crack.

"*Where is my car*?" Lynn felt herself mouth. The voice seemed to echo deep within the cavern of her senses.

The disheveled woman moved past the young man's car to the middle of the dotted puddles of light. The silhouette of a being shadowed at the doorframe of the room. Sounds of some sort were emanating from the silhouette. Lynn could not distinguish anything—except the spotted lights eyeing her in the black abyss.

Time stood still. Lynn spotted her black Accord far off in the darkness. Instead of being parked in full view of the Skyline Parkway, the compact sedan was tucked next to a dumpster, amid a corner of pine trees.

Lynn ran to her escape. It felt as if she was moving in slow motion. She dropped her undergarments to the ground and clamored for the car keys hidden in her satchel. She looked at her trembling fingers. They had lost their sense of touch. She dumped the satchel over and disposed its contents on the roof of the Accord.

The ring of keys fell to the ground.

Lynn gathered the loop and unlocked the car door. She indiscriminately threw the rooftop objects inside the vehicle. Wet pine needles clung to the spot of tar goop on her foot.

"*Why didn't I park on the pavement*?" the cavern voice echoed.

The automobile veered out of the parking lot onto the Skyline Parkway. It rolled to a stop at the intersection of Hank Jensen Drive. Lynn shifted the car into neutral. She kept her foot anchored on the brake pedal. The population of Duluth was predominantly asleep. Lynn was unaware that the windshield wipers had never been turned on. The spotted eyes of the light poles and puddles followed the Accord. A string of traffic lights lined the length of Skyline Parkway towards downtown Duluth. Lynn sat and stared at the synchronized columns—reds turning to greens, to yellows, and back to reds. The pattern continued over and over in the darkened silence. The calmness of the eyes did not leave her.

"*I need to go home*," the voice echoed in the cavern.

Lynn considered her options. I can get home any number of ways, she thought. I can turn left, or right. No matter what course I choose I will get to my destination. I can drive straight ahead. There are left turns and right turns anytime ahead at any of the eyes. I will get home.

"*But where is home*?" the voice echoed.

Lynn knew going to her parents' home was not her destiny—regardless of the time. Perhaps I should turn around, Lynn thought. I could go back to the motel. He was such a nice young man. I stranded him there. Maybe we could just sit and talk. I can apologize for my behavior. One-night stands are not my being. Maybe we could start over again—from the beginning. We could get to know each other, without having to take our clothes off.

The column of eyes continued the rhythmic sequence of color change. Lynn's mind drifted to her friend, Monica. Monica's family had recently lost her younger brother to cancer. Monica's mother was having a particularly hard time coping with his death. A friend had recommended a book about reincarnation. Monica encouraged Lynn to read the book. It had provided her mother with an inordinate amount of peace.

"Your spirit lives on and shall one day return to experience another earthen journey," Lynn recalled the voice of Monica's mother. "We shall all see each other in future lifetimes."

Monica's mother had talked about the lessons a spirit attempts to learn during each lifetime. Other beings come into our lives to help us learn those lessons. Sometimes we may even teach a lesson or two to benefit someone else.

"My mother is convinced that my brother knew of his shortened life ending in pain before he ever came to this being," Lynn could hear Monica saying. "He blessed us with the lessons he taught. We know that someday we shall be together again."

The column of eyes continued to stare into Lynn.

"Yes," Lynn Cloud said aloud. "I am ready to go home."

XII

The Dot Game was buried inside a United Parcel Service package. Peter unfolded the University of Minnesota tennis jersey hiding the sheet. The garnet block lettered "M" was boldly embroidered the heart of the jersey. The Golden Gopher was proudly smiling behind the logo.

"Dear Dad," the note read. "You know I have never been much for sports, but I know how much you love them. I saw this shirt and thought of two things—Minnesota is my home—and thank you for being such a "good sport" to play the Dot Game with me."

Peter returned his gaze to the gawking Golden Gopher. The note continued.

"I have started seeing someone on a regular basis. His name is Marshall Monroe. We used to go to school together growing up, but never really knew each other. Monica and I ran into him at a party. It is amazing how well we hit it off. I will let you know how it goes. Love, Lynn XO"

Peter smiled, and picked up his pen. He could not waste the opportunity to retort for sake of allowing another man to inadvertently bruise his ego.

"Marshall Monroe?" Peter replied. "You have lowered yourself to dating a person named Marshall Monroe? I did not realize they had Cowboys in Duluth. Careful not to walk behind his horse when he comes a courtin'. Don't want to step in it!"

Well before the awakening at the Skyline Court Motel, Lynn and Marshall had been a one-night stand. Lynn had slept with him before learning months later that they went to the same elementary school.

Marshall lived at home with his parents in Duluth. He worked as a manager for a local drug store chain.

Lynn felt a sense of security in settling down with a steady boyfriend. Marshall was a jack-of-all-trades able to do any host of fix-me-up projects. A typical Saturday morning would be spent at Lynn's parents' house. While Lynn and her mom would sit in the backyard chatting, Marshall would help her father with the project of the day. The Cloud clan would troupe to Marshall's uncle's house in the afternoon to enjoy the Lake Superior beach.

Lynn loved that the Clouds loved Marshall Monroe.

Lynn Cloud broadened her sports horizons, too, as the Marshall Monroe relationship flourished. He was an avid competitive fisherman. Lynn began accompanying him to weekend fishing contests. Marshall and his friends would excursion together to one of the many lakeside campgrounds. At first, the absence of a morning shower and the clustered huddle passing around a marijuana joint at the campfire was alien to Lynn's being. It was perhaps though following a Saturday night fish fry that Lynn developed a security need for Marshall. One clammy August night, Lee, the fishing corps kingpin, began tossing unsuspecting guests off a pier as an after dinner charade. Unbeknownst to Lynn, Lee came up from behind, and grabbed Lynn for an indoctrination plunge. No one in the group, including Marshall, knew that Lynn could not swim. Her kicking and flailing at first were a welcomed reaction for initiation into their club. The beer totters reveled as she scrapped her fingernails across Lee's bare back.

Lynn felt she was going to die.

Screaming, "Marshall!" at the top of her lungs, only one person on the grounds could decipher the plea that she could not swim. Marshall sprinted down the pier—shouting translation to Lee.

"She cannot swim, Lee—let her down, let her down!"

Lynn grasped her savior tightly—embarrassed by the aftershock of quivers and tears.

She realized that you have to sacrifice some pain in order to take hold of the good.

Lynn framed a color photograph of Marshall holding up a champion walleye for the wall of her office. The double ribbon diploma was relegated to a back bookshelf. Lynn enjoyed telling her clients the mustached man garnished in the khaki outer wear was indeed her boyfriend. He cast the image of a macho man.

Lynn developed subtle ways to avoid the not-so-pleasant aspects of life with a steady boyfriend. Marshall also played in a summertime men's baseball league. The level of play was amateurish—even to the eye of a novice—but the games were taken seriously. Lynn was revolted to see beer-bellied men taking each other out with flying spikes on double-play balls. Heated obscenities generally preceded the regular testosterone match of pushing and shoving.

"Lynn what are you doing?" Marshall would exclaim after the games.

"Everyone was pointing over at you, wondering why you were sitting in the football field stands staring off at the lake?"

Lynn learned to smile.

"I am sorry, Marshall," Lynn would say. "I thought you were going to play on this field."

Peter opened the Dot Game. A photograph was inserted in the folds of the baby blue sheet grid.

Lynn was smiling at the camera. She was posed with her head protruding from a character prop stating "I complained about the food at Senor Frogs".

"Just got back from a weekend holiday in Acapulco," the note read. "Marshall and I had a great time."

Peter studied the Senor Frog model with the over-sized sunglasses. He could tell by the grin how happy Lynn was in her life."

"It looks like my friend is falling for the Cowboy."

XIII

The frequency of Dot Game moves began to slow down. Peter noticed the return mail would lapse from two to three weeks.

He felt obliged to the aloofness. The Dot Game would be buried into the pile of monthly bills Collins paid towards the end of each month. He did not wish to appear as a prying old man penning flirtatious quips to a girl love struck for another who was twelve years his junior. When he did write, Peter would go to the Walgreens Pharmacy next door to his office. The cards would be on the humorous side—usually from the "Missing You" section.

Peter always made mention of the Cowboy. Is he man enough to handle what he has got?

Lynn never referred to her new companion by Peter's nickname. Peter understood the lack of acknowledgement to his slight. Lynn was determined to make a life for herself in Duluth with Marshall Monroe.

Common ground was found as it had been in Hartford—on any topic that did not have to do with the personal relationships of either Lynn or Peter. It was okay to ask about personal feelings. Issues like sex or religion or politics were fine. Goings on after business hours was not. Lynn did not even know Peter's wife's name—nor did she care to.

The demise of the Brigadier Property and Casualty Insurance Company became the primary theme of the Dot Game. Prior to policy form changes in the early 1990s, pollution and asbestos liability was not specifically excluded from Brigadier's insurance policies. Claims for pollution contamination had been contested in the legal system throughout the United States. Liberal rulings, probably from Massachusetts jury panels, Lynn would jibe, were slapping Brigadier Insurance with multi-million dollar judgements to clean up properties Brigadier originally intended to insure for traditional perils such as fire. The company was forced to set aside loss reserves in excess of one billion dollars over a three year period.

Environmental and asbestos claims were not the sole Achilles' heel. Close to another half a billion dollar losses in several ill-advised investments in empty skyscrapers were crippling to Brigadier Insurance. Plimpton McAllister as Brigadier Chair looked into his crystal ball. He decided to change the long-term strategy of the century old insurance giant. The entire property and casualty division representing more than two thirds of the company was sold to its main competitor. With an aging population of baby boomers, Brigadier Insurance would devote its remaining resources to health and long term care insurance.

The sale to Travelers resulted in the layoff of over two thousand Brigadier employees.

The Brigadier Home Sales School lost its functional purpose. Ruth Meyer joined Sam Carvellas and Ralph Heffling amongst the ranks of unemployed. Tracey Benison accepted a position at the Brigadier transitional company. She found a job at a different insurance carrier within three months.

Peter wrote a long note to Lynn describing all the changes. The Brigadier Conference Center had been sold off to the Marche Learning Center. It was being converted and renamed to the Hawthorne Hotel.

"Looks like you are sitting on a collector's item with the double ribbon diploma," Peter wrote.

Peter reflected on the traumatic ordeal of his ribbonless certificate and hasty departure from Cromwell Country Club.

"There are some things that happened that night that I never told you," Peter included in his note. "I know you assumed that I won the blue ribbon too—but I didn't. The only section I did not ace was the one I thought you were going to pull me through—Personal Automobile. I have got to confess, when you were jumping around whooping and hollering I could not take it. I regret not sticking around to be with you afterwards at Teapot's. I kick myself now for having to feel like I had to get out of there."

There—I said it, Peter thought. He ran outside of his office to mail the card before he had any second thoughts about re-opening his heart to Lynn.

This time there was not a two to three week interlude between Dot Game moves. Peter could feel the tingle up the back of his neck when he saw the baby blue envelope in his in-basket within the week of his mailing.

Lynn knows how I feel about her, Peter thought, as he returned to his office to open her reply. Surely she is going to admit what a mistake it was to link up with Brian Fitzgerald.

A Post-It sticky note was the only attachment to the Dot Game.

"Dear Dad – I am getting married – Lynn".

The XO was replaced with a smiley face.

XIV

Peter perused the wedding cards at Walgreens. He could not bring himself to buy one. He purchased a springtime theme card instead.

It had been two years since he first met the girl with penny loafers. Two years—and no one but Marshall Monroe knew of the correspondence relationship between the two insurance agents.

Lynn's new lease on life meant disclosing all of her past to her fiancée. Marshall was told all of Lynn's prior relationships—and fleeting indiscretions. It was important for Lynn that there were no secrets.

"Peter Collins is a dear friend," Lynn flatly told Marshall. "Do not forget I have been friends with him longer than I have known you."

Peter was having a hard time conceiving of Lynn's upcoming betrothal. As a married man with two children, he could not explain what was attracting—and maintaining—his emotion.

Three months earlier, the New England Patriots made it to the Super Bowl in New Orleans. Peter and a few friends traveled to the Big Easy for the game. He took advantage of his former classmate's invitation and got together with Chris Tripoli. They went out one night for drinks to reminisce about the weeks in Hartford.

"Do you keep in contact with anyone from the school?" Chris asked.

"No," Peter deadpanned.

Lynn's name never came up in the conversation.

As Peter walked out of Walgreens with the springtime theme card, he thought why would I not have mentioned my friendship with Lynn?

"Well—I guess this is it," Peter wrote in the card. "With the time difference between Massachusetts and Minnesota it will be two o'clock here when you walk down the aisle on Saturday. I figure I will be just getting off the golf course at that very moment. Rest assured I will have at least two tequilas to toast your happiness. I bet you will be a beautiful bride.

XV

The first completed box in the Dot Game was garnered by Lynn Monroe the following January. Peter forked over the negotiated wager for the winner of the first box. He mailed a New England Patriots sweatshirt.

"Make it oversized," Lynn wrote. "That way I can wear it to bed."

Peter chastised the Cowboy's inability to keep his newlywed warm—regardless of winters in Duluth. Poking fun at the subtleties of Lynn's new life had become as much of a competition as the Dot Game. Either my jabs go right over her head Peter thought, or she is as dumb as a fox and lets them slide by. Peter assumed the later.

Lynn was proud to mail Peter a New Year's wall calendar published by the Duluth News Tribune. It contained monthly photographs of natural scenes around her home.

"Isn't Duluth beautiful?" Lynn wrote. A new business card reflecting the new surname was stapled to the calendar. Lynn Monroe—Boylston Insurance Agency.

"Throw out the old Lynn Cloud card you got at the Brig," the note instructed.

Margaret Ann Monroe was born on May 3rd. Peter had to assume that Lynn had her baby. It had been over two months since he had last seen the Dot Game.

For the past five years, the relationship was maintained solely through the United States postal service. Not since Cromwell had Peter heard the voice of his cigarette break companion. The birth could mark the end of our relationship Peter suspected.

Peter focused his attention to matters of his own family and his business. He would generally be out four out of the seven nights a week at either his children's extracurricular activities or business functions. He accepted the presidency of the Worcester Area Chamber of Commerce. It was a volunteer position with high visibility. His presence in the business limelight made his insurance business flourish.

Peter made a point of associating in business and community projects that were destined to be successful.

"People like doing business with winners," Peter justified his out-of-office activities to his partners.

Unbeknownst to Peter, motherhood did not become Lynn. The first trimester of her pregnancy was spent vomiting each day. At seven months she began spotting. She reduced her hours in half at the agency to comply with her obstetrician's order for bed rest.

Lynn mailed only three Dot Game moves during her pregnancy. Never once did she mention her nauseous state—nor did she reference the difficulty of moving day into a new split-level starter home. The occasional note would focus on her dismay of keeping a friendship with a registered Democrat from Massachusetts.

"How are you and the Kennedy's doing?"

Peter would ignore the conservative Republican's slight.

"So exactly how big is the bud growing on your belly getting to be," Peter would counter about the rose tattoo. "Don't tell me I am going to have to call upon the pony express to find out from the Cowboy."

Peter would don the father's cap too.

" I cannot believe you are still smoking while you are pregnant." Peter had quit smoking cigarettes a year earlier. He made no mention of the fifteen pounds he gained as a result.

"Lighten up," Lynn responded. She included a postal-flattened cigarette in her next card to him.

Margaret's birth was a twenty-one hour marathon. Lynn's doctors had an operating room at St. Mary's Hospital prepped for a Cesarean section. Marshall never left his wife's side. He coached Lynn through their Lamaze exercise and blocked his ears from Lynn's incessant bad-mouthing.

The Dot Game reappeared on Peter's desk the day marking six weeks from Margaret Ann's natural birth. Peter was surprised to see the baby announcement photograph in the Boylston Agency envelope. The little girl posed in her crib looked just like her mother. Peter compared the date of the postmark to that of the announcement. What is she doing back at work so soon?

Peter dug into his business card notebook. He pulled out the toll free 800 number and dialed the telephone.

"Yes, may I speak with Lynn Monroe," Peter confidently stated to the receptionist.

"And whom may I say is calling?" the voice responded.

"Peter Collins."

A tinge of anxiety rose up Peter's spine as he waited on hold.

"Peter," Lynn exclaimed. "I can't believe you are calling!"

"Lynn, you have the most beautiful baby in the world," Peter bubbled. "How could I not call to wish you congratulations?"

"Oh Peter, I just love her to pieces," Lynn said.

Peter Collins' heart melted. The voice from five years ago emanated through him.

Around Worcester, he was referred to as "Pee-daa". Lynn Monroe was the only person he could recall pronouncing his name "Pete-er" with a hard "t" and a doubly hard "r".

"I just love 'her-r-r' to pieces."

The words echoed in his mind amid the sound of Lynn's laughter in the background.

"Yeah?" Peter swooned. He felt intoxicated from the sound he did not realize he missed so much.

"Lynn, why are you back to work so soon," Peter asked. "I can get Ted Kennedy over there right now to petition for the same maternity leave rights as we have here in Mass."

Lynn roared.

"You can get Ted Kennedy 'ova hee-ya'," Lynn mimicked the accent. "Pete-er, you haven't changed a bit."

"Lynn, you always manage to evade my questions," Peter shifted the conversation back to his original purpose. "Now tell me, why are you back at work?"

"Because I am a lousy mother," Lynn revealed. "Peter I was going absolutely crazy staying at home by myself. I love being with my little peanut, but I am not the cuddly affectionate type. Marshall is better with that than I am. We have this fabulous lady who is providing our day care. I swear the baby looks forward to being held by her more than by me. Besides, Marshall does not make enough money for us to live on just his income. The last few weeks have been hell on us. I have to get back in the breadwinner's circle just to keep up on the diapers."

Peter swallowed at the revelation. He had reached his own level of financial security with a healthy six figure annual income and a strong investment portfolio. He pictured the Cowboy getting back to the ranch after a day's roundup—with a box of macaroni and cheese in his meal pouch.

Peter changed the subject.

"So what do you call Margaret Ann," Peter asked. "Margaret? Peggy?"

"We call her Maggie," Lynn chuckled. "My little Maggie."

Peter and Lynn chatted about the longevity of the Dot Game—and the series of humorous notes over the years. It was like a Monday morning rehash of a prior weekend at the Brig.

"Oh my gosh, Peter," Lynn remarked. "Do you realize we have been on the phone for over half an hour?"

Peter looked at the digital console atop his desk phone.

"Thirty three minutes, seventeen seconds," Peter recited.

"Thirty three nineteen—twenty—twenty-one," Lynn chimed from her console. "It is amazing how synchronized we are, huh Peter?"

"Yes, it is," Peter whispered. The telephone line went silent. Both Peter and Lynn gazed at the ticking seconds rolling by on their consoles.

"Perhaps I should be getting back to work," Lynn whispered back. "I promise I will not sit for so long on the Dot Game."

Peter noticed on Lynn's next Dot Game move that the smiley face had disappeared. The "XO" returned.

XVI

It took two months to realize what life would be like in the new millennium. Lynn mentioned the concept as an aside to her now frequent Dot Game moves.

"Do you have a computer?"

"I have one," Peter replied. He explained how his agency recently invested in laptops for all of the salespeople. "But I have resisted even turning the thing on."

"You should send me your email address," Lynn wrote back.

A month later Peter attended a introductory computer workshop held for the agency's office staff. The instructor wired his system to the outside telephone network. Peter learned how to click on Microsoft Outlook.

"See there on the left side scroll bar," the instructor pointed. "You have seventy unread messages in your Inbox."

The instructor showed Peter how to point to the scribbled "X" and click to delete unwanted messages. Most of them were stale from lack of feedback. Peter kept the cursor arrow on the "X" and methodically deleted the first page of meaningless messages. The second page of emails surfaced from the bottom of the Inbox as the top ones evaporated.

He almost clicked delete by accident.

"Monroe, Lynn—Hi. Are you there?—Tue 8/17/99 3:07PM"

"Wait," Peter beckoned the instructor. "I want to read this one."

The instructor showed Peter how to double click the message to open it to full view. There was no further narrative beyond the four simple words.

"Now, can I write back on this?" Peter questioned.

The instructor showed her student how to trigger the reply function. The cursor began flashing above the "Hi. Are you there?"

"Just type away and press 'File—Send' when you are done," the instructor smiled.

"Yes. I am here," Peter plucked. "Does this thing really work?"

Peter pressed "File —Send". He sat back in his chair and took a deep breath.

"How long does it take to hear back," Peter raised his hand.

"Instantaneously if the other person is there," the instructor replied. Peter's laptop cried "ding" just as the instructor finished her statement.

New mail has arrived, the blue reporting box appeared on the monitor screen. Do you wish to read it now? Peter expertly clicked "Yes".

"My, my, Dad—you sure are coming a long way."

XVII

Insurance agencies were chaotic during the holiday season. Almost seventy percent of all commercial insurance policies renewed on January 1st. Personal insurance, particularly automobile, renewed during January and early February. The holiday season was difficult for any insurance agent with a family at home. Christmas week was often spent in late night office sessions—strategizing new business sales presentations or negotiating renewals with insurance companies for existing clients.

Once the crunch times of underwriter negotiations and vehicle registrations were finished, office activity dropped to an absolute standstill. Veteran agents migrated with the snowbirds to Florida and points south for rejuvenation.

Lynn and Peter's emails were limited to one message per week during crunch time. Neither would make mention of missed family gatherings, nor the pressured panic in the office.

"Lynn Dear—how did you bring in the New Millennium," would be Peter's solitary query.

"Laid on my couch and stuck a straw in a now empty bottle of Champagne."

Discovering these small aspects of personal life made contact by email enjoyable. The once-in-awhile Dot Game card was never able to reveal such cherished images as Lynn sipping Champagne out of a straw.

Peter and Marianne Collins were accustomed to attending the gala black tie affair on New Year's Eve each year at the Worcester Club. The Worcester Club was a stodgy, century-old downtown private dinner club. The bulk of members so old that the club emptied and shut its doors for the night two hours before the perennial ball drops.

What a different way we live our lives, Peter thought, as he pressed "Delete" on his message screen.

By the first week of January, Peter's commercial activity hit its annual lull. It would be two more weeks before his scheduled flight to the family condo in Florida for ten days of beaching and golf. Lynn still had six weeks of the personal lines' blizzard of activity. Each morning she would arrive at her office at 7:30. The one-hour time difference on the East Coast meant Peter had a head start inputting his message for the day.

He has to be the most inquisitive person on the face of the earth, Lynn surmised.

Peter's good morning message evolved into a daily punch list of questions. Sometimes the queries were bulleted. Most often, they were numbered.

He knows I am disciplining myself only to email once a day, Lynn concluded, so he is emptying his holster with his one morning round.

She found Peter's questions varied dramatically from number to number, or day to day, depending upon whatever was on his mind.

"When was the last time you went to church?" could be followed by "How come you paint your own fingernails when for a few bucks a professional can do it a lot better?"

Lynn found it convenient to pick and choose which numbered question she felt comfortable answering. Peter would inevitably respond "What about #s 2, 3 and 4?"

Lynn would ignore the counteroffensive. She knew Peter would forget the issues with a whole new set of questions the following day.

It was Leap Day—February 29th.

Lynn and her young family did not mirror the insurance industry's pilgrimage to seek a mid-winter sun tan. Too many bills and fix-me-up projects filled the refrigerator magnets.

"OK," Lynn typed into her computer. "Boylston Agency is getting a free day out of this salaried employee. I do not want to be here! Let's talk."

Peter was surprised to see the invitation when he arrived back to his office midmorning from an earlier client visit. It was rare that Lynn would initiate a day's communication.

"Why should I talk with you, Queen of Deflection?" Peter toyed with his response. The coined nickname had become a synonymous with Lynn's evasive attitude toward emails. "You never answer all my questions."

"Today is Leap Day," Lynn offered. "This is a very narrow window of opportunity. The Queen of Deflection shall grant you this one time and one time only chance to ask any question you wish. Once five o'clock comes though, the window slams shut."

Lynn sat back in her chair after pressing "Send". She bit into her routine morning staple—a chocolate toaster tart. The computer sang "ding" before she swallowed the first bite.

"Anything?"

"Anything," Lynn resolved. She munched on her breakfast. She was in an adventurous mood. What pray tell will Peter consider his most pressing question, Lynn mused.

She was flustered by the unanticipated never-before-been-raised topic.

"Why do you call me Dad?"

"Because you remind me of my father," Lynn typed simply.

"Lynn, I am 39 and you are 27. That is not quite a generational difference if you ask me. Your father has to easily be in his 50s. So why the analogy?"

"I mean my real father," Lynn typed.

"'Real' father? What are you talking about?"

Lynn gazed at the screen. The open invitation was becoming bothersome.

"You remember my 'real father'," Lynn typed emphatically. She waited fifteen minutes.

"Lynn—I can honestly tell you I do not have the slightest clue what you are talking about. Who is your 'real' father?"

"Peter—you remember I told you about my real father," Lynn exasperated.

"You know what, Lynn—I swear sometimes you confuse me and your days at the Brigadier School with Brian Fitzgerald. Maybe you told Brian about your 'real' father, but you never told me."

Lynn stared at the reply. Maybe he was right, Lynn thought. Maybe I told Brian one night, but never did tell Peter.

"Peter—I NEVER told you?" Lynn checked.

"Never."

Lynn devoted the next seven minutes to a continuous punching on the keyboard.

"I always knew I was adopted. I was the first child of Norman and Evelyn Cloud. My adoptive parents never thought they could bear any children. Subsequent to my arrival they did have three children—my brothers Larry and Luke and then my baby sister. Even though everyone knew I was adopted, I was the oldest of the family and never felt like I was on the outside of the tent."

"On my nineteenth birthday I was sitting in the family kitchen eating an ice cream cone. The phone rang and I answered it. I swear to God for the next half-hour I sat on a kitchen chair and listened to the words of the caller. My ice cream cone melted entirely onto the floor."

"The caller told me that his name was Richard Nelson and that he was my real father. He told me that he and his wife Susan conceived me while they were in high school up north in Ely, Minnesota. My real mother Susan was sitting next to my father when he spoke to me, but she was too nervous to get on the phone."

"Richard told me he was seventeen years old and Susan was sixteen when she got pregnant. My father made mention of the fact that he was a big high school hockey star in Ely when Susan got pregnant. They originally planned to do whatever they had to in order to have and raise me."

"Unfortunately word got out around Virginia and the surrounding towns that Richie Nelson got his girlfriend pregnant. Whenever there was a hockey game, the crowds would chant 'Dad-dee – Dad-dee'."

"The pressure was bad—particularly for Susan sitting up in the stands. They decided to put me up for adoption three days after I was born."

"Richard and Susan eventually married after I was gone. They ended up having three additional children who are my natural brothers and sisters—Kyle, Kevin, and Kelly. They moved to Santa Fe, New Mexico, but never gave up searching for me. It took them years of trying, but the state of Minnesota would not allow access to my records until the day before they called me."

"When Norm and Evelyn Cloud from Duluth adopted me, they changed my name from what I was given at birth—Margaret Ann—to my present name—Lynn."

"That is why I named my first daughter Margaret Ann."

The Leap Day confession was exhausting. Lynn took refuge at the back entrance of the Boylston Agency building to have a cigarette. When she returned, the message was simple.

"You never told me."

"I am sorry Peter," Lynn slowly typed. "I thought I did."

"Interesting isn't it, Lynn Dear—your adoptive parents named their children Lynn, Larry and Luke. Your birth parents named their kids Kyle, Kevin and Kelly.

1. What is with that? Is that a Minnesota thing?
2. You didn't mention the name of your sister from your adoptive parents."

"My baby sister's name is Janet. Isn't it ironic that she is the only one who falls outside the letter scheme," Lynn reflected. "She is the only one I happen to have difficulty getting along with."

"All I can say is," Lynn continued. "I have been blessed with nineteen immediate family members between parents, siblings, nieces and nephews. It is something I would have never had before if it not been for that unexpected phone call."

"So you have to understand," Lynn concluded. "When I refer to you as my father, I am referring to my birth father. He is only five years older than you. From the first time I met him I could not get over how incredibly handsome he is—with blue eyes just like yours. He has become a very successful national sales manager in the computer industry just like you are with insurance. He carries a confidence within himself that is not seen too often—just like you."

It was over an hour before Lynn received a response. Perhaps Peter was on his lunch hour, Lynn speculated. She was unaware of Peter's decision to coerce a high school sweetheart to secretly have an abortion two decades before. If Lynn was a possible daughter figure, that "need" for love from a young adopted female—Peter Collins quickly refuted the notion from his conscience.

"Lynn," the ding finally transmitted. "I wish I knew that background before I bolted from Cromwell Country Club."

"Why?" Lynn could not understand. She waited fifteen minutes.

"I never had perspective on you referring to me as your 'father figure'. Quite frankly, I had a really hard time stomaching you at the Brigadier School with someone else."

It was after four o'clock in the afternoon when Lynn pressed "Send" to the message "A hard time about what?"

"About the fact that I am in love with you. I have never in my life wanted to be with another person as much as I want to be with you. If you have not figured it out—I am in love with you, Lynn."

Lynn considered the depth of the message in silence. The screen saver image flashed on—a picture of Maggie astride a rocking horse. Lynn fled to the rear entrance to garner another cigarette. Fortunately, there were a couple of telephone messages to follow up on when she returned to her desk.

The Queen of Deflection's window of opportunity closed shut when the "Send" command was pressed after five o'clock eastern standard time.

"Bet you have been sweating bullets for the last hour Peter," Lynn wrote. "I do know how you felt at the Brigadier School. I feel the same way too."

XVIII

The Queen of Deflection returned to her throne. As far as Lynn was concerned, the window of opportunity vanquished. Any attempts to delve deeper into the Queen's heart with numbered or bulleted pleas were thwarted by simply ignoring what was asked.

The email messaging returned to the mundane—mostly religion or politics. It was a Presidential election year. Lynn soft-pedaled her lobbying efforts. She had until November to see if she could get her liberal Democrat friend from Massachusetts to check an "R" instead of a "D" on a ballot.

"I cannot believe you voted for Bill Clinton," Lynn coerced. She was thoroughly disgusted with the leader of the nation. "The Senate should have followed Congress' suit and impeached him out of office."

"Lynn—I voted for Clinton the second time around. When he first ran, I voted for George Bush. Come his second term though, I felt Bill Clinton was better for the country than Bob Dole. I am disgusted with Bill Clinton too. Not so much for his extramarital activity—that is his business. More so, I cannot condone how he flat out lied to the American people denying a relationship with Monica Lewinsky. All I can envision is sending my sons to war to fight for our country and having Bill Clinton knowingly lie about a circumstance that could cost them their lives. I guess you could say I have always advocated my vote to whomever I deem the best candidate."

"Aw, come on you Kennedy sympathizer," Lynn retorted. "Don't tell me you ever voted for anyone other than a Democrat."

"Lynn—are you aware that since I was old enough to vote in 1980 the only time I ever voted for a Democratic Presidential candidate was that one time for Bill Clinton?"

Lynn viewed the message on the screen. It was getting late in the day on a Friday afternoon. The salespeople had earlier cut out of the office to get a head start on the weekend. The processing clerks were cleaning off their desks. The anticipation was mounting for the five o'clock stampede for the door.

Someone had already turned off the front waiting room lights. In doing so, they inadvertently shut off all the office lighting. Lynn sat in the dim room and smiled at the glowing monitor.

"Now Peter, you must be having a memory lapse," Lynn pecked. "Are you trying to tell me your first time ever vote was for Ronald Reagan? He was the most conservative President in the last half century!"

"I did not say I voted for Ronald Reagan."

"Then who?" Lynn typed. "Reagan's opponent in 1980 was Jimmy Carter, and he was a Democrat."

Lynn's office had now completely emptied. The overhead Musak system was turned off. Lynn slumped back in her chair. She closed her eyes for a few minutes. The dark silence was relaxing.

Lynn knew she was only moments away from the usual weekend whirlwind. Maggie was probably already buttoned up in her winter coat waiting to be picked up at the day care center door. Marshall had probably already called in the standard Friday night pepperoni pizza for Lynn to pick up at Vinnie's on her way home. Saturday morning would be devoted to Cinderella duty—scrubbing the bathroom and kitchen floors.

Maybe Maggie and I can go for a walk tomorrow afternoon Lynn dreamt. The ding awakened her conscience.

"Actually I voted for a lesser known Independent candidate in 1980."

"Who?" Lynn sent back. She closed her eyes again to return to the temporary state of peace. She knew she had to be going, but there was something blissful about the serenity of the darkened catacomb of complete quiet.

"John Anderson."

The name glowed on the lone source of light in the room.

Lynn's mouth dropped half open. Her mind raced in time and place—to a point in the space of a life long forgotten.

She was back in her third grade class at the Lakeside Elementary School. The Social Studies teacher was conducting a straw poll of students. The exercise was intended to show how the popular vote has one purpose in a Presidential election—to determine the final votes cast by the Electoral College. The teacher had two names written on the chalkboard—Ronald Reagan and Jimmy Carter. One classmate was extracting folded paper ballots from a shoebox. He was announcing each scribbled name. Another was making a mark on the board as each vote was cast.

"John Anderson," the boy with the shoebox uttered. He flipped the paper to the other side, convinced the name was written by mistake.

"Mrs. Ramsey," the boy at the chalkboard revealed. "We do not have a column for anyone else."

The teacher smiled and stood to her feet.

"Class... would the person who voted for John Anderson care to identify him or herself?"

The small bobs of hair at the miniature desks darted to the left and right. Lynn Cloud raised her hand. The teacher stepped towards Lynn's desk.

"Lynn dear," Mrs. Ramsey addressed the pupil. "Would you be kind enough to tell the class who John Anderson is? I am sure there may be a lot of children in this room who are not even aware that there is an Independent third party candidate in the election."

Lynn sat in a trance. The teacher's words echoed in a deep cavern of her being.

"*Lynn dear... Lynn dear... where have I heard that before*?"

There is someone here with me right now, the little girl sensed. *Who is that whispering to me*?

The silhouette in front of the school desk grew larger. There was a muffled sound coming from the shape. Lynn could not comprehend the words.

"Lynn, can you tell us who John Anderson is? Lynn, are you alright?"

Lynn could sense the voice echoing inside the cavern of her being.

"*I don't know*," droned from the little girl's mouth.

Who is that speaking inside of me, the little girl wondered? *Why are you here right now*?

Lynn stirred from her state of semi-consciousness.

"*I don't know*," the voice in the cavern mouthed into the abyss of the insurance agency office.

Lynn sat up in her office chair and rubbed her eyes. My God, she realized—the only time I ever heard that voice was when I fled from that roadside motel. But it came to me once before. When I was in the third grade. I forgot. *Why*, Lynn wondered? *Why do you come to me now after all of these years*?

Lynn's attention was drawn back to the lonesome glowing computer screen.

"John Anderson".

The wave of energy and enlightenment swelled.

"Peter Collins," Lynn proclaimed. "Do you realize that you are my soulmate?"

XIX

Peter had the weekend to reflect on Lynn's unusual revelation. How can one attribute a vote cast for John Anderson over two decades before as an omen of any sort?

"Lynn Dear," Peter entered onto his keyboard the following Monday morning. "Now I know why your practice of sleeping in on Sunday mornings and watching TV is promoting your avoidance of going to church. I am open to hearing anyone's philosophy on religious beliefs—so please educate this bias Irish Catholic mind. I have never been exposed in my learning to the concept of a soul-mate."

"Don't you believe in fate?" Peter's screen flashed.

"Hardly," Peter replied. "God gives man freedom of choice to do anything... jump off a bridge if you want! Is that fate? Every road you walk in life can take a right turn or left turn. Your decision is not fate. It is your freedom of choice. I know there is a divine plan that we all return to our Maker, but it is up to you what you want to do before you get there. So what does fate have to do with soul-mates?"

It took several minutes before the "ding" of a reply.

"Peter," Lynn wrote. "Many believe as I do that all souls pass from earth to a spiritual space of being. Maybe it is called Heaven. When we get there our souls are greeted by all of the other souls in our life that passed before us. There is no measurement of time in this continuum. While there, we have the opportunity to reflect and analyze both the positive and negative actions of our life on earth."

"The ultimate goal is to enlighten your soul to be nearer to God. The more 'God-like' a spirit can become, the higher one achieves God's fulfillment of creating man in his own image."

"Some souls can be more advanced in this journey. Most others are a lot less. God allows a soul to reincarnate back into a baby's body at birth to attempt to achieve a greater life lesson the next time around. If you believe in this concept, then it would be possible that each of us could have lived dozens of prior lives. That being the case, it would not be unusual when your spirit passes to be greeted by all sorts of soul-mates who may have been a spouse, sibling, or child of yours in a previous life."

"A soul-mate goes beyond sharing an earthen life together. It transcends to a higher level of being. It means the ability to spiritually share the common bond of love."

"I have always held a tainted view on the term 'soul-mate'," Peter extended his reluctance. "People use the term so loosely. I hear so many couples say they are 'soul-mates'—only to treat each other like crap. There is nothing more hypocritical than to see a pair of so-called 'soul-mates' say they cannot live without each other only to divorce when something better comes along."

"No doubt 'soul-mate' can be a relative term," Lynn qualified. "I view it this way. Think of all souls in this universe representing leaves on a huge, magnificent tree. All the leaves are somehow rooted together—to God. Some leaves aspire to reach the highest pinnacle in the sky. Some are hidden deep within the foliage—perhaps ignorant to their opportunity. Picture human creatures as leaves on a tree. While we are all a part of the same tree, some souls are closer to us than others. A couple who at one time thought they were soul mates perhaps was to some extent. They just happened to be leaves on opposite ends of the tree."

"You make soul-mates sound like something divine," Peter opined. "What does this have to do with fate?"

"The spirit tree also exists beyond earthen life," Lynn expounded. "In the other realm—Heaven, I guess. There are some souls who are on the same spiritual plane—perhaps extending on the upper most part of the tree nearest to God. Their incarnated returns to earth are probably in the form of what most people know as saints or heroes—destined to teach others on the tree how to aspire to grow nearer to God. For most of us, we share branches somewhere in the body of the tree. Decisions to learn life lessons on earth does not mean we all leave the spiritual tree together to live a shared relationship in the same family. Incarnations can come at various points in earthen time and place. We return to the same spiritual tree in the end however."

"Sometimes you can have two souls that share the same twig on that spiritual tree. Odds are that you would never see those two souls together as lovers on earth. For those aspiring to a greater good, it is probably selfish to ask God to allow such a thing. It can happen from time to time though. You hear about it in rare instances—with a parent and child, or husband or wife, or even two dear friends of the same gender. Most instances though, one would not even know their spiritual twig mate while on earth. They could pass you one day in a crowded shopping mall and you would not even recognize them—either because of their gender, the way they look, or who they may be with. That is where fate comes in. That one chance in countless earthen journeys where one does happen to encounter their spiritual soul-mate."

"What happens then?" Peter speculated.

"Bliss."

"According to your concept of fate," Peter postulated. "Are you saying, Lynn Dear, that we live on the same spiritual twig? That we have encountered our soul-mate beyond the traditional love we have known in our relationships with others in our lives?"

"The Queen humbly deflects, for now."

XX

Peter strolled to Walgreen's to purchase a friendship card. He mulled the cautionary words once invoked by his computer instructor.

"Do not type anything on the Internet that you would not expect to be printed on the front page of the daily newspaper. There is no such thing as privacy."

There were certain matters of the heart that were not appropriate to transmit via electronic mail. The Dot Game was better suited.

"Lynn Dear," Peter inscribed in the greeting card. "It has been six years since we last saw each other. I am desperately determined to see you again. Ironically, I figure if we were to pick a mid-way meeting point for you and me to travel it would be Buffalo, New York—the home of Brian Fitzgerald. I have given a lot of thought to the idea. Wouldn't it be prophetic to see each other in the city you were jilted from flying to a few years ago? Something tells me Buffalo is the right spot. It would certainly be fulfilling to me to be with you in Brian Fitzgerald's city. Could you imagine the look on his face if Fitzy ever caught sight of us in a restaurant or someplace!?!"

Peter anxiously awaited Lynn's response. He convinced himself that the idea was a fabulous one. The email response he received was not.

"Peter—I really think that it would be better if we did not communicate with each other for awhile."

Peter slammed the top of his office laptop shut. Fine, Peter fumed. If she wants to play fickle with me, I can be as stubborn as the next guy. Peter Collins bundled his computer hardware in its portable case. The agency information systems director had been requesting access to the laptop for several weeks in order to install some upgrades. Heretofore, Peter resisted the thought of being unable to communicate on the computer with Lynn for the two-week prescribed upgrade period. This ought to fix her canoe, Peter cursed as he stormed from his office.

After receiving the note with the Dot Game, Lynn realized that Peter did not understand her reference to him as her soul-mate. He belittled their relationship by suggesting that they get together to make her former lover jealous.

He cheapened their relationship.

Peter was miserable without the daily contact. His wife, Marianne, knew something was bothering her husband. As always, Peter was close-mouthed about things outside of the home that was not going his way. He felt it was his duty not to air dirty laundry—whether it was finances, or problems with a client or colleague.

Peter's father had once told him not to bring the problems of the day home to the dinner table.

"Can you recall me ever coming home in a bad mood in front of your mother or brothers and sisters," Peter would recite the paternal words to Marianne.

"That may be so," Marianne responded. "But did your father proceed to drink a full half gallon of scotch in four days time?"

Peter aborted the notion of a rendezvous in Buffalo. In ten days time he retrieved his laptop. He resigned himself to not expecting any messages from Lynn when he plugged back into the online network. He scanned the Inbox for mail. Three lines down held the voice of his heart.

"Hi," the heading read. "I am weak."

It was the sole statement in the body of the message. Peter studied the time and date the note was sent. It had been transmitted three days before.

"You are back!" Peter typed excitedly. The reply was instantaneous.

"Peter—do you really think a trip to Buffalo is appropriate?" Lynn mailed back. "Do you think that is a place I would truly feel comfortable?"

It dawned on him. What an absurd idea it was to think Lynn would see any joy in a trip to Buffalo.

"I guess it was a pretty silly idea," Peter confessed.

"I missed hearing from you the past ten days," Lynn responded. "Can't we just go back to the ways things were before with your daily dose of numbered questions to the Queen of Deflection?"

Peter complied—for no more than a week. He was right back on the saddle of the "when-are-we-going-to-see-each-other" horse. Lynn could begin to feel her will being defeated.

"Lynn—I am traveling to Chicago the end of October to an insurance convention. Do not worry. I will be the only representative of my agency who will be there. No need to feel uncomfortable meeting with me. Here is the deal… I will forward a plane ticket to you. All you have to do is reply favorably with three simple words… 'I love you'."

He had laid the gauntlet. He resolved not to communicate with Lynn again until he received a response.

Life as a young mother, newlywed, and career woman was becoming increasingly more hectic. Maggie interrupted recent nights of slumber cutting new molars. Marshall's post-Saturday workday hours suddenly seemed more and more difficult to track. A high school chum told Lynn about a rumor circulating that Marshall had struck a flame for a new employee at the drug store. The Boylston Agency announced their decision not to replace an office support person in Duluth. The back flow of work was overbearing.

The personal messaging stalled to an abrupt halt for the entire workweek. Peter absently clicked on Microsoft Outlook when he returned to his office following a Friday luncheon. He did not know Lynn discovered a gray hair on her head coming back from her morning cigarette break. There was one solitary image on the screen.

"I love you."

XXI

Lynn escorted the victim of a minor fender bender towards the front door of the Boylston Agency office.

"An insurance adjuster should be in touch with you before the end of the day to set up a time to look at your car," Lynn assured. The relieved client shook Lynn's hand and exited the office. Two of the other women in the office were giggling at the front counter as Lynn returned to her office.

"Going to Chicago, Lynn?" the women pried. Lynn felt like she was standing in the lobby with no clothes on. She could feel the color flush from her face.

"Pardon me," Lynn stammered. One of the smirking clerks produced the fax pages from behind her back.

"Who is Peter Collins?" the second conspirator asked raising a suspicious eyebrow.

Lynn reached for the dangling pages. The cover sheet was a customized "From the Desk of Peter L. Collins" letterhead. Attached was an Internet plane ticket purchase confirmation. Bold capitalized letters affirmed "Lynn Monroe—Nontransferable—Nonrefundable."

Lynn marched to her office. She kicked aside the small potted plant abutting the doorway. She never shut the door to her office. In this instance, the door shut loudly. She dialed the toll free number listed on the fax cover sheet. The receiver picked up after one ring.

"Peter, what did you just do?" Lynn amazed. She could hear herself laughing. I am so nervous all I can do is laugh she tremored. Peter laughed back.

"I meant what I said," Peter boasted. "Your message was very easy to understand."

"But I was only kidding," Lynn laughed.

"No, you were not."

"Yes, I was," Lynn slowly uttered.

"Too late now," Peter shrugged. "Looks like you have a date to see me in the Windy City."

"Oh My Gosh," Lynn speculated. "How am I going to tell Marshall?"

"Just tell him you are going out of town to an insurance convention."

"I cannot lie to him," Lynn demanded.

"You will not be," Peter assured. "There really will be an insurance convention going on."

"You know what I mean," Lynn slumped into her chair. "It is important for me to tell Marshall the truth."

"Use a little discretion, Lynn," Peter counseled. "You can express the trip in such a way to Marshall without having to compromise yourself. Does Marshall feel it is necessary to account for all his goings on when he makes a business trip?"

"As a matter of fact he is out of town right now—at a trade show in Colorado," Lynn spoke softly. She looked up to Marshall's fish picture on the wall. "He is probably with his girlfriend right now for all I know."

Lynn sat quietly at her desk. She appreciated the pause on Peter's end of the line.

"You did mean what you wrote in the message, right," Peter asked in a hushed tone. Lynn let the nervous question sink in.

"Yes."

"So will you come to Chicago?" Peter tried to restrain his plea.

"Yes."

"Aw, this is great Lynn," Peter exhaled. "I am so happy we are going to see each other again."

"Okay, okay, I have to go," Lynn composed herself. "Oh My Gosh, what am I going to tell Marshall?"

XXII

The coughing became so violent it threw Peter from his bed.

"My God Peter," Marianne woke from a sound sleep. "Are you alright?"

Peter pushed himself off of the floor. He stumbled barefoot into the bathroom. Coughing in his sleep had become an unconscious routine. Coupled with nightly toots of scotch, it was not unusual that the coughing would precede choking from the esophagus.

Peter found himself on many nights of late sleeping alone. Marianne would seek refuge in the spare bedroom to escape the incessant snoring.

"Is Daddy going to die," his youngest son would ask. The boys could not understand why their father—a Rock of Gibraltar for so many years of their lives—would go to bed prior to nine o'clock each night. "Dad always used to tuck us in. Now he cannot even stay up until our ten o'clock bedtime."

Marianne was worried about her husband. He was smoking again—in excess of a pack of cigarettes a day. His evening drinking had gone well beyond a cocktail before dinner. He had gained over twenty pounds since turning forty a year earlier. Marianne could tell Peter was stressed out. She could not put a finger on the exact cause. Perhaps this is merely a phase Marianne conjectured. We will all get through this. Her anecdote was to assume the role of a doting housewife.

Peter did have a sense that something was wrong with him physically. Unbeknownst to anyone, he contacted his physician and requested a lung x-ray. He had heard that people will cancer into their body if they convince themselves of it. The doctor could not explain the tightness Peter was experiencing in the right side of his back. God forbid I have a lung tumor, Peter fretted.

Lynn once joked that the determination to meet in Chicago was because he was going through a mid-life crisis, Peter reflected. Was it possible, being smitten with a younger woman for over six years, was indeed a mid-life crisis?"

The anxiety of communicating with Lynn and not seeing her face to face was taking a toll on Peter's psyche. The knot in his back and dull chest pains around his heart heightened the sense of urgency to see her in Chicago.

The lung x-ray results came back negative.

"There is absolutely nothing wrong with your lungs," the doctor reported. "There are some test results from your physical examination however that do cause me some concern. Your cholesterol level is a bit too high given your family history for heart disease. I would recommend trying you on Lipitor, but your liver enzymes count is off the charts. You do not happen to drink liquor, do you?"

"Yes, I do," Peter replied matter-of-factly.

"What type of alcohol do you drink?" the doctor asked.

"Scotch."

"What—just a social drink—or perhaps one before dinner," the doctor nodded.

"No."

"Well, then, approximately how much?" the doctor's eyes widened.

"Oh, I would say about six drinks a night—seven days a week."

The doctor was a longtime friend of the Collins' family. He was well aware of the financial reputation and social standing of his patient. He was shocked at Peter's laize-faire attitude about his well being.

"Well let me tell you something Peter," the doctor dropped his clipboard on the exam room counter. "You are drinking yourself to death."

Lynn's agreement to fly to Chicago changed Peter's focus on things as he left the doctor's office. The lung x-ray was negative. He may have pushed the envelope, but had been given a second chance.

He made the best of it.

Peter purchased a nicotine patch kit on his way home from the doctor's office.

"Would you like me to pour you a drink?" his wife dutifully asked once he pushed the remote button to close the garage doors.

"No, Marianne," Peter instructed. "For now on, no more drinking during the week."

The absence of the malt whiskey blend resulted in Peter losing three pounds in the first week. He wished it had been more so that he could return to the former Brigadier School buff Lynn had remembered before the scheduled trip to Chicago. Unfortunately, the waistline does not respond as well as the lungs for a reformed smoker.

The Collins family noticed a marked turnaround in the health of their patriarch. The snoring bouts and fits of coughing and choking seemed to end with the first nicotine patch. Marianne slept an entire night in the master bedroom.

The nicotine patch did not address Marianne's continuing dilemma. Her husband remained soft spoken and withdrawn. There is still something bothering him she would confide to friends at midmorning coffee.

Peter did have a new source of stress, and it was coming from Lynn directly.

"You are going to tell your wife you are meeting me in Chicago," Lynn dared by email.

"Lynn Dear—I am not asking you to tell me what you say to your husband," Peter replied. "Why press the issue with me?"

"Because the basis of why we are seeing each other means everything," Lynn stated. "If you think that our reuniting with each other means some wild sex session in Chicago you might as well forget it."

"Lynn—you are confusing the hell out of me," Peter was flustered by the demand. "Are you saying we have to forfeit our marriages and our families just to see each other."

"I am not saying that at all," Lynn' email flashed. "What does it say about how you think about me if you cannot be honest with your wife?"

"Let me guess," Peter typed. "You have already told Marshall that you are meeting me in Chicago."

"YES. I DID," Lynn resorted to the Caps Lock key. "Maybe married couples of the 90s are more with it than married couples of the 80s. Marshall has always known about you. He knew about our friendship at Brigadier School and about our Dot Game since the time he and I started dating. He has no problem with me maintaining my friendship with you. I told him you were going to be in Chicago and that you thought it would be a way we could see each other again. We could hang out at all the jazz clubs. Maybe even find a place where you could do some Karaoke. Marshall knows you are a riot! And he does trust me to visit a male friend for a weekend without having to worry that we will sleep together."

XXIII

Lynn Monroe could be a royal bitch. She readily acknowledged the label, tagged from observations made by family, friends and co-workers.

Marshall had four years of practice absorbing the wrath of what happened when things did not go his wife's way.

"Marshall, you were absolutely fine with this a week ago," Lynn flung her arms in the tiny kitchen. "You go away on a business trip for three days up north, and now you come home telling me this?"

Marshall turned his back to the flailing arms routine. He resumed Maggie's spoon-feeding.

"I have given it a lot of thought," Marshall reiterated. "I do not think it is healthy for you to go."

"Wait a minute," Lynn backpedaled. "I am leaving for Chicago in three days. Are you telling me you do not trust me? You go off to Colorado last month, and you and I both knew your old flame was going to be there. Did I stop you? Turn around and look at me! Did I stop you?"

Marshall turned from the baby's high chair prompted kitty corner between the two-seat kitchenette table. Maggie started to cry over the raised voices of her parents. Marshall's upper lip was puffed. Lynn realized she had her husband's attention.

"I said, don't go," Marshall demanded.

"Are you asking me, or telling me," Lynn challenged amid the loud sobs in the corner. Tears began to well above the puffed lip.

"For Maggie and me, I am begging you, don't go."

Lynn double-clicked the Inbox icon. The programmed voice cue announced "You've Got Mail Baby!"

"Just to set the record straight," Peter declared. "I have told my wife that I am expecting to meet up with an old friend from the Brigadier School while I am in Chicago. If the weekend is going to be filled with jazz clubs and no sleeping together, I quite frankly do not think I need to say anything more beyond that—do you? If so, hopefully our seeing each other Friday will be just what we hope it will be."

XXIV

Peter Collins was a born salesman—with a certain degree of qualification. The art of a deal is oft times buried in detailed minutia. The flamboyancy of an extroverted salesman can frustrate not only their administrators, but also foul opportunities. Peter was always cognizant of this potential flaw. He would never omit a detail that could taint a well thought out plan.

Peter foresaw some potential problems with Lynn when he first searched the Internet to buy her a plane ticket from Duluth, Minnesota. The ticket purchase clarification flashed on his computer screen. "Specify airport in Chicago." He pressed the "Help" icon. "Choose between Midway Airport or O'Hare International". A city map line showed the distances of the two airports to downtown. While Midway appeared closer, O'Hare was the only available option for incoming flights from Duluth.

Not a big problem, Peter thought. He keyed his preference for the larger airport. I am landing there, too. His agency office had already purchased his plane ticket in advance. The chartered flight of insurance agents was scheduled to depart Logan Airport in Boston at ten thirty in the morning. Arrival time for the three-hour flight to O'Hare was a little after noon central standard time.

The charter's arrival time posed a potential second problem. Peter was headstrong to make sure he arrived in Chicago ahead of Lynn. Any successful salesperson will tell you the most vulnerable time in sealing a deal is the post purchase confirmation with the buyer.

"Yes! You have made the right decision!"

There could be nothing worse than grabbing a down payment check from a new sale and bolting away to celebrate victory. It is too easy for a buyer to have second thoughts whether or not they have done the right thing.

He was determined to meet Lynn right at the arrival gate. The consequence for not doing so seemed clear. All it would take would be the lonesomeness of an alien airline terminal—a simple phone call home to the Cowboy—a spontaneous change of heart—and a skip back onto the return express flight to Duluth.

The number of flights from Duluth to Chicago was limited. Most of the departures left early to mid-morning. All landed in O'Hare well in advance of Peter's East Coast flight. The remaining option was to choose a mid-afternoon departure for Lynn. It would arrive in Chicago just after five o'clock.

He chose the mid-afternoon flight.

The next set of connection problems dealt with getting from O'Hare to the downtown Chicago Marriott on Michigan Avenue. Peter was shocked. The map line revealed a seventeen-mile commute from the outskirts of O'Hare to downtown.

"I am kind of held hostage by the charter itinerary for this insurance agents' convention," Peter emailed. "There is one group shuttle bus transporting us to the Marriott. We are all checked in at the same time once we reach the hotel. I think it will be impossible for me to wait the afternoon at the terminal for you to arrive. What I plan to do is this. Once I get registered at the hotel, I will jump a cab back to the airport. I should be able to get back and forth in plenty of time. If for any reason I am not at the terminal gate when you arrive, please do this. Hail a cab, and have him take you to the downtown Chicago Marriott. I do not care what it costs. When you get there, call up to my room. I will pay the fare. If you have to pay, I will just reimburse you. That is strictly Plan B though, because I am determined to be at that gate."

The last problem was by far Peter's worst. He had heard only Los Angeles had more traffic congestion than Boston. No one told him about the seventeen-mile clogged artery between O'Hare and downtown Chicago.

The agents' shuttle bus crept at a virtual snail's pace upon exiting O'Hare. It was well after two o'clock by the time all the baggage and reveling insurance people had been gathered.

The agents gave no notice to the lack of movement. The bus was fully stocked with an open bar of refreshments and cold appetizers. The hull rocked with music and laughter. Peter paced the inner aisle way—sipping a Bloody Mary and checking his wristwatch.

"What time do you think we will be downtown?" Peter ventured to the bus driver. The antennae of the Sears Tower looked as if you could touch them, but the line of vehicles to the horizon showed they were still miles away.

"Friday afternoon," the driver scrutinized. "Not much before three thirty."

Peter did the mental math. At this sluggish pace, he may not have his room key until four o'clock.

"Let me ask you, Buddy," Peter figured. "Is there any kind of express service that can zip me back to the airport? I need to pick up a friend at around five."

The bus driver laughed.

"Have another drink, my friend!"

XXV

The lobby of the downtown Chicago Marriott was a grandiose marbled arena of massed humanity. Peter stood patiently in the agents' queue for his room assignment.

"Smoking or nonsmoking?" the front desk attendant asked.

It had been over two months since Peter's last puff. He thought of Lynn, and promptly replied "Smoking".

The attendant furrowed his face as if he bit a lemon. He hurriedly played his fingers over the service keyboard.

"Mr. Collins, the room assignments for your group are on the forty-first and forty-second floors," the attendant informed. "Those are all nonsmoking suites. If you want to downgrade to a smoking room, I am afraid we will have to separate you to the twenty-fourth floor."

"That is fine," Peter shrugged. Perhaps it would give Lynn and him more privacy, he thought.

Peter collected his carry on luggage. He skirted past the piano bar to the hotel elevators. A couple of his convention colleagues entering the car feigned a look of surprise to see their well—known competitor depress button 24.

He passed the card key through the bar code slot above the doorknob and entered the room. The accommodations were a fraction of what he knew had been reserved at the top floor suites. A king-sized bed took up a bulk of the confined space. The bathroom was sparse and cramped.

Peter drew the wall length curtains to view the city skyline. Rather than a view, a large roof top air compressor hummed in front of the glass. It was not quite the love nest he imagined. Peter resigned.

The hour was late. Plan B was deemed to be in effect. Hopefully Lynn had the presence of mind to grab a taxi and head to the hotel.

A wave of nausea overcame his mind. Was it the claustrophobic environs of the miniature room? Whatever the reason, Peter realized an urge to telephone Lynn's office. Maybe they can give me her cell phone number, if she has one, Peter's mind popped. I know she cannot have the phone on during a plane flight, but maybe by chance I can catch her off the plane to assure Plan B.

Peter pressed the telephone buttons for an outside line. He punched in the number for the Boylston Agency.

"Thank you for calling the Boylston Duluth office," the receptionist welcomed on the first ring. "How may I direct your call?"

"I am trying to reach Lynn Monroe," Peter started.

"Hold on. I will put you right through."

Peter fell onto the desk chair jammed against the massive bed. He stared helplessly at the outside air compressor.

"This is Lynn," the voice identified. Peter dropped his face into his hands.

"Lynn? What are you doing there," Peter stammered.

"Where are you, Peter?" Lynn asked.

"I am in Chicago. I am at the Marriott—waiting for you." The telephone line went silent for a few seconds.

"You did not take the flight," Peter asked rhetorically.

"I called the airline last night," Lynn whispered. "I asked them to postpone my trip voucher."

"Last night?" Peter wondered. "What happened last night?"

"I sat chain smoking on my back deck late into the night," Lynn remarked. "I was back there again at six o'clock this morning. Marshall told me to go if that was what I really wanted to do—but I could tell that I should not. When I came to the office this morning I honestly did not know if I would hop up to the airport at lunchtime to still catch that flight. The decision was totally up to me. I decided I should not go."

Peter sat in a stunned silence.

"I am sorry, Peter," Lynn continued. "I have been thinking about you nonstop. I know I will be thinking of you all weekend while you are in Chicago."

"Yeah," Peter whispered. He hung up the telephone.

"Front desk," the Million Dollar Man barked into the telephone. "This room stinks. Please call a porter here at once. Give me back my assigned suite."

Peter grabbed his unopened bags and heaved them into the hallway. He could not survive another moment quarantined in the minuet concubine. As he waited for the porter, Peter turned the corner into the vending and ice machine alcove. He reached into his pants pocket for a couple of singles to buy a soda. The machine blinked red at each selection. It was completely empty.

Peter scoped both sides of the unoccupied hallway. His bags would be safe if he ran up the fire stairwell to the soda machine on the floor above. He hurdled the steps two at a time. The entry doors at each floor above and below were locked.

Peter could not return to the alcove on floor 24. He stood in the grab gray stairwell and ogled the slit of void space extending up and down between the handrails.

How the hell did I get myself in this situation, Peter scolded himself. He had to get up on the tips of his toes to view the tiny alcove through the small wired meshed glass squared in the fire door. It would be impossible to hear a porter's steps in the hallway. Perhaps a shadow, anything, would appear to assist him from his plight.

Peter banged methodically on the door with the ball of his fist. His right knuckles began to redden. The ache was a soothing salve. After about five minutes, Peter lost track, the porter's head peered from the side of the alcove threshold.

"Those are my bags in there," Peter yelled. The porter scurried into the alcove to release the trapped guest.

"Every door in this stairwell is locked tight," Peter shouted to no one in particular. "This is a goddamn liability hazard you know!"

"Mr. Collins," the porter stated. "These doors are locked for security purposes."

Peter could sense a return of sanity when the porter addressed him by name. He looked blankly at the uniformed black man.

"Come with me, Mr. Collins," the porter finally smiled. "Wait until you see your suite on the forty-second floor."

Peter absently followed the porter to the elevator station. Atop the forty-second floor, the porter proudly pointed to the double-door suite at the end of the exclusive hallway.

"Welcome to Chicago," the porter announced as he flung open both doors.

Peter walked in ahead of the porter. The suite bore walls of open glass on three sides. Peter walked to the far window. He loomed over the architectural magnificence of the Wrigley Building and the headquarters of the Chicago Tribune. Scanning to the left was the blue aura of Lake Michigan extending beyond the Navy Pier. The porter walked past the guest in the living room to the adjoining dining room.

"I will gladly take your things upstairs to the sleeping quarters," the porter offered. "The control switches to turn on the spa up there can be tricky. I will show you that too."

The porter waited for a response from the inert.

"Unless you want me to leave these things right here."

"Whatever," Peter muttered. He stared beyond the river locks to the edifice of Soldier's Field. The porter laid the bags at the foot of the dining room table. He traversed to the large bar area abutting the enclosed wall.

"Would you like me to pour you a drink, Mr. Collins," the porter invited. "Looks to me like you could use a little unwinding from your trip. The bar is fully stocked with whatever you fancy."

"Double Dewars on the rocks," Peter replied. He did not turn from the window. The porter dutifully poured the scotch whiskey into a lead crystal tumbler. He placed it on the glass living room coffee table. Peter turned and extracted a twenty from his gold money clip.

"Thank you for rescuing me," Peter extended the gratuity.

The porter departed. Peter returned to the far glass wall. It was possible to open one of the sliding panes. He unlocked the window hinge and pulled the aluminum frame.

The window was designed to open no more than an inch or two.

Peter could feel the room conditioned air escape from behind him out of the slit. He stood tight up against the opening to view the image below. The angle of the elevation was such that he could not see straight down to the street level.

Boy, Peter thought. If ever a time to jump out of a window, it is right now.

XXVI

The downward swirl of Marshall and Lynn's fifty-two month marriage spiraled like a flushing toilet.

Lynn returned to the modest split-level family dwelling an hour after Peter hung up the telephone in Chicago.

Marshall did not bother turning to acknowledge the black Accord's appearance onto the paved driveway. He continued to wield a sledgehammer against the concrete walkway arcing towards the front entrance.

Lynn got out of the car and primped herself to negotiate open the awkward double-width wooden door on the detached two-car garage. She exhaled the mandatory grunt to expunge the rubber strip sealing the door bottom from the cement floor slab.

As usual, Marshall had the yard tractor positioned in Lynn's garage space. Lynn's shoulders slumped. She retreated to the backseat of the Accord to retrieve Maggie from her strapped confines.

Maggie held onto her mother's hand. She asked if they could walk around to the front of the house to see Daddy working.

"Maggie!" Marshall shouted as the pair emerged from the back of the driveway. He dropped his sledgehammer and ran to pick up the infant.

"How is my number one girl," Marshall elated, tossing the toddler up in the air. Father and daughter gleefully laughed upon Marshall's catch.

"Marshall, what are you doing?" Lynn asked softly, looking at the half-smashed walkway.

"Thought you were going to Chicago," Marshall quipped never taking his eyes off of his daughter.

"I told you last night I wasn't going," Lynn reminded her husband. "That does not explain why you are ripping apart our front walk."

"Gotta fix the water leaking into the basement," Marshall leveled his little girl above his head. Sweat stains circled his armpits and neckline. "We can't finish the downstairs until we re-route the outside drainage."

"Marshall, this is too big of a job for you to take on by yourself," Lynn viewed the mess. "We have plenty of professional contractors who do business with the agency that have the equipment to do this job in no time. Can't we call someone?"

Marshall placed Maggie back on the driveway, next to the silhouette he did not care to regard.

"What's the matter, Lynn," Marshall challenged. "Are you saying I am not man enough to do this job? Or is it that I do not make enough money to hire this out?"

Lynn grabbed her daughter's hand. She quietly walked to the back haven of the house. The box of Vinnie's pepperoni was forgotten next to the baby's seat in the back of the Accord.

Lynn opened the glass slider off the deck into the back entrance of the house. Amos, the Monroe's golden retriever, anxiously awaited his exit to pee.

He could not even let the dog out, Lynn marveled.

Maggie ran straight down the narrow hallway to hang a newly crayoned picture on her bedpost. She had graduated from a crib to a twin bed. The bedpost was filled with coloring book renditions of her favorite children's TV show's characters.

Lynn turned from the tiny dining room area into the even smaller kitchen nook. A familiar smell of burnt bitterness hung in the air.

She ambled to the corner of the far counter, and depressed the orange illumined button. Once again, Marshall had left for work that morning without checking that the coffeepot was off.

Lynn shook her head at the crusted inch of brown crud smoldering the bottom of the pyrolite pot.

He is going to burn this house down, Lynn pondered. She doused the sludge under the kitchen tap—squirting dish liquid concentrate to soak up the damage.

I have salvaged this poor pot before, Lynn mused. She left the project in the sink for later recovery. Lynn fell into a deep sleep as soon as she reclined on the black leather living room couch.

She dreamt back to her last year as a teenager. Lynn Cloud had defied her adoptive parents. She was dating a town roughneck two years her senior. They were at a friend's house party whose parents were out of town.

The roughneck ditched Lynn at the party—driving off in his red Camaro with some less-than-desirable friends. He did not tell her where they were going. Lynn loitered in the front yard with Monica Chambers and some acquaintances. About an hour later, the red Camaro returned with a full load of hooting rebel rousers. A cloud of pot smoke rose from the vehicle as the car doors opened. The roughneck pitched an empty beer can across the front yard as he exited the driver's seat. He ran around and unlocked the trunk of the car. Six cases of lager were jettisoned for the reveling gang.

"*Eric, everyone here is underage*," Lynn dreamt yelling. "*You can't bring beer and pot here*."

Lynn grabbed the case-totting boyfriend from behind. The roughneck dropped the beer back into the trunk. He grabbed Lynn into a bear hug and tackled her to the ground.

The revelers cheered and the girls screamed at the pair rolling around on the lawn. Lynn was so angry she wrestled her beau using all her might.

The roughneck pinned Lynn's arms beneath his knees and straddled the high-pitched foe. The shouting ended when Eric cold cocked his girlfriend soundly across the jaw.

Lynn's dream state fast-forwarded to her adoptive parents' house. Her brother Luke was standing behind the blinds of a side window.

"He is still there," Luke reported. "That red Camaro has been sitting in the same spot in front of the house for the past five nights."

Lynn had enough of the intimidation. She abruptly opened the front door of the house and sprinted towards the red Camaro.

"*Get the hell out of here*," she dreamt her scream. The red Camaro did not expect the sudden ambush. Lynn could see the interior dashboard light up. Eric hurriedly turned the ignition.

Lynn had developed a loping stride with her long thin legs while running track at Duluth East High. She visualized herself sprinting after the fleeing vehicle as it peeled rubber down the road away from the scene.

The dream continued to pan. Lynn could see herself running back to her parents' house. She got into her rust bucket compact and raced after the Camaro. Lynn witnessed her image exiting the rust bucket and running up to Eric's darkened house. She was not aware that Eric's parents were not at home.

The front door was thrown open before Lynn could reach for the knocker. A flailing fist crushed her nose—careening her off of the stairs. She could taste the salty blood streaming from the front of her mangled face.

The shadowed image was screaming. The roughneck grabbed his prey by the long mane of hair on her nape. He dragged her face down into the unlit house.

Lynn's conscience recalled awakening in Eric's bedroom. Her arms and legs were shackled to the corners of the bed with clothesline. A sock was stuffed in her mouth. She could barely breathe through the blood-clogged nostrils. The roughneck stood above the mattress waving a leather sheath. A bright silver colored stiletto emerged from the sleeve.

The roughneck cut the shoulder straps apart from the tank top. Lynn could feel the prick of the knife at the base of her belly button. The metal sliced the center of the tee shirt to her neck. The point of the blade moved to the button hitching the flared blue jeans.

"*Bitch,*" the voice sounded as the fly was sheared from its seam. Each leg of the dungarees fell victim to the onslaught. Tattered denim fell to the sides of the bed. The muffled body lay trembling in an eggshell pair of bra and panties. The blade ripped through the undergarments. The image could feel the chill of the stiletto against a quivering neck.

"*I could kill you right now, and no one will ever find you, Bitch!*" the voice echoed inside the cavern. The knife pressed harder and harder against Lynn's throat. The softest of swipes under the pressure would sever the carotid artery.

It was a different penetration now—more violating than the stiletto. The slow banging sound of a drum beat in the far distance.

Lynn knew she was being raped. Her conscience was recessed deep within the cavern. The violence and hatred surrounding her reverberated throughout her being. The drum continued to drone.

She was raped every hour, on the hour, throughout the night. Each violation was preceded by the silver threat to the throat. The drum continued its beat.

Lynn could feel the rawness of her wrists and ankles in her dreamlike state. The sensation of blood trickled from her nose, her face, and between her legs. The noise of the drum became louder.

Did he rape me with the knife, the cavern lolled.

"*You will be home soon,*" the voice from the cavern echoed.

The drum was beating at a fevered pitch. Lynn could feel herself running naked out of the house—the beat of the drum following dramatically at her heels. She ran away from the structure into bright sunlight. The spirit was there to save her.

It was Peter.

Clad in his navy blue business suit, the soul-mate enveloped the caverned being into his muscled arms. The beating sound did not stop.

Lynn's eyelids popped open. She was back on the black leather sofa.

Cold beads of perspiration dotted her brow.

The rhythmic pounding of Marshall's sledgehammer continued its assault outside the bay window. Lynn caught her breath. She stared at the stucco ceiling.

"Peter".

XXVII

The email voice cue giggled into the airwaves.

"You've Got Mail Baby!" the stud voice announced. Lynn double clicked the blue rectangular window.

"Lynn Dear—Just because you decided not to go to Chicago—does that mean you are forfeiting the next move in the Dot Game? Too bad! We were so close to crowning a winner."

The rush of crisp enthusiasm perked the insurance agent up in her seat.

"For the past week I did not think you ever wanted to talk with me again," Lynn typed.

"I must admit I was pretty disappointed," the screen flashed. "I still cannot quite understand your hesitancy to go. Chicago is so full of life. You would have loved it."

"I got scared," Lynn confessed.

"Scared of what? Me?"

Lynn collected a wide array of thoughts and emotions that troubled her mind that first week of November. Hopefully, I can assemble these into some kind of reasonable order she challenged herself.

"Peter—I love you and I know you love me. I feel that your expectations of meeting were different than mine. Remember when I told you I discovered we were soul-mates? To me we have something very special between us. Your ego was so strong leading up to the trip. I could sense there was no way to corral your expectations beyond a sexual encounter. That is not why I wanted to see you."

"Making love with you was definitely in my equation," Peter responded. "I do not think it was naïve of me to think that our sleeping together was implied. I asked you to come with the 'I love you' invitation."

"Thank you for being honest with me," Lynn tapped onto the keyboard. "It was implied with you—but not for me. That is why I was so up front with Marshall—and so disappointed that you could not do the same with your wife."

"Lynn—if I am the so-called soul-mate you presume I am—then why do you have the impression that had you come to Chicago, I would not have been sensitive to your wishes? How do you think I would have reacted if you told me there was no way you would feel comfortable making love? What—did you think I would throw you out of the hotel room into the street?"

"At the time—yes," Lynn transmitted. "That is why I was scared."

"You know me better than that," the screen responded.

"I said 'at the time'," Lynn qualified. "Aside from Brigadier School, I have never traveled on an airplane by myself. That one episode is still a nightmare to me. I still get scared thinking about walking unattended in an airport or big city. The other thing was the idea of meeting a man I have not seen in six years to spend a weekend at this humongous hotel in a foreign place. What if things did not go right? It has happened to me before."

"Happened to you before?" the screen asked.

"When I was nineteen years old, I was physically attacked," Lynn revealed. "This instance—right here—right now—is the first time I have ever come out and admitted it—and I am admitting it to you, Peter. I have never breathed a word of what happened to me to anyone—including Marshall. It was the most horrible experience of my life. I thought I was going to be killed. It was buried so deep within me for so many years. It was probably the driving force keeping me from Chicago."

"That realization did not surface until I had missed the flight," Lynn continued. "It dawned on me after that I should have gone to you. I do not think I could ever come out and tell Marshall about what happened to me. I do not think he would understand. Please keep this between us."

"Thanks for the perspective," Peter replied. "Perhaps in time I will figure out what a soul-mate is."

XXVIII

The Dot Game was sealed in a 10x13" business size manila envelope. The Duluth time stamped postage metered $1.26. She forgot to write "Personal & Confidential" on the face.

"I am sorry Mr. Collins," the mail clerk hesitated at the executive's office. "I did not realize the package was personal until after I opened it."

Peter noticed the gaping hole at the top of the package. He blushed slightly at the sight of the unfolded Dot Game.

"I swear I did not read anything, Mr. Collins," the clerk chirped. Peter regarded the fidgety person at the foot of his desk. He could tell from her anxiousness that the frail woman knew she has stumbled upon something that was not for her eyes. He was convinced that she lacked the gumption to peruse the contents beyond the dog-eared grid. As absurd a sight the correspondence doodle game appeared, even the naïve could not associate an impropriety with one of the agency partners.

"That is quite all right, Kathy," Peter assured. "Shut my door please."

Peter pulled the Dot Game sheet from the top of the delivered contents. Lynn had successfully maneuvered to complete five squares in the lower right corner of the game. The loopy "L"s centered each created box.

Peter placed the sheet on his ink blotter. He extracted a lengthy typewritten letter from the open envelope. Peter fanned the pages like a hand of playing cards.

My goodness, Peter observed. Lynn has not typed me a formal letter in years.

January 7

Dear Peter,

You laughed at my email last week when I told you my favorite television programs are the Sunday morning news magazines. Remember I told you, my idea of a perfect Sunday morning is to cuddle under the covers with Maggie on a cold winter day and watch the news magazines?

I did take your suggestion this morning. I changed my Sunday routine. I told Marshall that I wanted to go to Mass as a family. I figured maybe you were right—to give the Catholic Church another chance. Like you said, it would be like revisiting a restaurant where you may have had a bad meal.

Marshall had no problem with the idea. I guess he will do whatever I say as far as religion is concerned.

We got all dressed up. Maggie was so cute in her nice little bundle. We drove over to St. Mary Star of the Sea. Marshall and I had not been there since our wedding day.

They have a different priest there now. Maggie was so well behaved—sitting quietly in the pew munching on crackers. I noticed Marshall was not totally disinterested. He sat there and listened courteously. I am sure he would go back every week—if I said that was what I wanted.

Here lies the dilemma… I have no interest whatsoever in going back. It was so boring! Hello? Is anybody home?

Peter—I have to explain to you further the beliefs I have developed over the past five years.

Remember I told you about my best friend Monica who lost her brother to cancer the year we met in Hartford? Her mother was so devastated. Someone had recommended to Monica some books for her mother about reincarnation. Monica has always experimented with parapsychology.

The books Monica's mom read did wonders for accepting the premature death of a child. I know skeptics say desperate people fearing death cling to unconventional hopes—but what is belief in God in the first place?

They say if you read five books on any given subject, you can be considered an expert. I have read more than five parapsychology books and will be the first to admit I am no expert! I have formed some very definite ideas on certain things though that I want to share.

So many people who have survived a near death experience describe seeing a great bright light—a tunnel way for the soul to pass to the other realm. It is on the other side of that tunnel where we are greeted by the loved ones who proceeded our passing. It is God's way of making us feel loved and welcome coming back to our eternal home.

We do not stand around and hug our favorite relatives the whole while—though we can as long as we want, because time as I told you before, it is not measured there. Once our soul acclimates to the familiar surroundings from which we came, we have the opportunity to review and analyze the lives we had just led. The soul's ultimate goal in being nearer to God is not to have been "more like God" on earth, because we already ARE God. The assembly of all souls together as one makes up God's creation. The purpose of each earthen journey is to FORGET we are God and EXPERIENCE that which God in Heaven cannot—the opposite of love, the opposite of peace—and to collectively make a difference in creation.

Most people seem to spend their entire lives running in the hamster wheel—totally out of touch with what they are supposed to be trying to fulfill on earth. It is probably not until they pass into that tunnel of light that they realize it is too late.

If people and societies, have to discipline themselves to the regimen of going to church in order to remember the purpose of the journey of their souls—then great if that helps them. Jesus did say I am there whenever two or more are gathered in my name. But don't tell me folks who do not go to church will not be welcomed in the other realm—no way!

Our God is a loving God. We all mess up in our lives—some a lot worse than others. Fathom that God's divine plan for man is to be created in his own image. In order to perpetuate God's love for man and creation, wouldn't it make sense for God to allow a soul who has messed up in dealing with the opposites of love and peace in a lifetime to have another chance?

Is this where we get the concept of original sin? I do not know. What I do know is the difficulty I have with the teaching about Adam and Eve. We are not born with sin in our hearts. That is one of those Judeo-Christian "keep 'em feeling guilty and they'll come back for redemption" things. It is not possible to "mess up" in a lifetime. Your idea of "messing things up", like skipping Teapot's the last night in Hartford or missing a weekend in Chicago, may have been the backdrop for a perfect life learning experience.

Many say that if God is Man, and Man is God, then Heaven in a certain dimension is right here on earth. Each soul opts to incarnate into a body to hopefully realize a new life lesson. The lessons can be simple—like seeking enlightenment through the arts—or more complex—like learning to be kinder, humbler, or more loving.

Did you know surveys show over half the population in the United States and Canada believe in reincarnation? For the first six centuries after the crucifixion of Christ, the Old and New Testaments were littered with references to reincarnation. It was not until some Catholic Pope came along during the Dark Age of Christianity and had them stricken from the Bible.

Many of us have lived dozens of prior lives leading up to this current earthen journey. Can you imagine the number of spouses you may have had—husbands and wives assuming you have also lived as the opposite sex? How about the numbers of brothers and sisters or even children?

Can you imagine the hoard of loved ones over generations and past lives waiting for you at the end of the tunnel? Who would you want to greet first?

Parapsychologists have done all sorts of research in this area. Most of it is through a hypnotic process called regression therapy. It if from this research that the concept of soul-mates has developed.

Picture yourself greeting your loved ones from lives you did not remember until you returned to the realm. Some souls would stand front and center determined to greet you first. Others would be surrounding that one soul while many would perhaps be a row or two in the distance.

Here is the linchpin of a primary soul-mate. That one other soul is hoping to seek the same level of enlightenment to God as you are. When the welcome and life review process is completed in the realm, there is a period of reflection. Again, time is not measured. The period can last for seconds, where a passing spouse decides to reincarnate to a widow's newborn child, or centuries.

During reflection, souls that are at the same level of enlightenment seek to understand how to best perpetuate God's eternal love. Some souls seek out a reincarnated life opportunity where hopefully they can realize their life lessons together. Other souls may take a dramatically different course—like incarnating into a child destined to have a premature life just to assist others in their life lessons, or incarnating at a totally opposite end of the earth's geography and culture, or deciding not to reincarnate at all.

Have you ever listened to an elderly person fondly recall one particular friend or relative—be it a grandparent, or an aunt or uncle, or even a spouse? Chances are that fondest of memories was experienced with a primary soul-mate.

Unless you are incarnated into an immediate family, the odds can be great whether or not two souls on the same spiritual plane might meet up during their earthen voyage. If time is not measured in the realm, those souls may even incarnate decades apart in human terms.

With the freedom of choice that you advocate is given to a being's every decision, two souls of the same spiritual plane can take very separate paths during their earthen lives. That is probably why two soul-mates could indeed virtually pass each other one day on the street and not even realize each other's existence.

That gets me to my second profound phenomena—that of the Spirit Guide. Some religions refer to them as Guardian Angels. These are souls that have achieved such an enlightened state of God that they do not have to incarnate any longer. They actually look out for souls in their care to assist in our life lesson while we trod through our earthen travails. Some human beings evoke their Spirit Guide quite often through meditation, or even unexpectedly during so-called "moments of truth." Others may be oblivious to their existence. They can reject the presence of their Spirit Guide when it does try to appear.

There have been odd times in my life Peter—too varied to mention here—when I can recall my Spirit Guide coming to me. It is difficult to explain the experience. Let's just say these moments have confirmed my belief that you, Peter, are my primary soul-mate.

It is hard to rationalize the circumstances that led to our life paths crossing. It is even harder for me to think out why our paths crossed in the first place!

Our Spirit Guides know the life lessons we have set out to achieve. Who knows if we are fated to realize these life lessons together.

And what does "together" mean? We are half way across the country apart. We are raising our own children—other souls who decided to incarnate to the opportunities we can provide.

In the end, these are the reasons that prevented me from meeting you in Chicago. I could not identify how our meeting under those circumstances could foster our life lessons.

At this point you have probably decided that I am certifiably crazy. I do not know if we are destined to ever see each other again on this earthen voyage—or if there is even a purpose in doing so.

I do know you will be the one soul front and center when I cross to the realm home. Then we will hold each other for an eternity.

Love,

Lynn XO

Peter read the letter a second time. He placed it over the Dot Game sheet and moved the computer keyboard to the middle of his desk.

"Lynn , got your letter. I have known for a long time that there was something special between us that I could never quite put my finger on—but past lives?" Peter puzzled as he typed.

"The premise that as soul-mates our paths would cross is amazing! When

I was born my father was an intern physician stationed overseas in Germany serving in the U.S. Army. My mother was a registered nurse. They had been trying to conceive a child for over two years and had almost given up hope. They had started the paperwork to adopt a German baby right at the time they found out my mother was pregnant with me."

"Isn't it a stretch to consider if we were on the same spiritual plane that I would arrive in West Germany twelve years ahead of you?" Peter speculated. "And how would you rationalize deciding to incarnate to a teenage couple in northern Minnesota out of wedlock? How could a soul anticipate being put up for adoption three days after incarnation? Could skew a life lesson pursuit, don't you think?"

"Please do not think I am being condescending," Peter leveled his fingers on the keypad. "Your beliefs about me are quite flattering—and could very well be the reason why I do love you so much and want to see you. It is just contradictory to my lifelong personal parochial upbringing in a typical Irish Catholic family. I do happen to cherish the rites of the church. It fulfills my soul and hopefully steers me to right directions. I do not hold much validity to a Spirit Guide though beyond my faith in the Blessed Virgin Mary. I can probably relate to some times in my life when I could feel Her presence through a novena or prayer. That is a special relationship I have. It probably goes against what a small group of reincarnationists believe."

Peter instructed his mouse to send the message. He slid the keyboard back to the corner of his desk and pulled out the Dot Game.

Peter analyzed the grid to calculate his next move. Only about a third of the squares were initialed. He discovered the area where Lynn was forced to yield a three-walled open space.

Big mistake, Peter ogled. He completed the box of the space and stoically scribed a "P" in the secured cube. The move opened a vast pattern of squares over the entire left side of the grid.

Peter proceeded to close each new square with a methodical "P". He smiled with glee as the pattern twisted across the row second from the top.

The open available area of three-sided enclosures came to an abrupt end. Peter sat back in his executive leather chair and examined the near-filled grid. An almost equal area of vacant space remained on the right side of the sheet.

Peter gawked at his only remaining move. Enclosing any of the two-walled area on the right side with a dissecting third bar would cede the remainder of the game to Lynn.

Peter grabbed a pencil from his desk drawer. He nervously counted the "P"s to date versus the loopy "L"s. He could visually see more "P"s than "L"s, but he has to factor the final boxes that would be filled after the posting back to Duluth.

Peter counted 95 "P"s. He added the number of boxes across the top of the game and multiplied them by the number of vertical ones.

A 196 box game Peter dropped his pencil. Lynn will win again—101 to 95.

XXIX

Lynn had been avoiding the trip to her gynecologist for months. Postponing another lunch hour appointment would prompt another telephone call to the Boylston Agency as was the case two weeks earlier.

Dr. Rebecca Montagne had been a longtime friend since school days in Duluth. She too had her first daughter within two months of Lynn having Maggie.

Lynn and Marshall bumped into the Montagne family several weeks earlier visiting Santa at the DeWitt & Seitz Marketplace. Rebecca was noticeably pregnant with another child.

"You have to stop canceling your appointments Lynn," the doctor playfully scolded. "We have to talk."

Lynn tried to shade her cringe at the doctor's remark. Marshall did not know his wife had been postponing appointments.

Lynn climbed into the back of the full-sized GMC Suburban to strap Maggie into the rear child seat. Marshall ground the ignition to liven the frozen starter. The four-wheeler appeared to be a good deal three months prior at the used car lot—but the signs of weathering five previous Duluth winters with another owner showed once the mercury fell below zero.

"It is my busy time of year Marshall," Lynn headed off the anticipated inquisition. "I have every intention of seeing Becky at the end of January."

"You are still on the pill, aren't you," Marshall's upper lip puffed.

Lynn nodded. Marshall focused his attention to the arching clearness surfacing from the defroster at the bottom of the windshield.

"I thought we decided to try for a brother or sister for Maggie before she gets too old," the gloved driver whispered.

"I am not cut out to be a mother," Lynn griped. "You know what a hard time I had carrying Maggie. I do not think I could stomach it again."

Lynn fastened the final buttons on her navy blue business suit. She departed the examination room. This was the part she dreaded. Lynn swallowed. She tapped on the half-opened door leading into Dr. Montagne's office.

"Sit down Lynn—sit down."

Lynn daintily sat on the plush-cushioned armchair across from the doctor's desk. She crossed her stocking legs as if the hostess had not seen the innards of her being five minutes before.

"Everything in your exam checks out fine," the doctor folded her hands on the desk. "Did you have any questions for me?""When are you due?" Lynn tactfully veered the conversation away. Dr. Montagne looked down at her plump belly and smiled.

"March 17th."

Lynn mirrored the nodding assent.

"That is why I wanted to talk with you Lynn," the doctor tilted her head. "Have you given consideration to having another?"

"If it were up to Marshall I would be a baby pumping machine," Lynn remarked. "I don't know, Becky. I am such a lousy mother. I could not wait to get back to work after Maggie was born. Quite frankly, I will not feel cheated if I never experience all the sickness and pain again."

The doctor stood from her chair and waddled to the front of the desk. She leaned her behind against the desktop.

"I know exactly how you feel Lynn," the doctor counseled. "So many of my patients have felt the same way, but I have found a vast majority reach their late thirties or early forties and suddenly change their minds."

Lynn Monroe laughed.

"Becky, are you trying to sell ice to an Eskimo?"

"Think about what I am saying Lynn," her friend advised. "In my professional opinion you will have a very difficult time carrying a baby to term once you reach thirty-five. Your proverbial biological clock is ticking. There are a lot of research articles I could give to you showing all the benefits of mothering children close in age. Maggie is at the perfect stage for another baby in the house."

Lynn crushed the cigarette with her shoe on the stone step of the Boylston Agency's back door entrance. Rebecca Montagne's words continued to ring in her ears. She retreated to the confines of her office without bothering to check in with the receptionist at the front counter.

A small stack of mail sat in the "In" basket. Lynn fumbled through the pile, and seized the greeting card postmarked "Personal and Confidential" from Worcester, Massachusetts.

Lynn eyed the photograph of Whistler's Mother on the face of the card.

The profile of the hard looking bonneted matron sat stationary in the wooden rocking chair. The folded Dot Game fell to the desk as Lynn opened the card. She unfolded the sheet to confirm the terminal moves she anticipated. The ride side remained available as predicted.

Lynn gazed at the large capitalized letters Peter printed at the bottom of the sheet.

"1/17/01 – YOU WIN!"

The victor brushed her fingertips over the dated notes scribbled on the right margin of the sheet.

"6/3/94—First move of the Dot Game—by me! Lynn Cloud".

"4/23/96 —Lynn Cloud bites the dust—do Mrs. Rhinestone Cowboys know how

to play?"

"1/30/97—Lynn gets the first box!"

"3/9/97—Peter gets the first box!"

"4/1/99—Lynn gives birth—now 2 against 1—only one move at a time!"

"10/23/00—Bring game to Chicago—we will finish it there!"

Lynn returned to the greeting card. It was designed blank for a writer's creativity.

Two words were penned.

"Now What?"

The ring of the telephone aroused Lynn from her meditative state. It was the familiar voice.

"Hey, how did you make out at the doctor's office?"

"I have decided to go off the pill, Marshall. You are right. Now is the time to have another baby."

XXX

She was in one of her moods again, Peter fumed—but this time, it appeared to be different. The more succinct Lynn's message, the higher the chance she was fed up. But fed up with what?

"I have decided we cannot speak with each other anymore," Lynn stayed late at the office the night before to type the message. She knew the email would intercept Peter's arrival the next morning. That way he would not form his "What shall we talk about today" morning hello.

"My marriage has been the pits since the aborted trip to Chicago. I hope you understand," the message ended.

Peter felt as if he had been kicked in the gut. Why was it whenever feelings were strongest, something intervened? But what this time?

Peter closed his laptop shut and picked up the telephone. He called the C.N.A. Insurance Company regional office in downtown Boston. When the requested underwriter answered his four-digit extension, Peter reverted to his aura as the Million Dollar man.

"John, heard you want to get together to go over some accounts," Peter's ego took control. " I cannot think of a better day for me to get out of this office. Are you available for lunch? My treat."

Within the hour, Peter was speeding down the Route 2 artery toward the Cambridge side of Boston. His thumb continuously clicked the radio station control on the steering wheel of his Lexus sedan. Why are there so many commercial breaks on talk radio, Peter brooded. The thumb continued to click.

Peter's workday invariably involved hours behind the wheel of what had become a mobile sales office. When not speaking into his dashboard mounted cellular phone unit, he would focus on one of the six stations programmed to either twenty-four hour news or talk radio.

The advertisers were generally the same for the half dozen stations. Must be identical target markets Peter conjectured. Two separate jingles—one for replacing your worn mattress and another for auto glass—were running concurrently on five of the six stations. The head aching coincidence made the driver's mood even more ornery.

Lackluster underwriting results coupled with a nosedive in the stock market created a hardening of insurance premiums. The major insurance companies mandated a direct edict to their staff underwriters. Writing new business and retaining policies were no longer a priority. Increase rates across the board. If you cannot demonstrate at least a minimum fifteen percent hike in a commercial account's premium, then find another job.

Most business' most costly property and casualty insurance line is workers compensation. The coverage provides medical benefits if an employee gets hurt on the job plus covers lost wages if unable to work because of the injury.

State laws require any business that has employees to carry workers compensation insurance. The premium a business has to pay depends on the perils of the job. A roofer pays a lot more than an office of secretaries.

States set workers compensation rates based on how much is paid out in claims compared to how much premium the insurance company collects. Regulators monitor insurance companies not to make too much money in writing workers compensation. The insurance companies meanwhile siphon millions of dollars to lobbyists who complain that rates are not high enough.

Massachusetts' workers compensation rates had been decreased thirty-two percent by the insurance commissioner over the previous two-year period. For insurance company underwriters to keep their jobs with the fifteen percent increased premium mandate, the falling workers compensation rates had to be taken into account. Other lines of insurance such as property and automobile had to be increased close to forty percent to meet the internal directives.

The hardening economic cycle was a double-edged sword for Peter. His personal income was rising merely because of the increase in insurance rates. Trying to explain the rationale behind the arbitrary decisions of a large insurance carrier was another story. Peter could envision the reactions his top clients would have to the tens of thousands of dollars jump in a program with little or no changes from the year before.

A dull ache throbbed in Peter's skull as the C.N.A. underwriter ran down the list of accounts facing double-digit rate increases. It was not so much the threat of a client finding another insurance agent Peter feared. It was more the anticipation of less than amiable client meetings.

Plus the inability to share a workweek and day-to-day life with Lynn.

The aura of Lynn completely overwhelmed Peter's mind. As the mundane monotony of the day's business meeting progressed, the sense of her existence hung in Peter's conscience. Peter could see the underwriter's mouth moving. He could feel himself nodding at words and scribbling an occasional note. The notion of ceasing the relationship with Lynn however muddied his brain to a state of numbness.

Peter departed the C.N.A. offices at five o'clock in the afternoon. He knew the trek back to Worcester would take about two hours regardless if he took the Mass Pike or Route 2. There was no way to avoid the mass exodus of commuter traffic out of Boston.

The Lexus joined the herd of bumpers inching along the banks of the Charles River. Some drivers darted in and out of the Storrow Drive lanes to gain the benefit of a car length or two. The weaving would not amount to much of a benefit in the stressed drivers' estimated times of arrival.

The sealed windows of the Lexus incubated Peter from the chaos of rush hour. He kept the radio off and stared blankly at the rolling ribbon of red taillights.

The stream of working humanity trickled to their twilight destinations around the suburban towns of Concord and Acton. Peter kept his cruise control setting at the 55 mile per hour speed limit. Normally the mechanism was gauged at an even twelve miles per hour over any posted limit. Peter always figured any speeding violation could be fixed by a number of law enforcement or legal contacts. At this point, he was in no hurry to get anywhere. His family was used to eating dinner regardless of what time he arrived to the house. A sporadic flow of more anxious travelers zipped by in the passing lane.

Peter absorbed the melancholy tranquility.

The cruising Lexus passed the Route 2 intercept of Interstate Route 495 and motored along the foothills of Harvard, Massachusetts. A road sign atop the highest elevation of the foothills declared "Leominster—10 miles." Peter always set his arrival time home to the green metal landmark indicating where he would pick up Interstate 190 to Worcester. This day the spellbound driver was oblivious to the reminder.

The uppermost point of Route 2 after the landmark provided a panoramic aerial view of the Montachusett basin. The Nashua River flowed through the region—once the primary natural resource to old industrial cities like Fitchburg and Leominster lying north of Worcester. Mount Wachusett, a glacial mountain at the foot of the Mohawk Trail back dropped the geography. It stood as a pinnacle between Worcester and the gateway west to the Berkshires.

Peter watched the slow descent of the sun over the acme of the mountain. The orange ball shot off an array of red and purple hues against the wisps of clouds covering the summit's crown. The hues darkened in color as both Peter Collins and the sun continued their predestined paths.

For the first time since childhood, Peter could feel tears welling from his eyes.

"Lynn, I miss you so much," he mouthed.

A weather front was quickly forming in the horizon. Massive darkness flowed over the northern crest of the mountain. Peter gazed at the spiraling funnel of blackness. It was not the conventional brewing of a thunderstorm. Perhaps it could develop into a tornado or microburst Peter speculated.

The cloud arced to the zenith of the sky. It hung without any further motion. Peter pulled his vehicle into the breakdown lane and rolled to a stop. He turned of the motor.

The perfect image of a woman had formed in the cloud line. Her arms were fully extended to the hues of red and purple. Golden rays layered the flowing gown created within the reminder of the fallen sun.

"Lynn—it is you," Peter marveled. "I know it is you."

XXXI

It was a fitful attempt to slumber. Peter laid wide-awake staring at the neon glow of time kept on the bed stand clock radio. 3:20… 3:21… 3:22.

Marianne was deeply asleep. As was always the way, the back of her head faced her husband. Peter wished it was Lynn.

Dinner that night had been difficult. Peter willed his self-discipline not to show the emotions of the day. He could not bring himself to describe to Marianne or anyone in his family the vision of the woman in the sky. The notion of the family patriarch overcome by something more abstract than the Dow Jones Industrial Average was too foreign to comprehend.

Besides, Peter reflected as the clock face glowed 3:23, how would Marianne ever understand the feelings I possess for another woman?

Peter rolled out of the bed. He stepped into the sentinel of neatly arranged slippers at his feet. Marianne rolled onto her back and resumed her light even snore. Peter stepped into the walk in closet and scavenged his robe. He traveled knowingly in the darkness down the stairs to the kitchen.

I have to express my thoughts in writing, Peter resolved. I do not want to run the risk of waking in the morning and not remembering these thoughts I need to convey.

February 28, 2001

My Dearest Lynn,

I cannot believe the funk I get into whenever we feel we are getting too close to each other and decide to take a breather.

Your email to me this morning—oops, I mean yesterday morning because it is 3:43AM while I am writing this—really knocked me for a loop. I felt like a zombie today trying to function. The idea of not having you in my life devastates me.

Do you remember Sisyphus from Greek Mythology? Sisyphus was the king of ancient Corinth who tricked Death. He was eternally condemned to push a rock endlessly up a hill. The rock always rolled back down to the bottom of the hill before the task could be finished. Every time he neared achievement of his goal, it would crumble, only to force him to try again. My love for you makes me feel like Sisyphus—so near yet so far away. Are we eternally condemned for tricking the realm—for discovering the concept of soul-mates? It makes me wonder about things like perseverance. Did Sisyphus ever receive a sign not give up hope, or is it indeed an eternal damnation?

A sign came to me—an omen of sorts. I experienced it this afternoon on my way home from Boston. The sun was setting and the view was spectacular. All of the sudden this huge, dark cloud appeared from behind the mountains miles away. It formed into the image of a woman. It was like when Jesus went up to the mountain and transfigured into a brilliant robe of white light in front of his Apostles.

Lynn—the image was you—I know it was. I do not know if this was actually a Spirit Guide experience like the ones you mentioned happening to you at critical moments in your life—but it sure was something special to me. I swear I will never be able to look at a sunset again without thinking of you shining in the west.

As you know, today is Ash Wednesday—the beginning of Lent. In the past I would give up small sacrifices for Lent—no morning coffee, or no chocolate (I do not eat chocolate in the first place). Remember how miserable I was in my letters the year I gave up drinking scotch? Well in order to properly discipline myself—I have decided upon the following Lenten sacrifices:

Replacing scotch whiskey with water. I need to lose the weight I gained when I gave up cigarettes.

No Lynn Monroe. I do not know why my feelings exist the way they do—nor can I predict what will happen to us in the future. All I know is that if we are truly soul-mates for all eternity, reflecting upon what we have without direct communication for forty days and forty nights cannot necessarily be a bad thing.

Giving up personal vices for Lent always seems to make the Easter message of new beginnings more meaningful. My love for you, however, is not a vice. It's power goes beyond anything I have ever experienced throughout my entire life.

The next forty days will be hell for me—but I have the resolve to get through it. Know why? Because after Easter comes in mid-April, I am coming to Duluth. I must see you even if just once. I need to hold your face in front of my own. I need to look deeply into your eyes. If we have lived past lives together, then maybe something will trigger when we look into each other's eyes. Do you know I cannot ever recall you and I ever really making direct eye contact when we were at Brigadier School?

Maybe nothing will come of a trip to Duluth. It may just end up being a way of saying goodbye and moving on with our own separate lives. Whatever the case, I need to remember what is inside your eyes. I will never let your eyes pass me by if our lives cross in a future lifetime. I will remember.

Peter proofread the pages on the yellow legal pad. I will sign this when I am ready to mail it in the morning he determined. Peter returned to the darkened Master bedroom. The pad of paper was concealed into his night stand drawer.

XXXII

"Marshall, you get out of bed and shut the door if it is that important to you," Lynn pulled the goose down comforter over her naked lean body.

"I do not want Maggie waking up and walking in on us in the middle of it," the blue wool-socked husband said. He tiptoed in his flannels to the bedroom door. "She could be psychologically affected by catching her Mom and Dad like this."

Lynn rolled her eyes. She had hoped her announcement to have another baby might jump—start the otherwise unremarkable bedroom activities. Ever since moving into the modest split-level, Marshall's urge to "do it" with his wife occurred no more than once a month. Even when "it" did happen, it was a quick pant with no kissing—followed up by an exhale resembling a grunt.

Lynn ditched the February flannels in a concerted effort to retrieve the excitement once had as newlyweds. When Marshall retired to watch TV in bed, Lynn would slip into the small bathroom off of the bedroom to garnish a Victoria's Secret teddy.

She spent the past week shivering under the covers trying to arouse her husband. "I do not think Maggie is sleeping yet" was the standard response. It chilled the mood to a temperature worthy of the coldest Duluth winter.

"Marshall honey, will you please take those socks off," Lynn implored. "They may be soft on the inside, but they are scratchy on the outside."

"Your toes are always cold when my feet touch yours," Marshall removed his briefs and jumped onto the mattress. "Besides, my toes are freezing."

Lynn reached and held her husband tightly.

"Lynn, go brush your teeth," the mate coiled. "Your cigarette breath is raunchy in the morning."

Lynn threw the bulky comforter off the end of the bed. The two naked bodies were exposed save for the pair of wool socks.

"Hey!" Marshall shouted.

Lynn stood away from the mattress to let her husband survey her slender trim body. Instead, he scurried to retrieve the pile of goose down. Lynn retreated to the bathroom for a cursory brush over. The diva returned in less than a minute exhibiting her fresh pearly whites.

"There," Lynn smacked a kiss on her husband's lips. "Is that better?"

Marshall grasped his wife by the shoulders and pushed her arm's length from his torso.

"Wait a minute," Marshall furrowed his eyebrow. "Didn't you start your period last weekend when we had dinner at your parents?"

"Yeah, so?" Lynn replied absently.

"Well, you are not going to be ovulating for at least another week."

Lynn's snow boots crunched on the salt pellets strewn about the Boylston Agency's front walk. Her dress shoes hung from a plastic shopping bag at her fingertips. Winter weather ruined leather soles unless worn only while in the office.

"Was the Personal Lines meeting cancelled this morning?" the receptionist greeted. "The Cloquet office never called to tell me."

Lynn dropped her bag to the ground.

"The Personal Lines meeting—I forgot all about it," Lynn lamented. The frazzled agent turned back to the lobby's storefront style window. Marshall's Suburban had already pulled a U-turn. Lynn could see the exhaust smoke speed off to Maggie's day care center.

"Marshall drove me in because the driveway was icy," Lynn sounded as if she needed to apologize for the decision. "I better call Cloquet to let them know I cannot make it."

"Doesn't Marshall have a car phone," the receptionist bubbled. "Maybe he can scoot you back home in time to get the Accord."

The nonevents of the morning did not inspire Lynn to acknowledge the suggestion. The "What" No kiss?" remark Marshall made as Lynn hiked her dress to scale down from the four-wheel drive truck was still regurgitating in her mind. That would be the day he would ever think of getting the door for me and helping me out.

"No—forget Cloquet," Lynn decided. She hopped on one foot to secure the second dress shoe strap and marched toward her office. "I have some things to catch up on."

Lynn settled in at her desk. The dripping boots were tossed into the corner. She picked up the telephone and pressed the speed dial button programmed for the Boylston Agency headquarters. The recorded phone greeting forced a short voice mail stating that her presence at the meeting set to begin in a few minutes would be impossible. She hung up the receiver and promptly punched the toll free 800 number. This line will definitely pick up Lynn conjured. They are an hour ahead of us.

Lynn's agitation stirred to a froth. No one was as irksome as the Massachusetts' receptionist. No calls could be put through to Mr. Collins unless name identification was provided beforehand.

"This is Lynn Monroe speaking," Lynn recited in rapid-fire anticipation of the irksome script. "Yes, I will hold, and yes, Mr. Collins knows the nature of this call."

A sense of calmness oozed through Lynn's veins as she waited for the call to be transferred. The coined greeting "Good morning, Peter Collins speaking" made the frigidity melt.

"Hi," Lynn offered.

"Lynn? Is that you?"

"Didn't the receptionist tell you it was me?" Lynn questioned.

"Of course not, they never tell me who is on the phone."

"Then why do they make me have to tell them who it is?"

"I am surprised you are calling me," Peter ignored the jab at his office personnel.

"Don't you have to shut your door to talk to me," Lynn stammered. "You always say, 'hold on a second, let me shut my door'."

"Shut my door?" Peter puzzled. "Why shut my door? I love the spontaneity of getting a morning phone call from you."

Lynn's defenses relaxed. Would Marshall ever posses that self-confident assuredness? She thumbed the diamond stone portion of her wedding band towards her inside palm.

"Lynn, is something wrong?"

"No," Lynn's tone hushed. "I just wanted to hear your voice."

"Does this mean you are reconsidering the 'non-communicato' pact?"

"I guess so," Lynn conceded. "I do miss hearing from you."

"Actually, I am feeling like a dolt right now," Peter confessed.

"A dolt?" the comment made Lynn laugh for the first time in days. "That must be one of those ''Baa-stin' expressions. What is a dolt?"

"A dolt is someone who was up at four o'clock this morning writing a four page letter to you," Peter stated. "I mailed it first thing this morning, not thinking you would call."

"A letter?" Lynn's spirits rose. "You sent me a letter?"

"Ooh yeah," Peter bellowed. "I sure did."

"Can you tell me what is in it?" Lynn asked. "I do not think I can wait three days for the mail."

"Lynn, I had an incredible out-of-body spiritual experience last night driving back from Boston," Peter beamed. "My letter will tell you all about it. Let me just say I do not think I will ever be able to watch a sunset again without thinking about you."

"Peter, you should not relate me to a sunset," Lynn said.

"Why not?"

"Because sunsets are permanent," Lynn frowned.

"Sorry," Peter shrugged. "I am on too much of a cosmic high to think otherwise."

"What else is in the letter?" Lynn changed the subject.

"Well, first of all, I told you I was determined to abide by your wishes," Peter complied. "Not to have contact with you was going to be my Lenten sacrifice for the next forty days."

"Yeah?" Lynn acknowledged the seriousness of Peter's voice.

"Yeah," Peter whispered. "Does this phone call mean I should just stay off the scotch instead?"

"Yeah," Lynn whispered back.

"There was on more thing," Peter leveled his tone. "I have decided after Easter I am flying to Duluth. My letter will explain why I have to see you."

XXXIII

"Is that all you are going to eat?" Peter's agency President selected a cushioned chair facing away from the basketball court. "The beef tenderloin is out of this world."

Peter thrust his fork into the last leaf of salad. He chewed slowly.

"I am trying to lose a few pounds," the star salesman answered. The President observed the segregated slices of cucumber on Peter's china plate.

"Don't like cucumbers?" the President carried the conversation. Peter smiled at the chief executive's perception.

"They say cucumbers are one of the hardest things for your body to digest," Peter laughed. The two insurance executives peered out of the agency luxury box at the half-filled Fleet Center arena.

"I remember when you could not get a ticket to a Celtics game in the old Garden," Peter mused.

"I appreciate the partners coming down to the game tonight," the President nodded. "I know basketball is not your thing. It really fries my ass paying all this money for a luxury box and having so many of our clients saying 'no' to a freebie to the Celtics."

Peter turned his swivel chair from the game and viewed the scattered group of five partners. The living room suite could accommodate sixteen. One partner sat alone on a stool chatting with the hired bartender. Two others were involved in a serious looking conversation near the coffee table.

Peter gulped a swig of his ice water and reflected on his day. Lynn had emailed him that morning. She resigned herself to his upcoming trip—chalking it up to fate.

"I do not believe in 'fate'," Peter typed in response. "We have all been blessed with freedom of choice. The freedom to take a left turn or right turn whenever there is a fork in the road. Sure there may be a pre-destiny for all of us—God's master blue print. We will all get to the end of our planned journey—but how we get there is up to the willing decisions we make."

"No, Peter—it is fate," Lynn countered. "It is fate that caused us to meet and fate that has brought us to this point in our lives. We do not have full control over what happens to us when you come to Duluth."

"Lynn—do you remember the Bible story of Jesus going to visit his friend Lazarus," Peter recalled. "He was so upset to learn of Lazarus' death before His arrival. It was an accident that Jesus did not accept as 'fate'. He went into the house where Lazarus lay and commanded he rise from the dead. Jesus exercised His own freedom of choice."

The huge crowd roar at a three-point basket stirred Peter from his thoughts. He panned the luxury suite at the group of men who had become like family to him. Was it fate that brought these souls together to enjoy such a fruitful earthen existence?

Peter stood from his chair and ambled over to the pair in deep conversation.

"Have you ever been to Foxwoods?" the managing Executive VP smirked.

"No," the head of underwriting laughed. The pair took healthy swigs on their tumblers of scotch.

"What are you drinking—water?" the Executive VP acknowledged Peter's invitation to the conversation.

"Never been to Foxwoods?" Peter ignored the traditional barb at his Lenten sacrifice. "We were all down at Foxwoods last fall."

The head of underwriting laughed.

"That is just it," the partner placed his hand on Peter's shoulder in confidence. "Everyone has been to Foxwoods. It is the largest casino in the world. Sometimes though we all have a need to escape. To do things that we do not want others to know where we are, or what we are doing."

The Executive VP winked at his star salesman.

"Have you ever been to Foxwoods is our little code," the head of underwriting continued. "Lets say it is our way of knowing to give a partner a little wiggle room from explaining his whereabouts. No questions asked."

"Hey, fellas," the President beckoned from the bar. "Gather around—I have a few presents to hand out."

The group encircled the agency head. The assembly beamed at the pile of large white envelopes appearing from beneath the bar. The ceremony had become an annual ritual.

"Once again we have qualified for a ton of trips from the insurance carriers because of last year's banner sales production," the President grinned. He handed the top envelope to the Executive VP. The second was placed next to his tumbler on the bar.

"Jim and I are taking the two-week cruise around the Mediterranean this June—and no—it is not up for negotiation."

The President handed the third packet to the underwriting head.

"Andy has been with us twenty years in September," the agency head reasoned. "I asked him what trip he and Debbie would like to choose and they opted for Tahoe."

"I have three packets left," the President gestured. "Peter, you has such an outstanding production year that we want to give you the one week golf package to Scotland at the end of April. David, you and Phyllis can have dibs on your annual jaunt to Bermuda. John, we have a four day getaway at the end of this month to the Atlantis Resort in the Bahamas."

"John, how would you like to pinch-hit for me in Scotland?" Peter Collins queried. "I am going to be out of town the end of April, so the Bahamas might work better for me."

The golf enthusiast partner traded envelopes with Peter before he could change his mind.

"Peter, are you sure you want to forfeit teeing it up at the Old Course," the Executive VP marveled. "It is the chance of a lifetime."

"Have you ever been to Foxwoods?"

XXXIV

Marshall's mother was psychic. She could read people's minds and predict the future. Spirit Guides could be evoked practically at will to assist in counseling a soul.

Marshall was reluctant to tell Lynn about his mother's strange notions when they first met. Even as a kid growing up, Marshall would avoid bringing friends to the house. His mother was often outspoken in making assessments of anyone crossing her threshold.

Mrs. Monroe gave Lynn the creeps. Dabbling in parapsychology was always a fulfilling learning experience with her friend Monica. The mother-in-law on the other hand was not constructive with her abilities. She often used her talents to reprimand her daughter-in-law's direction in providing a home for Marshall and Maggie.

From the first day Marshall's mother laid eyes on her granddaughter, she was convinced the baby had similar psychic gifts.

"She is going to be a star," Mrs. Monroe doted to her son.

Lynn became accustomed to the mother-in-law's snub whenever she came to visit—be it unconscious or otherwise. Just as well, Lynn assumed. She spends all her time gushing over Maggie. It beats the way she used to stare at me sideways before the baby was born repeating "something is wrong—I do not know what, but something is wrong."

What really riled Lynn was the way Marshall would heed his mother's advice. It usually came in the form of a doom and gloom warning.

"Lynn, stop taking my mother so seriously," Marshall would scold.

"Me taking her seriously? How about you?" Lynn would bawl. "I saw that look on the side of your face when she said Maggie does not get enough motherly love."

Lynn decided to push the envelope. She invited her mother-in-law to dinner on a Tuesday evening. Both Marshall and his mom were flattered by the unexpected gesture of midweek generosity.

"Oh, it is no bother at all, Mom," Lynn assured. "It will be a simple chicken casserole. I can whip it together when I get home from work."

Lynn followed the recipe directions on the mushroom soup can to the letter. She reflected on her day's email conversation with Peter as she stirred the ingredients.

"Lynn Dear—you are going to have to help me with hotel reservations," Peter opened. "You know the area better than me."

"What type of hotel are you looking for," Lynn remembered her giddiness in replying.

"Given the room rates in Chicago, I am sure whatever you consider the most first class in Duluth will be fine. You do not have to tie me into one place though. I would not mind spending a night or two on a lake, or someplace tranquil."

The Monroe family courteously chewed on the rubbery noodles. Every few moments Marshall and Maggie would eye the guest's ice cream cake thawing on the kitchen counter for dessert.

"So tell me, Lynn," Marshall's mother inquired. "What is new in your life?"

Lynn placed her dinner fork at the place setting as if on cue.

"Actually Mom, I received some great news," Lynn dabbed the corners of her mouth with a paper napkin. "A very dear old friend of mine is coming to Duluth at the end of the month to visit for a few days."

"How marvelous," Mrs. Monroe smiled. "What is her name?"

"It is not a 'she', Mom," Lynn corrected. "It is a 'he'. His name is Peter Collins. He is a lot older than Marshall and me—forty something I think. Anyway, he and I were classmates at an insurance school I went to in Hartford years before I met Marshall. We have stayed in touch from time to time ever since. He has become a very successful insurance agent. Wouldn't you know it, he takes so much time off now during the course of the year traveling to different places that he surprised me by saying he wanted to check out Duluth for a visit."

Lynn bit her tongue to slow her speech. She knew she was hurrying through her planned soliloquy. She glanced at her husband seated at the head of the table. As expected, Marshall was searching his mother's countenance for a reaction.

"Isn't that a nice surprise," Mrs. Monroe widened her eyes. "It is so nice that the both of you still maintain some lifelong friendships. Will he be staying here?"

"No, Mom," Lynn overlooked Marshall's blank stare. "I have done some scouting around. At first I checked the Hawthorn Suites, but they were booked solid. The closest place to us is at the bottom of the hill at Best Western Edgewater. I reserved the first two nights there. That way I can show off my handsome husband and Maggie. The second two nights I booked up at Superior Shores."

Marshall frowned at the mention of Superior Shores. It was rated the most romantic resort in the state of Minnesota. Lynn and Marshall had taken two getaway weekend trips to Superior Shores. The first was on their wedding night. It befitted the resort's romantic label. The second had been a complete disaster of bickering.

"I am sure your friend will be suitably impressed when he sees how pretty it is here," the mother-in-law surmised. "Maybe I will be lucky enough to meet him while he is in town."

Lynn was satisfied. No fire and brimstone erupted from her soothsayer relation. Marshall's attitude would mirror his mother's perception.

"Lynn, I really do not care that Peter Collins is coming here," Marshall told his wife after his mother left the house. "The two of you can do whatever you want over those four days… on one condition."

"Sure," Lynn turned wiping the last of the dishes.

"You have to promise me you will come home every night."

XXXV

"Check out Superior Shores on the Internet," Lynn typed the next morning. "Let me know if it is the waterfront kind of hotel on a lake that you are looking for."

Peter keyed the web search "Superior Shores". The aerial photograph illuminated the italic slogan encased in quotations "Most Romantic Resort in Minnesota".

Peter swallowed.

"It looks perfect," Peter tapped on the keyboard. He sat back and imagined what the rustic suites would be like alone for a weekend with Lynn. His mind shifted to the home front.

Marianne was thrilled about the upcoming trip to the Bahamas. Her husband omitted the tale about the forfeited golf junket for two to Scotland.

"I have to go to Minnesota the week after we get back," Peter mentioned nonchalantly.

"My goodness, two trips in the same month," Marianne glistened. "We are regular worldwide travelers, aren't we?"

"Going solo on number two," Peter said flatly. "I have a meeting scheduled with an insurance executive out there."

Peter's laptop dinged with the signal that new mail had arrived. He opened the window revealing Lynn's long narrative. Peter resorted to his half moon reading glasses. Wordy emails from Lynn were rare.

"Have you realized the basis for you coming to see me now is so much more appropriate than Chicago? Initially, I wanted to book you in this real swanky hotel in Waterfront Plaza. It may not be the top floor of the Chicago Marriott, but you would have found it suitable. Then I remembered how you love to gamble. There is a new casino resort that opened recently about two hours north of here. I was going to make a reservation there, except I hate driving home in the dark late at night. Superior Shores is only about an hour north in Two Harbors. That is a lot more manageable."

"There is one favor I need from you," the message continued. "We do have to get together with Marshall for at least one of the nights. I have been completely truthful with him about where we are going and what we will be doing. He has been amenable to the fact that I will be seeing you, but I have noticed he gets real quiet sometimes. I know he will feel a lot better about the whole thing if I tell him you want to make a point of meeting and spending some time with him. XO"

Peter was befuddled by the contradictions of the message. He centered the keyboard on his desk.

"Lynn—I do not mean to be as subtle as a train wreck, but you have to confide with me on this one… You have made reservations at a place dubbed the most romantic in Minnesota, but then refer to driving home at night? Then you ask me to chum up with your husband? Have you given any thought to the odd chance that we could make love while we are together? What do you think the probability – 0%, 5%, 10%, 50%, 100%?"

Peter pressed the "Send" command and sat back in his chair. He could not function until he received a response. The ding signal was almost immediate.

"0%" Peter read. "Do you hear me loud and clear—0%! Anything else would change everything forever."

XXXVI

The Monday morning anxiety of the visitor's arrival to Duluth simmered like a pot waiting to boil.

"I cannot understand why you have to go to Minnesota," Marianne griped. The return from the Bahaman sun focused the spouse back to reality. "You never had to go there before."

"St. Paul Insurance Company is in Minnesota," her husband informed. "They have a large construction insurance division. They probably would like to know how to write more contractor business in New England."

Everything is just said is true, Peter said to himself. Is it lying if St. Paul has absolutely nothing to do with what I am doing?

"Then why do you have to stay over the weekend," Marianne scrutinized. "Since when do business meetings extend over a Saturday and Sunday?"

"They don't," Peter admitted. "The airfare costs a thousand dollars more without a Sunday night stay over."

Peter satisfied his conscience—no untruths there.

The setting in Duluth was not much better. Marshall decided to skirt a late winter weather warning by departing on a three day business trip to the Canadian border the night prior. He did not bother a kiss goodbye beyond a quick peck to Maggie's cheek.

The volatility of the air stream over the Iron Belt region caused heavy horizontal rains to ice as soon as it hit the ground. Lynn and her little daughter woke the next morning to a landscape resembling a crystal wonderland.

Lynn had to kick on the garage to loosen the ice chips freezing the overhead door shut. Beads of perspiration trickled underneath the back of her coat as she heaved the mammoth door above her head.

Lynn frowned at the sight of Maggie running towards the little Honda Accord. I wish Marshall left me the Suburban, Lynn thought and shuddered. I hate driving this car in bad weather.

The black compact slid at a forty-five degree angle down the driveway. The salt bucket was long since empty. Marshall did not expect ice so late in the season. What little residue of sand lying on the driveway was covered with the glistening frozen precipitation.

The Honda caught its tread when it reached the city treated road. Lynn clutched the gears to drive without bothering an attempt to step back up the ice surface to close the garage door.

The journey lasted no more than fifty feet. A large tree blocked both sides of the roadway. Lynn punched the heel of her hand against the steering wheel.

"Looks like we are going nowhere for a while, Maggie," Lynn said with a slump.

Maggie and her mother gathered handfuls of street sand and made a small game of dropping tracks tire widths apart up the icy driveway.

"Stay here at the mailbox while Mommy tries to get the car back in the garage," Lynn advised the toddler.

Maggie ran up the treaded tire prints as the Accord reached the safety of the detached garage.

"Mommy and Maggie Day?" the two-year old implored.

"Mommy and Maggie Day," Lynn surrendered. "Come on Sweetie—Mommy has to call the office."

The dinette light did not illuminate when mother and child entered through the back deck slider.

"Great," Lynn looked to the ceiling while flicking the light switch. "No electricity."

The furnace is off too, Lynn calculated. She picked up the kitchen wall phone. The sound of the dial tone was relieving. The agency office line picked up on the first ring.

"It may be awhile before I can get in," Lynn reported. "There is a huge tree blocking the end of my road."

"Do not bother trying," the associate replied. "There is a state of emergency for the eastern side of the city. Power lines are down everywhere. We are not going to open the office today—hopefully things will be back to normal tomorrow."

Lynn pulled on the kitchen drawer to find the telephone book. She searched for the number to call the Department of Public Works. The fallen tree at the end of the road had already been reported.

"Yes Ma'am, we have that one listed," the voice confirmed. "Not quite sure when we will get there."

"Come on Maggie, let's get our jammies back on," Lynn brightened. "We can get comfy-cozy in Mommy's bed."

Mother and daughter could feel the chilling air above the goose down comforter. The prospect of a prolonged lack of heat was not Lynn's primary concern. She fretted that she could not access her office laptop. It was Peter's first day back from the Bahamas. Surely he would be trying to make contact.

Lynn reached for the bedside telephone. She punched the toll free 800 number recalled from memory. The telephone rang while she and Maggie kept the blankets over their heads. It was uncomfortable answering the receptionist's identification requirements with Maggie lying at her side.

"I am sorry," the receptionist returned to the line. "Mr. Collins is in a meeting. I am told it expects to last until noon."

Lynn and Maggie slept lightly through the morning hours. At lunchtime, they spooned melted ice cream from the thawing refrigerator freezer. The thermostat read fifty-five degrees. Lynn tried reaching Peter a second time. The response was unchanged.

"I am sorry. Mr. Collins' meeting is still in session."

Maggie picked up on the requested name. The toddler twirled around the living room floor adorned in her winter hat, mittens and coat over footed pajamas. She sang "Pe-terr—Pe-terr—Pe-terr."

The irony of the situation caused the worn out mother to fall to her knees. She laughed and joined the melody at eye level. "Pe-terr—Pe-terr—Pe-terr!"

"Sweetie, do you know who Peter is?" Lynn smiled. Maggie nodded her red-topped head.

"No, you do not," Lynn laughed. "Peter is Mommy's dear friend and you will get to meet him this weekend."

"I do know Peter, Mommy," Maggie continued to nod. Lynn paused and eyed her little daughter.

"What do you mean Maggie? How do you know who Peter is?"

"I can see him in you when we sing songs in the car."

Blinking yellow lights flashed through the bay window. It broke the trance-like state between the two hugging bodies. Lynn stood up to view the municipal truck crew sizing up the scope of lumber debris.

"Maggie, we cannot stay here tonight without electricity," the flustered mother decided. "As soon as the street is clear we will drive over to Grampy and Grammy Cloud's house. I am sure they will have heat on their side of town."

Lynn disregarded the unanswered phone at her adoptive parents' house. The car heater will be warmer than here Lynn mused. Maggie and Amos the dog climbed into the Accord.

The cross-town journey took close to an hour. Even during the busiest of traffic times the four-mile trek would never exceed fifteen minutes. Lynn was forced to alter her route three different times. London Road was closed to traffic at the 40th Avenue East intersection. The orange diamond shaped sign emblazoned "Detour—Work Crew".

Lynn veered up a residential side street to back track to a native known short cut. She did not remember the severity of elevations until the Accord began losing traction with the road.

Norman and Evelyn Cloud's residence was shadowed in darkness when the Accord arrived. Lynn searched the plethora of keys dangling from her spiral ring. The copper colored Yale key for her parents' kitchen door was color-coded with a yellow sleeve for case of emergency.

Mother, daughter and dog entered the darkened house. The light switches did not work. Lynn dropped the overnight bags on the kitchen table. She shouted "Hello?"

Maggie and Amos stayed close to their guide. Lynn picked up the telephone and dialed her brother Larry.

"Mom and Dad decided to spend a couple of days in Minneapolis when they got back from Vegas," the brother comforted. "They are not planning to drive home until Wednesday."

"There is no way I am going to venture home on those roads," the sister exhaled. "Magg, Amos and I will put up here for the night."

"Fire up the wood stove in the living room," Larry suggested. "It will warm the house in no time."

Lynn lit the stove. She showed Maggie how to rub hands near the flickering flame.

"Let's take our bath, Maggie dear," the mother offered once the heat surfaced. She paced to the whirlpool bathtub off the master bedroom. Every drop of tepid fluid stored in the inactive hot water heater was drained into the tub.

The girls remained silent absorbing the warmth of the bath. Maggie did not bother asking for the tub toys Grammy kept in the adjoining closet. She could tell her mother was exhausted. Lynn rested her head against the tiled wall and closed her eyes.

"Maggie says it will be pretty," the little girl assured her weary companion. Lynn did not open her eyes.

"What will be pretty, Sweetie?" the mother drawled.

"For Peter," Maggie caused her mother's eyes to open. "Maggie says it will be pretty for Peter."

XXXVII

The red message light on the telephone console blinked brightly. The fluorescent lights ceiling lights activated as Lynn tripped the motion sensor inside her office. She smiled in gratitude to technology—and the welcomed return to the twenty-first century.

"You have… seventeen new messages," the voice mail system informed. "To listen to your messages, press one…."

Lynn placed the receiver back to its cradle. The agent could not recall the last time the office was closed two consecutive business days due to weather. Duluthians are a hearty breed when it comes to cold and snow. Ice, however, is a different story. Lynn's day promised to be chock full of property damage claims—and the lengthy stories detailing the ordeals. You can count the number of times on your hand that a homeowner ever actually has an insurance claim. It is often a moment of truth for the insurance agent. Advertisers always brag that their service is extraordinary, bar none. God's Speed to an agent who is not responsive when an incident ever actually happens. A disgruntled claimant can be more detrimental to an insurance operation than the storms themselves. The city of Duluth has a population of less than thirty thousand households. Word travels fast—especially a negative one.

The rubber was hitting the road for the Boylston Agency. No one attended to making the first pot of coffee in the employee break room—though for most it would have been their first hot beverage since the storm began. The staff entered the office at Central Entrance and manned the telephones.

Lynn could not begin her day until she made contact with her guest for the weekend.

"May I please have his voice mail," Lynn requested. Excuses about meetings and outside appointments were driving her batty. In this instance, he had yet to arrive to the office.

"Hi! It's me!" Lynn rejoiced at the cue to leave a message at the beep. Hearing Peter's recorded voice was an aphrodisiac. "I do not know if you saw the News, but we had an awful ice storm here. Our office has been closed in case you have been trying to reach me. I really wanted to reach you, but I do not know where you are. Please call me when you get in, okay?"

Lynn organized a steno pad from the corner of her desk. She took a deep breath. Proper preparation was needed before embarking on the transcription of recorded pleas for assistance. The telephone rang.

"Young lady, I have a tree sitting right across my living room floor."

Claims callers held on three different lines. The receptionists kept sliding scribbled notes under Lynn's nose. No, they were not content speaking with a receptionist. They demanded to speak with the Personal Lines expert.

Lynn filled an entire steno pad with salient policyholder information. She shuddered at the re-emergence of yet another receptionist note of interference. The deliverer tapped the pink square of paper with her pencil for courteous effect. "Long distance—line 4".

Lynn abruptly ceased the caller's droning complaint about not having coverage for melting ice flooding the basement. She disconnected the call with a simple click of the transfer button to toll free long distance—line 4.

"Peter?" Lynn asked hopefully.

"What?" the voice balked. Lynn realized it was her husband. She quickly regained her composure.

"Marshall," Lynn chuckled. "I am sorry. My phone has been ringing off of the hook all morning with claims. I thought they said it was someone else."

"Lynn, I need the account number and expiration date for the credit card," Marshall ignored the faux pas.

"Where are you?" Lynn cropped the ear piece on her shoulder. She reached for her pocketbook.

"I am still up north," Marshall informed. "I want to buy a generator for the house."

"Honey, the newspaper reported that all the stores are sold out of generators," Lynn replied.

"Not in Eveleth," Marshall provided. "My customer up here has one sitting right in front of me."

"But Marshall, the electricity is back on," Lynn groaned. "We do not need a generator now."

"It's for next time," Marshall reasoned. "It will be good to have a back up in the future."

"Those generators are so bulky, Marshall. Where are we going to keep it?"

"In the garage."

"Where Marshall—where?" Lynn exasperated. "There is so much junk in there now I cannot even open my car doors."

Lynn could sense her plea was falling on deaf ears. Marshall's customer could be overheard detailing all of the useful features of the equipment. Dammit, Lynn scolded. Once again her husband was wedged between a rock and a hard place—mentioning to a customer that he needed something only to have the customer flip the table. Marshall would not make a sale—the customer would.

Lynn recited the sixteen-digit account number. She did not have the nerve to ask how much they were being fleeced for the generator. Instead she promised a hot supper on the table by six o'clock. Her head shook as the phone idled on its stand.

"Lynn—line 4 again," the speaker on the console scratched. I forgot to give him the expiration date Lynn thought. She would not make the same greeting mistake twice.

"This is Lynn."

"Aah you looking fa me," the Bostonian voice asked.

"Peter!"

"Oh, man, am I glad to hear your voice," Peter beamed. "You've had quite a time of it with that ice storm, huh?"

"It has been an event," Lynn downplayed.

"Nothing worse than an ice storm," Peter mused. "You must be inundated with claims."

"I figure I have over fifty, and it is not ten o'clock yet."

"Is the airport open?" Peter asked.

"It is," Lynn happily reported. "It is over fifty degrees outside today. You would never know we had a storm. The forecast is sunny and warm for the balance of the week."

"I cannot wait to see you tomorrow," Peter's voice softened. "I have been so stressed out not being able to talk to you these past ten days. I have this knot between my shoulder blades that will not go away. I would not care one bit if we did not do one thing this weekend. All I feel like doing is crashing out."

"I feel the exact same way," Lynn mellowed. "You know what I want to do? I want to lie on your hotel bed for four days and hug you."

XXXVIII

The livery dialed the ten-digit number into the limousine telephone in accordance with the rider's wishes.

"Turn off the speaker, Angelo," Peter instructed. "This call is private."

The plexiglass divider rose from the driver's bench seat.

"Lynn, I am on route to Logan," Peter greeted. "You will be at the gate at seven-thirty?"

"I will."

"Then I will see you in a few hours." Peter disconnected the telephone call.

Mid-day traffic to Boston along the Mass Pike was light. Peter detested the chaos of early morning flights. Better to hire a private limousine and book for the afternoon to avoid the bustle of anguished humanity.

Angelo Corsi ferried the Collins family on their frequent excursions for years. Most often, Peter would engage the driver in a lively conversation about the Red Sox, or how deprived their grandparents were when they came over on the boat. It was a rarity, Angelo probably thought, that Mr. Collins would elect to keep the divider sealed.

Peter hopped from the limousine to the curb. He stuffed a wad of cash into Angelo's hand in exchange for the two small pieces of carry-on luggage. Angelo did not have to count the bills. This was one regular customer who always tipped handsomely.

"Monday—five o'clock— right here," Peter waved.

The American Airlines terminal was jammed with passengers waiting to board the 3:20 Flight 1527 to Chicago. Peter sat in a vacant lounge chair and arranged the connecting boarding pass to Duluth in a self-help book titled "How to play Baccaurelet". He peered into the carry on gym bag stuffed with magazines and a continuing education insurance textbook. If the meeting with Lynn turns out to be a disaster, at least I can study for my CPCU exam, Peter thought.

The counter staff at the American Airlines gate began reciting a host of incentives for ticket holders agreeing to be bumped for a later flight. An executive seated across from Peter pulled the cellular phone from his ear and disconnected his call. He masked his approach to the counter so that it would not look like a full-scale gallop. An upgrade to first class on the 4:40 flight was too good to refuse.

The offer had few takers. Peter watched the elderly couple seated next to him hold their hands in anticipation.

"Ladies and gentlemen," the counter person announced into the hand held amplifier. "American Airlines will offer two round trip tickets anywhere in the continental U.S. to anyone agreeing to board the 4:40 flight."

The blue-haired woman grabbed her mate's knee.

"Harold, let's take it," the woman gushed. "We can fly Jimmy and Sandra home from San Francisco for Thanksgiving."

The elderly gentleman cautioned his wife to sit still.

"Sounds like a pretty good deal to me," Peter could not help from interrupting. "Provided you will not miss a connecting flight."

The gentleman ignored the unsolicited comment. He stared at the counter gate.

"Not too many takers on that one," the old man observed. "Don't worry Marjorie, the pot will sweeten. Get your things ready."

The counter staff glanced curtly at one another. The holder of the hand held returned her attention to the script on the acrylic clipboard.

"Ladies and gentlemen, American Airlines is offering two round trip tickets anywhere in the continental U.S. plus a seven hundred dollar cash voucher...."

The insurance agent laughed. The couple sprinted to the counter before the representative finished her sentence.

Peter boarded Flight 1527. He settled into his standard requested window seat above the right wing. Call it superstition, Peter thought. His travel agent still made a habit of questioning his odd choice. Just because the majority of male travelers prefer aisle seats, Peter reflected on the premise that he was not your typical "pretend in front of everyone aboard you fly all the time so act nonchalant". He liked to look out the window.

Peter adjusted the earphone headset to the music console stationed in the arm of the seat. He fiddled through the dial trying to find a suitable medley of songs. Never much inclined toward music, Peter settled on light rock.

The skies over the northeastern part of the country were perfectly clear. Peter stared out the window the entire flight. He tried to count the fifteen hundred miles that separated him from her.

Peter turned his attention to the left window of the fuselage as the airplane descended to reveal the city skyline of Chicago. Images of the ill-fated trip six months prior popped into his mind. The paralytic limbo of the shuttle downtown. The endless hours spent emptily looking out the hotel window. It seemed so long ago. It seemed as if it was still happening.

Peter disembarked the Boeing 727. He walked up the tunneled taxiway to the overhead chart mapping the multitude of connecting gates. Gate A28 was on the other end of the huge American Airlines terminal. Peter estimated it would take about ten minutes to walk to the far end of the building. No problem Peter calculated. The flight to Duluth left in forty minutes.

Peter slowly strolled down the massive corridor. He watched the hoard of passers by. So many people—all looking so different—and hurrying in varied directions. Why is it I have never laid eyed on anyone that even remotely resembles Lynn, Peter wondered?

Gate A28 was a miniature runt of its larger brethren. It was unilluminated and devoid of humanity. Peter sat quietly with his back to the wall in the middle of the tiny two-row seating column. I must be in the right place, Peter folded his hands on his lap. The counter placard displayed "Duluth—6:05PM".

A blond longhaired man about Peter's age entered the velvet roped seating area. He took the front column chair closest to the taxiway door. Peter eyed the wardrobe of blue jeans, matching denim jacket and worn brown boots. The cowboy pulled a twenty-ounce Big Gulp soda cup to his mouth. Peter watched as the straw navigated between the handlebar moustache. Peter wondered whether the cowboy knew Lynn. Is that how Marshall dressed?

Peter looked down at his blue button down oxford Polo shirt and khaki Dockers. His tan western styled leather golf belt matched his sockless pair of tasseled loafers. I will probably to stick out in Duluth, Peter frowned.

A middle-aged couple appeared. They sat straight-backed to Peter's left. The husband height was well in excess of six feet. His wife was petite—no more than five foot one. She had to weigh less than one hundred and ten pounds. Their haircuts were identical—short cropped and parted on the side. Must be a two-for-five-buck special, Peter figured. They were the epitome of a Norman Rockwell couple from the Midwest. The woman wore neutral tones of blush and lipstick. Almost an intentional ploy to downplay any natural beauty. Both their mouths remained closed—maintained with thin, pursed lips. Their eyes tended to focus down as opposed to up—indicating they were more thinkers. Dreamers, on the other hand, gaze to the sky before speaking. Their blanched countenances held red spots on each side of their noses created from the pads of their wireless lensed glasses. The spine of the wife's book held a single crack towards its cover. Obviously, she was not much of a reader. The husband sat with a blank stare. If he did leaf through the token magazine in his hand, it would only be to scan the pictures. My God, Peter imagined. What if they were Lynn's parents? Or worse, what if that will be the life Marshall and Lynn come to lead?

Peter sat back and tried to relax. The companions of cowboy and couple were too Americana. The Duluth placard was subconsciously overwhelming. *What was he heading to?*

A woman appearing well to do approached the column of connected chairs. A young blond, close to looking like a sister but sure to be a daughter, bounced at her side. The mother was smartly clad in a bright peppermint stripped sleeveless blouse. Her hair was richly colored and coifed. Both of the women toted large shopping bags brandishing Macy's and Bloomingdale's. Now that is how I picture Lynn. Peter smiled.

A half a dozen other passengers appeared from nowhere at the gate right as the American Eagle flight was announced to board. Peter hurried to claim his right wing lucky window seat.

"Excuse me, can we check those bags for you?" a voice offered. The sound came from a narrow opening between the ramp way and jet. Peter looked down to find a uniformed stewardess. She was stooped below the floor ramp.

"These are carry-on," Peter replied with a confused manner.

"I know sir, but the cabin is very small. We can valet the bags for you right when you exit in Duluth."

"Would you mind if I kept my gym bag?" Peter asked as he surrendered the small nylon suitcase. "It has reading materials in it."

The same stewardess soon appeared in the tiny fuselage. She paced the aisle counting the small number of passengers. A hand set was not required to address the group.

"Ladies and gentlemen, we are a little unbalanced. Could we please have a few of you up front kindly move to the left rear of the airplane?"

The band of strangers absently turned to one another. No one moved.

"Please folks," the stewardess implored. "The pilot cannot depart the gate until we have a balanced load."

The stewardess viewed the cast of blank stares. She expertly turned to a gentleman sitting alone in the front seat. He easily tipped the scales in excess of two hundred and seventy five pounds.

"Sir, if you will agree to move to the back of the airplane I will be happy to provide you with a complimentary beer."

"Tell you what," the hulk bellowed. "You give complimentary beer to all my friends in this here airplane, and you have yourself a deal."

"Deal," the stewardess grinned. "Complimentary beer and wine for everyone."

The group of flyers applauded as the hulk shifted to the rear of the plane. This must be what people call Midwest charm, Peter assumed.

XXXIX

Lynn cursed the broken tip on her fingernail. She reached her hand back into the Suburban, and angrily tugged the other rubber floor mat to the driveway. A cloud of sand pebbles and salt pellets dusted the top of her shoes.

Lynn bent over and appraised the worn remains of the driver's side mat. Constant heel friction had formed a frayed hole in the upper right corner. The frazzled cleaner picked up the shabby rubber and threw it on top of its passenger side companion. A second cloud of particles settled on the crated generator that had become a storage pedestal in the center of the detached garage.

"That outside water line has not been opened yet," Lynn heard her husband call from the bathroom window. "That pipe could still freeze if we get another cold snap."

Lynn looked dejectedly down at the yet-to-be-attached garden hose.

"Do you think you could go downstairs and turn on the valve?" Lynn dropped her shoulders.

"You do it," Marshall countered. "You are the one so concerned that the truck is a mess."

"Thanks a lot."

"And I would not turn that water on next to the vacuum cleaner cord," Marshall went on. "Unless you think your friend might like to see you with a frizzy Afro."

Lynn scrubbed the interior of the vehicle. Fumes of ammonia mixed with Lestoil burned at her nostrils. The plastic bucket of noxious water turned a dingy brown as the season of winter treading and cigarette smoke came clean. She did not bother to put the shabby floor mats back into the front seating area. Why should we keep this vacuumed carpet in good shape for the next owner, Lynn figured? This is special occasion enough.

Once satisfied with the inside presentation, Lynn shifted her attention to the outside of the Suburban. Maggie's child seat remained anchored to the back seat. It was going to have to stay there. There was no way to jimmy the knotted belts buried deep within the seat cushion without Marshall's help.

Chances for that were longer than hitting the lottery.

Lynn tore another fingernail while she scoured the greasy wheel rims. An edge of the steel wool became stuck in the crack of the nail. A tingling shiver shot up Lynn's spine as she tried to pull the pad without any further damage. Marshall casually walked by the scolding spouse on one knee into the garage.

"That grease is on the axles for a reason you know."

It was after six fifteen when Lynn rinsed the soapsuds off of the Suburban.

"Look at the knees of your pants," Marshall laughed. He resumed bouncing Maggie in his arms on the deck. "I cannot believe you actually washed the roof of the truck."

Lynn marched past her critic to take a quick shower. How am I going to have enough time for nail polish to dry she fretted?

The sight of the ironed clothes on top of the bed was relieving. At least I had the sense to get these laid out before I got all grimy.

Lynn stepped into the shower stall. The steamy head of water absorbed the chill from the outdoor air. Her mind drifted to a comment Peter made during their conversation the day before.

"How are we supposed to greet each other?" Peter joked. "Do I run at you like the sailors on Vee Day and embrace with a leg-flying kiss, or do we merely shake hands?"

"No kissing," Lynn recalled herself saying. "Do not forget, I live here. There could be someone at the airport that I know."

Lynn moved to the bedroom. She pulled her best pair of laced ivory lingerie from underneath the laid out bibbed overalls. She knew Marshall had already scrutinized the selected welcoming outfit. The bibbed overalls gave the appearance of kicking around with an old pal. There was no way he would have checked for the hidden lingerie.

"What should I bring to wear?" Lynn reflected on Peter's follow up question.

"I feel most comfortable in blue jeans," Lynn remembered stating. She smiled as she notched the brass buttons on the sides of her pants with her fingers.

"Blue jeans?" Peter bawked. "I do not think I even own a pair."

Lynn rushed past her family dining on ready mix macaroni and cheese. She stood before the wall mirror and stroked a comb through her wet hair. I am not going to give in to Marshall's guilt trip of slumming it on macaroni and cheese while the vagrant mother hits the road.

Lynn relaxed in the Suburban as it made its way cross-town to the airport.

The evening commuters had already found their way home.

Lynn pulled into the short-term parking lot while tossing her cigarette butt out the window. As planned, she reached into the armchair console between the bucket seats and pulled out a pine tree air freshener wrapped in cellophane. She pulled apart the pre-cut plastic wedge at the top of the cellophane to expose the hanging elastic tip of the tree.

Lynn sniffed the inside of the vehicle. Still a hint of cigarette smoke she sensed. She pulled on the tree so that it was halfway out of its wrapper. That ought to do it. She dangled the freshener from the far side directional stick on the steering column and headed into the terminal. Her wristwatch showed 7:11—just right. Slow your pace. Take a breath.

Lynn was not aware of her subconscious direction. Any previous occasion to visit the airport would have instinctively prompted a confident stride through the automatic front doors. Lynn for some reason found herself detouring to the handicapped concrete tunnel way bunkered to the right of the main entrance. Did Larry say Mom and Dad were flying or driving home from Minneapolis? She took the elevator to the second floor arrival concourse.

Lynn checked the ceiling mounted television monitor. American Airlines' only scheduled flight arrival from Chicago was reported on time. The windows in the arrival area pointed only towards the parking lot. Lynn could not see the jet land.

She stood against the back glass partition of the arrival gate and swayed side to side on the balls of her feet. She examined the tacky glow of her freshly painted lilac nails.

XL

The express jet soared over Wisconsin. Peter resumed his stare out the window. The stewardess methodically served the beverages down the middle aisle. Everyone seemed to be accepting beer.

The peppermint bloused mother and daughter sat diagonally in front of him. Peter smiled as the pair lowered their hospitality trays. They giggled in anticipation of a free alcoholic libation.

"Do you have a white Chablis?" the confident mother asked. The women's eyes lit up at the sight of the cute six-ounce wine bottles. They toasted the plastic cups.

"Sir, can I offer you a beverage," the stewardess addressed Peter. "Complimentary beer or wine if you like."

Peter's body yearned for a cold beer. I could use a drink right about now to beat down these butterflies in my stomach Peter reasoned.

"Mineral water will be fine," Peter found his voice blurting. The last thing you need is numb senses when you see Lynn his conscience counseled. Beer on the breath would not be too flattering.

Peter turned his attention back to the brown barren landscape. It was good I did not end up renting that car in Chicago six months ago to drive up to Duluth to meet Lynn, Peter thought. As the crow flies there were no major roads on this route. You cannot get there from here.

Peter set his gold Rolex back an hour to Central Standard Time. Twenty minutes before we land. The peppermint mother and daughter pulled winter sweaters from their shopping bags. Welcome to the Great White North!

Butterflies danced in Peter's mid-section. These women are putting on sweaters, and I feel like I am perspiring to death. Peter checked his oxford shirt. He shuddered at the sight of the large arcing armpit stains. Oh my God, Peter panicked. My suitcase was checked into storage.

Peter unlocked his seatbelt and fled to the rear lavatory with his gym bag. His original plan was to wash up a bit before landing. Now he found himself pawing through the toiletry bag praying for some way to evaporate the wetness. He resorted to splashing cologne underneath the pitted shirt. A red wind shirt embroidered with his country club logo sat below the pile of magazines and books. Peter tugged the wind shirt over his head. At least the gross part of the oxford shirt will be hidden. The cologne will hopefully mask any body odor.

Peter returned to his seat and aimed the overhead blowers toward his neck. He felt as anxious as a schoolboy about to get a report card.

The massiveness of Lake Superior appeared below the wisps of clouds along the Wisconsin shoreline. Peter turned to the left side of the cabin to see if the Duluth skyline was on that side of the craft. Would it be as visible as Chicago? He had spent the prior evening reading an old Compton's Encyclopedia about Duluth, Minnesota. The Aerial Lift Bridge was noted as the most famous geographic landmark. The angle of the small cabin windows was such though that Peter's view was limited to the Superior waters out the right side of the plane.

Peter was amazed how brown and murky the lake waters first appeared. The Wisconsin landscape looked almost swamp-like.

As the plane neared its destination, hues of rich blueness emerged from the massive depths of Duluth Harbor. The sun shined on the city like a Shangri La.

Peter always envisioned Duluth having a flat terrain with winter winds whipping off of the waters. The small jet however looped its descent over a vast hillside of development on the Minnesota side of the lake. The view was breathtaking.

Peter squinted at the dotted homes of Duluth. I wonder if Lynn's house is one of those, Peter speculated.

The plane flew over about five miles of the Duluth terrain before making its sharp descent to the landing strip. Peter's first notion of civilization on the ground was an archaic snowplow truck abandoned at the far end of a private flying club hangar. There were no other signs of humanity.

The Duluth terminal was a clean trimmed modern architectural building. Its size led Peter to believe that perhaps they would exit the plane via a mobile stairwell to the pavement. Perhaps Lynn was waiting somewhere outside? Peter craned his neck to sharp angles against the window to survey the area. All of the building's windows were heavily tinted to prevent sun glare. Peter could see no one.

The passengers sat silently as the craft rolled to its final stop. Peter ditched proper protocol. He immediately stood and hurried to the front exit door. I have waited too long to see her again, Peter reasoned. There will not be one wasted second over these next four days.

The stewardess had disappeared. Peter waited patiently at the door wondering who was going to open it. The co-pilot emerged from the cockpit and excused himself around the anxious passenger. He calmly unlatched the exit.

Peter stepped out of the fuselage to encounter the stewardess valet the stored luggage. All the surfacing black pieces looked identical. Peter stood above the woman as each suitcase was placed on the loading bridge. The other passengers maneuvered around him, picking up their own bags and meandering up the Jet way.

Peter could sense his frustration reaching a crescendo. He was going to be the last person through that gate. He had traveled over fifteen hundred miles in the past four hours – and Lynn was only fifty yards away!

"Ma'am?" Peter stuttered. "Do you have my bag?"

"Sir, I took yours off first," the stewardess pointed. Peter looked at the remaining black suitcase isolated at the front of the exit door. The orange valet sticker blurred his recognition. God, am I nervous!

Peter grabbed his bag and ran up the ramp to the gate. It had been too long coming.

The gate was crowded with well-wishers greeting the earlier group of passengers. The maze clouded Peter's vision for a brief second.

There—standing like a beacon in the back of the welcoming area—was the tall creature Peter last saw seven years before.

BOOK III

"Did the purple cluster say anything else?"

"Almost two centuries have past on earth since you last incarnated."

"Eternity. Who keeps a clock—other than mankind?"

"Not in this realm... The earth is very different from what you remember."

"The anguish of life. It is painful... the sight of me... black veiled—a widow who died—weeping for a dead husband. Barren to conceive—unable to provide him children. I knew my life path was set to be useful. He did too—working as missionaries. Our inability to have a family is what catapulted him to start an orphanage. Then he left me to illness. I felt so abandoned."

"Your husband did not welcome your return home?"

"Blue lights seem to teach lessons in every realm. Mine was obviously not to depend on him for ascension—neither here nor earth. Living within the Pillars must give the Blues sanctuary from our unenlightened yellow tinged ways."

"The cluster knows how much you love the prospect of ascending to live within the Pillars. Perhaps another attempt at a selfless incarnation will teach us both to tame the human ego. When we return, the yellow fray may instead be blue. We will be able to go through the Pillars as true Blue soul-mates."

"Maybe we can incarnate together—as twins perhaps."

"The cluster encourages a nobler attempt for us at independent enlightenment."

"The thought of returning to the American frontier is worth considering. There was a beautiful Indian girl we cared for...."

"A lot has changed there. The Motherland seems to be calling my return—so many wrongs to be made right. Maybe we should be inclined to journey this time on separate paths. Chances are we will not meet. We will not know each other exists."

"Go then if you must. We are back here sooner than mortal bodies could ever fathom. Who knows, I may decide after all to follow you."

I

The three minutes it took for the passengers to disembark seemed to freeze the scene beyond slow motion.

Where was Peter?

Lynn could feel herself begin to panic. Do not tell me he got second thoughts at the last minute.

She carefully studied the faces of the people around her. It had been seven years. Maybe we will not recognize each other.

The footsteps rumbling up the stainless steel runway seemed to gain volume in Lynn's ears. The crowd of people resumed their normal motion as Peter burst through the metal frame doorway.

Lynn had envisioned this moment for weeks. She could imagine herself opening her arms wide and exhibiting her toothy smile. She would wait for her love to walk up to her. She would ask, "What took you so long?" and squeeze him with all her might. She would peck both sides of his cheeks—the way the French do.

Instead, Lynn was frozen like a statue. No one said it would take three minutes. No one said everyone in this terminal would slow to a crawl. And since when did people burst into a room, with a rumbling stainless steel drum roll? Oh My God! Look at how tanned he is, Lynn awed. No one in Duluth had a suntan like that. Lynn felt pale.

The visitor recognized his hostess in an instant. Lynn's eyes widened as Peter ran past the groups of people toward her.

"I made it," Peter shouted. He dropped his bags to the carpet and grabbed both of Lynn's shoulders.

Lynn was astounded by the forward kiss to her lips. She did not mean to tilt her head away—but she did.

He did not seem to mind my hesitation, Lynn reacted. Is my smile too thin? Am I even smiling? Does he have any idea I nervous I am? Oh My God, he is even more handsome than I remembered. He has a couple of gray hairs in his sideburns! He looks so distinguished!

The image of Richard Nelson, her natural born father, popped into Lynn's mind. Do I know anyone here? A client perhaps? My God, they will think he is old enough to be my father!

"Hi," Lynn could hear the sound come out of her mouth. "Are you ready to go?"

Peter scrambled to pick up his bags. He had to trot to catch up with the long-legged stride.

"Aren't the escalators over there?" Peter called. Everyone else was leaving the gate arrival area in a different direction.

"We are taking the elevator," the fast-paced guide shouted back.

Peter came to a stop a third of the way down the mezzanine. He stood in front of the plexiglass sign marked "Elevator". Further down the corridor, Lynn took an abrupt left turn into what she must have remembered as the elevator station. Peter squinted to the sign indicating where Lynn entered—"Men's Room".

"Oh shit!" Lynn exclaimed to the befuddled gentleman standing at the urinal. She pivoted her heel and retreated to the corridor.

Peter Collins calmly pressed the down button. He never did laugh at me, Lynn realized.

The pair waited for the elevator car as if nothing had happened.

Peter followed Lynn to the parking lot. Her pace had returned to normalcy. Peter walked past the menagerie of pick up trucks and vans toward a row designated for compact cars.

"Which one?" Peter looked.

"It is over here," Lynn cut between the cars. She pointed to the glistening GMC Suburban.

Lynn pressed her remote key control to unlock the vehicle. She expertly swung open the large rear tailgate, and returned to the driver's door before her guest slung his bags in the back.

The stench of evergreen was overwhelming. Lynn snatched the pine tree wrapper and threw it to the ground. My God, I hope he does not say anything.

As safety conscious risk management professionals, both driver and passenger locked their shoulder belts into place. Lynn could sense though that Peter was sitting sideways in his seat. He was staring at her as the Suburban rolled out of its space.

"You always drive this vehicle?" Lynn heard him ask. She could feel herself nod.

"Boy, is it big. Look how high we are above the road."

Lynn slowed behind the small queue waiting to exit the parking lot. She could still feel the eyes upon her.

"Lynn, I am so happy to be here with you," she heard him say. She could feel his fingers touching her arm. The attention of the booth attendant was still two pickup trucks away.

"Here," Lynn interrupted. "I bought you some souvenirs of Duluth."

Lynn bowed her head to the middle console. She handed Peter four postcards. One was a fog-shrouded photo of the Aerial Lift Bridge. Another was of the cliffs off Lake Superior. The third was of the black bears at the Duluth zoo. The last was an animation of Minnesota's state bird—the loon.

The postcards were a needed distraction from the tenseness. Lynn continued to feel her head nod. Was it in reaction to the pulsating throb in her brain, or just the embellishment of acknowledging Peter's research about the Aerial Lift Bridge?

"So this is the state bird, huh? The loon?" Lynn's attention returned to the conversation. Peter stuck the photo of the lake cliffs in the driver's face. "This one is my favorite."

"That is where we are going tomorrow night," Lynn informed. "That is the view from Superior Shores."

The mention of the resort sent a painful sting through the back of Lynn's head. She could feel Peter's hand rub between her shoulder blades.

"Geez Lynn, you are so tense. What is the matter?" Peter asked. "Christ, your back is all hunched over like a hump back, and the skin around your neck looks green."

Lynn had forgotten Peter's propensity to state whatever was on his mind. Her head pounded as the truck entered the traffic flow.

"Peter, there is something I have to tell you," Lynn cast a quick glance to her right. "I have been having some awful dizzy spells over the past couple of weeks. A couple of times, I had to go home early from work."

Lynn acknowledged Peter's concerned stare.

"My doctor has diagnosed a very rare disease in me," Lynn continued.

"Oh my goodness Lynn, what is it?"

Lynn looked into Peter's eyes. Oh My God, *they are so blue*!

"Peter, I have Meniere's Disease," Lynn stammered.

Why was he laughing?

"Meniere's Disease," Peter chuckled. "What are you so worried about? I have Meniere's Disease too!"

"You have Meniere's Disease?"

"Of course I do. I never told you about that?"

"No," Lynn marveled.

"Do you know much about it," Peter asked.

"Just what the doctor told me. That it is an imbalance of the inner ear, and that there is no telling when it will go away."

"Very true," Peter concurred. "You know it is the disease of geniuses. Albert Einstein had it. It hit me unexpectedly about twelve years ago. I had to be rushed to the hospital the spinning was so bad. I vomited and dry-heaved for three days straight. What are you taking for it?"

"Valium."

"Valium? You need anti-vert medication to steady your equilibrium. The doctor did not prescribe Meclazine? That is the miracle drug for Meniere's. I never leave home without it. Even got some in my bag."

"You are carrying Meclazine right now?"

"That is the fun part about Meniere's," Peter smiled. "You never know when it is a coming. Why don't you pull over right now? I will give you one."

Lynn shook her head at the dashboard. This was too eerie a coincidence. The doctor had told her the odds of finding another person with Meniere's Disease was over a million to one.

"I think I need some water," Lynn pronounced. She commandeered the truck into a Spur gas station quick mart. "Want one?"

Lynn could tell Peter was checking her out as she moved inside the little store. The satisfying grin on his face affirmed the approval of what he saw.

Lynn handed Peter a plastic bottle of water. She extracted a package of Ultra Light 100s from the middle console.

"I guess 'when in Rome'," Peter mused. "Can I have one too?"

"I thought you quit?"

"I did. Eight months ago," Peter smiled. "I just think my old Brigadier chum could use a smoking companion right now."

Lynn shared the light with her passenger.

"Where do you want to go now?" Lynn offered. "To the hotel?"

"No, the sun is setting. Let's go someplace to watch it go down."

Lynn pulled right out of the Spur parking lot into traffic. The Suburban sped west up the gradual incline of the East Central Entrance. She turned off the divided road into the ShopCo parking lot. Neither spoke as the sun disappeared below the skyline. They inhaled on their cigarettes and reflected.

"So you equate me to the sunset?" Lynn broke the silence.

"Yes, I do," Peter looked into her eyes. "I want to spend each of the next four nights watching it with you."

Lynn flicked her cigarette out the window.

"So what do you want to do now?" she asked.

"Show me your life, Lynn," Peter held her hands. "I want to know everything about Duluth that makes up your life. Where you grew up; where you live now; the route you take to get to work every morning...."

Lynn smiled.

"Gee, and I was wondering what we were going to do with each other for four days," Lynn laughed.

Lynn found herself excitedly accepting the challenge.

"My parents do not live far from the airport," Lynn realized. "Do you want to see their house?"

Lynn instinctively took a series of turns through the residential neighborhoods. The sight of fallen tree limbs from the ice storm returned the driver to her previous state of anxiety.

"I wish you could be back in a month's time," Lynn whispered. "It is so beautiful when everything is green."

The Suburban scaled a barren side street barely paved with material inadequate to withstand a heavy snowplow season. Lynn's shoulders slumped as she pointed to Norman and Evelyn Cloud's brown ranch house.

"I did not realize how many trees fell in their yard when Maggie and I spent the night," Lynn frowned. "My father is too old to clean the yard by himself."

Lynn quickly remembered how the Million Dollar Man could change a subject from something negative.

"So this is where you grew up?"

"Actually, no," Lynn said. "My parents moved here a few years ago. I grew up in the neighborhood around the corner. Want to see it?"

The Suburban passed by a small five-room cape painted a pale lime green with white trim. A basketball backboard was nailed to the two car detached garage. The driveway was a single slab of cement frost heaved with numerous cracks.

"That is where I grew up with Larry and Luke," Lynn gestured toward the right side of the Suburban. She gazed at the wavy curls on the back of Peter's head, and wondered what kind of house Peter grew up in?

"So that is where your long legs learned their basketball prowess?" Peter joked. He turned to face Lynn. Lynn's eyes seemed to dance as she forced her attention back to the street. She had not traveled this side road in years. The memories were intoxicating. Had Marshall ever asked to see where she grew up?

"See, right there?" Lynn exclaimed. "That is the Lakeside Elementary School. Monica and I used to go there. We used to walk up and down this hill every day."

"Let me guess," Peter rationed. "In three feet of snow?"

The Suburban continued its destined path. Lynn could feel herself suddenly become sullen. Please let this moment pass she found herself plead. It did not.

"Hey, a Catholic Church," Peter pointed demonstratively. "I cannot read the sign. What is the name of it?"

"Saint Mary's Star of the Sea," Lynn uttered. "That is where Marshall and I got married.

The dizziness returned to the back of Lynn's head. She turned the vehicle into the eastbound lane of the Central Entrance. The Suburban came to rest in the breakdown lane.

"Peter, I am not feeling so well," Lynn grimaced. "Can you please drive?"

"Why don't we head to the hotel," Peter consoled. He exited out the passenger door.

II

There were two hotel buildings on each side of London Road that carried the franchise label Best Western Edgewater. The reservation receptionist was instructed not to disclose this nuance to unknowing tourists telephoning for accommodations. Visitors to the Edgewater West facility were treated to the omnipresent view of Perkins Restaurant and a cookie cutter Burger King. The Edgewater East building provided a flanking image of the same area. A returning guest or native Duluthian knew to specify the waterfront side of the East building. Those select rooms catered spectacular views of Duluth Harbor, and the expanse of Lake Superior to the north.

Peter was fortunate to have the advanced preparation by his hostess.

"You are on the lakefront side of the hotel," the front desk receptionist confirmed. "Room 1020."

"Ten-twenty," Peter questioned. "Does that mean you have ten floors in this building?"

"No sir—that would be the first floor."

It is said that Irishmen generally walk ten feet ahead of their women. The adage popped into Peter's mind as he strode the narrow hallway to Room 1020. Was my woman obediently following my lead, or were doubting thoughts caused her to flee without him knowing?

A person can change a lot in seven years time, Peter reflected. He once read that one's physical being was totally converted every seven years. The mostly water and chemical matter that that comprise a human body was completely replaced in that period. New matter replaced old matter. New bone cells replaced old bone cells. New organ cells replaced old organ cells. Your external flesh, hair, and even your eyes were totally transformed. Could your soul change too?

Lynn was not the person Peter envisioned since the Brigadier School. It was a process of calculated elimination that led him to recognize his long-term pen pal at the airport terminal.

The long flowing hair that used to drape the twenty-one year old's head was gone. Lynn sported a matronly pixie-cut hairdo. It used to be that Lynn would only don her eyeglasses if she had to read the amphitheater white board. A frameless pair of spectacles now windowed the brown eyes Peter had fallen in love with. He knew the tiny lens were the current fad in eyewear—but geez! They sure made her look grandmother-like.

The most disconcerting feature Peter found with Lynn was her posture. The lack of facial makeup came as no surprise. The natural beauty of her countenance never needed artificial enhancement—but the bowing of her frame was marked.

Peter reflected on how Lynn always wore flat shoes. Her five foot nine inch frame would tower over most male counterparts had she worn heels. Nevertheless, she had always carried a very erect stature—walking confidently with her shoulders back. The shoulders that Peter found now slumped forward. Was it just because of the stress of him being here?

Peter swung the hotel door inwards to let Lynn pass into the room. Nubs of black hair were visible on the nape of her neck—the foundation of the former shoulder length flow. It had probably been a couple of weeks since she last went to the hair salon, Peter surmised. He thought of his wife Marianne's mandatory weekly pilgrimage for beauty maintenance—and of the Midwest couple waiting at O'Hare.

Lynn walked to the far side of the room. She opened the rear wall door that revealed a cement slab outdoor deck. She lit a cigarette and gazed at the harbor lights reflecting off of the water.

Peter mounted his gift assortment of postcards inside the bottom frame of the wall mirror. The customization made the institutional quarters seem a little more like a home. He grabbed a clean shirt from his bag and took refuge in the bathroom.

"Maybe I can change to one of the upper balcony rooms?" Peter suggested as he joined his companion on the cement slab. "They look like they have better views."

"Actually, I like the location of this room," Lynn motioned to a side walkway leading to the presence of the Suburban visible in the parking lot. "I felt uncomfortable thinking about having to walk in and out of that lobby."

A chilling breeze blew in off of the water. Peter followed Lynn's lead into the tranquility of the room.

"So, is there anything you would like to do?" Peter gestured with his arms. "Didn't you mention Duluth has a casino here in downtown?"

"They do, but I have never been there," Lynn stood between the pair of queen-sized beds. "It is in a kind of seedy area."

Peter viewed the fluorescent clock radio centered on the bedside lamp stand. It read 10:20."

"What time do you have to be home?" Peter asked meekly.

"The bars close at one," Lynn stated matter-of-factly. Peter could tell the response was rehearsed. "Marshall will think we are hanging out catching up on things until then."

"So what do you want to do?"

"Stay here," Lynn's shoulders pushed back. Her frame resurrected. She toed off her shoes and walked barefoot to the TV. Peter watched aimlessly as the remote was scavenged from the top of the set. Lynn moved to the window side of the bed and propped all its pillows to one side. She lay atop the covers and patted the open side of the mattress to her left.

"Peter, grab those pillows on the other bed and come over here with me."

The expectation of obedience to the order was exhilarating. Peter knocked his loafers to the floor. The prone pair admired the set of extended bare feet.

"I thought you hated red," Peter commented on the glossed metatarsals.

"It is appropriate for toenails," Lynn smiled at Peter's memory.

"Welcome to Duluth—and thank you for choosing Best Western Edgewater," the main menu of the cable system announced on the television screen. "We hope you enjoy your stay."

Peter leaned over to face his long awaited partner.

"Lynn, would you mind if I took off your glasses?" Peter propositioned. "I have flown fifteen hundred miles to look into your eyes."

Lynn handed the fragile frames to Peter. He placed the glasses on the bedside lamp stand and rolled again onto his back. Lynn wiggled closer to the middle of the mattress. Without a word, Peter and Lynn took each other in their arms. Motionless, they stared deeply into each other's eyes.

She could not recall ever seeing eyes so blue. Peter was enraptured by the deepness of brown that opened to a place experienced in a continuum he knew existed before. Without the aid of prescription lenses, Lynn's eyesight was keener at closer distances.

"Do you know you have gray hairs?"

The couple began to kiss—slowly at first, and then more passionately. The union was pure. It exuded the rightness of being. Why had it taken so long to realize?

The pair fell victim to the forces of animal instinct. Within a few short moments, the couple shed their upper clothing. The bibs of Lynn's overalls hung awkwardly down beneath the loins of the clinging romantics.

Peter kissed the lobe of Lynn's left ear. He caught signal of the uncontrolled pant, and glimpsed at Lynn through the corner of his eyelash. Her eyes were closed, but he could tell her mind was in a place well beyond. She arched her back upwards and released a loud audible moan. He had never witnessed a lover so inviting.

Peter moved his lips below Lynn's neck. Lynn's hands touched her lover's ears lightly as the roaming head moved down towards her navel. Peter could feel the rhythmic pulse of Lynn's wanting hips.

Peter's guided head discovered the laced top of the ivory panties. The image of the magic area exposed so many years ago at the Brigadier Conference Center rolled into memory. Peter raised his head for a moment to appraise the cherished site.

"Hey! What happened?" Peter rose to his elbows. "It's gone!"

"What?" Lynn exhaled. The exclamation startled her to a sitting position. "What is gone?"

"Your tattoo is gone," Peter informed. "Your rose tattoo."

Lynn fell back on the pillows. Her awestruck face revealed the surprise of a captured prankster.

"You mean the rose tattoo I had at the Brigadier School?" Lynn's grin widened.

"Yeah," Peter nodded rising to his knees. His concentration remained focused on the plain flesh above the stretched lace. "The matching one you got with Brian Fitzgerald."

Lynn covered her mouth with her hands. A high degree of pressure was needed to suppress the laughter.

"That was a fake tattoo, Peter," Lynn burst. "Brian and I never got tattoos. I was pulling a practical joke on you because I knew you were so smitten with me."

Peter stared in amazement. The joker patted the back of her ear like a movie star diva.

"You mean to tell me when my cards referred to the blooming rose on your belly while you were pregnant with Maggie that the joke was on me?"

The bantered foreplay resurrected Lynn's spirit.

"Yup," Lynn beamed. She bounced off of the bed.

"I did get one a couple of years later," Lynn exposed a full pedaled version on the side of her right hip. "I did not want to tell you though, because your cards were always so preoccupied with my mid-section."

Peter propped his elbows next to his ears on the bed pillows. The transformation into a joyous woman was awesome to behold.

"Come on and get your jacket," Lynn bubbled. "Let's go outside and share a cigarette."

The frigid air did not detract from the lively conversation spanning the following two hours outside the shade-drawn hotel room. Peter reveled in the enthusiasm of Lynn's newfound spirit. It was a little after one o'clock in the morning by the time Lynn acknowledged she had better get going.

"Oh, and one more thing," Lynn caressed as they hugged and kissed goodbye at the edge of the dark parking lot. "No more after-shave this weekend."

"What do you mean?" Peter asked.

"Your after-shave," Lynn beamed waving her palms in front of her face. "It is bad enough that you whisker-burned the hell out of my cheeks tonight, but now I am going home smelling like 'boy'."

III

Human clocks do not adhere to time zone mores. Peter had never been a deep sleeper. No matter what time he retired in the evening—as early as nine o'clock or as late as a two o'clock in the morning party—he inevitably awoke precisely at 6:20am.

Peter opened his eyes and scoped for the time on the digital clock—5:15. He rolled onto his back and stared at the stucco ceiling. With him in a foreign place, who would be the one to roost his sleeping family back home?

Marianne had always been a late morning riser. Her children were cut from the same mold. Peter envisioned the chaotic scene waiting to unfold. Who forgot to set an alarm? The school bus will be here in twenty minutes! Hurry up and get dressed! Don't forget to brush your teeth!

Peter surveyed the empty room. The serenity of the setting was surreal.

There could have been a host of excuses cited for not making the weekend excursion. A charity foundation board that Peter served on had bestowed a leadership award to an esteemed business colleague in the community the night prior. The nonprofit group, like so many others, automatically expected that Peter would reserve an implied fifteen hundred dollar table of ten. Even when he disclosed to the group that he had been called out of town, they still expected a table commitment. This time Peter declined that, too. A short congratulatory note handwritten to the award winner was satisfaction enough for sending regrets.

Little League opening day was slated for Saturday. Peter pictured the Mayor of Worcester questioning his whereabouts before throwing out the ceremonious first pitch. Marianne's voice reverberated in his head. Everyone including your sons will be asking where you are?

"There comes a time when our sons are going to have to learn their father will not always be standing at the sidelines watching them," Peter recalled his reply. "Sometimes you have to trust to go it on your own."

The remote control was still lying on Lynn's pillow—just as she left it the night before. Peter reached for the gadget and pressed the red power button.

"Welcome to Duluth," the blue screened menu greeted. "And thank you for choosing Best Western Edgewater. We hope you enjoy your stay."

Peter turned the television off, and then on again. The canned message reaffirmed his decision. He rose from under the bed covers exposing a plaid pair of long pajama bottoms. He traipsed barefoot into the bathroom for morning relief. A miniature complimentary coffeemaker sat at the corner of the sink. Peter splashed water on his face as the two-cup pot brewed. He mixed a concoction of powdered condiments into a Styrofoam cup and exited to the concrete outdoor slab.

The sun was dawning over the northwestern banks of Wisconsin. The rays emitted a predicted balm. The temperature was already above sixty. If Duluth was considered the nation's icebox, then a first time tourist would not know it. The forecast was to stay above seventy degrees through the weekend. Peter sat down on the vinyl-ribbed deck chair to witness the panoramic invasion of color. Lynn's package of Ultra Light 100s laid on the matching round end table. Peter ignited one of the remaining sticks. He inhaled deeply. Eight months may have elapsed since his last sequence of habitual tobacco, but his body reacted as if it never missed a day. He scrunched his toes on the cold concrete.

Duluth, Minnesota was slowly waking its dreary head. Sets of semi-trailers loaded with timber trudged their way between the final concrete divide of Interstate 35. A couple of joggers plodded the pedestrian concourse on the lakeside of the expressway. A solitary motorboat equipped with fishing gear putted parallel with the margin of the bank.

Peter absorbed the atmosphere that defined Lynn's livelihood.

He wandered back to the room door once the last of the cigarettes were exhumed. It was locked.

Was it something with this relationship, Peter frowned. The knob did not cooperate with his twists. He slumped back into the deck chair. The notion of circling the perimeter parking lot to the front lobby for another key card was not inviting.

Peter eyed the four-legged aluminum walking cane posted as a sentry to the cement slab of the room next door. Was that there when I first came outside, Peter wondered? Maybe my neighbor was an early riser too.

Peter tiptoed to the bay window next to his own. The curtains were closed. Still asleep, Peter figured. He could hear a shower running though. I will give the door a light knock when the shower stops, Peter surmised. That way they can call a room attendant.

An elderly lady with strong Norse features limped from the room about twenty minutes later. The sight of the tanned bare-chested man caught her by surprise.

"Could you do me a big favor and call up to the front desk?" Peter fired as quickly as he could. Most women this age would have retreated to their sanctuary like a tortoise. This woman did not. "I seemed to have locked myself out of my room."

The limping lady obliged with a head-shaking chuckle.

"They said they will be here in about twenty minutes," the Norse limper returned. "How long have you been out here?"

"Oh, not too long," Peter refrained. "It has actually been quite nice sitting out here. I watched the sunrise."

Another older woman with a severe case of pillow head emerged from the room.

"Okay Marge, where is the hunk you said is here to get me out of bed?" the woman stepped onto the slab. The sight of the bronze pectorals caused the woman to shriek back into the room. "Jesus Christ Marge! You were not kidding!"

"Don't mind Phyllis," Marge managed a proper handshake of formal introduction. She, too, was now locked out—a travail more humorous than clamorous. "She has not seen a man still around come morning in years."

Phyllis re-emerged—totally unfazed by either her impulsive reaction or bed head. She was armed with a battery-operated blender. The munitions were placed on the matching round end table.

"Well, Mr. Guest to our party," Phyllis palmed the extended hand of the male visitor. "We can celebrate the lack of pockets in your pajama pants for a key card with a nice frozen Marguerita."

"Is it even seven o'clock yet?" Peter gawked.

"It is cocktail hour somewhere in the world," Marge announced.

Peter politely asked to be omitted from partaking in the salted tequila. He surrendered by accepting a LaBatt's Blue beer from Phyllis' accompanying cooler.

A tattered uniformed hotel employee with a pimply face appeared along the rear walkway just as Phyllis heaved the remaining ice water from the cooler onto their third girlfriend lolling in bed. The teenager hesitated in shock as the aged women glowered over the resulting scream.

"Bet this happens all the time," Peter laughed as he directed the helper to the barred steel door.

"No," the boy could not get his eyes off of the plastic cups of yellow drinks. "Never."

Peter showered and dressed in a pair of golf shorts and matching shirt. He slipped on his tasseled tan loafers and rejoined the partying triumvirate. Doris, the ice watered victim of the trio, was seated with her friends swallowing her second Marguerita. The group of women stared at the bare legs of the short panted man. Doris nodded in acknowledgement. The golden color of the thighs and calves matched the earlier report on the chiseled torso.

"You are not from around here, are you?" the girls giggled in unison.

"Why do you say that?" Peter played the game. The women ogled as Peter cracked open the second LaBatt's left on his end table while he showered.

"First of all," Phyllis informed, "every pair of short pants in the state of Minnesota are still in winter storage during the month of April."

The triangle toasted the revelation with a clunk of plastic cups.

"And second of all," Doris chimed appraising Peter's legs. "No one in Duluth has a tan line this time of year."

"And third of all," Marge reprimanded with a wagging forefinger. "You asked me to do you a big 'fay-vaa', not a big 'fay-vore'."

"Truth be told," Peter confessed. "I am from Boston."

"Boston? With all those people?" Marge continued the interrogation. "What is someone from Boston doing here?"

"I have come to see the bridge," Peter smiled. He pointed to the daunting spectacle of the Aerial Lift Bridge. What was meant as a half-hearted shirk ended up being a reasoned response. The women turned to gaze at the engineering marvel as if it were a religious icon. The landmark glistened in the early morning sunshine like an attracting magnet.

"The Aerial Lift Bridge is one of the greatest creations of mankind," Marge confirmed. "Are you an architect?"

"No," Peter felt his brow furrow. The respect the women held for the fabled gateway was overwhelming. "I happen to be an insurance agent. I am here visiting a friend I used to go with to insurance school."

The women told of how they all worked together at Family Life Picture's worldwide headquarters in Minneapolis. Peter warmed the conversation by stating that he was aware of the company, and its reputation. The company did photography even in Boston for yearbooks and youth groups.

"Marge is the boss of our unit," Doris revealed. "We specialize in providing archived photos for missing children cases and for families victimized by premature death of their youngsters."

"I never thought about it, but your records are a valuable resource, aren't they," Peter realized. Whatever joy comes from a job can also carry a certain amount of heartache. Chances are, Peter thought, these women have seen more pain than most. If so, it was masked by the plastic yellow cups. "I can imagine your jobs can be both rewarding and disheartening at the same time."

"It is," Marge nodded. Peter could tell she was the leader of the group. "That is why each year we take a girls-only weekend to the Norwegian Riviera."

"The Norwegian Riviera?"

"Duluth, Minnesota," Doris exclaimed broadening her arms to the crystal blue harbor. "It is the Norwegian Riviera."

"But do not tell all those people in Baa-ston," Marge bribed with another cold LaBatt's. "Only we hearty-blooded Minnesotans know about this little piece of Eden."

The casual tone of conversation was interrupted by the telephone. Phyllis was in the midst of her lecture on the dimensions of the bridge. She was just moving on to her next topic relative to the frigidity of the lake waters. Peter excused himself from the discourse. He knew who was beckoning the call.

"Hi," Lynn welcomed. "Did I wake you from a lonesome slumber?"

"Well, if it is not Mrs. Monroe," Peter toyed. "Can Lynn come out and play today? She has already missed the first two hours of our Norwegian Riviera cocktail party."

"Cocktail party?" Lynn puzzled. "And where did you hear about the Norwegian Riviera?"

"Thought you could keep it a secret, didn't you," Peter bubbled. "My girlfriends told me—here, at the cocktail party."

Lynn shook her head at the bits and pieces of Peter's tale of morning events as she hung up the telephone. How was it that no matter what the circumstance, Peter inevitably became the life of everyone in his wake?

Lynn cleared the rest of the breakfast dishes abandoned by a family who already started the day's trek. Images of the Monroe exodus to Disney World the previous winter floated in her mind. Marshall was so introverted. He shunned any contact with folks from neighboring rooms in the resort. Heaven forbid he could muster a hello at the shuttle buses or at one of the facility swimming pools. Maggie's hand was gathered whenever an inviting parent would offer their child's friendship at the baby pool or swing set.

Those people all seemed so nice, Lynn remembered. She could imagine what that trip would have been like with Peter. He would have had the whole hotel group in Mickey's Parade marching down Main Street, USA. The vision made her sigh.

The merriment of the ground level enclave was clearly audible as Lynn crossed the parking lot to the cement poured walkway.

"Lynn, I would like you to meet my friends—Margie, Phyllis and Doris," Peter stood poised with his arm around a gray haired woman holding the battery operated blender. "Doris was just about to give a dissertation about all the possible attachments that can be invented for this handy piece of portable equipment."

Lynn shielded the uproar of new laughter and meekly sat down at the empty deck chair next to the tabled LaBatt's. There was a sense of relief not recognizing any of the female party. She could still see though the women's educated intuition to check out the diamond wedding ring on her finger. The rapid glimpse to the gold band on the gentlemen's finger was even subtler. She would not want to be a fly on the wall for their topic of speculation later on, Lynn figured, and tightened her mouth.

"One thing that could stand improvement with this thing is a longer battery life between charges," Doris exclaimed. Even Peter noticed the lecturer was nice enough to draw attention away from the visitors' ring fingers. She depressed the black plastic button to demonstrate the sporadic deadening purr. "Then again, maybe a constant stopping and starting would be useful for the special attachments I have in mind."

Lynn politely refused a Marguerita. No, the fact that it would have to be on the rocks because the blender was out of action did not influence her decision. Peter stopped his drinking with the third beer.

The group continued its chat. Guests at the hotel made known their awakening by tossing pieces of bagels and muffins from the continental breakfast out from their upper balconies. A flock of menacing seagulls began diving at the morsels regardless of the humanity at ground level. Was the feeding ritual coincidence, or protest to the revelry? A break up appeared imminent. Lynn's own version of "how to" relative to dealing with garbage eating birds rather than blenders cued the party's end.

"Have you ever heard of feeding seagulls instant rice? The kernels blow up in their gullets and they die."

IV

Lynn excused herself from the circled gathering. She went into Peter's room. Her friend comprehended the signal. Bid adieu to the sorority from Minneapolis.

"You are going to Two Harbors today, too?" Lynn could still overhear Doris' glee. "Where are you going to be?"

"Superior Shores," Lynn could hear Peter's reply. She cringed at the mention of the name. Natives knew of the resort's romantic label. She hoped Peter did not suggest trying to rendezvous as a group up there. Lynn squeezed closed her eyelids.

"I am sure you will find Lynn and me somewhere around the bonfire at sunset," Peter waived naively. He entered the room and closed the door behind. He mindlessly stood beside the television and looked at Lynn—lying prone on his bedcovers.

"Peter, please draw those shades," Lynn whispered. She placed her hand over her forehead. "I do not want those neighbors of yours peeking in."

Peter fumbled with the connecting halves of the curtains. No matter which way he tried, the lined material would not overlap. A slit of sunshine still appeared. He jammed the writing table against the radiator to hold the flimsy wall cloth tight. He turned to face his bequeathed with an eye of triumph. Lynn did not share the sense of accomplishment.

"Lynn, are you okay?"

"Yeah," she lied, then thought better of it. "My Meniere's is acting up. I have felt dizzy all morning."

She could feel his body joining next to her on the bed. She kept the anxiety of returning home to Marshall eight hours earlier to herself. It was an unsavory feeling—walking into the split-level's Master bedroom—seeing her husband fast asleep in the king-sized bed. She felt cheap removing her overalls. Her bra strap and panties were twisted to one side. She debated whether or not to shower before entering the bed. Rinsing the perceived scent of the out-of-town visitor would have been too tell-tale. She crept to the far edge of the bed and prayed that Marshall would not wake up. She was convinced that she reeked of Peter's musk. She could not admit she laid half awake the entire night—thinking how she wished to be sleeping in the arms of another—in the hotel footed at the bottom of the hill.

Lynn showered and dressed at dawn. She prepared a full breakfast for Maggie and Marshall—a rarity for any weekday, except for this one, that she was taking off. Perhaps the smell of bacon grease will cover the aroma of Peter's body, she hoped. It seemed to permeate her being.

The dizziness came on with Marshall's strategic appearance. Instead of meandering into the kitchen as always from the hallway, he entranced the adjoining dining room—proudly carrying the two-year-old daughter. He said nary a word—until Maggie was securely strapped to the high chair. The toddler commenced her routine and began chewing on the daily wedge of white toast waiting on the plastic tray.

"You got in late last night," Marshall noted to his wife's back stationed at the griddle.

"Would you like bacon, sausage, or both?" Lynn averted the opening jab.

"He is twelve years older than you," Marshall emphasized. "What the hell is that dirty old man doing in my backyard hitting on my wife?"

Lynn dropped the spatula onto the griddle. The metallic cling pronounced for effect.

"Marshall, he is a long-time friend," Lynn reminded. "I want to visit with him as much as he wanted to visit with me. Please do not start this."

"Do not start what?" Marshall implored. "That your husband takes offense to a married man spending a weekend with my wife? I bet if I call Massachusetts right now his wife would not even know where he was!"

Lynn grabbed the kitchen counter for support. The wave of dizziness buckled her knees.

"You can ask him that question yourself directly when we meet for lunch today," Lynn replied. She refused to face her interrogator.

"Lunch?" Marshall balked. "Did you really think I was going to meet the two of you for lunch? And what Lynn—were we going to ask for a booth? Is that what you are planning to do? And which side of the booth would you sit on? Do you have that one figured out too? The side of your husband, or the side of your 'dear old friend'."

Lynn turned to face the pent-up husband as he gestured quotation marks with his fingers. Maggie absently stared at the toast crumbs on her bib.

"You said you would meet us for lunch," Lynn stated. "Peter already said he was looking forward to meeting you. I am telling you—you have this all wrong."

Lynn rolled so that her back abutted Peter on the bed. Her eyes remained closed.

"Peter, will you hold me? Please. Just hold me?"

He calmly draped his arm over Lynn's back. His hand completely enveloped the skinny wrist. The bodies spooned in natural rightness.

"*Please*," the soft voice repeated. "*Just hold me*."

V

"Lunch is off with Marshall today," Lynn offered as the pair exited the hotel parking lot. "I guess he has a busy month-end at work."

Lynn glimpsed to see if Peter detected a fabrication. There was a look of relief instead. Was it from avoiding the luncheon, or the need to make a quick dash from Room 1020? The heavy petting had stirred the pair's sexual drive almost beyond control. A fresh change of scenery was needed to sidestep the unfathomable.

"So, it is your call what you would like to do today," Lynn continued. "We cannot check into Superior Shores until four o'clock."

"How about swinging by your agency?" Peter brainstormed. "I would love to see where those Dot Game moves emanate."

Lynn hesitated at the suggestion. It was still a day of commerce in downtown Duluth. The idea of a co-worker or client catching view of Lynn cruising with a male friend was not enticing. Besides, they would have to pass Marshall's drug store along the way. The potential for chaos was unimaginable.

"My office is way over on the other side of town," Lynn apologized. "I was planning to take you by there tomorrow. You said you wanted to see the bridge. How about we go down to the lakefront instead? Do you know how to drive a standard?"

Lynn tossed the set of keys over to her companion. Peter caught the ring and smiled at Lynn's model-like pose against the black Honda Accord.

"Hey!" Peter remarked. "So this is your version of my old sedan!"

Peter opened the trunk of the Honda to store his overnight bag for Superior Shores. A similar bag centered the compartment.

"Don't get your hopes up," Lynn countered the optimistic look. "It is a mere change of clothes. I figured you could keep my car while you stay over at Superior Shores. Marshall said he would come to pick me up tonight. All I have to do is call to let him know when."

Lynn admired Peter's confident stride as he maneuvered to the driver's side of the car. She noticed he could depress the floor clutch without adjusting the bucket seat. Their bodies were of near equal height.

Peter revved the accelerator and slowly eased up on the clutch. The vehicle lunged forward and conked out.

"Thanks for parking on an incline," Peter let out a laugh. "I swear, I think I know what I am doing."

Lynn exhibited a patient sense of humor as the fumbling stick shift ground the Accord's gears out of the parking lot. She was able to relax by the second set of traffic lights on London Road. Peter always did seem to demonstrate an ability to adapt to a situation, the passenger mused.

Any inkling of dizziness had evaporated. Lynn found herself thoroughly enjoying the role of tour guide and navigator. Never had she encountered such an inquisitive subject—including Maggie. Area landmarks that blend into every day life in Duluth, Minnesota sprouted to vividness.

"Who is that guy sitting on the bench?" Peter pointed as they parked at the Downtown Lakewalk. Lynn noticed the large bronze statue facing Canal Park Drive. I have lived here my whole life, Lynn thought, and never realized the existence of that statue. The first thing he noticed at Canal Pier was something most people pass. Lynn slowed her pace to absorb the sight of Peter running up to the mounted bronze placard.

"Albert Woolson—February 11, 1847—Watertown, New York—August 2, 1956 —Duluth, Minnesota," Peter recited. "Battery C First Minnesota Heavy Artillery—Last Union Survivor. Wow Lynn, can you imagine that?"

Lynn stood with her arms crossed behind the reader. She analyzed the weathered features of the town father.

"Can you imagine the life opportunity availed to this man?" Peter looked up to the hills of the downtown district. The architecture skyline was like none he had ever seen before. "Isn't Watertown, New York a port city on Lake Ontario?"

Lynn shrugged.

"I think it is," Peter nodded. "This guy probably sailed the Great Lakes, ending up here at its furthest tip in Duluth. Heavy artillery—the Iron Belt? Seems to make sense, huh? He could have made his fortune anywhere in the world, traveled the country in the war even, but no. He chose to make Duluth his home—for one hundred and nine years. Unbelievable!"

"All that and a bag of chips," Lynn stepped to face her friend. The plight of their relationship reflected in the yearning pair of eyes. Maybe it was not one hundred and nine years, but it felt longer. Peter's Adam's apple motioned a hard swallow.

"You have not experienced Duluth until you try our famous onion rings," Lynn gestured to the nearby French Fry shack.

VI

The little black Accord rolled over the metal surface grid of the Aerial Lift Bridge and lumbered down Minnesota Avenue. Lynn munched on the lunch of fried food and pointed to shoreline homes of interest.

"Telly Savalas used to live there," the navigator motioned to the modern looking A-frame.

"Come on," Peter viewed the glass enamored home. "Kojak is from Duluth?"

"I do not know if he was originally from here." Lynn snapped an onion ring in two. She fed the first half to Peter. "But he knew where to settle down in retirement."

A more modest house was pointed out further down the road.

"Marshall's aunt and uncle live there. Marshall actually grew up in the house next door before his parents moved to California. That is where I mentioned we take Maggie and Amos in the summer."

The Accord was instructed to turn left at the end of the road to and empty public lot.

"Come and see the beach," Lynn jumped out of the car leaving her sandals behind. She headed towards the planked boardwalk scaling the posted dune revitalization area.

Peter joined Lynn at the wooden steps at the end of the boardwalk. The beach was completely isolated. Lynn cupped her hands in an effort to light a couple of cigarettes.

"When you told me you went to the lake on summer weekends," Peter admitted viewing the endless stretch of reddish-brown granules of sand. "I never envisioned a beach so much like the Atlantic coastline."

"I had a sense you did not quite have a handle on Lake Superior," Lynn observed. She handed Peter a cigarette—not taking her eyes off of the white-capped fresh water. "To me, this is home."

Peter turned and headed back towards the car. Oh My Goodness, Lynn feared. He did not just flick a whole cigarette into the revitalization area, did he? Or did he? Did I touch a nerve? She slowly followed Peter's reflective stride. The appearance of the cigarette nestled in his hand softened her curiosity.

"Let's go to my house," Lynn suggested in hopes of changing the mood. "You said you wanted to see my life."

Peter started the car and headed back down Minnesota Avenue to South Lake Ave. He negotiated the Aerial Lift Bridge as if he were a life long native. Lynn placed her hand atop his on the stick shift.

"Take a right at the top of Canal onto the expressway," Lynn said. She was determined to convert her guide into an accomplished veteran of Duluthan street lingo. "This is the precise end of Interstate Route 35, you know. Route 35 runs from the Mexican border town of Laredo, Texas all the way north across six states, dissecting the heart of America. Almost two thousand miles of roadway ends right here in front of the Best Western Edgewater. See that? You can tell all your friends in Worcester that you stayed at the end of the rainbow."

Peter contained his focus on the highway. Lynn digested the slow nod of acknowledgement. The prophetic words hung in the air. What was more compelling? Lynn's inspiration—referring to the end of the rainbow, or her pronunciation of Peter's hometown—"Wis-ta". Lynn knew she inadvertently adopted Peter's accent. The same thing happened when Peter annunciated "Albert Woolson—Watertown, New York. The variation of "r"s at one time was an attractive appeal. Now their language was blending. The couple looked in unison to the corner hotel unit numbered 1020.

"Maggie and I take this route everyday from day care," Lynn stammered. She fought to keep the "This is My Life" tour theme.

The Accord exited the highway and began to scale the residential Duluth hillside. The commute reminded Peter of his own. Over fifteen hundred miles from Worcester, yet almost identical terrain.

Peter followed the series of instructed turns left and right through the maze of neighborhoods. Lynn's finger settled at the final left turn. Peter immediately noticed the directional sign for Northland Country Club.

"Golf course," Peter amazed. "Lynn, you never told me you lived on a golf course."

"We don't," Lynn answered. "The golf course is about a half a mile up a different street. Seems everyone in the neighborhood belongs there though, but us."

"Marshall does not play golf," Peter asked.

"Oh, he does—he loves golf," Lynn replied. "He sits at our picture window every Sunday morning in the summer watching the neighbors pick each other up to head over for a morning round."

"So why don't you join?" Peter wondered.

"Because it costs something like five thousand dollars to get in," Lynn excused.

"What is five thousand dollars if it is something you want to do," Peter blurted. "If it were me and I wanted to play golf on weekends with my buddies in the neighborhood, then I would set that as a goal for myself. One descent sized incentive, even in the drug store business would pay for a membership."

"Marshall does not quite think along the same line as you do Peter," Lynn downplayed. "He really is not much of a businessman."

"Didn't you tell me once that you were the breadwinner of the family?" Peter recalled.

"I am," Lynn affirmed proudly. "That was why it was so important for me to get back to work after Maggie was born."

"How much do you make?"

Lynn smiled and looked out of the side window. Peter's boldness knew no bounds.

"You do not have to tell me if you don't want."

"I will if you will," Lynn challenged.

"You sure you want to know?"

"Marshall makes thirty thousand dollars a year," Lynn sputtered. "And I make thirty-five. I am awfully proud of that extra five, you know. How about you?"

"Me?" Peter deadpanned. "The flat salary on my renewing book of business is a buck and a half a year. That is what I use to cover the household bills—tuitions and stuff. My new business commissions puts another fifty grand in my pocket a year. Not that I see the whole thing though with taxes and so forth. That money is geared towards fun things like vacation trips and country club memberships. My partners' bonus at year-end is usually another fifty. I use that portion for investments."

Lynn sat in silence as Peter bantered dollar figures incomprehensible to her Duluthan world.

"You know, last year I invested my whole bonus in a high tech company that was supposed to enter into an exclusive government contract with China to introduce the Internet. The deal went bust and I lost my entire bonus. All I have to show for it is a nice capital loss deduction for this year's tax return."

It would take Marshall and me over four years to make what Peter earns in one, Lynn tried to conceal her coil in the car seat. How in God's name would we ever have an extra two thousand dollars left over after every month for "investments"?

The Honda turned into the split-level's driveway. Peter adroitly noticed the pile of rubble in the front yard.

"What have we here?"

"That is our old front walk," Lynn muttered. "It is in the process of being replaced."

"Looks like it has been there for awhile."

"Marshall started it last fall, but had to stop because the weather set in."

Peter and Lynn got out of the parked car. They headed toward the back deck.

"So this is where the chain-smoking debate whether or not to go to Chicago occurred," Peter recounted. He placed his hand on the stair rail and looked off into the wooded backyard. It looked so different than Michigan Avenue from the forty-second floor. "I have wondered for the longest time what it looked like. For you to stand here that morning trying to decide. I never pictured it like this."

A passenger jet soared directly over the solitary pair. The noise was deafening.

"The flight pattern out of the airport for planes heading to Chicago passes right over our house," Lynn yelled above the noise in the sky. She followed the jet's tail stream—rigid and narrow at first, then vaporizing into the atmosphere. "See the double plume of white condensation? Maggie calls it the 'skywriters'. Seeing the skywriters that morning? That was probably the toughest thing."

VII

Golden retrievers love to sniff a foreign crotch. For that matter, any crotch will do. Lynn seemed embarrassed by the intrusion. She tried to block the dog's exit through the slider by locking her knees.

"This is Amos," Lynn yielded. Her attempt to pocket the house key while simultaneously seizing the pet's collar was fruitless. "He does not react well all the time to strangers."

"Oh, it is okay," Peter bent over to pat the animal. "I wonder if he can smell my golden retriever on me?"

Peter began to scratch behind the dog's ear. Amos had been in the "who-goes-there" mode. The masculine touch, however, had a titillating effect. The canine slowly acquiesced to the welcome. Peter boasted at his accomplishment.

"See that, he's a sucker for me!"

Lynn gathered Amos by the scruff of the collar. She marched the dog outside to the backyard run. Peter backed away to allow Lynn to do her business. Marshall was in all likelihood Amos' master. No way, Peter thought, did Lynn want him striking up a warm rapport with her husband's dog.

Peter leaned on the deck railing. He waited for Lynn to come back. Better to allow her to enter the abode first, ahead of the invited guest.

Peter stepped into the small area designated as a dining room. To the right was a tinier kitchenette. Straight on was the formal living room. The walls in every room were painted white.

"Marshall does not allow shoes on the living room carpet," Lynn conveyed. She slipped off her sandals in a routine fashion and meandered barefoot down the beige carpeted hallway towards the bedrooms. "But he is not here; so do not bother. Make yourself at home. I need to use the bathroom."

If he had his druthers, Peter did prefer to keep his shoes on. He walked into the living room and viewed the framed group photographs on the wall.

It was the first time he ever saw the image of Marshall Monroe. In many respects, the man was nothing like Peter imagined. He had sandy blonde hair. Why would I think he would be dark featured like Lynn? He was also about an inch shorter than his wife. Gee, and I thought Lynn deserved a high-in-the-saddle Cowboy about six foot four. Peter squinted closer at the photograph without removing it from the wall. Was Lynn wearing heels to appear taller than Marshall?

"I see you found my favorite family picture," Lynn observed returning down the hallway. "Can you recognize any people?"

"Well, it is easy to spot you," Peter answered. He pointed to Lynn standing in a hip length wool coat with a long black scarf at the far right side of the group. She sported her trademark broad toothy grin. "And I figure this must be Marshall and Maggie next to you."

Peter noticed the little girl opted to hold her father's gloved hand, even though the mom's was available without a glove at her side.

"This picture was taken last New Year's Day outside my adoptive parents' house." Lynn said. Like Peter, references had turned to "houses", not "homes". "I like it so much because my birth parents were visiting from New Mexico and they are in it too with all of my brothers and sisters. Can you spot who my real father is? The one I said reminds me of you?"

Peter scanned the large group. By process of elimination he discounted the very young from the very old in the setting. Four people down from Lynn's left were a forty-something, tanned couple. Both had dark colored hair. The man, who appeared a little shorter than his partner, looked to have some sort of a curly permanent.

"This one," Peter jabbed the glass with his forefinger.

"You are right," Lynn exclaimed. "Can you see how I associated the two of you?"

Peter forfeited an opinion on the coifed hairdo. He smiled and motioned towards a side wall table.

"Are those more pictures?" Peter questioned. He wanted to get off the father-figure subject.

"Those are from my wedding."

Peter picked up the framed photograph of bride and groom. It was a professionally mounted pose. The garbed pair's faces pondered over an invisible object. A floral bouquet was superimposed at the invisible spot. Peter could envision the spot was where the overpaid photographer stuck up his finger and said "Focus right here and think about the life ahead of you."

"Gee, you do not look very happy," Peter speculated—seeing perhaps what he wanted to see.

"No, Peter," Lynn replied. "You are wrong there. My wedding was a very happy day."

Peter placed the picture back on the side wall table. He followed Lynn's shadow down the hallway.

"There's our bathroom," Lynn spoked a visage to the right. "Maggie's room is over here across the hall, and the Master bedroom is in the back corner."

Lynn and Peter stood at the jamb of the Master bedroom. A brass iron king-sized bed dominated all but a two-foot horseshoe around the room. It was evident to Peter that if the adjoining bathroom door were open too wide, it would hit the foot of the bedpost. A matching door to its it flank indicated the existence of a small closet. I would get claustrophobia in there, Peter thought to himself.

Lynn walked past the absorbing visitor into what appeared to be an extra bedroom. It was the only room of the house that was not picked up clean.

"This is Marshall's study," Lynn stated as she pointed out the assemble-it-yourself computer desk with accompanying PC. "You can tell Cinderella does not spend much time in here."

Peter followed his guide into the square messy room.

"You never saw my photo book from the Brigadier School, did you," Lynn quizzed. She pulled a large white three-ring book off of the shelf. "Look, I wanted to show you. I must have two rolls of photographs from Hartford. Peter, you are not in one single picture. Can you explain that? I do not have one picture of you."

Peter cradled the bulky book in his left arm. He flipped open the cellophane picture pages with his right. The first set of pictures was of Lynn hamming it up with Brian. Peter did not want to appear too discourteous—ignoring the painstaking travail of a love lost.

"Most of these look like shots from your weekend road trips," Peter offered in response. "I was never around for any of those."

The last set of pages was dedicated to the final night at Cromwell. Even Craig Hinson made the journal—boasting his double ribboned diploma. Peter resisted the urge to close the book.

"Look at the final picture," Lynn laughed. "See the guys carrying me back from Teapot's? Boy, I was not in good shape that night."

Peter had enough. He closed the book and replaced it to the shelf. Lynn crossed her arms. She realized her memories of Hartford were different.

"You have not seen our downstairs project," Lynn changed the subject. "Wait until you see our construction-in-progress."

Peter followed Lynn down the center stairwell that split the house in two. The downstairs floor was drab gray concrete.

"We are trying to do something worthwhile here," Lynn stepped into the middle of darkness to draw the light bulb strung from the ceiling. "Our goal is to shoot to have these rooms finished by the Fourth of July. My family is flying in to spend the holiday weekend with us."

Peter paced the barren area. He stopped in front of a large contractor's leather hip belt. It was chock full of hand tools. A worn pair of steel-toed work boots sat next to the pile.

"Looks like someone left these behind," Peter said.

"Those are Marshall's," Lynn replied.

"Marshall's? Marshall totes around tools like these?"

Peter reacted to Lynn's slow nod.

"How long has he been at this project."

"Since we moved in," Lynn attempted a half-hearted deflect.

"And how long has that been?" Peter asked rhetorically.

"Three years," Lynn stated. "He putters around with different parts of it whenever we drum up the money."

Peter walked past the rehab area.

"This appears finished," Peter motioned towards a completed full bathroom. Lynn walked over and flicked on the inside light switch. The illumination revealed a large built in Jacuzzi bathtub.

"This is where Maggie and I take our bath every night," Lynn smiled. "The upstairs only has a stand up shower stall."

Peter glanced from the tiled floor in the bathroom to the carpeted steps on the other side of the basement.

"You have to traverse this area in bare feet during the middle of winter?" Peter pointed to the sawdust covered cement floor. "I cannot believe the woman I adore is scampering underground on this floor in the middle of February when it is thirty below zero outside."

"That is the fun of it Peter," Lynn touched his elbow. "Maggie and I make a game out of it—running on tippy toes to get upstairs into our jammies."

"Does Marshall freak out if you track sawdust on the precious living room carpet?"

Lynn's hand fell from the elbow.

"Peter, what is the matter?" Lynn whispered.

"This is the matter," Peter waved his arm across the half-completed room. "It is the not-joining-the-country–club because 'we do not have the money', the we-didn't-finish-the-front-walk because 'the weather set in', the we-can-get-twenty-more-years-out-of-the-carpet-if-no-one-wears-shoes mentality, the let's-putter-around-the-basement-for-three-years-until-we-drum-up-the-money routine. All of it! All of it is the matter!"

"That is what I mean, Lynn, about setting goals," Peter continued his rant. "Not to half-heartedly 'shoot' to finish the basement by the Fourth of July, but to commit to make the money to get what you want. All Marshall has to do is what he is supposed to know best. If that happens to be managing a drug store, then he should devote his time to managing a chain of drug stores! It is just like insurance. The best use of my time is to sell insurance—period, the end. I know the business and people seek me out for my expertise. That way I make the money to have an expert mason come to my house to install a front walk—not half-heartedly, but professionally! It is cheaper for me to have a landscaper take care of my yard than for me to sacrifice the time to do it. And this downstairs area? For two grand—which can probably be made on one signing bonus with a descent company—you could have a contractor bang this out in a week."

Peter could see the effect of his monologue. Not only on Lynn's forlorn face, but on the ego combating the spirit inside him.

"What is the matter?" Peter repeated. "The matter is that I am pissed! I have dreamt for seven years that you spring boarded your life after Brigadier School into a euphoric state of bliss. Running from the tub to the jammies every night with Maggie—well, that is bliss… This other stuff though, Lynn… I don't know."

VIII

Meniere's Disease creates an odd sort of dizziness. The initial signal of onset is ear ringing. The ringing is high pitch—low volume recessed way in the back of either the left or right ear. The pitch remains constant, but the volume increases. It blossoms to both hearing organs within moments. A sufferer will then experience an aura of bright specks zipping across the cornea. The feeling of falling backwards comes practically at the same time. The back of the cranium begins to rotate like a spinning Frisbee. One must attempt to anchor equilibrium against the nearest supporting wall. Falling to the ground—a misfortune that can result in serious potential injury—can create a sickening enough condition to induce severe vomiting. There is the illusion that your whole body is gyrating. The ear ringing does not cease.

Lynn knew the sensation was not a Meniere's attack when she stepped onto the outside deck and spotted the deer. Her ears were reacting to the situation, but it was not a pitched ringing. It was more like the hollow loll of a vacuum. No time—no space—no dimension. A different realm. She could hear her voice as if it were miles away in a cavern.

"*Look Peter—a deer.*"

Behind the detached garage was a wooded patch buffering a back nine golf hole at Northland. Fallen saplings camouflaged the large hornless beast. It was not the tannish brown of most deer. Rather, the coat was more of a gray and black.

The deer froze its stance like a statue. The eyes focused on its witness. Lynn could sense the penetration of the glare. The air did not move. It was soundless.

"*We do not get many deer around here,*" she could barely hear her voice. It was an echo. Peter stepped past her to the driveway pavement.

"Look Lynn—another deer. Hiding—see there? Further in the back."

Lynn could not collect her stare from the fronting animal.

"*Look Lynn—can you see it?*"

Lynn could perceive a shadow pointing. She knew the silhouette. It was more than her friend. The eye of the deer penetrated her consciousness. He is the one—your soul-mate—your sense of being.

"*There—the head is peeking out from the thicket.*"

The light touch on her shoulder spontaneously pulled her being out of the cavern. Peter's eyes were focused directly into her.

"Do you see?" Peter's voice delivered at a normal tone. "The smaller one that is in the back?"

Lynn looked again to the wooded patch. Both of the animals were in clear view. Their sights were set on the pair. *Is Peter sensing what I am*?

"The color of those deer are a lot blacker than what I see in New England," Peter concluded. "I notice the trees in the woods are not as big either. They do not have the big thick trunks I am used to seeing. Maybe it is because of the climate. The wind and cold probably necessitate rejuvenating life cycles. What do you think?"

Peter walked to the car before Lynn could muster an answer.

IX

"My girlfriends at Edgewater suggested the North Shore Scenic Route to Two Harbors rather than the highway," Peter mentioned as the Accord headed north. "Do you have a preference?

"I am not up for much driving right now," Lynn adjusted the tilt mechanism on her seat. "Route 61 will still take a half hour."

Peter noticed Lynn's glimpse to the speedometer. The needle was a smidgen above the seventy-five mile per hour bar. The Accord did not seem to welcome the alien pad on the accelerator. The car delivered a slight rattle of protest.

"Do you always drive on the fast side?" Lynn tried to appear casual. Peter released his foot from the gas pedal. The Accord's rattling ceased at a steady five miles per hour cruising speed above the posted sixty-five mile per hour limit.

"Don't you ever get calls from clients asking you to fix their speeding tickets?" Peter broached the subject diplomatically.

"What do you mean?" Lynn asked.

"You know," Peter prompted with his hand. "A prominent client gets pinched for speeding. They call you to see if you can make a phone call."

"Does that happen to you?" Lynn quizzed. She appeared surprised at the suggestion.

"Not often," Peter said. "From time to time it can occur. You have chits in your pocket for the cash you contribute to police associations or the local polls. I guess you learn to pick your spots. If I had my druthers, getting someone a low numbered license plate at the Registry is easier than straightening out a ticket. It is not quite as sleazy."

Peter glanced at Lynn to observe her response. The setting sun cast a low twilight on the horizon. Its beams inadvertently struck the crystal of Peter's gold Rolex. A corona of light the width of a shirt button jumped along the roof on Peter's side of the compact. Lynn's focus followed the sporadic diffraction.

The bent light darted indiscriminately against the gray cloth of the Accord's inside roof. A prism of color bordered the laser depending upon the angle of light. Lynn seemed caught up with the nuance—particularly as the sunlight shifted with the motion of the automobile. The ray did not have the ordinary prism of color. The corona's edge would glisten a sharp gold—then turn to blue. Was it the cloth that was creating the blue fray? It could not be because the blue would appear for a microsecond—then zip back to gold. Where were the reds and purples? Why only yellow and blue?

Peter regarded the crystal culprit clasped atop the steering wheel. He jiggled his wrist with a slight twitch. The ring disappeared through the driver's side window. Lynn directed her stare to the source. Peter continued to drive—pretending nothing had happened. Within a moment, Peter could tell Lynn was no longer enamored with the watch. She was staring at his wedding band. The gold arched from the ring finger of his left hand stationed on top of the steering wheel. The pressure of the ring's base against the wheel caused the top of the band to protrude a half moon between Peter's finger. He wished he could hide the object, but that would have been too obvious.

"Fixing tickets and sleazing license plates sound like a liberal Democratic way of doing business," Lynn mustered the nerve to proclaim. "Don't get too cavalier on this road Peter. Flashing the Massachusetts State police decal in your wallet will not do you much good. Though it would be entertaining seeing you try."

Peter got the point. He slowly motored to the franchised strips that cropped along Two Harbor's city line.

"Mind if I pull into that liquor store?" Peter bobbed his head to the emblemed sign cornered at the first crossroad. "I think a little champagne is in order to christen the hot tub."

"I usually do not drink anymore," Lynn weathered. "I get drunk on two glasses—but what the heck—why not?"

Peter drove through the intersection and pulled into the parking lot. He parked the car along the far edge of the blacktop reserved for parking. New town—new environment—Peter popped out of the car with a confident gait.

"Would you like to come in?" Peter offered. He felt like the cash was burning a hole in his pocket. I am not in the confines of the Monroe house anymore, Peter thought. I can spread my wings.

"No, thank you," Lynn preferred the safe confines of the vehicle. "I will stay here and wait for you."

The cash register attendant suspended the transaction with the solitary customer to eye the visitor as he walked into the rustic store. They could tell he was not a native of Two Harbors.

Peter could see the purchase of the Old Milwaukee beer ball had been put on hold. His preppy wardrobe was now the center of attention. Certainly a question would not interrupt the sense of limbo Peter ascertained.

"Do you have any Dom?"

Peter was impressed by the unblinking matter-of-fact comeback by the counter person.

"No, we do not," the dungaree clad woman responded. "Any champagne will be on the top middle shelf behind you."

The duo at the counter continued to watch. Champagne was not a fast moving choice in the establishment's inventory. Peter grimaced at the dust covered bottles.

"Anything on ice?"

"Maybe some in that cooler on your left."

Peter settled back on his haunches to view the selection on the bottom glass shelf. Neither of the two, labeled brands of champagne rang a bell. They both must have been there since New Years, Peter supposed. Standing straight up on the shelf instead of on their bellies no less. Each was priced at $7.99. Peter grabbed the all-black bottle.

"Champagne glasses." Peter rose and turned towards the check out counter. "Do you have any?"

This time Peter did interrupt the beer ball transaction. The pair turned from their business.

"Oh, I am sorry," Peter admitted his faux pas. So much for taking the liberty of thinking folks were impressed with me, Peter condescended to himself.

"That is okay," the woman behind the counter leveled. "We do not sell champagne glasses."

The hiking booted customer armed the beer ball under his flannel shirt. A courteous nod goodbye was granted to the attendant before perusing the cavalier customer one last time. He exited the store.

"Is there a store in the area that might sell them?" Peter continued—not bothered by the inspection.

"The only place that might sell them is Pamida—first right back up the hill," the lady pointed with her left hand while ringing the black bottle purchase with her right.

Peter slipped the purchase into the back seat of the Accord. Remnants of the orange price tag hung gummed to his thumbnail. He was appreciative that Lynn did not check out the credentials of the slim brown paper bag. Marianne would have torn into the package in seconds. Anything of alien origin would have been immediately discarded. Peter would have had to drive back to Duluth to find an appropriate winery.

"Have you ever heard of Ayleeda?" Peter asked. He turned the Accord left—back up the street mentioned at the counter.

"Ayleeda." Peter repeated. "The woman in the store said they might sell champagne glasses there."

"Peter, we do not need champagne glasses," Lynn countered suspiciously. She was unsure whether Peter's confusion was a Freudian slip. "Paper cups or even the glasses they give you in the room would have been fine."

"Hardly," Peter retorted. He negotiated the turn into the large mall parking lot promised by the check out person. "Champagne is more memorable when properly served."

Lynn burst out laughing as the discount retail store surfaced over the crescent.

"Ayleeda?" Lynn chuckled. "You mean Pamida."

The ignorance swept over Peter's head.

"Do you think they sell champagne glasses there?"

"Yeah," Lynn sensed a small sort of victory. "Plastic ones!"

"Well you sound like you are well-accustomed to the plastic housewares section of the store," Peter teased. "Would you mind searching out champagne glasses? I need to run into the bank next door to cash some travelers cheques."

Lynn was at the far end of Pamida when Peter entered the store. The sight caught Peter in his tracks.

To a casual observer, the routine of a woman scrutinizing items on a store shelf would seem a mundane occurrence. Peter—observing Lynn—in what was a staple of everyday life was more foreboding. Peter stood in silence and watched as she pondered the varied offerings on the shelf. This was what Lynn has looked like over these past seven years. This was what she will continue to look like after he left to go back. She was ten paces in front of him, and he missed her already. God I cherish this memory of what she is doing right now, Peter thought. God, please do not let me ever forget this vision of Lynn—and her trek through life.

Peter inhaled deeply through his nose. The Big Gulp cowboy surfaced from a corner aisle and blocked the path to Lynn. His emergence was alarming. The Big Gulp cowboy from the airport sans straw between the handlebar moustache! Peter stood in shock. It had been less than twenty-four hours, and what were the odds that Peter would ever cross this dude's path again? And a half an hour north in Two Harbors, no less! Peter could not believe it! Big Gulp was still wearing the exact same outfit he had on the day before. Peter could identify that plaid flannel anywhere! Big Gulp did not seem to recognize Lynn. Well, that was good, Peter calculated. At least he was not a best buddy of Cowboy Marshall. But Christ, Peter figured. Here he was going back to Worcester at the end of the weekend. He would be yearning for this Madonna at the shelf. Meanwhile, this jamoke would be walking the other way, in Lynn's same realm. Where was the justice?"

Big Gulp was oblivious to his surroundings. He did not recognize the stunned prep with his mouth agape. The billboard for denim absently walked down another aisle.

The irony had a marked effect.

"Almond chocolates." Lynn broke the silence in the store. She displayed the large tan bag at eye level. "Do you like them?"

"I do not think I have ever seen them before," Peter senses blurred.

"You will like them." Lynn conjured flatly. Peter viewed the expressionless look on Lynn's face. Forget about my travails, Peter shook his head. Lynn was just as deep in thought standing at that shelf as he was running into Big Gulp.

"These all right?" Lynn produced a scalloped corrugated box containing four long stemmed flutes. "They do not have two to a box. I hope you do not mind having to buy four."

The couple joined the queue at the lone register illuminated for business. A gum-snapping middle-aged woman stood behind the revolving rubber belt. She curiously surveyed the odd assortment of discount coupons presented by the customer in front. This could take a few minutes Peter reconciled his watch. Check in time at Superior Shores started in five minutes. He patiently waited next to his companion.

Big Gulp was standing outside the front window of the store. Peter knew who it was. The droopy moustache with the slackened jaw was unmistakable. The woman friend next to him mirrored his dull demeanor. Peter shuddered at what he thought he saw. Those are not nubs on the back of that woman's neck, are they? The duet lumbered past the glass. Don't stylists in the Midwest use clippers on women to shave the nubs off their necks? Peter viewed Lynn's nubby nape. The finality of fate seemed fatalistic... overwhelming.

Lynn's hands were full between champagne flutes and the almond chocolates. Peter leaned over and smacked a kiss to the back of Lynn's neck. It was almost more of a bite than a kiss. The tip of his tongue and teeth brushed the prickly cropping.

"Don't do that," Lynn muttered beneath her breath. Her body convulsed like there was an ice cube down her blouse. Peter leaned over again. He whispered audibly into Lynn's ear.

"Let's give 'em something to talk about, Lynn Dear," Peter toyed. "Let's roll a quarter down the aisle and see this line in front of us get in a Pamida pig pile for it."

Lynn was certain the fronting patrons heard the lewd remark. Did the cash register person just peek at me, too? Oh my Goodness, did she know me from somewhere?

Lynn could feel Peter's breath on the back of her ear. She turned and bellowed.

"Peter—stop it!"

Lynn stepped up to the front of the register. The two items were set on the rubber belt.

"Plastic," Lynn instructed in advance of the standard inquiry. She gathered the sales receipt and stormed out of the store—leaving Peter to wait for change from his ten. A spare key buried in her pocket book allowed entry into the Accord. Chivalry from the driver was not necessary.

"Peter, that was rude and disrespectful," Lynn scolded as soon as she unlatched the driver's side door. "Not so much to the poor ladies at the register, but to me!"

"What do you mean Lynn?" Peter attempted to downplay. "I was only joking."

"The two of us are buying Champagne glasses. We are flitting around the Pamida registers minutes before check-in time down the street at Superior Shores. Think about it," Lynn stated rhetorically. "What do you think the people in that store are saying about the two of us? And what do they think about me? For all I know one of them could be friends with my parents. They could be calling them right now."

X

Website photographs of the Lodge Suites at Superior Shores did not do justice. The actual rooms were a lot more elegant. Guests entered their quarters through hallways framed in bare pine. The elegance was simplified in the design. Bare pine—with ink lot numbers were still in print on the planks near the elevators. The suites opened to a kitchen area—equipped with modern convenience—including a full-size refrigerator, stove and cabinetry complements. Beyond the kitchen island was a large living room outfitted with an L-shaped plaid cushioned sofa. A coffee table centered the seating area. The highlight of the space was a propane-fired fireplace encased in native stone. A television was housed on the knotty pine bookshelves to the left of the fireplace. A dining table and chairs sat at the far end of the living room—next to wall-length windows facing the shores of Lake Superior. A sliding glass door between the TV and dining chairs accessed a large wooden deck that had a gas barbecue grill with accompanying outdoor furniture.

The pinnacle of the Lodge Suites was the massive bedroom area to the right of the kitchen and living room. Knotty pine paneling matched the welcoming rooms. The masonry of the dividing wall accommodated a glass-enclosed view of the fireplace from both sides. An identical television set up was mounted at the foot of a king-sized bed. The bedroom walls were also full-length panes sporting the waterfront scenery. The crescendo of the bedroom was a large hot tub spa that has a capacity for four adults—but was meant for two. The faucet to the spa was double any institutional size. The tub could be completely filled in no less than three minutes.

Tradition abounded for visitors—mostly Minnesotans who kept it secret—at Superior Shores. The resort was a destination spot for lovers of varied ilk. Were you a newlywed? A couple celebrating an anniversary? Trying to salvage a relationship on the rocks? Minnesotans winked their oath to the magical aura of love that happened at Superior Shores. The stories were well documented—a trademark of the setting's lore. Weather worn shore stones and scraps of driftwood graced the fireplace mantles and hearth baskets. Messages were scribed on the mementos. Etchings of love, gratitude, and good fortune greeted the lucky readers coming in a future time. More descriptive details were archived in the diaries at each living room coffee table. Whether it was a walk along the shore, sitting by the nightly bonfire, frolicking in the hot tub, or sleeping in total silence, one thing was sure to happen at Superior Shores—magic.

Peter paid cash at the Registration Desk for the night's stay. The lecture about rudeness since exiting Pamida did not elicit any comment about the "Welcome Lutheran Convention" lettered on the Resort's blue roadside entrance marquee.

Peter found it unusual that the woman at the Registration Desk mentioned three times during check-in that video rentals were available in the adjoining gift shop. The lobby was filled with numerous clusters of early registration arrivals. Peter assumed that they were all Lutherans. The nearest cluster of All-American bred faces took notice of the solitary gentleman standing at the front desk. The movie offering was repeated. We can add anything you choose onto your room tab. What were they doing here, Peter speculated? Were they questioning why he was checking in alone? Was Lynn supposed to come into the lobby with me too? Were the movies in the gift shop all X-rated? With his luck, the Bible-belters were just aching for a fish to bite—probably at pornographic bait.

The location of the suite came as a bit of a surprise to Lynn. Earlier visits had always been spent in the easternmost point of the resort facility. Those units contained spectacular cliff side views of the Great Lake.

Lynn assumed the room assignment in the far west side wing was because of the single night reservation. Partakers of the weekend getaway packages must have gotten preference in room allocations.

Peter was very much impressed with the ambiance of the environs. He quickly sought the freezer compartment of the refrigerator to chill the bottle of champagne. Accustomed to the floor plan, Lynn Monroe walked straight to the bedroom. She tossed her pocketbook on the bed.

"Oh, there is a marsh between us and the lake," Peter could hear Lynn comment as she opened the bedroom shades. Peter dropped his head to the floor as if he had heard it a million times before. He pulled the champagne bottle from the freezer before he even had the chance to close the door.

"What are you doing?" Lynn bubbled as she appeared from the bedroom. A canvas tote bag hung from her shoulder.

"No problem," Peter acquiesced stuffing the champagne bottle back into its brown paper bag. "We can switch."

"Switch," Lynn bewildered. "Switch what?"

"The room," Peter concluded. "The marsh is between us and the lake. If you want a better waterfront view, go ahead and call the front desk. No problem."

"I would never do that," Lynn scoffed. She skipped into the bathroom and closed the door. Peter stood statuesque in the kitchen alcove. The bottle was still gripped half in, half out of the brown paper bag. How embarrassing. A creature of habit, Peter had assumed Lynn would do what Marianne certainly would have done. Call the front desk and demand satisfaction. His marriage had become a ritual of exchange. This table will not do, can we have the one in the corner? I ordered the dressing on the side, take it back. Stop eating that meat, I know it is not done enough. Your mother always leaves the price tags on, because she knows I like to return.

If Peter was concerned that Lynn caught him thinking she was like Marianne, then he needed a little more fine-tuning. Since first sighting the deer in the backyard, the echoed tinny sound of the cavern tolled within Lynn's inner being. Her original plan was to cruise the North Shore scenic route along Lake Superior to Two Harbors. The echo changed her senses.

The notion of meeting up with Marge, Phyllis and Doris at the bonfire was revolting. Lynn realized the contradiction while she stood at the shelves at Pamida. Chastising Peter at the registers was merely to settle him down. Blow the thought of singing around the campfire after a quickie out of your mind.

Lynn was experiencing something with Peter that she never knew existed. She could not stop looking at him. For a time too long to remember, she doubted it was possible to be compatible with a man who exuded a strong personality and charisma—like her own. Actually sitting in the Accord next to Peter was an unexpected sensation. She realized the advanced reservation to Minnesota's secret weeks before was to satisfy a subconscious yearn. I need to be with Peter. I need to feel him.

Lynn stripped out of her blue jeans and pulled on a tiny navy blue bikini stringed with white piping. Perhaps she could throw Peter for a loop, coming out wearing just the bikini, Lynn mused. She appraised her body in the mirror—and felt a pang of inferiority. What if she came out of the bathroom, and actually started kissing him passionately. What if he looked at her, and laughed?

She camouflaged the swimwear with a baggy pair of gym shorts and a tee shirt. The glossy red toenails were the extent of her eroticism. Peter was still fidgeting around in the kitchen when Lynn opened the bathroom door. She bent over the tub of the spa and opened the water tap.

"Sounds like Lake Superior is rolling in," Peter remarked from the kitchen. The roar of the faucet waters was indeed loud.

Peter entered the bedroom. He carried the plastic ice storage bin from the freezer.

"This should make a good makeshift wine bucket," Peter pronounced. He laid the champagne bottle on the bed of ice cubes. "Looks though like any chance of a good time is flowing right down the drain—fast."

Lynn regretted changing into the flop-around outfit. She rose from fingering the water temperature and looked down at her naked legs. She did not think Peter had ever seen this much of her body in plain daylight. Lynn fretted. Maybe he did not find her quite so appealing.

Peter skirted behind to Lynn's right. He placed the impromptu champagne bucket next to the water tap and retrieved the large rubber stopper lying on the top corner of the tub. She could feel the brush of his body against her own.

"Mind if a liberal Democrat conserves some of the earth's natural resources," Peter suggested. Lynn's appearance of being a veteran old hat of the Superior Shores' Lodge Suites was somewhat thwarted. Peter stuffed the stopper over the drain. "Besides, that blue bikini I can see under your tee shirt has me so pent up that I cannot wait to christen this hot tub with you."

Lynn watched as Peter too took refuge in the bathroom to change. Did most visitors to Superior Shores go to another room to change? Or were piles of castaway clothing the standard? Did Peter say "pent up" or "horned up"? Lynn knew how she felt. Maybe he felt as insecure as she did.

He did not. The tub was only half full when Peter emerged—clad in a solid hunter green pair of swim trunks. Lynn remembered folks at Brigadier saying Peter had been a well-known athlete in his younger days. If he was, he rarely seemed to mention anything. She never imagined such a muscular frame.

"You sure are big," Lynn marveled as Peter dropped one leg into the water. He pinched the skin on both sides of his waist.

"What do you mean?" Peter did not bat an eyelash. He was obviously not the least bit intimidated by the suggestion of being a little overweight.

"Not that," Lynn amended. Her eyes rolled in panoramic appraisal. "I mean all over—your legs—and your arms—and your chest. You are just—big."

Peter ignored Lynn's attempt to flex her biceps for effect. He leaned across the tub and took hold of the wet champagne bottle. He began to pick at the neck of foil covering the cork. Lynn stood purposeless at the foot of the spa controls. She had hoped to manage into the tepid waters and have a jet spray of bubbles covering her body before Peter got out of the bathroom. Now the table had turned. Peter leaned back against the wall of the tub. Whether or not the jets were on to make bubbles seemed to be no matter to Peter. He could tell she felt awkward.

"Lynn, will you please bring a couple of those champagne glasses in here from the sink?" Peter asked. "I would like to propose a toast."

Peter synchronized his aim to coordinate with Lynn's return with the glasses. The cork hit the targeted mark on the ceiling.

"So what are we toasting to?" Lynn gawked at the blemish in the stucco overhead.

"Here's to you turning on the jet spa dial and taking off those God forsaken shorts to join me in here."

XI

Half a glass of bubbly and the cavern began to widen. Lynn sat silently at the opposite end of the swirl. She could see the animated mouthing of Peter's face. Her head nodded from time to time in recognition of the words, but her conscience was elsewhere. Peter's fondling massage of her feet was setting her into a seducing trance.

She bent her elbows and began to jimmy out of the hot tub.

"Ten minutes? That's it?"

"I hate it when my fingers and toes get all pruny," Lynn excused. Why couldn't she focus on anything, but his smiling face? She stepped on a large fluffy white bath towel. The folds of her conscience began to unravel. "I prefer to lie in the bed instead."

Lynn retreated to the bathroom carrying her gym shorts. Peter refilled his champagne glass and mulled Lynn's prolific words. Most people he knew, would say, "lie *on* the bed" Peter considered. He guessed if you weathered enough Duluth winters, you became accustomed to lie "in' the bed. He glanced at the abandoned flute on the other end of tub tiles.

"Care for anymore of this?" Peter offered holding up the black bottle when Lynn resurfaced. He could see the bikini bottoms hanging over the bathroom sink. Lynn had on just the blue stringed top and the gym shorts.

"Nah," Lynn waved. "I told you I am not much of a drinker."

Lynn walked across the room and turned on the television with the hand held remote control. She lowered the volume on the animal kingdom documentary to muffle the sound in the room. Without a second thought, she pulled the covers down from the bed. A quick tug on the drawstrings and the soggy bikini top fell to the floor. She remained at the side of the bed. Exposing her perky breasts was no longer a concern.

"Peter—please turn those jets off and come in here with me."

Peter did not have the luxury of gym shorts. He returned from toweling in the bathroom wearing his pair of khaki golf shorts. The tub drain gurgled the last of the water. Peter climbed into the right side of the bed.

"I normally take the left side of the bed," Peter commented. He tried to get comfortable with the button-closed golf pants.

"That is funny," Lynn faced Peter under the sheets. "I normally am on the other side too."

Lynn rolled from her position.

"Here is a solution," Lynn moved on top of Peter. "How about if I stay right here?"

Exploration. Naked exploration. The cavern echoed over and over. Exploration. Naked exploration. Lynn began kissing Peter lightly on the lips. Let me love him. Let me be with him. Let me feel him.

Lynn brushed the tip of her tongue over the edges of her lover's mouth. She yearned to explore—beyond his lips—with her tongue. She fought to constrain the urge. Please give me the strength to maintain some semblance of control.

Lynn closed her eyes. She could feel the breath of her man on her face, her neck, her arms, her shoulders, her breasts. Her body juices responded to the arousal.

"Please Peter—don't," Lynn reacted to the tugging on her gym shorts.

"Please," Lynn could hear Peter's plea.

"We can't," Lynn breathed.

"Please, Lynn—please."

Lynn opened her eyes. She met the focus of her soul-mate. It was in their eyes. A mutual cavern. A lost sense of being. An ageless infinity of rightness.

She could feel the gym shorts fall to her ankles.

The initial thrust penetrated the essence of Lynn's life—and being. She exhaled an audible moan that sounded like it came from the deepest recess of the cavern. She welcomed the entry—an entry to her soul—with a pulse of her hip.

"Peter," Lynn voiced. She could feel her finger tips dig into her mate's shoulders.

"I love you, Lynn," Peter whispered.

The third thrust clashed like a clanging symbol. In a flash, images of Marshall and Maggie, and everyone in Lynn's extended family photograph jolted into her mind. The vacuum of the deer-induced cavern evaporated within a split second. Lynn Monroe—wife, mother, business-person—was being violated. The physical intrusion was not what this visit was supposed to be.

Lynn repulsed from the bed. She felt foolish—running bare ass into the bathroom. Her rose tattoo jiggled on her hip. Fortunately, the bathroom door locked with a flick to the knob.

Lynn evaluated her reflection in the mirror. What did you just do, she lamented. You broke your promise to Marshall. You broke your wedding vow.

Shivering fingers wiped the tears with a small hand towel. Lynn ignored the sound of Peter's voice on the other side of the door. Lynn surveyed the room. Two wet bathing suit bottoms were the only apparel available. She did not care if she never came out of that room.

The roar of the hot tub faucet returned to the suite. Lynn refused to get teary-eyed again. She could hear Peter plopping back into the jet swirling spa.

It took a few minutes, but Lynn mustered the composure to face her travail. She emerged from the bathroom with a large shower towel wrapped around her body. She regarded Peter's sullen face.

"Lynn," Peter begged. "Please tell me what is wrong?"

Lynn ignored the question. She straddled the rim of the hot tub and placed her feet in the motion-filled waters. She pretended the tub tiles were not cold as she sat on her bare buttocks.

She was fully aware that her seated position exposed the fullness of her crotch. She did not need the shift of Peter's eyes to the open pubic area to confirm her lost sense of sanctity. Lynn followed Peter's look to the slightly exposed shadow between her legs. With slumped shoulders, she pursed her lips.

"Doesn't matter much now—does it?"

"Lynn, please. Sit down inside the tub."

"No," Lynn looked up to the ceiling. "I don't think so."

Lynn silently removed her feet from the tub and retrieved her bikini bottoms from the bathroom sink. There was no sense of discretion as she pulled on the wet covering.

Lynn returned to the spa waters. She hugged her shins so that her knees would stay above the water. The last thing she wanted was physical contact with the suitor on the other side.

It was a blighted episode. So why then, Lynn fought with her inner conscience. Why was she so captivated by looking at him? His magnetism was endless.

She slowly shook her head.

"*You let me down.*"

XII

The Superior Shores Resort & Conference Center did not provide room service. Visitors to the get-away facility customarily brought their own provisions. The full kitchen and outdoor grill areas catered a festive backdrop for personal cooking and libation.

Personnel at the front desk were used to getting calls from the likes of Peter Collins. No, sir, room service is unavailable—no matter who you are, or think you are. Kamloops Restaurant is your only option should you wish to order food. Yes, the staff there can box a dinner, but you will have to go to the restaurant part of the lodge to pick it up. No, they were not permitted to deliver.

Peter trudged down the labyrinth of hallways from Room 261 to access the five star dining room.

How did she not know this was going to happen Peter wrestled in his mind. He brooded at the maitre'd stand as the hostess pursued a requested bottle of beer. The impulse decision to add a bottle of beer to his order, like so many other decisions Peter seemed to recently fathom, seemed to inevitably create a tangled web of unanticipated consequence. The hostess did not seem to heed much concern for the guest as Peter considered carrying the open long-neck coupled with the weight of a cheeseburger and roast beef sandwich packaged in flimsy corrugated trays. You were supposed to be smart enough to know. Superior Shores Resort & Conference Center did not provide room service.

The thought of having to make two trips back and forth from Kamloops with the food was discomforting. The last thing Peter wanted to do was to leave a meal at the entrance table of the restaurant and manage the card keys two times through the door instead of one. Marianne entered into his reasoning process. You what? You left a dinner unattended back at the restaurant? Are you nuts? Who knows who could have tampered with it? Leave it there.

He could still visualize Lynn's sojourn image—lying static in the mammoth bed. The resignation of accepting a roast beef sandwich was followed by the continuous blank stare at the nature documentary on the television mounted in stone. A black widow spider was devouring its spent male lover.

Damn, Peter scolded as he made his way back to the suite. A zero percent chance that we would make love? How could she have expected that?

Lynn had propped herself up against the bedpost like an invalid. She checked out the leanness of the red beef without muttering a word. Her first acknowledgement of sustenance was a nibble against the corner of the sourdough bun.

Peter Collins had lost his appetite. He resigned to a high back chair between the bed mattress and a hand carved wooden bear against the window. He lit a cigarette and took a pull on the long-neck beer bottle.

"You are not supposed to smoke in here," Lynn stated. She did not look up from her continued exam of the dough's consistency. Peter cracked the side window panel open. A rush of frigid air blew into the room.

Lynn must have had thick blood under that skin, Peter observed. She did not flinch at the gust from the drapes.

"Have you ever cheated on your wife before?" Lynn asked. Her stare froze to the television screen as she chewed on the sandwich.

"Depends on what your definition of cheating is," Peter blew the tobacco smoke towards the window opening.

"Don't give me that liberal Democratic 'definition' crap," Lynn turned to face Peter. "You are either honest with yourself or you're not."

"If you are asking me whether I have ever had sexual intercourse with someone other than my wife since I have been married, then the answer prior to tonight was 'no'," Peter stated. "If your definition of cheating includes something less than intercourse, then I may not be quite so unequivocal in my reply."

"Elaborate," Lynn fixed her stare to the confessor.

"It was about twelve years ago," Peter began. "There was an office Christmas party that kind of rolled into an after hours thing at a fellow employee's house. My wife was eight months pregnant at the time, so I happened to be there, solo. As it turned out, this attractive young clerk was there, who I guess you could say was enamored with hobnobbing with the corporate Vice Presidents. She was flirting with me and doting on with all these fluffy complements. Toward the end of the evening, folks at the house were saying she had too much to drink and that she should not be driving. She asked me if I would give her a ride to her father's apartment where she was staying. I would be lying to you if I said I did not realize that she wanted to get a little frisky. Needless to say, we made out in the parking lot outside her father's apartment. It was not much beyond the standard teenage necking routine."

"That was it?"

"Yup."

"And did you ever see her again?"

"That was the ironic part I could never understand," Peter reflected. "It bothered the heck out of me that I had this lapse in judgement. Who was this person that all of the sudden came into my life unexpectedly and caused me to breach my wedding vow? I mean the circumstances could have been dire—my marriage, my family, my job. And do you know what was so disconcerting? This girl seemed so cavalier about it. When I subsequently saw her in the office during the weeks that followed, she tactfully acted like nothing ever happened."

Peter studied his intertwined fingers. "Fortunately after a couple of months, she moved off to another job somewhere. I never saw her again."

Lynn cracked a thin smile.

"Did you ever have a same-sex experience?"

"I beg your pardon?"

"You heard me," Lynn's smile broadened. "Did you ever have a homosexual experience?"

Peter glanced up to the ceiling.

"Oh God," Peter retorted.

"Come on," Lynn encouraged. She sat up on the mattress. "Spill the beans."

The truth-or-dare challenge was shaking Lynn out of her funk. The need for honesty to atonement was not what Peter anticipated when he had escaped to Kamloops for relief. He looked down to his lap and fiddled his hands.

"Okay," Peter surrendered. "I guess the closest thing to what you are suggesting happened when I was in high school."

Lynn's eyes brightened in anticipation.

"There was one summer night when a group of about six of us on the football team all slept over one of our teammate's house. It was unbearably hot outside. Around eleven o'clock at night, we all decided to raid the swimming pool at an apartment complex down the street to go skinny-dipping. After about ten minutes of splashing around we could hear the cop cars coming. So we all went running back up to the house and turned off all of the lights. We all went scampering into the different bedrooms. Like fools we jumped under the covers to pretend we were asleep—as if the police would actually come storming into the house. Anyway, I found myself dripping naked with one of my buddies lying on top of me. For thirty odd seconds we laid there not moving while the glow of the blue cruiser lights rotated on the ceiling. When the police finally left the neighborhood, we realized how awkward the situation was. We ended up jumping out of the bed and getting our clothes on."

"That's it," Lynn marveled.

"That is it," Peter assured.

"Are you sure?"

Peter laughed at Lynn's fascination.

"Hey, you asked for my closest rendition of a gay experience, and that was it."

Peter threw his arms from his side for effect. The color was returning to Lynn's cheeks.

"How about you?" Peter turned the table.

"How about what?"

"Have you ever cheated on Marshall?"

"No." Lynn looked down and pursed her lips. Peter grimaced at his stupidity.

"No—no," Peter attempted to quickly shift the downward spiral of the conversation. "I mean gay situations for you. Have you ever had a lesbian experience?"

Lynn's head remained bowed. Peter could have kicked himself.

"Come on, Lynn," Peter could feel himself bailing. "Fess up—have you ever been with a girl?"

Lynn regained her composure. A memory must have triggered her awakening, Peter observed.

"As a matter of fact," Lynn's personality came to life. "My girlfriend, Monica, and I used to get pretty goofy when we were in high school."

"Yeah…" Peter lured Lynn from her cocoon.

"You have to understand," Lynn's voice began to perk up. "Where we went to high school there were not a lot of guys one would consider a good catch. It was not unusual to get hit up on by some real dorks whether it was a dance or a house party. One night we were getting propositioned from a couple of Duluth's finest dregs. The only way we could get them to leave us alone was by telling them we were lesbian."

"It was so funny," Lynn became animated. "These guys started challenging us to prove it."

"So what did you do," Peter questioned with a sparked interest.

"We looked at each other and did not bat an eyelash," Lynn chuckled. " We just started kissing each other."

"Kissing each other?" Peter's eyes widened.

"French kissing," Lynn qualified. "It was a riot! At first these guys stood there in awe. Then they got totally repulsed and split."

Lynn seemed to enjoy the lasting shock the story carried on its present audience.

"These turkeys inevitably showed up at a number of parties we would be at," Lynn continued. "Monica and I would get such a kick out of overhearing the side comments that we were lesbian. Whenever the right moment presented itself we would spontaneously break into French kissing—without even mentioning the idea to one another. Our friends knew it was nothing but a gag, but it sure was a good way to avoid the undesirables."

"Is that all there is to the story?" Peter playfully raised an eyebrow.

"I swear," Lynn let out a hearty laugh.

"Are you sure?"

"Yes, Peter—I am sure."

Peter stood from the high back chair and gazed down at the smiling face. He removed his golf jersey.

"What are you doing?" Lynn watched the shirt sail across the room.

"I want to make love to you the right way," Peter announced. He dropped his pants to the floor. "The way we should have done it the first time."

Any previous doubts were exhausted. Lynn lay motionless as Peter methodically removed her clothing.

Rejuvenated exploration. Rejuvenated naked exploration. Rejuvenated naked exploration—by both parties. Lynn began brushing the tip of her tongue on Peter's lips.

"What exactly are you doing?" Peter asked. He rolled his lover on top of him.

"Call it 'the move'," Lynn grinned. She resumed the intimate tongue brushing.

The second penetration was smoother—more natural. The lovers ceased their kissing and savored the rhythmic pulse of their hips.

Lynn pressed her hands on the mattress assuming an almost push-up position. She stared at her man as the rhythmic sensation continued.

Peter was mesmerized by the countenance of his long-awaited lover. Never had he loved anyone like this in his lifetime. Lynn's face was the most beautiful sight he had ever witnessed. The aura began to form.

The oval of Lynn's face began to transfigure into a white brightness. The intercourse transcended into an out-of-body experience. He had been with her before, Peter realized. He was with her when they were home. They were home—right then—for all eternity.

The bright glow of Lynn's face remained for the next few minutes of lovemaking. Peter could feel Lynn accept his love as deeply inside her as she did his ejaculation.

She resumed "the move".

XIII

Lynn towel dried her hair after stepping out of the shower. The casualness was infectious. Peter appraised the naked body as it negotiated the bedroom carpet to the waiting tote bag of fresh clothes. The rose tattoo wiggled—rather than jiggled—with each bouncing step.

"What are we going to do if you just got me pregnant?" Lynn wondered. Peter could detect a hint of anticipation in Lynn's voice.

"I told you before I had a vasectomy," Peter couched his response. He was hopeful the reminder would dissolve any potential fear.

"Vasectomies are not one hundred percent fool-proof," Lynn pronounced. Peter's suspicion of Lynn's desire to bear his child heightened. "How do you know whether or not you are still fertile?"

Peter stood and hugged Lynn's bare body.

"Answer me," Lynn twirled the hairs on Peter's chest. "Did you ever go through the follow up testing to see if the procedure worked? Most men don't, you know."

"Cripes Lynn," Peter flustered. "I wasn't going to go back with a cupful."

Lynn checked the time on Peter's wristwatch.

"Marshall is at home waiting for my phone call," Lynn said. "He said he would drive up here to get me. You can keep the car here and drive back in the morning."

"I'm not staying here tonight without you," Peter held Lynn from behind. "And God forbid you have to ask someone other than me to go back to Duluth."

"I was hopeful you would say that," Lynn turned and held her man. "I do not think I could face Marshall right now."

Lynn dialed her residence after she dressed. Peter retired to the outside deck to have a cigarette. The intent was to give the caller some privacy. He kept the door ajar however to catch a few words of the conversation.

"Hi, it's me," Lynn identified from the bedroom telephone. "No, I am all set. Peter decided to go back tonight too…no, he is going to drive back…

yeah, we had fun—had dinner from the restaurant, and so forth. How is Maggie?... really? So you are all set?... that is okay, you do not have to wait up—I should be there in about an hour or so... okay. Bye."

Peter closed the door softly at the call's conclusion. He was relieved not to hear the perfunctory "I love you, too."

The couple performed a courtesy clean up of the suite's surroundings—even though they did not need to. The exercise kept sanity to the situation—and prolonged a departure. Peter found the leather bound guest diary on the living room coffee table. He moved to the dining room table and perused the many romantic messages archived by lovers of a mutual vein. Travels to this oasis were impressive.

"Lynn, did you happen upon any kind of writing instruments while we were here," Peter called. "We need to leave a special momento of our visit."

A rummaging of the suite produced no results. Peter resorted to the stub of a golf pencil he found buried in his carry-on bag. He promptly dubbed a sixteen square Dot Game.

Lynn sat next to him. They alternated the lead stub to scrawl each move. In two short minutes, the grid was filled.

"It would take us a year to get this far with the mail," Peter studied the book. "It is easier being together, huh?"

Peter could tell the telephone call affected Lynn's attention. More "P's" surfaced on the squares than "L's".

"Well, what do you know?" Peter counted the results with his finger. "I finally won a Dot Game after seven years."

"Violets are blue, and Roses are red," Peter scribbled his inverted victory poem.

"Lynn and Peter sure enjoyed this bed—
Our night was one of fulfillment and
Peter's Final Victory—
We leave with forever thoughts
For the Rest is History."

XIV

The index finger initiated the customary navel spiral. The rotation would start slow—close to the belly button. Methodically, the arc would widen. The probing would swirl towards the elastic waistband of the silk panties. The stimulus in most instances roused the sleeping body by the time the pubic hairs were touched. Once the mission was complete, the finger would move on—inside to other anatomical areas of fascination.

Lynn had tossed and turned the entire evening. She was in a less than snoozing state when the finger cued the neighboring intention. She squeezed her eyes shut tighter—and prayed for the finger to go away.

The rotation became wider. Lynn decided to throw caution to the wind. In a first-time-ever attempt, she exhaled a hacking snore and rolled zombie-like from her side to her belly. The maneuver was a success. The finger and its owner disappeared from the bed. Lynn never found sleeping on her belly comfortable. On this occasion, she played opossum.

"Rough night last night," the toothpaste filled mouth called from the bathroom. The crisis had ended. Marshall never risked confronting his wife's morning cigarette breath after brushing his own teeth.

Thank Goodness, Lynn thought. Her back was killing her in that position. She dramatized the roll over to semi-consciousness.

"What time is it?" Lynn rubbed her forehead to demonstrate the apparent deepness of her slumber.

"Seven thirty," Marshall stepped out of the bathroom in his pair of gray sweat pants. He gazed at his wife. "God, you look like hell."

Lynn focused on her bed-head critic. Your tongue is a pencil without an eraser, she remembered her mother's warning whenever she dawned the urge to sass.

"Guess I drank too much champagne," Lynn absorbed the insult.

"Champagne? What were you doing drinking champagne?" Marshall shook his head. "You know you do not drink champagne. That stuff gives you a headache."

"I know—I know," Lynn held the sides of her head. A scolding for confessing to champagne was nothing compared to the rest of the story. Whatever he says-goes–as far as Lynn was concerned.

"So what time did you get home?"

"It was after midnight," Lynn closed her eyes. "Probably around one o'clock or so. There were these women from Minneapolis staying next door to Peter at Edgewater. They were already having a cocktail party when I picked him up yesterday. It was that kind of a day."

Lynn's actual arrival time home was at 12:36 that morning. Marshall knew this was the case because he was awake when she came into the bedroom. Marshall always trusted his wife implicitly. She was honest—sometimes too honest to a fault. Leave it to Lynn, Marshall thought, to err on the side of one am.

"Well, I have to get Maggie to our swim lesson on time," Marshall ceased his interrogatories. "Listen Lynn, I was thinking. Maybe I was a little hard on you yesterday, about not wanting to meet your friend for lunch. Maybe we can meet today—for breakfast after the swim lesson, or something."

Lynn rose from the bed to perform her motherly duties. She reached Maggie's bedroom to find her daughter already dressed in a pink one-piece bathing suit. A playtime dinosaur was printed across the front.

"Honey, your flip-flops are on the wrong feet," Lynn said standing at the doorjamb. She crossed her arms like an educator. Maggie looked down at the plastic flowers glued to the top of her foot straps.

"Would you like to take them off and put them back on yourself?" Lynn acknowledged the independence of trying to dress yourself as a two-year-old.

Maggie continued to look down at the flower pedals.

"Would you like Mommy to help you instead?"

The daughter remained still.

"Maggie, are you listening to Mommy?"

The toddler's chin made a slight quiver.

"Maggie, is something wrong? Are you upset with Mommy?"

The little girl raised her head to see her mother's face. The corners of her mouth formed a pout. The chin quivered at a rapid pace.

"Mommy loves Peter." Maggie began to cry.

Lynn closed the bedroom door. She walked past the whimpering girl and sat in a wooden tea set chair. She hid any emotion.

"Yes, Maggie." Lynn whispered to the back of the infant's head. "Mommy loves Peter. But you know what? Mommy loves Maggie… and Daddy… and Amos… and Grammy and Grandpa…."

Lynn watched as her daughter turned to face her in the backward footwear. The little chin shook conspiratorially from side to side.

"No." Maggie's chin abruptly dropped to the breastbone. "Mommy loves Peter."

XV

Non-members were required to leave their driver's licenses at the entrance desk when visiting the downtown Duluth YMCA. The pimply-faced volunteer analyzed the pair of laminated cards lying on the Formica counter.

"What kind of driver's license is this?" the teenager picked up the odd colored card.

"Massachusetts," stated the man next to Lynn Monroe. The security buzzer sounded to access the mezzanine level of the swimming pool area.

"Are you sure you want to do this?" Peter Collins repeated for the third time that hour.

"It is the perfect time to meet," Lynn assured. "It was Marshall who suggested it this morning. He is going to be so wrapped up in Maggie's swim lesson that your introduction will be light lifting. Besides, my mother is supposed to drop by this morning too. I want everyone to meet you regardless of how uncomfortable it may be at this moment in time."

The couple made their way down the short hallway to the door marked "Pool". Lynn stepped ahead and confidently turned the knob.

"One thing, though," Lynn counseled. "If the invitation to all go out for breakfast comes up, say that we have already eaten.

The door led into a rectangular viewing room for spectators. A glass window on the left wall overlooked the large Olympic sized swimming pool. A short robust woman no more than five foot two walked quickly over to the entrancing duo.

"Oh, my mother is here," Lynn spontaneously advised.

"The lesson just ended," Evelyn Cloud beamed as she clasped both hands of her daughter. "Maggie was so terrific. You know how all the children make such a production out of the water being cold? Well, Maggie did not even wait for any coaxing. She jumped right in the water ahead of everyone else like a determined little soldier. You should have seen her kicking those little feet."

Evelyn acknowledged her daughter's receiving smile. Determined little soldier, huh? Lynn avoided asking if Maggie had done or said anything else.

Mrs. Cloud turned her attention to the guest standing in the room.

"And you must be Peter," Evelyn beamed repeating the double handed greeting. "Seven years you and Lynn have been friends. It is so nice that you have been able to come out to visit. Lynn has been so excited about you coming."

Peter's striking appearance startled Evelyn. Her adopted daughter was like none other of the family children. Lynn always seemed to add a flair of her own independence. Evelyn had become accustomed to the flexibility needed to relate to Lynn's unconventional approach to life—and relationships. This friendship, however, with such a chisel-featured character was difficult to understand. Evelyn fought the impulse to peer up and down at the new acquaintance.

Lynn could sense the strained apprehension in her mother's steady grin. She walked over to the viewing window and stared out over the empty pool.

"Where do you think they went?" Lynn asked.

"I believe they went off to the heated kiddy pool to warm up," Evelyn welcomed the change of topic back to her granddaughter.

The trio peered out over the span of the recreation area. The dialogue digressed to an accounting of Peter's activities since he arrived in Duluth.

"I think I will go try to find them and let them know we are here," Lynn stated to break from the scene. "I will be back in a minute."

Peter and Evelyn watched as the yellow-slickered common denominator in their lives went down the stairwell to pool level. Evelyn continued her obligatory smile.

"Lynn tells me you work at the Wells Fargo Bank," Peter aimed the attention away from himself towards the smallish woman. There was no doubt Lynn had been adopted. Evelyn's features bore no resemblance to his soul-mate.

"Yes," Evelyn acknowledged. "Twenty years as the main receptionist. Have you ever heard of Wells Fargo?"

"Well, you are part of Wells Fargo of San Francisco, aren't you," Peter stated.

Evelyn was impressed by the recognition. "Not too many Easterners know about Wells Fargo."

"I own some stock," Peter shrugged.

Evelyn's eyes brightened at Peter's casual style. Her follow up question was interrupted from the opening of the stairwell door. Lynn led her family nucleus into the spectator room. Marshall followed at her heels carrying his two-year-old daughter. Peter stepped towards the father and child wrapped in a laundry beaten multi-patterned beach towel.

"Marshall," Peter extended his hand. "We finally meet."

The first thing Peter noticed was the extraverted shake of the finger-brushed blonde haired man. Peter digested the visage of receding hair conservatively scrapped to one side. The rectangular shaped wire-rimmed eyeglasses were several years out of style. It was that Midwestern presence that was so prominent at the airport.

Marshall Monroe was bland—too bland to be Lynn's husband.

"Maggie, can you say 'hello' to Peter," Lynn touched the toweled shoulder of her small daughter. The group focused their attention to the little face covered by a pair of dark sunglasses. Disney characters loomed from the corners of the plastic frames. The little head bobbed slightly—the chin touching the breastbone.

"Maa-ggie," the mother bent forward and whispered. "Can you say 'hello' to Peter?"

The daughter's head snuggled into the nape of her father's neck. The family members chuckled at the unexpected wave of bashfulness. Lynn reached over and removed the pair of sunglasses. The piercing eyes of the little girl focused directly at the visitor—who was not a stranger.

"Hello, Peter," Maggie's small voice chirped matter-of-factly.

"Hello, Maggie," Peter smiled. He shook the palm of the tiny hand. "Did you enjoy your swimming lesson with Dad?"

The riveting eye contact ceased. The toddler returned to the nape of her carrier. The group offered a doting laugh.

"So," Lynn directed to her husband. Maggie was freaking her out. "What do you have planned today?"

"I mentioned to your Mom that I would bring Maggie up to the house to clean the yard," Marshall replied. "She is going to watch her while she takes her nap so I can cut up all the tree limbs that fell for your father."

"What about our yard?" Lynn queried.

"Their place is in worse shape than ours," Marshall glanced to his mother-in-law. "I should be able to tackle our yard in the afternoon. How about you?"

"Peter wanted to see my office," Lynn answered. "We are going to head to that part of town."

"Did you want to go for breakfast," Marshall resurfaced his early morning idea. Lynn's eyes quickly darted to Peter.

"Gee, we already ate," Peter declared the scripted instruction.

"Perhaps we can meet up later," Lynn killed the issue with a motion to the exit. Marshall dutifully stepped in line with his wife. They proceeded side by side out the door.

Peter stuffed his hands in his pockets and watched the Monroe family walk out together. He hoped Evelyn did not pick up on the difficulty he had trying to swallow.

"Do you really think Wells Fargo Bank stock is a safe investment?" Mrs. Cloud's question broke Peter's wayward thoughts.

"They are one of the largest commercial banks in the country," Peter pocketed his driver's license. "I think their dividend performance in this marketplace makes them stable for the foreseeable future."

"I am only two years away from being eligible to collect Social Security," Evelyn confided. "I do not know if Lynn told you, but her father has not worked for several years because of a heart condition. We just came back from a week's vacation to Las Vegas. I do not know if I have the heart to tell anyone the real reason for our trip. Lynn's father and I have this sinking gut intuition that we are not going to have enough value in our Wells Fargo stock for me to retire. Vegas was kind of a whim."

Peter slowed his stride in line with Evelyn's along the concrete sidewalk. They happened to stop in front of the glass exterior of the Wells Fargo's Superior Street office.

"That is my desk right there," Evelyn pointed at the smoke tinted window panel. Peter scoped the modest reception desk.

Evelyn turned and looked off down the sidewalk. Lynn was holding the back door of the glistening GMC Suburban open, while Marshall adeptly secured Maggie in the child safety seat.

"I don't know what we would do without Marshall," Evelyn pondered. "Norman would be out in that yard all by himself today trying to clean up those trees. He would have died from a heart attack by now, if he did not have Marshall."

The short robust woman no more than five foot two turned to Peter, and smiled.

"Marshall is the only person I know who can get Norman off of his feet. That kid is the only one Norman thinks is capable to do his chores properly—the first time."

XVI

"I heard such a funny story the other day," Lynn recalled. The black Accord rolled to a stop at the Central Entrance intersection. The passenger side of the street was cornered by a row of retail stores.

"That is where I go for my dry cleaning," she pointed to a drab storefront. "My friend who works there told me this woman newscaster from the local TV station came in and asked if they mended clothing. My friend told her they did. So the woman drops a small plastic bag on the counter and says she needs a garment re-stitched. Know what it was? A torn teddy! The lacing looked like it had been ripped to shreds."

Peter smiled at the exuberance of Lynn's narration.

"Here is this woman who everybody recognizes in town trying to save a few bucks to salvage the integrity of her underwear," Lynn laughed.

Perhaps his frustrating message about people wasting time and money yesterday at the house had an effect, Peter thought.

"Want to hear the funny part?" Lynn continued. "The teddy was still soiled when she brought it in!"

Peter recognized Lynn's insurance agency. The logo on the sign matched the long identified baby blue corporate letterhead. The aluminum framed window casings resembled any cornerstone insurance office in America.

"Let me turn the corner to show you where I park on the back street," Lynn said. "It will give you an idea of the way I normally come into work in the morning."

Peter appreciated Lynn's token of revealing her routine of everyday life. He was unaware of Lynn's caution not to park street front. She did not want to chance having a co-worker spot the parked Accord and drop in.

The back alleyway to the rear Employee-Only office door reminded Peter of East Hartford, Connecticut. Garbage from a neighboring two family blew along the ground. Lynn stepped around the broken metal desk chair. Its back was missing—exposing a rusty steel frame. No one would steal such a piece of junk.

"This is where I sneak out to have my cigarettes," Lynn revealed. She fumbled with the metal padlock on the steel door. Peter surveyed the dozens of flattened cigarette butts lying around the broken chair. They all appeared to be of the same brand. Peter was about to say "You have got to be kidding me," but thought better of it.

Lynn walked inside the building negotiating three rickety wooden steps into what appeared to be a darkened basement.

"Lynn?" Peter called uncertainly.

"The light switch is on the other side," Lynn shouted back. Peter could hear her footsteps accustomed to the dark. A tug on a ceiling string illuminated a bare light bulb.

"You could break your neck coming into this place," Peter watched his steps over the uneven concrete floor.

"It is not so bad once you get used to it," Lynn smiled. "I am usually the first one in each morning so the light gets turned on for everybody else. I usually have the first pot of coffee made, too."

Peter regarded the makeshift coffee counter constructed with two by fours and particleboard. An array of chipped coffee mugs sat next to an antiquated automatic coffeepot. Everything was stained brown.

"I can see why you are not a coffee drinker."

Lynn opened the hollow paneled door to the professional office area. The appearance was significantly more impressive.

"My office is second on the right," Lynn continued ahead. She walked into the neatly arranged waiting area designed specifically for customer service and turned on the office lights. She joined Peter in the room he assumed by her point was her office.

"Peter, you have to promise me something," Lynn entered the office and circled behind the desk. "If anything ever happens to me, you have to get to this desk drawer."

Lynn sat down in her high backed leather simulated chair. With two hands she heaved a large pentaflex folder from the storage drawer. The contents were over a half a foot thick.

"This is everything you have ever sent me." Lynn plopped the folder on her desktop.

"You have got to be kidding me," Peter could hear himself finally say.

"Nope. Wanna look?"

The contents were stacked with most recent correspondence on the top—including the completed dog-eared Dot Game. Peter replaced Lynn in the chair and began leafing through the dozens of cards and letters. Recollections of Craig Hinson and Brigadier lawyers swelled back as Peter perused the oldest of letters. He sat silently reading word for word the card he mailed days before Lynn's wedding. The pain of penning "Congratulations" flooded his memory.

"You saved everything," Peter noted even the postmarked envelopes.

"Everything."

The gas station attendant did not comprehend the foreign language. Lynn walked up from the side cooler and placed two bottles of water on the counter. She burst out laughing.

"What did you say?" the attendant questioned.

"Is thee-ya a paa-k around hee-ya?"

Peter looked to Lynn in bewilderment.

"We are looking for the entrance road to Jay Cooke State Park," Lynn translated guttering the "r" in "park".

"Not from ar-round he-er, are you," the station owner observed. Peter could tell he was being made fun of.

Jay Cooke State Park traversed the banks of the St. Louis River. Melting snows had flooded its banks. The rapids of the roaring waters were more violent than Peter had ever witnessed.

Where does all this water go?" Peter scanned through the passenger side window. He declined to drive after the teasing at the gas station.

"Iowa." Lynn said flatly.

"So this is where all that water comes from when they show the flooding Midwest on the news."

"Didn't you know Peter," Lynn cut a smirk. "Iowa is Minnesota's septic tank."

Peter noticed the car was stuck in first gear.

"Whaddya say we go back to the hotel and take a nap," Peter suggested. "All this tourism is tiring me out. I am an old man you know."

"Peter, do you remember who Jay Cooke was from your American History," Lynn kept her focus on the winding road.

"Never heard of him."

"Really," Lynn reset the rear view mirror. "I thought you East Coast power magnates kept tabs on each other."

"Cooke—scmoock," Peter placed his hand on Lynn's knee. "Let's go back to the hotel."

"No," Lynn returned the hand to its owner. "I took you here to the park for a reason—to learn of the folly of Jay Cooke. Jay Cooke was a banker from the East Coast who financed the Union's victory during the Civil War. He took all the money he made during the war and invested in building the Northern Pacific Railroad right through here to Bismarck, North Dakota."

"So was that his folly?" Peter challenged. "An Easterner thinking he could find fulfillment in the Great Northwest?"

"Look at the river," Lynn motioned to the half mile breadth of raging whitecaps. "You tell me."

"Come to think of it," Peter looked back over his shoulder. "I did not see any railroad tracks around here."

"Because we are driving over them," Lynn professed. "They paved over them. Cooke went bust before he could ever finish his folly."

"Are you saying he was a victim of his aspiration?"

"No," Lynn considered. "It was probably more timing than anything else."

"Like asking you to go back to the hotel room with me?"

"Peter, I made a decision after last night," Lynn revealed. "We are not going to do Superior Shores ever again. I am not going to let that happen."

"Well, then what are we going to do for the next two days?"

"Whether you have noticed it or not, Peter," Lynn stated. "You have not so much as stopped to take a breath from all your constant talking since we left Superior Shores last night. Quite frankly, I am perfectly content hanging out with you listening to your babble."

"Babble?" Peter mocked. "All my prolific tales are nothing but babble?"

Lynn placed her hand on her friend's thigh and smiled.

"Believe me Peter—I love your babble. I cling to your every word. Just keep babbling."

XVII

Lynn recommended Grandma's Saloon & Grill for lunch. The harbor side restaurant on Lake Ave was a landmark for any tourist to Duluth. The pub style restaurant was renowned for its collection of 1950s restaurant sign memorabilia. Peter had mentioned his stomach was feeling somewhat nauseous. Lynn suspected it was because he had not had one bite to eat since his arrival on Thursday evening.

For the second time in less than twenty-four hours, Peter fiddled with the sesame seed bun of another cheeseburger that he could not bring himself to eat. He suspected the nausea was due to Lynn's decision to shut him off.

The waitress checked in twice after the food was served to the wooden booth to see if everything was okay. Failing to gobble down Grandma's beef must have been taboo to Midwesterners Peter fumed inside.

"Actually everything is not all right," Peter responded to the second inquiry. "I prefer to drink bottled beer from a small glass. If I wanted to slug from a weighted beer mug I would have ordered a draft."

The waitress was stunned by the unusual complaint. She glanced quickly to the surreal occupant across the booth. Lynn sat silently with pursed lips.

"A small glass?" the waitress tried to qualify the request.

"Yes." Peter formed a small circle with his forefingers. "A small glass. Not like that goblet you served her soda in, and not like this five pound mug. A small, thin glass… and I like to fill it only half way at a time."

"I am sorry, but I do not think we have any small glasses like that."

"Fine." Peter surrendered with his hands like a Western villain. "In that case everything is fine."

The waitress walked to a peer at the bar station shrugging her shoulders.

"Peter," Lynn looked across the booth. "Is everything all right?"

"I suppose not," Peter folded his hands. "Maybe you can explain something to me. Before I came here you told me you were convinced we were soul-mates. When we told each other how stressed we were leading up to seeing each other after all these years, you said we would spend the weekend in bed holding each other. Last night was the most amazing night of my entire life.

I swear, when we were making love your face turned angelic before my very eyes. We have forty-eight precious hours to still be together. After that, who knows when we will ever see each other again? So how can you decide never to let last night ever happen again?"

"Because Marshall trusts me," Lynn frowned. "And I already broke my promise. Never have I ever lied or withheld anything from him and I do not intend to start now."

"So what if he asks you if anything happened while I was here?"

"I will probably tell him," Lynn said. "That is why it has to stop right here and right now."

The waitress returned to Lynn's beckoned hand signal.

"Could you please do me a favor?" Lynn pointed to Peter's cold burger. "And wrap this up to go?"

For the first time ever, Peter glared at Lynn.

"I beg your pardon, Lynn Dear," Peter staccatoed his voice. "But I do not believe in doggy bags."

The waitress rolled her eyes.

"Please take this away," Peter nudged the plate to the edge of the booth. "It does not need to be wrapped."

"Booths are made for mates to sit on the same side too," Peter slid out from his end of the bench. "Sitting opposite in booths is sacrilegious."

Saturday afternoon was devoted to shopping. Peter gave in to Lynn's wish to remain in public places rather than drape-drawn hotel rooms. Peter said he wanted another Minnesota Gopher jersey like the one Lynn gave him years ago. Maybe he could even find sizes for his sons. The couple crossed Grandma's parking lot to the DeWitt & Seitz Marketplace. Lynn recalled buying the first jersey at a specialty store selling Minnesota items there.

Peter hated shopping. After his outburst about beer glasses, doggy bags and booths though, he figured he had better not press his luck. He obediently followed up and down the herbal scented aisles of knick-knacks—and other items he considered junk.

There was no more college sports shirts in any of the stores. Lynn recalled that it seemed only around Christmas season when items like that was stocked.

"How about something like these slippers?" Lynn suggested. She held up a pair of fluffy brown slippers with moose heads at the toes. Floppy ears drooped like Bullwinkle on each side. "Larry's fiancée's birthday is coming up. I bet she would love these. They live in California now. These will make her think of Minnesota."

They exited DeWitt & Seitz with the solitary bag of moose head slippers. Lynn was determined that more time had to be killed.

"There is a much larger mall up by the airport," Lynn took the challenge of finding shirts for Peter as an acceptable affair. "They have so many stores there I am sure we will find sports shirts."

The Accord motored into the cookie-cutter shopping center generic to Anywhere, USA. The prerequisite two loops around the lot were needed before finding an available parking space.

"See that Walgreen's store?" Lynn pointed to the pharmacy abutting the main mall entrance. "I used to work there as a teenager. Do you know when I was working there I was so self-conscious about being adopted? I always had this premonition that I would meet one of my birth parents there. I knew I had been born in Ely, Minnesota—which is only about an hour north of here. This mall is so big for the area that it is not unusual to find folks driving that kind of distance to shop. Whenever someone would pay with a check, I would scrutinize the address to see if they were from Ely. Then I would analyze their faces to see if their features resembled mine."

Lynn reached and held Peter's hand.

"When I finally met my birth parents, my mother said to me 'I know you from somewhere'. Then she jumped up and shouted. 'You are the girl from Walgreen's! I knew it was you'!"

XVIII

Peter wished he had eaten his cheeseburger. The hoard of shoppers mulling in the multitude of franchised stores made him feel claustrophobic.

The sporting goods stores only carried the "authentic" game jerseys of professional sports teams. Any uniqueness of an "authentic" jersey no longer existed. Every store had them.

Even the J.C. Penney store was bland. The clothing wear was identical to the same store in Worcester, Massachusetts. So much for a shopping mall highlighting local flavor, Peter mused.

The only retailers with goods sparking Peter's interest were the jewelry stores. Lynn was wearing a very unique Indian necklace that she said had been given to her by her psychic mother-in-law.

"I am an Aries," Lynn responded to the idea of Peter buying her something as a momento to their reunion. "Aries do not hold much stock in gifts."

Lynn realized there was no chemistry in a day of shopping.

"Let me use the Ladies Room," Lynn surrendered amid the swarm of traversing people. "Then we can leave."

Peter took a seat on a bench across from the public restrooms. He was glad to be off of his feet. Maybe we are soul-mates, Peter conjured, but that does not dispel the fact that he abhorred shopping malls.

Peter observed the rows of diners seated against the fishbowl walls of an Applebee's diagonally across from the bench. Everyone seemed to be wearing J.C. Penney clothes. The static noise of foot traffic in the mall foyer muffled the sounds inside the restaurant. Patrons were beaming over the menus of Buffalo wings and entrees being simultaneously offered in thousands of fishbowls across the country. A party of four exited the eatery. Each was carrying leftovers in Styrofoam boxes. God, he felt depressed. Peter bowed his head.

When he opened his eyes, he could see Lynn standing outside the Ladies Room. She was speaking with a blonde haired woman a head shorter than her. They made their way to the bench.

"Peter, you are not going to believe who I ran into in the Ladies Room,"

Lynn greeted. She had more of a serious look on her face rather than a smile of surprise. "I would like to introduce you to my friend, Monica."

Peter immediately stood to his feet.

"Monica, it is a pleasure meeting you," Peter gladly shook the woman's hand. "I cannot believe we bumped into you. Didn't Lynn tell me you live in Minneapolis? That is over two hours away, isn't it?"

"It was a last minute thing to come up," Monica analyzed the features of the person who had mesmerized her best friend. "I hosted a cosmetics party at my apartment several months ago and the make up orders finally came in. I was going to deliver the items my mother bought to her house down the street."

"I was also going to drop your stuff at your house." Monica redirected her attention to Lynn. "I expected I would only see Marshall there though. I thought you said you would be at Superior Shores on Saturday?"

Lynn blanched at the breach of confidence. "We decided to change our plans around."

"Well, if you are on your way out Lynn," Monica refused to delve on the inquiry. Like a true friend, she adroitly changed the subject. "I will get your bag of cosmetics out of my car and give them to you now. It will save me a trip over to Marshall's."

Monica walked ahead to a row of automobiles in the lot several yards to the left of where the Accord was parked. Peter was glad Lynn decided to walk next to him, instead of venturing with Monica to her car.

"I thought you would have been more excited to see Monica," Peter said. "Talk about a coincidence—that I would get a chance to meet your best friend."

"The first thing she asked me in the bathroom was if anything had happened between us," Lynn frowned. "I could not lie to her."

"So you told her?"

"That is just it," Lynn explained her sullen look. "I told her that 'I couldn't say'. She knows. I did not have to say a word. She knows me too well."

Monica approached the Accord carrying a small parcel of creams and lotions. Lynn gathered the belongings and laid them on the back seat of the car.

"Excuse me, but is that a tattoo on your hand?" Peter noticed the yellow daffodil across the top of Monica's right wrist.

"Yes, it is."

Peter took the liberty of leaning close to Lynn's friend to examine the ink pattern.

"That is all bone," Peter appraised the artwork. "I bet that hurt some when you had it done."

Monica tilted her head and smiled appreciatively at Peter.

"Of all the comments, and most times criticisms, I hear from men about my daffodil, you are the first one that ever wondered how it felt." Monica half-winked her eye. "I think I know now why you and Lynn are attracted to each other."

"You do?" Peter appealed. "Then I wish you would explain it to us."

Monica turned her attention from Peter to her dearest friend in the world, and then back again to Peter. She could sense the couple's magnetism. She could also see how the last thirty-six hours created a quandary of turmoil.

"Only time will tell the road to your futures," Monica kissed Peter and Lynn's cheeks in an impromptu bear hug. "Sometimes there is no rationale for two people realizing they are meant for each other—regardless of the circumstances. Whatever is meant to be will come to pass."

XIX

The red message light was blinking on the bedside telephone when Peter returned to Edgewater. He hesitated. It could not be Lynn calling from her car phone. He had just left her.

Images of Marianne, or the kids calling to talk to Daddy, popped into Peter's mind. Events of the past two days prompted Peter to hope that was not the case. Peter picked up the receiver and pressed the button for the Front Desk.

"Messages please," Peter requisitioned in an authoritative tone.

"No telephone messages, sir," the receptionist responded. "An envelope was dropped off for you. It is waiting at the Front Desk."

Peter hung up the telephone. His first premonition was Marianne—but how could she send him something in such a short time span? Wouldn't she call instead? What if she found out about Lynn Monroe? But then again, how?

The tightening of Peter's sphincter signaled a more likely candidate—Marshall Monroe. Shirking the breakfast invitation at the YMCA was probably not a very good move. Peter envisioned a crudely written note—"Stay away from my wife you old scumbag or I will kill you."

Peter double-checked his pants pockets to make sure he had a key card to get back into the room. Getting a "drop dead" message is bad enough without locking yourself out of your room two times in one weekend, Peter fretted.

Peter waited in the ground level hallway for an elevator car to take him to the lobby. The confines were void of humanity and claustrophobic. He glanced at his wristwatch—four-thirty. Peter exhaled a sigh and repressed the already lit elevator button. Do not think you have to baby sit me the whole time I am in Duluth, Peter recalled telling Lynn prior to his visit. I will be perfectly happy hanging out at a quiet place on a lake. Peter gazed at the unattended chamber maid bin filled with used linens.

"I was only kidding," Peter shouted out loud at the unmoving light above the elevator.

Peter could sense prior to being dropped off back at the hotel that Lynn was anxious to get back home—even if it was just for a couple of hours.

"I feel guilty leaving Marshall to take care of Maggie all day," Lynn said when they left the shopping mall. "Knowing him, he has been on the go all day cutting up trees."

The thought of not seeing Lynn again crept into Peter's mind as he approached the Front Desk. Why did he agree to Marshall joining them for dinner that night? Peter scolded himself. He pictured Lynn's arrival home. You are staying right here, the husband would command. I already left that creep a note to stay the hell out of our lives.

The teenaged receptionist could not find the envelope.

"The person you spoke with just finished his shift," the girl flicked through an assortment of papers on her side of the counter. "Did he say what the envelope looked like?"

A fellow Peter assumed was a hotel manager appeared from the side office.

"Are you the gentleman from Room 1020?" the manager asked. Peter assented with a single nod. "Your envelope is here inside my office."

The manager handed the rectangular envelope to the hotel guest. Peter could not contain his anxiety. He tore open the envelope and sat at the lobby couches. He pulled out the single page contents.

The postcard photograph was a close-up view of the Aerial Lift Bridge.

"Had to check out before we could say Good-bye. Wasn't it the best! Good luck with your interest in 'the Bridge'. Yours in Lust—The Girls from Room 1018."

"Is everything in order?" the manager called from the counter. Peter stuffed the postcard back in the envelope and smiled.

"Yes… quite."

XX

The outside door to Room 1020 was wide open. Lynn tapped gently on the frame.

"Peter, are you there?"

"In here," the voice shouted from the bathroom. "Come on in, I will be out in just a sec."

Lynn turned off the unwatched television and viewed the postcard display on the mirror. Peter emerged from the bathroom—a towel covered his face.

"I inadvertently put after-shave on my face after I showered," Peter rubbed his hidden cheeks. "Had to wash it off… don't want Marshall to smell 'the boy'."

Lynn rushed across the room and hugged Peter tightly. The onrush caught him by surprise. He fumbled with the face towel to capture Lynn's greenish eyes. They were red at the corners. Peter followed the trembling body as it sat hard upon the bed.

"I hate my life," Lynn Monroe sobbed.

Peter could feel the tears moisten the shoulder of his shirt. Lynn continued to weep. Peter was able to reach for a box of tissues on the desk in front of the mirror. He stuffed a Kleenex into the hand around his neck.

"Did you hear what I said?" Lynn dabbed the tissue ball against her nose. "I said I hate my life."

"Did something happen when you got home this afternoon?" Peter asked meekly.

"It is everything." A tear dropped from Lynn's cheek and landed on the bedspread. "I cannot tell you how hard I worked to clean the Suburban before you got here. Now look at me. Marshall takes the truck for one afternoon. I get in it tonight and now my clothes are covered in dirt."

Peter looked down at the navy blue coordinated pants suit. God, she looked fantastic, was his first impression. He did not want to acknowledge that he could not detect any dirt.

"Know how you questioned why we did not call a tree service company to clean our yard?" Lynn's crying had stopped. Anger was rising in her voice.

"Well, the city came out today and said they would chip up and take away any debris in people's yards at no cost. All you had to do was drag any droppings to the edge of the street. So you know what Marshall does? He decides to go out and buy a two thousand dollar tag-a-long trailer for the Suburban. He says you cannot count on when the city will get around to cleaning up the neighborhood. He prefers to make his own trips to the dump. Said it would be handy to have a trailer around afterwards for odd projects."

Peter sat silently and stared at the melancholy face. There was no need to say "I told you so". He had made his point the day before.

"Peter, you were absolutely right." Lynn blew her nose. "We waste two thousand dollars on something when a couple of neighborhood kids could have pulled the branches to the roadside for a few bucks. I asked Marshall where he was going to keep the trailer because the generator was already blocking my space in the garage. He has it parked on the side of the garage now. Christ, it is so big and ugly. It takes up half of my backyard."

Peter stood up and got a bottle of water left over from Superior Shores from the mini-refrigerator. He opened the bottle and handed it to Lynn who took a big swig. She handed it back. Peter returned the gesture.

"Perhaps a nice dinner will make you stop thinking about the trailer," Peter consoled.

"That is the other thing." Lynn dropped the tissue wad into a small waste paper basket. "I told Marshall you offered to treat us to dinner tonight. We never go out anywhere to eat. There are so many great restaurants in Duluth we have never been to. I told him you said to pick any restaurant we like to say thank you to him for watching Maggie this whole time. Know what he said? 'Let's go to Vinnie's for pizza. It is nice and quick and that way I can pick up Maggie early from your parents'."

"I can do pizza." Peter pacified. He swept a stray eyelash from Lynn's soggy cheek.

"Lynn, I never noticed your eyes are green. I always thought they were brown."

"They turn green when I cry," Lynn surrendered as she walked to the outside door. "Come on, Peter. He is waiting for us at the house."

The GMC Suburban looked like it had competed in a four-wheeling derby. Mud was splashed over all the side window panels and hood. Clumps of caked dirt molded to the shape of work boot soles fell from the floor mats when Peter opened the driver's side door. Lynn was not kidding. The vehicle was a mess.

"Dirt." Lynn bellowed as Peter turned the ignition. "That is all I can smell—dirt! And look at this—there is not a drop of gas."

Peter drove to the adjacent filling station. Lynn was about to correct Peter's error in choosing the full-service island instead of self-service, but caught herself. Peter got out of the vehicle and slipped a hundred dollar bill into the attendant's hand.

"Fill it up with Super," Peter whispered from the side of his mouth even though Lynn could not hear with the windows up. "And keep the change for yourself provided you can get the front and back windows of this thing spotless."

Peter went into the station convenience store. He returned moments later with a couple of packs of cigarettes—ne regular sized Lights, one the longer Ultra 100s. Two attendants were busy scrubbing at the Suburban's windows. Dried bird droppings and speckles of dead bugs retarded their progress. Lynn stared straight through the windshield as if either oblivious to the effort, or embarrassed.

"I bet you own a beautiful house," Lynn said to Peter as he remounted the vehicle. She continued her blank stare beyond the dashboard. "Will you describe it for me?"

"It is a four bedroom colonial," Peter spoke softly. "With a two car attached garage. That is one aspect about houses in Duluth that amaze me. With the winters that you have, I cannot figure why all of your garages are not attached to the house?"

Peter pulled out of the gasoline station. Lynn pointed up ahead at the set of traffic lights for Peter to take a hard left turn. The Suburban began to scale the hillside neighborhood of upscale residential homes.

"Do any of these houses look like yours?"

Peter scanned the surroundings. He could not bring himself to say his house in Worcester was nicer.

"You know what distinguishes my house that makes it so tough to compare with others," Peter deferred. "The exterior woodwork. We have a flat roof over our garage that I suppose would not be too practical with snowfall in Duluth. What is neat is this custom built railing that spans the perimeter of the roofline. The contractor we had do it made sure to use a pattern of rails that no one shopping at some home discount warehouse could copy. I like it because I know I will not find it anywhere else."

The Suburban rolled to the stop sign at the intersection of East Second Street and North 26th Avenue East.

"Does it have pillars?" Lynn gazed at the white wooden columns fronting the corner brick house. "That is my favorite house in the whole city of Duluth."

"No," Peter viewed the handsome home propped high above road level. "My home does not have pillars like that."

"I have always dreamed of someday living in a house with pillars," Lynn touched the back of Peter's hand. "I dream that if we were together, we would belong in a home with pillars."

The twilight of the setting sun cast an eerie color over the landscape above the house. Traffic was nonexistent. The Suburban sat motionless at the intersection.

"Why do you think pillars are so special?" Peter asked.

"They seem unattainable," Lynn replied without hesitating. Her stare radiated beyond the framed outline of the dwelling. "When Marshall and I first got married, we canvassed St. Louis County hunting for houses. We bopped between real estate agents and developers trying to find our dream home. It is amazing how you can settle for less. Whenever I would mention pillars to a real estate agent, they would look at Marshall and me and fight from laughing. I would ask what was so funny and they would say something like 'older houses with pillars are usually out of starter home range'. And you know what developers building new neighborhoods told me? You cannot find house plans nowadays that have pillars. They cost too much for people constructing new, and most folks prefer putting the money into something more useful—like bathrooms. I asked if pillared houses are ever built anymore in new subdivisions. They said no way. A house with pillars hurts its value and is tougher to sell. If you have a house on a new street with pillars, folks tend to gobble up the neighboring houses around it that don't have pillars. The old 'buy-the-worst-property-in-the-neighborhood' idea – the lesser house's value increases to that of the nicest home. As a result, the pillared one droops to its lowest common denominator."

"Just like people," Peter mused.

"What?" the observation broke Lynn's train of thinking.

"Nothing," Peter laughed. He redirected his focus to the dome light on the roof of the Suburban.

"What did you say?" Lynn poked Peter's side. The amused reaction to her confession startled her.

"I was thinking," Peter chuckled as he shook his head. "I have bought a total of two houses since I married Marianne. Neither time did she ever even see the house before I bought them. In both cases, I came home in the evening and announced 'Guess what? We are moving—I bought us a new house'."

"I can add one more item to the things that I am going to change when we are finally together." Lynn pointed for the Suburban to drive straight on.

XXI

The tag-a-long trailer was big and ugly. The base exceeded twelve feet from hitch to tail. The width was just narrow enough so extensions did not have to be installed on the Suburban's side-view mirrors. Four-foot stainless steel poles pointed at each corner. It made the transport look grotesque.

Marshall was hunched over the contraption when Lynn and Peter strolled over from the Suburban. He was earnestly trying to bore a hole through the steel floor with a cordless drill.

"What are you doing?" Lynn and Peter accidentally recited in unison.

"The plywood wall panels rattled a lot when I carted your parents' brush to the dump," Marshall reported. He did not bother to look up. "Some reinforcement bolts should make it more sturdy—if we ever want to use it for camping or something."

Lynn looked over at Peter and mimed "Help!" Her companion stuffed his hands in his pockets.

"Hope you don't mind, but I called ahead an order to Vinnie's," Marshall ceased his drilling. He carefully stored the drill in its portable chest and closed the clasp. "That way we do not have to wait for our food when we get there."

Marshall wrapped his spare arm around his wife. He paused in front of Peter—half for effect, half to garner any reaction to the Monroe domain. Is he breaking my stones, Peter thought? The husband proceeded to escort his wife to the house. Peter Collins ambled a respectful five paces behind.

Lynn cut a hard right through the kitchen as soon as she and Marshall entered the sliding glass deck entrance. Marshall ignored the flinch as his clench was unsealed. He set to arranging his tools on the dining room table.

"Can I offer you a drink?" Marshall addressed to his guest as Peter passed toward the living room. The visitor stopped at the crest between the linoleum dining room floor and the off-white carpet. Should he take his shoes off before stepping on the rug?

"If I had my druthers, I would love a Scotch," Peter heeled at one of his loafers. "But if you do not have any, a cold beer will be fine."

Marshall cast a sidelong glance at the request. He marched onto the carpet in his work boots and used the manual button on the television to turn it on. Peter wedged his foot back into his shoe.

"I think all we have is juice," Marshall retreated to check out the refrigerator. "Would you like some juice?"

"Our order is already in at the restaurant," Peter conjured. He walked onto the carpet and sat on the black leather couch in front of the TV. "I think I can hold off."

"You like Seinfeld?" Marshall pointed the plastic jug of colored water toward the sitcom on the screen. "I reckon Lynn has memorized every single episode."

"It is my favorite program on network TV," Peter blurted without regard. He recognized the comedic scene. It was a classic. Funny, Peter thought, I never knew Lynn and I shared the same favorite program.

"I am not much for it," Marshall looked at the monitor with disdain. "I suppose you have to be from the East Coast to appreciate that New York City humor."

"Do you watch the cable movie stations?" Peter decided to shift the discussion down a different road—unaware that Lynn was listening from inside the hallway bathroom. She knew the likelihood of any chemistry between the two men in her life would be remote, but it soon became obvious. Aside from her, Peter and Marshall had absolutely nothing in common.

"We only get three local stations with our antennae," Lynn announced entering the room. "Monthly cable fees are pretty high."

Peter looked to Marshall for a reaction. He expected the man-of-the-house to come up with some macho retort to excuse the appearance of a tight household budget. There was none. No doubt, Lynn wore the pants in this family, Peter concluded.

"Marshall, Peter and I are going to take the Accord after we eat tonight," Lynn informed. "I had no idea how much of the dump you tracked inside the Suburban."

Marshall obediently followed the Honda to Vinnie's. Peter could glimpse the mud-splattered Suburban behind them on certain turns through the passenger side-view mirror. Lynn would occasionally peek too at the truck through the rear view. Both kept their hands bound to their sides. Even the slightest twinge of wanting to physically touch was camouflaged. The arrangement seemed awkward.

Vinnie's Pizzeria was only a half-mile drive from the Monroe residence. Besides the implied "keeping one's hands to themselves" in the Accord, Lynn's prior hesitation of being seen in public so close to home with Peter seemed to dissipate once everyone got out of the vehicles in the parking lot. Perhaps Marshall's presence would dispel any rumor or innuendo.

Peter was sensitive to the spectacle of walking into Lynn and Marshall's favorite hangout. He waited at the side of the Honda for Marshall to join up with his spouse. No problem this time walking in behind them, Peter determined. He noticed, however, that Lynn was making a point of centering herself between the two men as they proceeded to the door. Peter still found himself dragging back a step.

Peter was as well known in Worcester, Massachusetts as its mayor. There was not a public establishment in the city where at least half of its occupants would shout "Hey Peter!" as soon as he appeared. More often than not, folks would approach him no matter who he was with or how he was dressed, business or otherwise, and feel compelled just to strike up a conversation. Peter had conditioned himself to those regular instances. He would casually listen for a key notion or reference to something to tip him off to who it was that was coming up to him. The exercise was almost like a game. Popularity was refreshing.

Peter rehearsed in his mind a couple of standard replies for any of Marshall or Lynn's inquiring friends in the pizza parlor. It was important, he figured, to refer to Lynn's friendship as generic. Thinking about what the situation would be like if it were Worcester instead of Duluth, he was resolved not to embarrass either of the Monroes.

Marshall and Lynn stepped into the eatery. They meekly surveyed the smattering of empty booths and tables. Both the diners and employees at the ovens viewed the entrants with blank looks of nonrecognition. Lynn ambled through the half-filled seating area. Marshall walked to the counter and uttered "I called in earlier? Monroe?" He spelled out his last name.

Marshall joined Peter and Lynn standing in the middle of the dining area. He displayed a small tab of numbered paper. "They said it will be a couple of more minutes."

"Do you want to sit at a booth or a table?" Lynn asked her husband. Peter was amazed at the couple's sense of uncertainty.

Marshall overlooked the variety of seating choices tailored for four. "Let's sit against the back wall," he pointed to the only large function table. It was big enough to accommodate a party of twelve.

“Let me go up front and buy some beers,” Lynn decided. She knew Marshall would not think of buying anything to drink at Vinnie’s other than soda pop. Peter would go out of his mind. Besides, avoiding Marshall as he figured a seating arrangement for three at a table for twelve made sense.

“Can you bring me the change? I haven’t paid for the pizza yet,” Marshall announced in full earshot of the patronage. “I spent the money you gave me this morning.”

Lynn returned a few minutes later to the banquet table. She toted two mugs of red ale and a diet soda. The soda had an extra paper cup over it.

“They told me they only serve beer in these mugs,” Lynn pulled the extra cup off of her drink. “You may want to pour your beer in here.”

“That’s okay,” Peter was genuinely flattered by the sensitive gesture. He figured it would be better to mirror Marshall’s draught rather than switching to a cup like Lynn’s. “These mugs are plastic—nice and light. I do not mind these.”

Peter and Lynn burst out laughing. They toasted the containers with a tap of plastic and paper that was supposed to resemble a “clink”. Marshall mimicked the salute.

“I do not get it,” the husband warily eyed the two.

“Inside joke,” Lynn chuckled. Marshall noticed she had yet to take her eyes off of Peter.

“I am not much for inside jokes,” Marshall warned. The levity cued Lynn to the side of the table where she should be seated. She maneuvered to the chair next to her husband. A recounting of the lunchtime experience seemed necessary. Lynn recited Peter’s peculiarities with the waitress at Grandma’s.

“You do not believe in bringing home leftovers either? What’s wrong with that?” Marshall eventually turned and questioned Peter. He reminded Lynn of an interested child getting into a bedtime story, when moments before fighting about going to bed. A Vinnie’s employee delivered an extra large tray of pizza with the works to the table. The offering was big enough to feed a small army.

“I guess I should explain myself,” Peter shrugged his shoulder. He watched as Marshall littered salt over the entire pie. “Back in Mass, we have this Italian restaurant that has a partial liquor license—that is, customers can bring their own wine, or what have you. It sounds corny, but the idea of saving a couple of bucks by bringing your own bottle is immensely popular. The restaurant has this unique reputation because any pasta dish ordered comes with about five pounds of macaroni.”

"Anyway, there is this bank president in town who is involved with a lot of the same charitable interests as me. He has this arrangement with the owner to hold court in the private function room whenever he wants to show off his peacock feathers. I am probably the only person in town who avoids the place like the plague. Be it one of these charitable functions or even an ordinary night, the sight of people sitting outside the restaurant to get in with their little brown bags really repulses me. Then, you have to see the people leaving afterward. They all walk out gloating over their Styrofoam package of soggy macaroni. Even the bank president will pour unused wine back into the jugs to bring home."

The pizza was being devoured as Peter detailed his story. Even he did not realize how famished he really was. Only a couple of squares remained on the tray.

"What about pizza?" Marshall pointed to the remaining food—knowing that boxing it later was a normal Monroe ritual.

Lynn and Marshall waited for Peter's reply. They held the same interested look.

"Pizza doesn't count."

XXII

Lynn hailed a table server to clear the tray. No, it was not necessary to wrap the remaining pieces. She pretended not to notice her husband's gaped gesture of protest.

"Lynn tells me your sons are pretty good ice hockey players," Marshall sipped his red ale. "I assume you played, too?"

"Years ago," Peter said. He wondered how such a topic could have come up between Lynn and Marshall. "I am nothing but a glorified chauffeur to hockey rinks now."

"How far did you go?" Marshall pried. Peter reckoned this was as standard a requisition for Minnesotans as "what school did you go to?"

"I guess my claim to fame was captaining my high school team senior year. We made it to the state championship game at the old Boston Garden," Peter said. He figured the buck was sizing up his foe's horns.

"Didn't play in college?" Marshall tried to downplay the feat.

"No. I opted for football instead."

A thin smile cracked on Lynn's face. Marshall acted as if he could not see it.

"Is that where you played?" Marshall motioned his chin to the Athletic Staff emblem and mascot sewn into Peter Collins' jersey.

"This?" Peter lowered his chin to the breast pocket embroidery. "No, this as a matter of fact was one of our rival schools. I happen to be their insurance agent now. They gave me this shirt for being a benefactor."

Peter wished Marshall would get off the "my dog is bigger than your dog" topics. Didn't the girl always fool you and run to the one in the end who was lying on the ground with the bloody nose?

"I played hockey as a kid," Marshall decided to float his boat. "One game when we were Pee Wee's was the district sectionals, to go on to the Minnesota State tournament. We had made it to the sectional finals—which was a really big thing around here. We were in overtime and this kid and I broke in on a two-man breakaway. This kid slid a perfect pass to me in front of an open net. I whiffed on the puck. We all got caught deep in the other team's end and they were able to dump the puck for a breakaway on our goalie. Needless to say, they scored, and we lost."

Marshall paused from his story. He circled his finger over the top of his beer mug.

"The next time we went out on the ice for practice the Coach called us all to huddle up around our net. He shouts out, 'Mun-row! Get out of here!" Marshall dramatized the banishment with a flailing stab in the air. "He told me to go down to the other end of the ice to skate with the 'B' team."

"So what did you do?" Peter calmly folded his hands on the tabletop.

"What could I do?" Marshall's eyes widened. "I got moved down to the 'B' team. It was the last time I ever played organized sports."

Peter looked directly into the eyes of Marshall Monroe. Was there a flame flickering in there or not, he wondered. Peter slowly shook his head.

"I cannot tell you the number of times I have heard stories like that," Peter consoled. "It stinks the way a Coach can confront you at the most vulnerable of times with a moment of truth. I have seen more sporting or business careers end that way."

XXIII

The awkwardness resurfaced when the trio walked out of Vinnie's. Lynn treaded in between Peter beside the Accord and Marshall's pace to the Suburban several spaces away.

"Can you call your parents with your car phone and let them know I am on my way to pick up Maggie?" Marshall requested of his wife. "I do not want them to worry where we are."

Lynn joined her husband at the driver's door of the Suburban. The distance was beyond Peter's earshot. Lynn's head produced a dutiful nod from time to time—acknowledging her husband's fears. Where exactly are you going tonight? What time do I tell your daughter that her mother will be home?

"Thank you for not giving me the money to pay for the pizza," Lynn said to Peter as she returned to unlock the Accord. "I forgot to tell you, Marshall was dead set against you paying for dinner."

"He is the 'caretaker', isn't he?" Peter watched as Lynn waited for the Suburban to back out of its space first. "I should actually be glad that Marshall is in your life. Since you have known him, he has not only been the caretaker to my soul-mate and her daughter, he also tends to everybody in your family."

"Everybody loves Marshall," Lynn stared at the Suburban's blinking directional light. "So tell me then, why am I so unhappy?"

"It is the moments of truth," Peter leaned back in the passenger seat. "Those times when we reach those crossroads in life and have to make a critical decision. Take the youth hockey story for instance. Virtually everyone has whiffed on a puck in some way, shape, or form at one time or another in their lives. Of course, a Coach or an elder is going to tell you to 'get outta here'. It is what you do at that critical juncture. Do you say 'go to hell—you know I can make that play if it ever happens again'? Or do you lower your head and skate to the other end of the ice?"

"He was twelve years old when that happened," Lynn excused.

"My first impression is that Marshall is content being the caretaker," Peter restated. "You are fortunate in the sense that he would always provide a safe and comfortable home. Do not expect him though to jump into the shark infested waters of the business world and make a million bucks."

"Maybe I thought there was more," Lynn whispered. She quickened the pace of the compact car. It zipped down the double lanes of London Road toward the shores beyond the Aerial Lift Bridge.

"I want to get to a special spot you are going to love," Lynn's excitement matched the speed of the car. "The sunset should be beautiful."

The rear of the Accord emitted a tinny echo as the back tires zipped over the metal road surface on the Aerial Lift Bridge. The shock absorbers gave a sense of weightlessness as the car crested from the metal grid to the graded roadway.

"Remember that boyfriend I was dating when I first got to the Brigadier School?" Lynn reminisced. "He was about six years older than me. The only reason I went out with him was because he let me use his Datsun sports car when he was in town. I used to love tooling around the shoreline with the roof down."

Lynn turned and smiled. It was the brightest gleam that Peter had seen.

"Ha-ha!" she cried.

Instead of pulling into the beachside public parking lots, Lynn took an unexpected right turn into Park Point—a rest area reserved for campers and recreational vehicles. The turnaround road fronted the backside maritime section of Duluth Harbor.

"We will have complete privacy here this time of year." Lynn lit two cigarettes in her mouth. She handed one to Peter.

"Looks like we missed the sun fall below the horizon," Lynn looked to the western hills of the city. "The sky is still pretty though."

Lynn did not know what she enjoyed more—the backdrop of red tower lights on the hillside antennae complementing the colors of dusk, or the look of fascination in Peter's face.

"I have a surprise for you," Lynn laughed. Peter had never seen Lynn so full of life. She checked the clock on the dashboard and turned on the car stereo. Tuning in a radio station required a turn of a knob rather than pressing the "seek" button.

"Every Saturday night there is a station in town that plays 70's disco music," Lynn said over the intermittent waves of static. "I do not know why, but the past few Saturdays nights I have made a point of tuning in. I kept thinking you would get such a kick out of hearing it. You know a couple of weeks ago I came down here just like this at the same time of night to hear some of the songs. I could not get the thought of you coming to see me out of my mind."

Peter tossed both of the cigarettes out of the window. He leaned over and kissed Lynn's lips lightly.

"I vowed I would bring you here on Saturday night to listen to disco music," Lynn panted.

"Why do you associate me with disco music," Peter continued to peck Lynn's lips.

"Because I was five years old when you were already out of high school," Lynn's breath shortened. "You were probably walking around in high-heeled disco shoes and leisure suits dancing the twist on Saturday nights while I was home watching Hee Haw."

"Ah, the twist was 60's—before you were even born." Peter's clench tightened. "There is no 'twist' in disco."

"There isn't?" Lynn's eye opened a brief second, then rolled back. Any concentration on a discussion was lost. Her mouth opened to receive Peter's.

"You do not know how to dance disco, do you?" Peter's eyes remained open. He could see Lynn was totally enraptured. The stick shift however was digging into his thigh.

"Hey," Peter backed Lynn's mouth from his lips. "You do not know how to dance disco, do you?"

"Of course I do," Lynn recovered slightly. "I used to dance with my girlfriends all the time."

"What? Line dances, like the Hustle and the Electric Slide?"

"No," Lynn furrowed her face. She did not want to admit she did not know these odd dance names. "You know—how you all gather in the middle of the dance floor? And well, you just—dance."

"That is not what I am talking about," Peter shook his head. "I mean pair dancing—man and woman."

Lynn sat erect in her seat—still kitty-corner to Peter. Any previous smile evaporated from her face.

"Besides swaying back and forth to slow music," Lynn whispered. "I do not think I have ever actually danced with a man who knew what he was doing."

Peter exited the vehicle before Lynn could comprehend what was happening. Her car door opened with Peter posed at its side.

"May I have this dance?"

"Peter, the battery will drain if we keep the car door open."

"Then roll down the window and shut it," Peter recommended.

Lynn took Peter's extended hand and daintily drew each foot out of the car. The near equal height matched their eyes almost perfect. Perhaps Lynn was a smidgen taller.

"Peter, please? Let's not do this," Lynn looked down at her feet. "I tried ballroom dancing classes once. I was so bad the gym teacher told me to go out for the track team instead. I swear I can feel people laugh at me behind my back—the way these lanky legs move."

"Moment of truth." Peter held out his hands.

"I am not exactly graceful on my feet," Lynn reluctantly took hold of Peter's left hand. She continued to stare at the ground as if it was covered with cow manure.

"Do you know how to ice skate?" Peter asked.

"I used to when I was a little kid," Lynn surveyed the sides of her feet. "But I always fell down. Last time Marshall took us skating I thought I broke my hip."

"Did anyone ever tell you not to look at your feet while you skate?" Peter whispered. "It is like falling face first into a wading pool."

"What?" Lynn looked up to Peter's face.

"Dancing is like skating. Focus straight into my eyes."

"When do I know it is time to start moving?"

"You are not wearing the pants in the family anymore, Lynn Dear," Peter led his partner back in forth in rhythmic three steps without releasing hands. "Just let your body submit to whichever direction my arms lead you."

Peter lightly squeezed the grip on Lynn's right hand cueing her to turn inside from her left shoulder towards Peter. The novice rotated flawlessly. Peter kept their arms at waist level instead of at the neck to avoid having to reach over his partner's head.

"No one ever spun me around like this before," Lynn giggled. She quickly adopted the sequenced steps of three.

"Probably because they were not aware that you have to spin tall women with your arms down."

"Have you had a lot of women in your life, Peter?"

"That is a dangerous road to go down," Peter returned face-to-face. "Have you ever seen the movie where the guy is coaxing the girl to admit her past escapades? He is all lovey-dovey with her and joking that it is no big deal whatever she did with other guys. Then the girl totally blows the guy away—telling a sex-tale that would make paint peel. The guy gets so upset he smacks her."

Lynn found her feet moving in manners she never knew existed. She was completely captivated by Peter's seemingly continuous babble. She had no response to the movie question.

"You are not buying that one, huh?" Peter laughed. Lynn shook her head no.

"Truth be told," Peter confessed. "I have had a lot fewer women in the truest sense of the word than you probably think. Sure, I may love to dance, or hug and kiss, but not too much else beyond that."

"I do not care," Lynn added the flair of kicking her foot in the twirl. "Right here, right now, at this exact moment in space and time—you are mine… and I am yours."

XXIV

Resisting temptation is a divine aspiration. The will of the mortal body can easily overpower matters of the soul—particularly when sands in the hourglass are visibly draining.

Both Lynn and Peter desperately yearned to experience the sensation of their insides being one again. The lights were off in the modest Edgewater room. There was complete silence. Lynn lay on the bed with her back spooned against her soul-mate. Peter softly kissed the lobe of her ear.

"Ssh," Lynn's voice was barely audible. "Hold me, and listen to the silence."

Peter ceased his foreplay. He laid the tip of his nose on the ear of his love. His right hand completely enveloped Lynn's thin wrist. The couple held their breath.

"Can you feel the peacefulness?" Lynn whispered. "I never want to forget this moment. I will never forget you… I will never forget the look in your blue eyes, or this strength in your hands. I will never forget how you felt inside of me. And God, I will never forget the feel of your hair."

Lynn reached her fingers to the soft curls on the back of Peter's head.

"God, I will never forget your hair."

The couple remained motionless in the vacuum of silence. Digits flickered across the neon clock radio.

"Peter?" Lynn checked to see if he was still awake.

"I am here."

"When did you first realize you were in love with me?"

"When?"

"Yeah."

"You really want to know?"

"Uh-huh."

"I don't think you will believe it," Peter whispered. "It is surreal to me."

"Tell me."

"It was the first day at Brigadier. I looked across the amphitheater and saw you crying. The second I saw you I knew. I was in love with you."

The revelation hung in the air. Neither said a word.

"You?" Peter stifled a welling sniff. "When did you realize you were in love with me?"

"I don't know."

"Really?" Peter shifted his body. Was Lynn's hesitation intentional? "You really do not know?"

"No." Lynn twitched her head. The love she held for Peter seemed to always be there—dwelling in a recess of her heart—since the earliest of childhood memories. How could she explain that he had always been with her, Lynn wondered? Since before ever meeting at the Brigadier School? How do you say, you have always been with me? How could one understand?

"*I honestly do not know*."

The bliss of serenity stayed in Peter's bed long after Lynn departed.

"Please, do not walk out to the car with me," Lynn had said—forcing herself to leave the tranquility of the room. "If I see your face in the light right now, I do not think I would ever go back to Marshall."

Peter could still sense Lynn's presence next to him on the empty mattress. Whichever way his joints moved, he could feel his soul-mate's union. He squeezed his right hand into a tight fist. Lynn's wrist was still there.

He fell into a deep sleep. Images of Lynn's face during the past two and a half days flashed into view like a slideshow. He knew her before, Peter drowsed, hadn't he? Where did he know her from before?

The transfiguration of Lynn's face while they made love at Superior Shores popped into view. Peter again marveled at the angelic glow of her glorious countenance. He squeezed his hand for reassurance. The wrist was still there. Yes, she was still with him.

The vision skewed into an eerie bizarre twist. The shadow of Lynn's eyes and mouth remained unchanged. The features surrounding the eyes and mouth began changing however—into a different person—a young boy?

Who are you? Peter could hear his voice. It was echoing—into a cavern he had never before experienced. It seemed endless, and deep. *How do I know you? How do you know Lynn*?

The visage of the boy transformed. *Please bring my Lynn back*, Peter squeezed his hand. *Thank God*, he dreamed. Her wrist was still with him.

The brightness of the face blinded Peter's vision. He fought to re-identify Lynn's presence. He could not.

It was a familiar face to Peter Collins. A face he committed to memory from picture books in the earliest of childhood. A face he prayed to for strength and sustenance. A face he loved. He knew the face as the Blessed Virgin Mary. Or was it? Why Blessed Mother would you bother with me—particularly right here—right now?

The aura of brightness could not overwhelm the intense feeling of love radiating from the smiling glow.

"*Do not be afraid*," the female voice echoed from the cavern.

"*What is your will for me*?" Peter's voice droned into the abyss. The countenance steadied its loving smile. *Are you my Spirit Guide*, Peter meditated telepathically. *Can the Blessed Virgin Mary be my Spirit Guide*?

"*What are Lynn and I supposed to do with these lives*?" Peter could feel his weepy panic echo in the cavern. "*We love each other, but each have families....*"

The glow of the face began to dim.

"*Do not be afraid*."

XXV

Maggie Monroe was a useful buffer. The reputed Queen of Deflection strategically utilized the pawn to challenge the onslaught of conflicting emotion.

Lynn's idea of taking her daughter to visit Peter was a welcomed relief for Marshall. The premise of mother and daughter going for a joint visit cemented Lynn's contention that she and Peter were indeed nothing more than friends.

The maneuver also avoided the potential for any morning repeat of the previous night's scene in bed. After the difficulty of prying away from Peter's arms nine hours earlier, Lynn was teetering on the edge. It would not take much to tell her husband she wanted to sever their five-year marriage.

Maggie was excited by her mother's invitation. It seemed an eternity since she took her nightly bath with Mom. Daddy would not acknowledge her mention of "Peter".

"What were you up to last night?" Marshall appeared in the kitchen. Lynn abruptly hesitated from putting on Maggie's prerequisite cartoon character shades.

"Why?"

"I went to put the stroller in your car," Marshall said. "When I opened your trunk the smell of cigarettes was incredible."

Maggie realized that while Daddy did not want to talk about Peter, Mommy did. As the car made its way down to the Best Western Edgewater, Maggie's perch in the back child seat allowed her to see her Mommy's reflection in the rear view mirror. She never looked so happy.

"Mommy," Maggie announced. "I like Peter."

"Mommy likes Peter, too."

Mommy's smile made Maggie smile.

Maggie could tell that Peter liked Mommy. She could not help burying her head on the bed cover when Mommy let her walk by herself into Peter's hotel room. They did not kiss like Mommy and Daddy do, Maggie noticed, but they sure smiled at each other a lot more.

I like it when Peter picks me up. It is funny that he is showing me the pretty pictures on the mirror that Mommy bought him. My cartoon sunglasses hide my eyes. He thinks I am looking at the pictures, but I am not. I can see Mommy behind us. I am doing what she is doing. I am not looking at the pictures. I am looking at Peter. Boy, he talks a lot more than Daddy.

Mommy told Peter our secret surprise. We are going to the park at Enger Tower. Peter says he does not know the park at Enger Tower. Wait until he sees! Mommy and Maggie love Enger Tower Park!

"Mommy, Enger Tower Park," Maggie stuttered. She did not know why Peter suddenly got out of the car. He was walking away.

"Sweet Pea, Peter is going to get a cup of coffee," Lynn assured. The motor idled outside the convenience store. "He will be right back."

Maggie did what Mommy did. She watched Peter stir the cup inside the store. Mommy likes to watch Peter.

"How come Daddy does not get a cup of coffee?"

Mommy laughed.

"Daddy and Mommy drink coffee in the house. Peter drinks coffee in cars."

"Is that his friend?" Maggie watched as Peter laughed with the gasoline man in the store.

"No," Mommy said. "Peter talks to everybody he sees."

"How come Daddy does not talk to everybody he sees?"

"Because Daddy and Peter are different."

Peter came back to the car with two cups in his hands. He put one on the roof of the car to open the door.

"Decaf, milk, half a sugar, right?" Peter handed the cup to Mommy. Mommy does not drink coffee in cars. Why is she smiling?

"Mommy and Peter drink sippy cups like Maggie?"

Peter and Mommy looked at the lids on their cups.

"Yes, Honey," Mommy chuckled. "I suppose we do."

"Oh, no," Mommy looked sad. "The tower gate is closed. Must be from all of the tree damage."

Maggie was going to cry.

"You know what?" Mommy said. The car began to spin around. "I am going to park out here on the street. There are a couple of other cars parked out here. It must be all right to walk up."

Maggie and her Mom watched Peter pull the stroller out of the trunk.

He knows how to open it fast like Daddy. He knows you are supposed to lock the foot brakes before putting Maggie in too. Mommy has to remind Daddy sometimes to lock the foot brakes.

Mommy walked around the wooden pole that gated the road. Peter rolled Maggie under it.

"Puddle," Maggie warned. *I better point my finger. Mommy says do not go through puddles! You will get sick.*

Maggie looked with horror at her Mommy. Peter rolled right through the puddle. And he splashed his feet in it too. He laughed when he did it. *Is Peter going to get sick?*

Here comes a family like Maggie with a stroller. There are two babies in it like me.

"Beautiful day, isn't it," Peter said from behind Maggie. *Mommy does not want to talk.*

"What a handsome couple," Maggie could hear from the Mommy and Daddy passing by. "They will have beautiful babies, that's for sure."

Are Mommy and Peter having a baby?

Peter is going the wrong way. He is taking me to the big stone tower. Mommy and Maggie do not go to the big stone tower. Mommy takes Maggie to the bell.

"This way, Peter," Mommy said. *Yup*, she is going the right way. *The bell is behind the little stone house.*

Mommy remembered my sippy cup—and my bag of crackers. I get to drink with my sippy cup, too. I am in charge of the cracker bag. Mommy never eats my crackers.

"Peter, you want a cracker?"

He ate it! Peter ate a cracker!

"Wan-na-nuther?"

Two! He ate two crackers!

"Okay, No more crackers until later," Maggie followed what Mommy says. "We will have more crackers until later, okay?"

"Okay," Peter said. *Peter is good. He does not pout for more crackers.*

"Mommy? Maggie will get you some flowers."

"Be careful with your running," Mommy says. "You do not want to fall down."

Maggie looked at her feet while she ran. Mommy says, "*Watch your feet*!"

Mommy and Peter sat on the bench next to the bell.

"This is your flower, Mommy."

"Thank you, Maggie," Mommy said. "This is a leaf, though, Sweetheart. Flowers look different than leaves."

"Maggie will get you another flower."

She returned with a leaf.

"Does Peter get a flower, too?" Mommy asked.

"No." Maggie said. "Flowers are for Mommy."

Why did I say that, Maggie wondered? *I like Peter. Peter would like a flower. I will surprise Mommy. I will get Peter a flower. Do not fall down though! Watch your feet! Mommy says watch your feet!*

Maggie fell down. *My hands! Oh no, my hands are all dirty! I cannot get Peter a flower. There are bees in my hands. They are stinging! And I cannot get Peter a flower.*

Maggie burst out crying. *I am sorry Peter. My hands hurt. I cannot get you a flower.*

Maggie ran up to the bench. *Mommy has her arms out—but I do not want to see Mommy. I want to see Peter. I want Peter to hold me.*

Thank you, Peter. Thank you for holding me. You are right. That rock sticking out of the ground is bad. It made Maggie fall. Thank you for spanking the bad rock. It is a bad, bad rock.

"Did you see that?" Maggie could hear Mommy say. "She did not want to come to me. She wanted you."

Maggie could feel Peter's head nod. *He is walking me around. He does not want to talk either. He is mad at the rock too.*

We are in front of the bell now. I do not want to cry anymore. It is a pretty bell, isn't it Peter? Mommy and Maggie like to come to see the bell. Mommy thinks about you, Peter, when we stand here.

Peter, why are you bending me down? Ooh, we are standing inside the bell! I can see light on the ground, but it is dark in here!

"Maggie, can you hear the bell?" Peter shook the car keys against its side. "The bell is ringing for Maggie."

You remember, don't you Peter? You remember before—when the bells were ringing. Mommy was with us there too. It was a happy place. And we listened to the bells ring.

XXVI

Lynn watched the scene unfold from the ornamental rod iron bench. She kicked stone dust over the rock jutting out from in front of the bench's right leg. Maggie would not want to see the protuberance again.

"Enger Tower." Lynn thought to herself as the dust covered the jag. "I have not been there since fourth grade."

Her mind flashed back to the history of Bert J. Enger—the mandatory subject of Social Studies classes in Duluth, Minnesota elementary schools for over seven decades. Enger came to the United States from his native Norway in the late 1800s. He was a meager laborer on Great Lake trade ships -eventually becoming rich as a merchant seaman. His success and love of life were not so much attributed to his dogged ethic toward work. Rather, his happiness—as teachers taught—was realized by appreciating the surroundings he truly considered home—Duluth, Minnesota. At the time of his death during the Great Depression, Bert Enger surprised the Duluthian town fathers by willing two thirds of his estate to the city. A magnificent tri-colored flagstone observation tower was constructed atop Enger's gift. Dedicated by Olav, the Crown Prince of Norway in 1939, the tower was a jewel—providing a panoramic view of the city along with the neighboring golf course and Leisure Park bearing its benefactor's name.

Enger Park was one of those places that a citizen of Duluth remembered visiting as a kid—usually at an end-of-school-year field trip—but soon forgot. There were too many other gems in the North Shore region to frequent. That was why, Lynn recalled, it was so unusual that Richard Nelson, her natural birth father would suggest picnicing at Enger Park for their initial visit after she turned nineteen. Was it because non-Duluth Minnesotans identify the landmark with the city from their own out-of-town childhood studies? Or was it a misconception that Duluthians only feel comfortable picnicking at their local yokel park?

"Enger Park?" Lynn repeated the reaction to her newfound father that day. "I have not been there since fourth grade."

"It is not the tower I am so much interested in," Lynn remembered Richard saying. "It is the Ohara Peace Bell. I feel we are destined to reunite at the Ohara Peace Bell."

Lynn paused in her reflection. She looked again at Peter and Maggie standing inside the squared concrete base beneath the bell. It was embarrassing at the time—telling Richard Nelson she did not know what he was talking about when he mentioned the Ohara Peace Bell.

"The Ohara Peace Bell," Richard proclaimed. "Don't you remember the history?"

The roots of the Ohara Peace Bell trace to beginnings in excess of three centuries. Its origin was within the Cho-ei Temple in Ohara, Chiba, Japan. It had at one time been considered the oldest remaining religious bell in Ohara. The bell was donated to the World War II Japanese government during a wartime scrap drive. Never used for its ore, the original bell was recovered by sailors aboard the USS Duluth at war's end. It was eventually gifted to the city of Duluth, Minnesota.

In 1951, the Dean of the Chiba University School of Horticulture learned of the salvaged re-existence of the bell. He petitioned then Mayor of Duluth, George Johnson, to return the religious symbol to its rightful home. The city of Duluth complied with the request and delivered the bell back to Japan in 1954.

The object was renamed the US Friendship Bell, a symbol of peace and friendship. The Japanese gifted a replica of the original Ohara Peace Bell back to the city of Duluth in 1994. It was dedicated at the highest elevation within city limits—atop the hills of Enger Park—housed within a six—steel post, brown shingled gazebo.

Richard and Mary Ann Nelson read about the replica bell in Duluth the exact same day Minnesota State authorities reported the whereabouts of their long lost daughter. What an irony, Richard remembered reflecting. Mary Ann and I pulled up roots years ago, to start a new life in Colorado. We wailed for our daughter to be safe and to someday be back with us. Then, while scanning the local Boulder newspaper, we learned of a Japanese bell coming back to Duluth—a wailing bell. For generations, Eastern culture erected bells on mountaintops to assist in meditations to the spirit world. They were called wailing symbols. Wailing in mourn for the souls of lost loved ones. Wailing in hope for the dawn of a new day. Then we learned our little girl was still there, where we left her. Waiting for us in Minnesota.

The Cloud clan accompanied the Nelsons that unifying day to Enger Park. Luke and Larry had to lug an extra picnic table from the tower deck over to the bell area so that everyone could sit together. Lynn found that she, too, was as captivated as Richard was by the bell.

"Margaret, I mean Lynn," Richard proclaimed as the two stood hand in hand before the cylinder. "We are home. We are finally home."

It began to rain. Forecasters predicted the chance of a sprinkle, but this was more than a mere sprinkle. Torrents of water fell from the sky. The party ran in unison for shelter under the eaves of the stone bathroom building. The remains of the picnic got drenched.

"It is not fair," Lynn scolded the wet skies. "We were having such a good time. This rain ruined everything."

"What do you mean?" Richard Nelson ran out from under the shelter. The Cloud clan looked in awe as Richard extended his arms and twirled amidst the soaking pellets. "Haven't you ever 'done rain' before?"

Richard Nelson ran across the sidewalk and jumped headlong into a gathering form of surface water on the grass. He rolled over onto his back and splashed like he was making a snow angel.

"This is a glorious day, Lynn," her birthfather marveled. "Come on everyone—let's 'do rain'!"

Lynn watched as Peter raced ahead towards the parked car at the gate—pushing Maggie in the stroller. The muscles in his legs rippled like a skater. Maggie was laughing uncontrollably as another puddle was compromised.

"*And he wonders why I told him, he reminds me of my father.*"

XXVII

The second surprise of the day was for Maggie. Lynn announced lunch at McDonalds before going back to the house. McDonalds was Maggie's favorite. Lynn walked up to the counter and ordered the standard fare—Hamburger Happy Meals. She smiled at Peter's willingness to partake in the same entrée.

Their relationship had solidified. Maggie took Peter's hand to escort him to her favorite table positioned strategically for the best view of everything going on. The traffic along the East Central Entrance was visible on the glass side of the booth. The Play Place indoor jungle gym was in full display on the other.

Peter instinctively grabbed a high chair with his free hand to bring to the booth. Maggie glared at the segregating cage. Without a word of acknowledgement, Peter dragged the chair back to the tray return station.

"Would you like the booster seat instead?" Peter pointed to the red plastic cube with vinyl straps. Maggie's focus remained unchanged.

"I want to sit like a big girl with Peter and Mommy," Peter could hear in his mind. He furrowed his brow at the strange phenomenon. Did she just say something to me?

"I assume Maggie wants to sit at her favorite booth," Lynn joined the group with a tray of multi-colored cardboard meal boxes. Her remark broke Peter's amazement.

"Does Maggie like to romp around in the jungle gym?" Peter asked as Lynn separated the meals. Maggie calmly looked at Lynn for a reply. Peter noticed Lynn's regard toward her daughter before answering.

"Maggie is not quite old enough to go into the jungle gym," Lynn stated matter-of-factly. Peter reluctantly looked at Maggie's reaction.

"It is for the big kids," the telepathic message said. Peter shook his head in awe.

"You are right," Peter asserted. "She is a star."

The couple watched Maggie's attack on the hamburger. It was implied not to break the sandwich into bite-sized pieces. Rather, the intention was to hold the whole bun and chomp like the adults. The results were still little bird-like chips on the roll.

Peter thought about asking Lynn whether or not it would be okay this one time to break her stringent rules about the jungle gym. What harm could come from Maggie trying out the Play Place? He would supervise.

The test worked. Lynn did not change her gaze from the passing cars. Maggie, though, stared at Peter.

You can hear me —can't you Maggie, Peter imaged in his mind.

"Yellow," Maggie pointed to the stripe on her straw. "White," she rotated the tube in her hand. "Red," the finger pointed at the final stripe.

Peter could tell Maggie was reluctant to play his game.

"That is right." Peter applauded the two-year-old's recognition of her colors. "What a smart girl you are."

Peter felt a bump against his sneaker. A red plastic ball from the gym's landing nest had rolled between his feet. He studied the netted area where the ball began its course. *How did that ball get through that netting*?

There were no children in the landing area of plastic balls. A couple of toddlers were at the opposite end of the conical entrance to the Play Place. *How did that red ball get here*? Peter looked across at Maggie.

"Red," the little girl repeated—giggling at the stripe on her straw. Peter picked up the ball from the floor.

"What color is this Maggie?" Peter held the sphere next to the soda pop.

"Red."

Peter picked up the little girl and carried her to the netting. He squatted to the ground and whispered.

"Maggie, how did this ball get out of there?"

Maggie Monroe smiled.

"Maggie, would you like to roll this ball back under the net if I hold the bottom up in the air for you?"

Maggie looked over her shoulder to her mother. Lynn sat stoically—admiring the chemistry between the two loves of her life. Peter handed the ball to Maggie. He pulled the elastic cord binding the net to the ground. Maggie knelt and rolled the ball back to its origin.

"Atta girl, Maggie," Peter marveled. He returned the mischief-maker to his arms.

"Congratulations, Peter," Lynn observed. "You are one of the few people I have met who can knock that girl out without having to drive around in the car."

Maggie was fast asleep on Peter's shoulder.

XXVIII

A wet wedge of perspiration streaked down the back of Marshall's tee shirt.

Lynn stepped around the pile of wood debris in the driveway to bring Maggie to her crib.

"Thanks for taking care of the little one," Marshall shook Peter's hand. "I was able to make a good dent in the yard this morning."

"My pleasure." Peter squeezed the callused palm. "That is one special girl you have."

"So what do you have planned this afternoon?"

Peter released the grip. He looked toward the bright burning sun.

"Lynn and I were thinking about heading to the beach."

"Good, you decided then," Lynn called back from the open kitchen window. "I will get my suit and a blanket."

Peter could see the seethe on Lynn's husband's face. His upper lip puffed as if stung by a hornet. This guy has had a belly full of me, Peter concluded. He stepped onto the back deck and paced its outline waiting for Lynn. Marshall stood sentry in the driveway with his puffed lip. Please Lynn, Peter conjured. Hurry up!

Lynn bounced out of the house and onto the deck. The outline of Friday night's bikini was visible under her tee shirt and cotton slacks. She was totally ambivalent to her husband's brood.

"Are you planning to come home for supper tonight," Marshall questioned. It was more of a statement than a question.

"Nope." Lynn reported. She cavalierly shook the winter's edge from the large beach blanket. "Peter promised us dinner at a nice restaurant and you opted for Vinnie's pizza instead. Tonight I am taking him up on his invitation. I am dressing up, too."

Lynn motioned for Peter's help to fold the corners of the blanket. My God, Lynn, don't you see the puffed lip? Lynn pretended not to care. She marched past the mud-splattered Suburban and tossed the blanket onto the back seat of the Accord.

"It is hot enough here to get the sun tan lotion," Lynn walked past Marshall. "But I think I will get a sweatshirt instead. It is generally a lot cooler on the beach than up here on the hill."

Marshall heaved a large branch into the tag-a-long. Lynn ignored the symbol of protest.

"Marshall, would you like some help with those big limbs out back?" Peter offered to calm the tension.

"No time," Lynn resurfaced from the house. "We have to go."

Peter and Lynn were the only ones lying on the beach. A group of teenage passersby casually tossed a football. The last day of April was not a high beach demand day in Duluth, Minnesota, regardless of the seventy-degree temperature. Wind gusts blew sand across their faces. They huddled together to light cigarettes. Lynn did not seem to mind the teenagers noticing their interlocked legs.

"Can you imagine living our lives together?" Peter asked.

"I can." Lynn joined his view of the spacious waters. "I do all the time."

"I always had an affinity for the water," Peter revealed. "I could see us living in a nice lake house along the Northern Shore."

"Not me," Lynn said. "I prefer escaping to Key West."

"Key West? Have you ever been there?"

"No. Have you?"

"No."

"I guess I have only seen it in pictures—no insurance agencies or commerce. Just a laid back lifestyle to relax and enjoy each other."

"Sounds like Massachusetts is out of the question."

"I do not know if I could be a member of the Peter Collins' fan club," Lynn said seriously. She held Peter's hand. "How do you think I will be viewed at your country club? I can see everyone being gracious meeting me, but can you imagine what they would say once we turned our backs? The men would chuckle. 'Good old Peter—looks like he snagged a young one'. And the women—many of whom would never reveal how friendly they are with Marianne—would snicker that I must be good in bed."

"Women's intuition's pretty sound to me," Peter tried to joke.

"How about your family?" Lynn continued. "Have you ever thought how, or if, your parents and your brothers and sisters would receive me in their homes? I would be an outsider—a family breaker."

"Then maybe we should make our own escape," Peter thought aloud. "A new environment probably makes the most sense."

"Sure," Lynn frowned. "I have thought about that, too. Seems every native of Duluth has thought about leaving at some point in time—migrating to Arizona, or California, or Florida."

"Florida sounds good."

"Yeah, until you go away to play in some amateur golf tournament."

"With you at my side," Peter leaned his torso into Lynn's. "Golf is not that important to me. I would have no problem giving it up."

"No, Peter, I would not want to do that to you. I want you to keep doing the things you love and excel in," Lynn began to stroke the locks on Peter's head. "I can just see myself though, wishing you well as you leave for your Saturday morning round. I would be fine for a couple of hours, but soon I would be missing my Maggie. I can see myself fighting to hide the tears when you got home."

"I was assuming Maggie would be with us."

"Then believe it or not, I would be crying for Marshall. He would be devastated without his daughter."

"From the sounds of it," Peter interpreted. "You have more or less resigned yourself to the notion that you are remaining here for the rest of your life."

Lynn sat up. She wrapped her arms around her ankles and pulled them close to her body. Her chin rested on her knees.

"For the past five years I have envisioned becoming the doting grandmother. You know? That apron clad cutout creature baking in the kitchen during the holidays? I can see all the little grandchildren running into the kitchen to find out what Grammy was cooking special for them in the oven. Funny thing is, I do not even know how to bake. I keep thinking—someday I need to have my mother teach me some of her famous recipes. How can you be the doting grandmother without the 'famous recipe'? Until now—until I met you."

"That can still happen," Peter tried to sound encouraging. He, too, sat up and emulated Lynn's look to the Great Lake for an answer. "Think there is much in the way of business opportunities for me here in Duluth?"

Lynn surveyed the hilly shores. She shook her head at the landscape.

"You would go crazy here trying to sell insurance. The agency I work at is one of the largest in the city. Even with that our highest paid producers make a fraction of what you make. You would become so frustrated—selling Businessowners Policies to the local pizzerias and dry cleaners."

"Depends on where you set your sights Lynn dear," Peter pointed to a behemoth steel barge passing under the Aerial Lift Bridge. "There are some pretty big looking shipping and gravel processing plants inside the harbor."

"None of the agents in Duluth write those accounts Peter. It is like we have no credibility—going up against the national brokerage outfits from Minneapolis. I am not saying it is impossible to write those accounts. I just think it would be difficult to find an agency here that you could even buy to equip you with the resources you would need."

"How about Minneapolis, then," Peter reached. "It is only a two hour drive from here. There are plenty of business opportunities there for us—and you and Marshall would still be able to be part of Maggie's growing up."

Lynn was flattered by Peter's suggestion. Has he really thought about the impact of pulling up roots, she thought? What about his kids, and his family?

"Peter, is that what you could see yourself doing? Working for a national brokerage firm?" Lynn rolled her eyes to the horizon. "They are different than local insurance agencies you know. No community pride, or giving back on special fund drives or neighborhood projects. Peter Collins is accountable to no one. You would not cut having to explain your whereabouts every hour of the business week to some bean counter type sales manager."

"I would do it, Lynn, if it meant being with you."

"Is that what you think our destiny is?" Lynn speculated. "The reason we are here right now in this time, in this place? For us to sacrifice everything around us in order to be with each other? And then to do what? To fall back to what we conditioned ourselves to be as most comfortable? Seeking replacement jobs at other insurance agencies? What will have changed, Peter? We would be jumping into a different hamster wheel— that's all. And instead of Marshall or Marianne running in the cage next door, it will be us."

"There is more to the notion of making our escape," Peter concurred. "It is finding that special calling to do what we really want. To pursue what one feels as their destiny."

"So what is your destiny, Peter?"

"There is a private country club in our area of Massachusetts that is probably the most exclusive and elegant in all of New England. I am generally lucky enough to get invited there once a year. I swear, unless you are able to trace your ancestry back to the Mayflower, you have virtually no chance of ever getting in."

"Is that what you feel your destiny is, Peter?" Lynn asked. "To become a member of that exclusive club?"

"No." Peter chuckled and shook his head. "That is the irony. There is a fellow there who is a retired President of a pretty well known savings bank. I am sure he has the wherewithal to be a member. You know what he does instead? He decided to tend to the flowers."

"Tend to the flowers?" Lynn was confused.

"Yes," Peter affirmed. "Tend to the flowers. He bought a rickety old pick up truck and arranged with the club to take care of all the flowers surrounding the entrance to the club. Let me tell you—these are some of the most beautiful flowerbeds you will ever see. He wears a floppy hat and it seems the same soiled pair of gardener's pants every time I see him."

"There are times I have stood on the first tee and watched him," Peter continued. "You almost have to change your perspective on things to see what is really happening around you. People aspiring to grab that brass ring—men and women alike—come zipping up to the clubhouse valet in their leased Jaguars and Mercedes. They inevitably have a cell phone glued to their ear to ensure that anyone who may be watching can appreciate how important they are. And the funny thing is—right next to them is the gardener. He will be kneeling on the bark mulch squirting fertilizer spray on his cherished petals. These people next to him often time look so frazzled and stressed out. And there the gardener kneels—either humming or whistling a tune. Most people do not realize who the old man is, or that he rose to rungs on the corporate ladder of success that they most likely will never reach. Once I saw this young guy from the lucky sperm bank looking down at the gardener with such disdain. The gardener merely smiled back at him and went about his appointed task. It was at that moment that I thought 'Buddy, you have got this thing figured out'."

"I guess that is why I said 'Key West'," Lynn reflected. "They must have gardeners in Key West."

"Do not mistake me," Peter qualified. "My allergies prevent me from being a happy gardener."

"Okay, then," Lynn could sense Peter's hesitancy in describing what he considered bliss. "What is it that would satisfy that soul inside of Peter Collins?"

"You will think I am crazy," Peter mounted his chin on his knees like Lynn.

"Try me."

"Really?"

"Yes, really—try me."

"School bus driver." Peter analyzed Lynn's reaction to be sure she did not laugh. "I have this urge inside of me to be a bus driver. I love to get up early in the morning, and the responsibility of driving people's children safely to school would truly inspire me."

"I can see me driving that yellow bus in bad weather and snowstorms," Peter mimed the flat-armed motion of negotiating the steering wheel. "Some kids would be sitting white-knuckled with worry wondering if we can make it home. Others would be rollicking around hollering and stuff—totally confident and secure in my abilities. That would really appeal to me."

"Why, Peter Collins?" Lynn's face lightened. "What happened to that macho ego? Ex-insurance executive turns school bus driver extraordinaire?"

"Every morning I used to drop my son off for school down the street from our house," Peter expounded. "There is an old, World War II vet who stands as crossing guard every morning without fail—rain or shine. He wears the commemorative cap from the ship he was commissioned to in the Navy. You can see the commuters' irritation when they have to slow to the schoolyard speed limit, or curse if they cannot beat his orange vest stepping from the curb with the octagonal red hand sign. Know what he does? He is a beekeeper in his spare time. He knows all the kids' names, and gives them a little jar of honey on their birthdays. It is so cute. My son used to say 'Mom, make sure not to throw out the honey jar. Joe needs the bottle back for my birthday next year'."

Lynn was experiencing a side of Peter she never knew existed. It explained the magnetism.

"One morning I am walking through the office, and who is seated with one of our Personal Lines customer service reps? Joe the crossing guard. I went up to him and asked 'Joe, do you know who I am?' He meekly nodded his head. I said 'Joe, I have always wanted to get out of my car in the morning and shake your hand for being such a great crossing guard. The kids in the neighborhood look forward so much to their jar of birthday honey—what a generous gesture. If there is ever a day you are sniffling with a cold standing there in the pre-dawn darkness getting splashed by speeding cars, please remember those little souls sitting in their warm kitchens biting into their toast coated with honey. They will be thinking about you. They will admire honey for the rest of their lives. They will see it years later on a country store shelf and will reminisce to their mate about Joe the crossing guard'."

"Know what happened next?" Peter tightened his dimpled jaw. "Joe began to cry. Right there in the office. The customer service rep? You could tell she felt somewhat ashamed for making this guy with a three-day beard wait so long to be helped. It does not sound like much, but seeking out those moments of truth? That is what 'escaping' is all about."

Peter removed his sneakers and socks.

"God forbid I travel all this way, and not put my feet into Lake Superior," Peter sought to relieve the direction of the conversation. He stepped around the remains of a long abandoned campfire and navigated the reddish-brown granules of sand to the lake's edge. The waters were frigid.

"Have you heard the new 'Thank You' song on the radio," Lynn called from the blanket. "It has been playing over and over in my mind today."

"Yes, I have," Peter lied. He was not up on contemporary pop music.

"I-I want to thank you," Lynn approached Peter from behind. She hugged his shoulders. "For giving me the best day of my life."

XXIX

They watched the final sunset smoking cigarettes at the Park Point parking lot. Neither had uttered a word. Peter seemed indifferent to the marked symbol of time. He was perhaps more captivated by the red dress Lynn decided to wear.

"Awesome," Peter marveled.

"It is a beautiful sunset," Lynn remarked.

"Oh, that too," Peter smiled. He reached for Lynn's hand. She drew it away.

Peter did not notice that Lynn picked him up at Edgewater after changing from the beach in a sparkling clean GMC Suburban. Marshall had devoted their beach blanket hours to restoring the truck to the glistening condition Lynn created three days prior.

"Your visit is coming to an end," Marshall rebuked the haughtiness of the weekend when Lynn returned to the house. "Figured the least I could do was clean up the mess I made with the truck so you can escort your friend during your final night in style."

Lynn had chose Bellisio's Italian Restaurant for dinner on the way back from the beach. It is centered square in Duluth's Canal Park downtown harbor district.

"It gets great reviews in the paper," Lynn remarked at the time. "And I have never been there."

Peter presumed the hand withdrawal was an early night signal to be discreet in a public place like Bellisio's. Lynn could always stand the chance of running into a business client or colleague. Or at least that was what he thought the signal meant. The pristine Suburban had gone right over his head.

Sunday evenings were not big nights out for restaurants in downtown Duluth. The maitre'd sat the couple next to two gentlemen, who were the only other diners in the establishment.

"Perhaps we can be seated with a little more privacy?" Peter suggested to the host.

"No," Lynn took the offered seat. The gentlemen were not acquaintances, but at least they buffered the chance of too romantic an evening. "This table will be fine."

The maitre'd rounded the opposite side of the table. He pulled the chair facing Lynn for Peter to be seated. .

"Thanks just the same," Peter selected his own seat to Lynn's right and sat down.

"This is not a booth," Lynn noted.

"Same rules for booths apply to couples sitting at tables set for four."

"Shall we start with a beverage this evening?" The maitre'd stood like a sentinel over the table.

"What are you going to have, Peter?"

"I was thinking about wine. Would you like to share a bottle of Chianti?"

"I am not too familiar with wines. Is that red or white?"

"It is a heavy red Italian wine—great with pasta. Two glasses, and you are ready for bed."

"I prefer white," Lynn deflected. The maitre'd handed Peter the house wine list. Peter hefted the thirty-odd paged cellophane wrapped binder.

"This will take forever for me to read," Peter's attention was more focused on Lynn. He handed the folder back to its owner without regard. "Tell you what, I am sure you have a nice Chardonnay in there that you can bring us."

"Any particular vintage, sir?" The maitre'd was taken aback by the cavalier response.

"Could you ask the bar manager for us," Peter glimpsed briefly. "We would like his recommendation for the best California."

"You did not even check the price," Lynn watched the maitre'd cut across to the bar. If Peter was trying to show off, it was not very impressive, Lynn thought. She could feel a moat building around her emotions. "What if it turns out costing three hundred dollars?"

She wished it would cost six hundred to teach him a lesson.

"I will let you in on a little secret," Peter unfolded the cloth napkin and placed it on his lap oblivious to Lynn's rhetoric. "Have you ever noticed the anguish a guy on a dinner date has when it comes time to pick a wine from the wine list? Most people, including me, have no idea what to order. They automatically read the prices on the right, and totally ruin their guests' excitement of enjoying a bottle of wine with this downtrodden frown."

Peter dramatized an accentuated puss for effect.

"They end up ordering a wine too expensive for their pocketbook, or they pick the cheapest one on the list. Maybe that is why maitre'ds seat couples on opposite ends of the table. So they can hide the cost of the wine."

"Now, if you were to ask the maitre'd, the waiter, or the restaurant manager to select the wine," Peter continued his theory. "Then you are sure to get socked with the three hundred dollar jobbie. They think you must be a big spender to seek them out for their opinion. Not only that, but they pool the tip on top of that, too."

"So, hence my secret," Peter noticed that perhaps Lynn was starting to unwind. "Who better to seek advice, but from the expert—the person who buys the wine? No one ever asks his opinion on anything. I have yet to find a bar manager not flattered by a request from the table. He or she is not going to insult you by picking the most expensive wine on the list. They are going to go out of their way to show you a great wine in their mind for the most reasonable price. They do not get tipped either, unless you want to."

The maitre'd returned displaying an ordinary bottle of Kendall Jackson.

"There—I know that one," Peter nodded for the cork to be screwed. "Sometimes it is better to be lucky rather than good."

Why was this happening to her?

Lynn gazed in amazement at the brimming spirit of confidence set before her. Marshall was probably in the middle of giving Maggie her bath at home. Just the way he washed the truck a few hours earlier. The secret elements of fine dining, like seeking out a bar manager to order the wine, would be as foreign to Marshall as towing a tag-a-long trailer would be to Peter. So why, Lynn wrestled, was she wedged between two such magnificent men?

Lynn sat back to allow the wine to be poured into her glass. She imagined Peter had a host of flamboyant words in store to toast the occasion. I wonder, Lynn thought. Would it be something he has practiced for months, one that he keeps inventoried for certain occasions, or would he once again rely on spontaneity. Lynn raised her glass in unison with Peter.

There was a simple clink.

The pair picked up their dinner menus—assuming that was the next thing they were supposed to do. The gentlemen's conversation at the next table was barely audible. A waitress was introduced by the maitre'd. She placed bread sticks and a plate of seasoned dipping oil on the table. Neither noticed the staple.

"Are you ready to order, or would you care for a few minutes?" the waitress asked professionally.

"I will have the mixed fettuccine," Lynn said. She handed back her menu before Peter could request extra time.

"The veal dinner special looks good to me," Peter surrendered. The waitress walked away without having to scribe for memory.

"What—no secrets to ordering meals?" Lynn tilted her head coyly. Peter swallowed a mouthful of the Kendall Jackson and played with the stem of his wineglass.

"You have gotten awfully quiet all of the sudden," Lynn observed.

"I was just thinking about twenty-four hours from now," Peter resorted to tapping a breadstick on the corner of the table like he was playing a drum. The nervousness enveloped like a wave. "Returning to the everyday routine will be a little tough to stomach."

Then do what I am doing, Lynn thought to herself. *Fight off this temptation to be together.*

"Life sure takes a strange twist once you hit your forties," Peter revealed. "And I do not mean 'mid-life' crises. Maybe it is the instant gratification society we live in today. I don't know. It is just that it seems people tend to throw away relationships so easily if they do not fit their fancy."

"Do you think that is the reason you had to visit me?" Lynn speculated, "to realize that there could be more than 'winning the chase'?" Lynn primed her fingers like quotation marks. "Maybe our seeing each other will make you realize all of the good aspects of your marriage to your wife."

"That is not it at all," Peter shook his head in defiance. "Marianne and I have seen so many friends of ours divorce—particularly over these past few years. There was one couple we were close to in our neighborhood. Their kids were roughly the same age as ours. So it was kind of natural that we socialized a lot together. Long story short, they were miserable for years before we ever met—stayed together for 'the kids'. The wife decides to move out. So what happens? The husband befriends a new live-in within a month—could not stand being alone. In no time we were back socializing with this brand new couple. It was like nothing ever happened."

"Is everyone happier as a result?"

"No. That is the irony I cannot understand," Peter lamented. "Certainly, alcohol has a negative effect on so many couples. These two renew the same arguments we used to hear with the old couple. Sometimes it gets very embarrassing. One night the ex-husband was in a real ornery mood. We were playing cards and all of the sudden he gets up from the table and storms into bed for the night. Marianne and I sat there watching this poor woman going through the same ordeal we saw before. So I mention all of these books I had been reading about parapsychology. I ask this person if she really feels her new significant other is her destiny? Her soul-mate? Know what she says? She says 'Yes, Mark is definitely my soul-mate."

"Peter," Lynn interjected. "How can you deem yourself fit to act as judge and jury in a situation like that?"

"Good question," Peter reflected. "I asked her how she came to know that Mark was her soul-mate? She told Marianne and me that for the six years prior to meeting Mark, she was a single mom living in a three decker tenement on Grafton Hill. She said the whole time she lived at or below the poverty line. 'No matter how bad a night like tonight might look on the surface—it still beats living in poverty', she told us. 'I do not care how bad or abusive this relationship may appear. I am not going back to where I was'."

"So in twenty-four hours I will return back to that setting in Worcester," Peter sighed. "And that is just one of many tales I could tell. So many people searching for happiness. And settling for something so much less—just to avoid a lower level of misery."

The waitress arrived with the tin-covered dishes. She arranged the setting on a side station to prepare service. A plate of orange and green fettuccine was placed in front of Lynn. Peter's veal entrée looked a lot more appetizing.

"This is not what I expected," Lynn surveyed the colorful presentation with her hands on her lap.

"Would you like to order something else?" Peter offered. The meal did look like something that would be served off the Kiddie menu. Marianne Collins had developed a knack over fifteen years of marriage for returning dinners—sometimes even making a mockery of it. Refusing attempts to salvage a fare to see if the cost would be deducted from the bill—particularly if she had her fill from soup and salad appetizers. Peter instinctively raised his hand. "Waitress, I believe there is a problem with the lady's meal."

"I would never do that," Lynn read Peter's mind and shuddered. She brushed her hand at the returning waitress. "No, this will be okay." She stabbed a noodle with her dinner fork and chewed.

"Are you sure?" Peter hesitated. He felt somewhat perplexed. Is it a Midwestern custom to accept your dinner as is? Or am I so naive that I would mistakenly assume Lynn would do something just because I am used to seeing someone like Marianne? He watched as Lynn made the best of her mouthful.

"Maybe I could try a piece of your veal though," Lynn winked—only after being convinced the waitress was out of sight.

Lynn admitted her choice tasted a lot better than it looked. While bites were shared from each other's plate, Lynn managed to devour a good portion of the colored macaroni.

"Back when I was a teenager," Peter watched the repetitive motion of his companion's utensil, "I got my driver's license and there was this classmate I was dying to ask out on a date. She reluctantly accepted. I was so excited about actually driving to her house to pick her up and take her to a movie. We went to one of those franchise restaurants first to get a bite to eat. The waitress asked for our order and my date says 'You go first'. So I order this big dinner. Then she says 'I do not want anything. I am not hungry.' I do not know if she was concerned about messing up her lipstick or what, but she was content to sit there while I ate by myself. I felt like such a dork—everyone looking at us while I ate and she sat there. Bottom line? She did not feel comfortable with the prospect of eating food and running the risk of making a mess with someone she really did not want to be with. Talk about nature's birth control. It did not matter how attractive a person can be on the outside. What was going on inside made it our only date."

The waitress returned to the portable ice bucket and refilled Peter's glass. Beyond the original toast, Lynn had not touched her wine. Her glass and the bottle still had about four fingers.

"Peter—let's get out of here. Right now." Lynn dropped her napkin next to her plate. Peter looked at his full glass of wine. She wanted to leave right now?

"Dessert or coffee?" The waitress stammered as she fumbled the wine bottle back into the ice container.

"We are all set," Lynn determined. "And no, we do not want to have anything wrapped to go."

Lynn leaned over to Peter and whispered.

"It is eight-thirty. I am not spending my last night talking about memories of our past. I want to make our own memories in the present."

The gentlemen at the next table were startled by the sudden upheaval of dining chairs. Lynn headed for the exit as if a fire alarm sounded. The waitress skidded out of sight, obviously in search of a check to settle. Peter dropped a hundred dollar bill on the table. As he traced Lynn's footsteps, the waitress appeared out of a corner. Peter glimpsed at the tabulated sum and realized the money he left was way too much.

"Sorry, we have to run," Peter quickened his pace. "Keep what is on the table—and tip the bar manager for me, too."

XXX

Emotions in conflict… moments of truth that encapsulate a lifetime. Forks in the road—which can forever shape the outcome of a future.

Peter drove the GMC Suburban back to Edgewater in less than five minutes. Stars illuminated the night sky. The occupants of the vehicle ran to the haven of Room 1020 like tormented victims of a blinding windstorm.

Lynn by now had adopted the second key card as her own. She tugged the magnetized strip from her pocketbook and opened the outside door to the room. A gust of reality swept across her body as she crossed over the threshold.

Peter stopped at the doorjamb and watched as Lynn purveyed the darkened room. She did not remove her pocketbook from her shoulder. She ambled between the two queen-sized beds and stared at the neon numerals on the clock radio.

"Almost nine o'clock," Peter announced. Lynn sat on the bed and folded her hands. She watched the digits change to 8:42."

"Peter," Lynn's eyes did not leave the clock. "I think I better be going."

"The bars are open till one," Peter stepped to the foot of the bed. He resisted the urge to sit. It would be too confrontational.

"That excuse flies during the weekend," Lynn closed her eyes. "But it is Sunday night. We have been together past midnight each of the last three nights. Marshall has been pretty tolerant to this point with the notion of our propensity to bar hop. He is sitting there at the house right now waiting for me to come home. Maybe it would be good if I surprised him with an early night."

Peter drew a deep breath.

"The mad exit from the restaurant led me to believe you wanted to get back here to be alone," Peter said. He sat next to Lynn on the bed.

"I did," Lynn admitted. "I wanted to make love with you."

"But…," Peter prodded.

"But we can't," Lynn resolved. "I cannot do that again to Marshall. If he asks me whether we had sex, I am going to have to tell him. One isolated lapse in judgement is one thing. Telling him it happened more than once is quite another."

"Telling him it happened more than once means that it was not a lapse in judgement," Peter stated. "It would mean we made our own premeditated decision to be together. It would mean a choice to leave our spouses because we know being together in this lifetime is the right thing to do."

"Marshall needs me," Lynn frowned. "Remember you once said the reason you loved me so much was because of the conversations we share? Marshall has said the same thing to me too. I am not saying I am more educated, but he says I am. He looks to me constantly for guidance and support."

"Everyone looks to me for guidance and support," Lynn threw her hands in frustration. "I wish everybody would leave me alone."

Peter sat silently as Lynn stood up and paced between the beds.

"For all I know you came out here purely in conquest of a good time," Lynn touched her fingernail tip to the Superior Shores postcard on the mirror. "Could I get in the pants of the girl who denied me at the Brigadier Home Sales School? I am in my forties now. My life is boring and I wonder if a twenty-nine year old could still get hot for me?"

"Well, congratulations," Lynn turned. "You did it! You can go back to Worcester, Massachusetts and keep this little secret to yourself. You can get out your old Brigadier Conference Center class photo and etch a little notch on the frame. You can stand around your office and one day point me out to all of your business partners and boast 'See that one? I got her!'"

"Is that what you think?" Peter whispered.

"I wonder?" Lynn scolded. "I wonder if you are honest enough with yourself. If you feel for me the way you say you do, you would come right out and tell your wife what has happened between us."

"I intend to," Peter sighed. "I want to be with you."

"If that is indeed the case, then making love right now is not going to make much of a difference, is it?" Lynn crossed her arms and leaned against the desktop. "You will be gone tomorrow, and I will still be here—with my life upside down."

Peter stood and opened his arms. He stepped forward.

"Please, don't touch me, Peter," Lynn hoisted the strap of the pocketbook like a chest protector. "I do not even want a goodbye kiss. I will be back in the morning to pick you up for the airport. Nothing will be different then, either."

Peter remained standing in the empty chamber. The second key card laid on the nightstand behind him. The clock radio flashed 9:02. He pressed the button next to him on the television.

"Welcome to Duluth," the voice canned on the screen. "And thank you for choosing Best Western Edgewater. We hope you enjoy your stay."

XXXI

To the naked eye, it was a solitary speck in the skyline near the Aerial Lift Bridge. The wings took shape as the speck ascended north. Their bodies formed in the air. It was a pair of black ducks—flying together along the banks of Lake Superior. The male duck flew a few feet above its mate, sheering the breeze for gentle passage.

It was six o'clock in the morning. Peter watched as the birds continued their journey across the rising sun. A corona of gold formed around the boundaries of their frames. Within moments, brightness blinded the view. Peter flicked his cigarette stub onto the rock embankment between Room 1020 and the lake.

Six hours until departure. Perhaps Lynn had reconsidered their relationship after a good night's sleep. Peter returned to the room and flopped to the floor. He did twenty-five pushups—pleading for the muscles in his upper torso to awaken. These final hours were not going to pass without making one last ditch effort to make love. Was this a conquest, Peter conjectured? He heaved through a second set. Was this my ego resisting Lynn's siren for honesty? Why was it so God-damned important for his peace of mind that Lynn assented to making love again—that very morning—before he left? Why was that cement needed so badly?

"Welcome to Duluth," the screen companion greeted. "And thank you for choosing Best Western Edgewater. We hope you enjoy your stay."

"Damn right I will!" Peter shouted. He marched into the bathroom to shower.

The first hint of idiocy crept in about three hours later. Peter analyzed how ridiculous he looked in the mirror—showered, shaved, and poised topless with nothing on but pajama bottoms. When was the last time he did two hundred pushups, he wondered. His arms ached. Where was Lynn?

The commerce of a new workweek was in full swing. Trucks and semi-trailers zipped along the expressway fronting the hotel. An air horn blasted in mockery at the topless man standing barefoot on the concrete slab outside Room 1020.

Peter went back into his assigned quarters and hunted down the Yellow Page Business Directory. Peter selected the largest landscaping firm advertisement in the book. Besides, the company's family name had a "Mc" in it with an Irish shamrock corporate logo.

"My bank will be contacting you within the hour," Peter told the party on the other end of the line. "I would like to wire transfer five thousand dollars for you to put in a stone walk, lamppost and shrubbery in front of a friend of mine's house here in Duluth. I will touch base in case the cost runs higher. Let them pick whatever they want."

The order was taken like it happened all the time. Another hour passed. Lynn was still not there. Peter jettisoned the pajama look. He dressed and packed his luggage. The bags were neatly placed in the closet next to the bathroom. Their owner sat alone—outside of the room.

It was after ten-thirty when Lynn appeared from the back corner of the parking lot. She had on her professional blue high-buttoned conservative business dress. Matching tights covered her legs.

"Bought you some breakfast," Lynn held up a small paper bag in front of her. "Couldn't eat it alone at my desk."

"Your desk?"

"I went into the office early this morning," Lynn battled the temptation to look directly at Peter. "I knew my work would be piled up after taking Friday off."

"I was hoping you would have come by here," Peter contained his whine.

"Figured you did," Lynn concentrated her focus on pulling a carton of orange juice from the bag. "I got up this morning. You know—the same Monday morning routine? We all got dressed to start our day, and I drove Maggie to daycare. I was just about to make the turn to come here. And Marshall passed me while I was sitting at the intersection. He was on his way to work. He tooted and waved like nothing happened over these past four days. I turned to the office instead."

"I have a gift for you," Peter handed the landscaper's name and number on hotel stationary to Lynn. "I made arrangements to have the front of your house finished the way you want. All you have to do is call them."

Lynn's shoulders dropped.

"You do not get it, do you?" Lynn refused to accept the paper. "Marshall would be so insulted. Call them back right now and cancel."

"Lynn, I want to do this—for you."

"Well I don't want it," Lynn walked past the outdoor patio table into the room to mix the coffee.

"I haven't called my bank yet," Peter backpedaled. "Nothing happens if the bank does not call them."

"Good."

Peter sat bent over in the plastic strapped lounge chair. He stared at the slab ground of concrete. Lynn cast a sidelong glance from the room to see the hurt of rejection.

"It is a sweet gesture," Lynn came out and rubbed the back of Peter's shoulders. "The time is not right."

"Seems the time is never right," Peter did not look up.

"You never know," Lynn circled the deck to the accompanying lounge chair. She pulled a foil package of chocolate-frosted breakfast tarts from the bag.

"I will be interested to see where we are in ninety days," Lynn tore at the ribbed perforation atop the foil. Her lips pursed to accent her conviction. "I predict one of two things are going to happen. Odds are fifty-fifty either way with nothing in the middle. Either we are going to be together—and I mean together as mates within the next ninety days, or we will be totally out of communication with each other forever."

"Pretty bold ultimatum," Peter studied the matter-of-factness on Lynn's face. "Sounds like you are still challenging whether I have been playing a game of conquest in coming here."

"I am not challenging anything," Lynn broke a square of the tart and offered it to Peter. It was the first time all day that she attempted to look at his face. She laid the square on the table when he refused to notice. "Remember you asked me the probability of our making love, and I said zero percent? That anything outside of that would change everything? Well, it has Peter. We cannot go back to the way we were. Playing Dot games and sending cutesy little cards to each other. Too much water has passed over the dam. We cannot maintain this type of lovers' relationship while being married to others."

Peter picked up the morsel on the table and broke off a tiny corner. He chewed it in his mouth, but could not swallow. A solitary duck flew across the lakefront. It flapped alone.

"Don't you wish you were a duck?" Lynn said quietly sitting back. The food became stuck in Peter's throat.

"This morning there were two—," Peter began to say. His emotions erupted. Tears welled from his eyes. He ran to the bathroom and took refuge against the door.

It was over. Whatever fate had collided in the path of these two lives had ended. The mystery of the past seven years doomed to the lasting memory of love lost. Peter thought of the stories he had heard of people recalling an elderly relative's babble while lying on a deathbed. Calling out the name of a love one that no one recognized. "Must have lost their marbles," the people would retell. A young one would be scolded at bedside for blurting an insensitive question like "Gee, did Grandpa love someone else other than Grandma?" Peter pressed his tear ducts to halt the stream down his cheeks.

"Are you going to live?" Lynn came into the bathroom. She placed her hand on Peter's back.

"No," Peter cried. Lynn laughed quietly.

"That is what I say every time Maggie starts to cry," Lynn quietly whispered while rubbing his back. "Are you going to live? You answered the same way she does. She always cries, 'No'."

Lynn guided Peter back into the bedroom. They sat and hugged on the bed. Peter's tears soaked the blue polyester shoulder.

"I love you, Peter," Lynn whispered. "More than you know. I do want you to take me. I want us to be together for the rest of our lives, but I am scared. I am scared that there will be a day when I will not be everything to you. I am scared that someday there will be a day you get mad at me and say I ruined your life—that you left your wife and your children and your career. I would not be able to live with myself if that ever happened. I should be of no bearing to what you decide to tell your wife—or even if you stay with her. You do what you have to do and I will do what I have to do. If we are truly destined to be together in this lifetime, then we will. I just do not want me right now under these circumstances to be the sole reason you decide to make a life change. And the same goes for you with me. Your decisions must be made in spite of me, not because of me."

"My Spirit Guide came to me Saturday night while I was asleep," Peter rubbed his eyes. "It never happened before, but I knew it was her. She told me two times. 'Do not be afraid'. And you know what? I am not. I am not going to be afraid. Neither of us should be. We will do the right thing. I just do not think you are giving my love for you enough credit when you knock it into a ninety day window."

"I do, Peter," Lynn smiled. I do know how much you love me, but I really do not think there will be anything in between. And I want you to know if it does not end up being option number one and you decide to stay put and not talk to me again? It will be okay. Nothing will ever take away the feelings we share for each other."

The stoicism of Lynn's external courage was ripping her apart inside. She walked across the room and sat at the round writing table next to the window. One more hour, she resolved in her mind. She could get through this.

"No wonder I cannot see," Peter exclaimed extracting a contact lens dangling from his eyelash. "You got me so upset my contacts popped right out of my head."

Peter hurried to salvage the dried chip at the bathroom sink.

"I know I have a spare set somewhere in my toiletry bag," Peter composed himself. "I better hustle though. It is already eleven-fifteen."

"Duluth Airport is not like Boston," Lynn leveled. "I guarantee there will be no line at the check in counter. I can get you there in five minutes."

Lynn raised her feet onto the opposite chair. Peter blinked his way over to the table and lifted Lynn's legs so that he could sit down. He lowered her feet onto his lap.

"My goodness Lynn," Peter pulled a shoe off of her foot. "Whose shoes are these?"

"They are mine."

"Your feet are swimming inside these things," Peter tugged off the second shoe. "They have to be at least two sizes too big."

Peter began to massage Lynn's feet. The red glossed toenails that played the day before with Peter on the beach tried to eke through the synthetic prison of blue nylon. Lynn ignored its plea. Her gaze zeroed in on Peter.

"I gained sixty pounds when I had Maggie," Lynn mused. "You never knew that reading the Dot Game, did you? I got up to a hundred and eighty nine pounds. My feet swelled so bad that none of my shoes fit. I got so depressed about my girth—I was convinced I would never get back my regular weight. So I threw away all of my old dress shoes and bought all new larger ones."

"Now, I have to be mindful when I walk," Lynn laughed. "If I am not careful, I will step right out of them."

"Lynn, that was more than two years ago," Peter bewildered. "You have not bought a new pair of dress shoes since?"

Lynn shrugged her shoulders.

"What can I tell you?"

XXXII

Lynn took nothing but side roads to the airport. Other than putting her foot on the accelerator to venture onto a new street, the Suburban rolled well below allowable speeds. Not that any were posted on trails such as these to begin with. The companionship would be over in minutes. Both looked blankly beyond the windshield. The grip of their hands atop the middle console was so tight that their knuckles were white—and bloodless.

"I could have sworn there was a house on this street with pillars," Lynn scanned each side of the Suburban. "Help me, Peter. See if you can find the house we can picture ourselves living in."

"That contemporary on the left is nice," Peter settled for Lynn's side of the truck. "I insure that house," Lynn followed Peter's pointed finger. "I took pictures of it inside and out. It has no pillars."

"You really want pillars, huh?"

"Listen, Buster," a tear appeared in Lynn's eye. "If we are going to go through what I think we are, you better believe I am going to settle for nothing less than pillars and two carats."

"Wait a minute," Peter played. "You never said anything about two carats."

"Save the money you were going to put on the front walk," Lynn chuckled. "I want a ring instead."

"I was meaning to mention," Peter regarded the hand on the steering wheel. "That is a pretty big rock you have on now."

"It is a full carat," Lynn informed without bothering to look. "When Marshall first hinted about marrying him, I said 'prove you are serious and buy me a carat!' Figured for sure it would make him go away. Damn if he did not call my bluff."

"Pillars and carats," Peter squeezed Lynn's hand even tighter. "If it is true about 'women scorned', I may be flat broke coming back to you."

"Don't try crying poor mouth to me, Peter Collins," Lynn demanded. "That is for the Million Dollar Man to figure out."

"Hold on," Peter countered. "You have not told me what you will be bringing to the table. What kind of dowry can I expect?"

"I decided I am leaving Marshall everything—including these shoes,"

Lynn reported. Peter could tell she had given the idea some thought. "All I will have is the six thousand dollar balance in my 401K."

"You have been working for almost ten years and all you have is six thousand dollars in a 401K?"

"Hey! I worked awfully hard to save that amount."

The side entrance to the airport surfaced along the flank of the road. Peter and Lynn noticed the freight hangars through the tree line at the same time. It ended the playful banter.

"Peter," Lynn gasped. She hardened the squeeze against the knuckles. "I promised myself this morning not to go into the terminal building with you. Please do me a favor? Let me stay in the truck."

The Suburban rolled beyond the designated parking areas and commandeered the entrance ramp to the main entrance. Lynn's prediction was accurate. Monday noon was not a heavy flight time at the Duluth Airport.

"There," Lynn stated like a schoolgirl completing a novice piano piece. She braked the vehicle abruptly and positioned both of her hands at ten minutes until two on the Suburban's steering wheel. Peter took a moment to look, but Lynn would have none of it. She balked at the notion of moving her eyes.

Peter exited the vehicle. He opened the back hatch of the Suburban. He pulled out his two bags and slammed the door closed. He proceeded to walk to the driver's side window. The pane slid open a crack only after a tap on the glass with his wedding band.

"Bye," Lynn chirped.

"Kiss me," Peter ordered.

"No."

"I said 'Kiss me'."

Lynn closed her eyes for the briefest of seconds. She leaned outside of the window. Peter planted the lightest of pecks on her lips.

"See you soon," Peter winked. He picked up his bags to leave. Lynn felt obliged, for once, to get in the last word.

"Let that kiss last forever."

XXXIII

Peter could care less whether or not he missed his plane. As soon as he crossed through the metal framed doorway, he knew the tinted glass made his figure invisible. He watched the truck negotiate the perimeter of the parking lot. What looked like such a behemoth vehicle moments ago now seemed miniature in the distance.

Please do not leave Lynn, Peter could feel his lips mouth. The truck continued to roll. Change your mind and come back to me. It is not supposed to end this way.

The grade near the exit of the lot caused Peter to lose sight of Lynn. He sprinted to the check out counter.

"Electronic ticket—Peter Collins," he blurted—quickly flashing his driver's license. The computer printed a boarding pass within seconds.

Peter scaled the moving escalator steps an extra two-at-a-time. He ran to the mezzanine to re-scope the parking lot.

The GMC Suburban was nowhere to be seen. Could she have changed her mind? Perhaps she hooked into short-term parking. Which side of the lot was that anyway?

The intercom bellowed.

"American Eagle Flight 307 to Chicago with connecting flights now boarding at Gate A."

Peter meandered to the gate area.

"Let me know when you are about to close the doors," he asked the attendant at the skycap. "I am waiting for someone."

Peter positioned himself at the beam-anchored chairs and prayed. Please Lynn, please—please appear from that escalator. A middle-aged couple rose from the belted stairway. A twenty-something daughter on crutches accompanied them. They slowly made their way to the gate. The daughter kissed her mother courteously goodbye. She grasped her father and held him tight. It seemed an inordinate amount of time.

"Sir, you are the last ticketed passenger to board," the attendant announced. The revelation shook Peter from his concentration on the escalator. The daughter on crutches must have got on the plane quicker than expected. Peter glimpsed to the escalator one last time. No Lynn. He staggered onto the plane.

The last remaining window seat was reserved next to the daughter on crutches. Peter was relieved that she did not appear talkative. She had tears mounted on her eyes, too.

Rain began to spit on the outside window. Peter felt as if he were in a hazed trance as the commuter transport backed away from the terminal. Remember what you see, Peter commanded his mind. The thought of the dying elder shouting the name of someone unknown enveloped his conscience. Do not forget what happened here these last four days.

The jet scaled above the tree line. My God—Peter's heart leapt—there is Lynn's house! He recalled the air route to Chicago. We must have passed over it on Thursday too, but I never knew it. He searched, but he could not make out any sign of the Suburban. Where is my diamond, Peter implored? He craned his neck to see more. Where is my diamond in the rough?

The jet sailed higher and faster into the air. Duluth Harbor was in full view—the Aerial Lift Bridge—and the beach. Lynn, I cannot do this, Peter touched his fingers on the fuselage window. I have to come back to you.

Sight of the ground was lost across the shores of Wisconsin. Storm clouds would camouflage the landscape until O'Hare.

"Lynn," Peter wailed. He pulled a handkerchief from his pocket.

The daughter on crutches ceased her crying. The fellow next to her was hurting a lot more.

BOOK IV

The quest of mankind—to transcend to be more—in the likeness of His own image. The lesson to be selfless—to vanquish ego over soul—the purpose to creation.

The lessons learned in prior trials sculpt the earthen canvas. The ability to shun the animalistic appetites of human nature—violence, envy, greed, and selfishness. The most basic of vices are curbed in early carnations—so long as souls are open to learn.

Selflessness is the most magnanimous of virtues—to forsake personal envy for the benefit of others. It is the intangible key to realize the glory of the realm—to enter the inner sanctum within the kingdom's Pillars.

I

There were no breaking news reports of a plane crash, so Lynn figured Peter must have made it home safely.

The final separation actually did not wax that melodramatic.

Peter's first email arrived the next morning.

"I am here. Duked the limo driver an extra twenty to get me to the Little League field before my son's game ended. Made it in time to see him make a diving catch at short in the last inning. He ran up to me afterward asking whether I saw him 'go horizontal'? The kid has great drive. No matter what happens, I know he will be all right."

Lynn chose not to reply to the electronic message. Acknowledgement signified a willingness to return to the old status quo. Peter had to come to terms with matters at home. The last thing Lynn wanted to do was fall back into a flirtatious relationship on the Internet.

Lynn left the office to pick up Maggie and get home early that second night—specifically to make dinner. It had been awhile since Marshall had come home from work to a home-cooked meal. Meatloaf and mashed potatoes seemed an appropriate cuisine to settle things back to a normal fare. Besides, the springtime weather remained balmy in Duluth.

"How about we take Maggie for a walk in her stroller?" Lynn brainstormed as she cleared the table. She yearned for a return to some semblance of order. "I can finish up these dishes after the sun goes down."

A few neighbors were puttering around their yards as the Monroes walked along the roadside. Piles of sand, munitions of attack on long-forgotten storms of the winter were heaped uniformly in front of driveways for the city sweepers. A new season was dawning.

Marshall and Lynn knew the names of most everyone who lived on the street. It was disconcerting though—walking now through the neighborhood. Heretofore, the Monroes had preferred to keep to themselves. Privacy in the past was in large part due to Lynn's philosophy not to get too chummy with her neighbors lest they become obliged at some point to deem it prudent for her to solicit their insurance. Nothing, she maintained, generated bad blood like a dissatisfied insurance claimant. The aura on the street was now even odder. The neighbors appeared stranger—more alien—or perhaps the paranoia oozed from within.

At the end of the road lived the Wilson's. Evoking a Norman Rockwell image, husband and wife were outside—rocking their daughter Maggie's age in her backyard swing. A vision of the Wilson's annual family photo Christmas card popped into Lynn's mind. Insurance was too hectic around the holidays to send picture cards, Lynn grappled in her mind. Why does everyone on this road feel like they have to send us one?

"Let's turn around," Lynn countered any chance of a happenstance meeting with the Wilson's. The threesome casually rotated their pivot on the pavement. A move they had mastered from habitual practice.

"Marshall! Lynn!" the familiar voice called from a side yard. It was Alice Perkins, the resident matriarch who made it her business to know everyone else's. "Is that little Margaret you have hiding in there?"

Marshall and Lynn froze in their steps. It was as if Alice Perkins could emit a force field to snare unsuspecting gossip. Marshall pulled back the sun cover shading the top of the stroller.

"Maggie, can you say 'hello' to Mrs. Perkins," Marshall prodded. Alice Perkins noticed the Monroes had found greetings easier when they asked their daughter to say hello first.

"My goodness have you grown," the older woman cooed rather than wait for any guttural recognition from parent or child. She bent down to touch Maggie's hand. "You were such a tiny little peanut last fall. Look at what a big girl you are!"

Mrs. Perkins rose to her feet. She propped her fists on her hips to admire the young family.

"Marshall, I have been keeping my eye on you," the matriarch wagged her forefinger. "Breaking your back working around that house. How is your front walk coming?"

"Just fine," Marshall reported. He knew Mrs. Perkins was more interested in knowing how long the pile of rubble that disgraced the view from her bay window was going to be there. He chose his words carefully—knowing they would be repeated later at each mailbox on the street. "I am shooting to have it done by Memorial Day."

"And Lynn, how are you my dear?" Alice Perkins nodded and shifted her inquisition. It was obvious Marshall's timeline for completing the walk was adequate. "You look so thin. Have you been feeling well?"

"Lynn has had a bout of Meniere's Disease," Marshall aimed to shield any barrage.

"Meniere's Disease? That sounds serious," Mrs. Perkins furrowed her brow—more to make sure she memorized the name of the ailment for future gossiping. "Have you had to be confined?"

"It is an inner ear imbalance that causes some dizziness," Lynn decided to speak for herself. "It can be treated with medication. I am feeling much better now. You probably have not seen much of me because I am normally at the office early mornings during the winter before it gets light. And it is usually dark by the time I get home."

"Well, it is a pleasure seeing you walk as a family on such a nice night," Mrs. Perkins observed. "How many years has it been since you moved into the house?"

"Right after we got married," Marshall replied. "Coming up on five years."

"Five years," the matriarch repeated. "You know, I have worried about how the three of you have been making out. Never home, and when you are, so busy with projects around the house. You never seem to have time to enjoy each other's company as a family."

Marshall and Lynn looked awkwardly at one another.

"It is important that you make time like tonight to enjoy the quieter moments," the street sage counseled. "Do you think you have ever really had the opportunity to develop as a husband and as a wife?"

"Who knows how much longer we even want to stick around as a husband and as a wife," Marshall stated flatly. "We may come to figure quieter moments are best enjoyed without each other's company."

Alice Perkins eyed widened in shock. The revelation prompted Lynn to let out what sounded like more of a snort than a laugh.

"Marshall," Lynn's teeth filled her grin. "Thank you so much for admitting how you feel."

Mrs. Perkins' mouth gaped to match her bewildered gaze. The woman almost lost her balance when Marshall began to push the carriage away, saying "Your welcome."

The Monroes made sure they were in the full security of their split-level house before rolling in laughter.

"Did you see the face on her when we hinted about divorce," Lynn closed the slats of the front blinds. "I bet you would get a busy signal from every telephone on this street if you tried calling right now."

Marshall deadened his laugh.

"I was not kidding," Marshall admitted. "I wonder if it might be better if we were apart."

II

Avoiding Marshall's overtures to make love would be impossible. The exercise was an absolute—a necessity to dispel the conjecture of Mrs. Alice Perkins.

The inevitable prevailed as soon as Lynn entered the bedroom. Marshall was already under the covers. The television set was off. His pair of briefs laid in a clump on the floor next to his side of the bed.

Lynn pretended to ignore the pair of underwear. She opened her chest of drawers and pulled out a pair of pajamas.

"Don't bother," Marshall levied before Lynn performed her nightly disappearing act into the bathroom to change. She stopped and stood motionless at the foot of the bed. The flannels hung limp in her arms.

"Strip for me," Marshall commanded. Lynn stood dumbfounded. Marshall had never been so bold. She was unable to move a muscle.

"What's the matter?" Marshall folded his hands behind his head. "Is there something wrong with a man asking his wife to strip for him?"

Lynn tossed the pajamas onto the corner chair. She unbuttoned her favorite pair of jeans—faded denims borrowed years ago from her brother Luke. A hole worn in the butt was her personal signature, next to the designer trademark.

The laundry beaten pants fell to the floor. Lynn stepped out of the heap. Without a word, she unzipped the back of her turtleneck. The blouse was heaved above her head—mussing up Lynn's hairdo in the process. Lynn stood meekly in her panties and bra.

"Four days of partying seems to have sapped your energy," Marshall stared at his wife's face.

"I do not feel comfortable doing this," Lynn fumbled her hands on her back trying to unhooked the clasp on her brassiere.

"Probably because you have been so strapped in this past week with your tits harnessed up the whole time while you were with your friend," Marshall smirked. "You must be pretty horny by now—what, with hanging around nightclubs and not having your hubby to do you at the end of the night."

"I do not think you are funny," Lynn turned off the overhead light. She tiptoed to her side of the bed and removed her panties. The covers were held extra high in the air to block Marshall's view as she slithering butt first onto the mattress.

Marshall grabbed the comforter with his right hand before it could fall again onto their bodies. He threw the quilted down to the back end of the bed.

"Marshall, what are you do—," Lynn tried to protest, but to no avail. In a split second her husband straddled on top of her. The tip of his manhood rock hard—slapping against her thigh as he took position.

Marshall had always been a sweet lover—content more with foreplay than the actual deed. Lovemaking occurred most often during episodes of "E.R." when there was an unlikely lull in the blast of background sirens and alarms—usually once every three or four weeks.

Marshall had never been so incensed. With the thrust of a hound dog, he drove himself as hard as he could into the dry love canal. The recipient winced. Lynn looked up to regard the man satisfied to hump with his arms in a push-up stance. His upper lip was puffed. He stared at the headboard while he accelerated the velocity of his violation.

Lynn rolled her face to the side of her pillow. This cannot be happening to me she shuddered. She clenched her right fist tight—remembering Peter's hand on the way to the airport. *Peter*! Lynn called out in her conscience. *Pretend it is Peter.*

The springs of the mattress squeaked a rhythmic whine. Visions of disco dancing at Park Point on Saturday night swelled in Lynn's head. She could hear the songs from the side door speakers of the Accord. *I am dancing with you, Peter*. Lynn recited in this nightmare of a trance. *You are with me right now and we are dancing.*

Marshall exhaled a loud grunt. He tightening his buttocks in place as his seed exhumed its body. Lynn opened her eyes. Beads of sweat dotted her husband's forehead. He never looked so intrusive.

"Get off of me," Lynn pushed the spent dampness of flesh to the other side of the bed. Tears began gushing from her eyes. "I cannot believe you just did that."

Lynn tried to extend her leg off of the bed. Her crotch ached in pain. She closed her knees in order to roll helplessly off of the mattress. She stumbled bow-legged into the bathroom. Her stomach ached.

She began ripping shards of toilet paper indiscriminately from the dispenser roll. Large swaths of tissue piled atop the toilet water as Lynn swiped at her insides to extract the mess. Incessant sobs blinded her ambition.

"What are you doing?" Marshall stepped into the bathroom. The silhouette cast from the bedroom lamp revealed his underwear back on.

"Leave me alone," Lynn screamed swinging her foot off of the toilet seat. She ran naked out of the side door of the bathroom into the darkened hallway. Maggie had begun to cry in her bedroom. Lynn ran away from the commotion—seeking refuge at the farthest end of the house.

Marshall stormed down the hallway flicking on every wall light switch he passed. The fixture over the dining room table was blinding as he discovered his wife cowering in the corner.

"You had sex with him, didn't you," Lynn's husband barked. "Tell me! Tell me right now! Did you have sex with that bastard?"

"Yes!" Lynn shouted, swabbing at her cheeks. "Yes, I did."

III

Peter heard nothing from his soul-mate. It had been almost a week.

He was tempted to call her on the telephone, but thought better of it. If she was unwilling to reply to the most innocuous of emails, what would be accomplished with a phone call? Talking comfortably—like in the old days—would be out of the question.

Peter knew why Lynn was avoiding him. She was headstrong. He had to come to terms with the actions of his visit. If he could not be honest with himself and come out in the open about his feelings to his wife, then there was nary a need to continue any sort of long-distance relationship.

The mystery of the Minnesota business trip mushroomed within a day of Peter's return. Why was it that Peter could not bring his spouse? It was never the case before—particularly if a trip extended over a weekend. Marianne was prepared to delve deeper into the aberration, but there was a more pressing issue of concern. Peter had once again taken up smoking.

"One of those things with this nasty habit," Peter excused the sudden self-anointed liberty of lighting up in the house. "I was dumb enough to put one in my mouth while I was out in Minny because it looked so appealing seeing the person I was with smoking."

Marianne was too disgusted to bother asking any more questions.

Peter got up the nerve to confess his actual whereabouts to his wife the following Sunday night. He knew she would be upstairs—probably watching TV in bed. She probably assumed he was downstairs—performing his nightly scotch-sipping ritual.

The lights and television were off, however, when Peter entered the master bedroom. He undressed and adroitly slipped into bed without making a ruckus.

"Marianne—are you awake?"

"Uh-huh," Marianne exhaled. After close to twenty years of marriage, turning from her backside to face her husband was not a requirement.

"Marianne, there is something I have to tell you," Peter conveyed to the motionless hump. "It is about Minnesota. It's been bothering me ever since I got back."

"What?" The sound came from the other side of the hump.

"You know how you kept wondering how I could not get a flight home if a business meeting was over on a Saturday?" Peter fought to find the right words. "Well, you were right. The trip was not business."

"I did not think so."

"You didn't?" Peter stared at the shadow cast on the ceiling. "Then why didn't you say something more about it?"

"Because I had a pretty good hunch on what you were up to."

"You did?" Peter breathed a sigh of relief. Perhaps it would be better for it to come out this way, Peter decided. Marianne could be the one to say it. She knew about his secret relationship for years. "What do you think I was doing?"

"Putting a contract out on somebody."

"What?" Peter sprang up to a sitting position on the bed. "You mean a contract, like on someone's life?"

"Uh-huh," Marianne admitted. Her head had not moved a smidgen.

"Why in God's name would you think for a minute that I would leave town to have a contract put out on somebody's life?"

"I know how upset you were in January when that client from the country club fired you with a Broker of Record letter to another insurance agent. When you called him a 'no good sonovabitch' in front of the crowd of people," Marianne recalled. "I saw the fire in your eyes when you told me he called the Insurance Commissioner's office and your agency President to complain. I said to myself right there and then. Knowing my husband, pal—you are a dead man."

Peter had to squeeze his eyes to remember the episode from six months earlier. Sure, the guy happened to be a pain in my side at the time, but what was the use of dealing with a scumbag? Better to move on. There were plenty of more scrupulous people to do business. Besides, the turkey's account did not amount to that much money to give it a second thought.

"I think you have been watching too many Mafia shows on TV," Peter resumed his stare to the ceiling. "The reason for my trip was nothing of the sort."

"Then where did you go?"

"Oh, I was in Minnesota," Peter found a second wind. "It was not business though."

"Oh?"

"I went to visit a friend, Marianne. Someone in the insurance field who I first met seven years ago when I went to the Brigadier Insurance School in Hartford, Connecticut. We have kept in touch ever since." Peter paused to remind himself to take a breath. "I spent the time visiting with her in Duluth."

The confession hung in the air. Peter searched for any kind of reaction.

"It was something I had to do. I wanted to see her again. It had been too long." Peter could feel the sudden urge to backpedal. His offensive was coming on too strong. Marianne's paralysis was too disconcerting. Any kind of motion or reaction would have been welcome. "It was a nice visit actually. I got to spend a day with her daughter... met her mother... even had dinner one night with her husband. It was nice—visiting with her family, and seeing where she lives."

There—I said it. Peter took solace in the moment. Lynn Monroe was not a fly on the wall. It was not exactly what Lynn would call complete and unconditional honesty, but at least there was no screaming and hollering.

"I got it off my chest," Peter announced to the pitch-black air. "I feel better now. I had to tell you."

The sound of a distant train lumbering on its track could be heard in the offing. Peter lay quietly on top of the mattress. The few minutes that passed seemed an eternity.

"So what's her name?" Marianne broke the eerie silence of the night.

"Lynn," Peter said.

"Lynn?" Marianne turned her head for the first time. She faced her husband's profile. "Lynn what?"

"Lynn Monroe."

"Lynn 'Munn-row'?" Marianne pronounced. "Yeah, right."

"It is," Peter was stunned by the sarcasm. "What? You don't believe me?"

"I know what you are up to, Peter Collins," Marianne replied.

"What—the contract?" Peter twisted his head. "You have got to be kidding me Marianne. I swear I was visiting Lynn Monroe in Duluth, Minnesota. Don't you want to talk about this?"

"Hardly," Marianne scoffed. She rolled over to return to her original position—her opposite cheek to the far end of her pillow.

"Well, I think this is something we should talk about," Peter mounted to his elbow.

"Sorry, I don't." Marianne tugged the bedcovers to her chin. "Goodnight, Peter."

IV

Another week had passed since Peter's prolific email admittance—"I told her". His reward came in the form of a cellophane wrapped cardboard cube. The office clerk could not contain that standard Cheshire cat grin whenever a delivery was postmarked Duluth, Minnesota.

Peter had to resort to a razor letter opener to slice the heavy seal. Inside the carton was a blank envelope without an address. It lay atop a pile of popcorn packing material. Peter opened the back fold of the envelope. It had not been licked closed. Connecting the loopy penmanship was like a hearing a favorite song.

Tuesday, May 8

Dear Peter,

I just read your message that you have told Marianne everything.

I have to say that I am feeling very relieved. I also have to confess that I told Marshall last week. I didn't know why I didn't want to tell you that—until now. I just didn't want you to tell her because I told Marshall.

I wanted to see if you would tell her on your own—and you did.

Any doubts I had about your intentions or character are gone.

Right now I know that I fell in love with a truly wonderful person.

Now… the next big subject. Where do we go from here?

What do we do with what we have received?

I truly want to thank you for giving me the best day of my life.

My time with you has given me a new starting point for

my life.

It has changed me forever. And wherever life takes me…

I'm not going to be afraid. I think you will understand, and agree, that we can't go back to the way we were. It's not right to carry on a relationship while we are working on our individual lives.

The enclosed gift is what I was buying while your plane was taking off at the Duluth airport. I have been holding on to it for the right time to send it. And I think that this is the right time.

Peter, if you ever get sad, tired, lonely, or afraid… just remember that your soul-mate is thinking of you and she loves you from afar.

Fly into the sunset, Peter—without a single regret or any guilt.

The one duck means that you need to do it alone.

Love Always,

Lynn

Do it alone, Peter read the last line a second time. What did she mean by that? Do it alone?

He stuffed his hand into the cardboard cube. The fake popcorn bounced out of its containment like a ravenous disobedient—spilling at random over the floor. His hand felt a hard animate object toward the bottom of the box. He extracted a ceramic duck— a "canard noir" actually—sitting like a decoy would on a serene body of water. It's side feathers were gilded in purple with a black tip centered on its orange beak.

Peter held the duck up in the air—surveying its dimensions. "Hand made in Canada by J.B. Garton" the red maple leaf sticker disclosed beneath the base. Peter placed the figurine next to his laptop computer.

"Do it alone," Peter repeated aloud. "How can she think such a thing?"

He picked up the telephone and punched the toll free number from memory.

"Lynn Monroe, please?" Peter asked to the voice at the other end of the line. He was transferred to Lynn's desk directly.

"This is Lynn," chimed the customary greeting. Peter melted hearing her voice.

"I love my duck. I hope you bought a matching one."

"Not telling," Lynn laughed.

"Lynn dear—I miss you so much," Peter exclaimed. "How is everything? Are you doing okay with Marshall?"

"I am doing."

"How about Maggie?" Peter continued. "Is Mag-pie doing okay?"

"As best as can be expected," Lynn refrained. "For about a week she kept asking me and Marshall—'Where is Peter? I want to see Peter. Is Peter coming?' I must say, Marshall's reaction was not too pleasant."

"How did he take it when you told him?"

"Like a caveman."

"A caveman?"

"Picture a caveman," Lynn sounded like a worn out schoolteacher. "How do you think a caveman would react after he found out another caveman had his woman?"

Peter frowned. The picture was not pleasant. He imagined a Neanderthal dragging his winch by the back of her hair—beating his club against the ground. He wished his ordeal with Marianne were as dire.

"How about you?" Lynn asked. "Was Marianne able to understand?"

Peter looked at the statue of the duck. It's eyes were mere dots of blank black paint. He felt guilty. No wonder Lynn had not been in touch with him.

"Lynn, there is something you have to know," Peter tossed a sheet of paper over the duck. "Telling Marianne was probably not as vivid as you may think."

Peter anticipated the pause on the other end of the line. He pressed his forefingers against his temple.

"Tell me," Lynn stated.

"I told her about you," Peter tried not to sound like a truant. "Who you are… where you live… and that I had to be with you."

"Yeah," Lynn prodded.

"Well, that is it," Peter lamented. "She does not want to hear another word about it. It is as if she is in complete denial. Have I actually told her we made love? Well, the answer is no. You know why? I cannot get that far into a conversation. She will physically remove herself from me anytime I begin to bring up you or the trip."

"You have to tell her," Lynn said. "For both of your sakes."

"Up to now, she will have no part of it," Peter accentuated. "Remember I told you about her girlfriend who refuses to leave an abusive relationship for fear of living in poverty? I swear she is determined to weather any infidelity in lieu of living below her usual standard."

Lynn cursed to herself.

"So what are you going to do?" Lynn asked. She noticed her fingers had crossed superstitiously.

"These last couple of weeks have given me the opportunity to reflect on a lot of things," Peter illumined. "There are some things that I have decided. I am not prepared to give up everything I have after what was just a four day weekend together. It is not fair to you, and selfishly it is not fair to me. Secondly, the only way we can be together in the short or medium term is if you come here. There is no way I can settle my affairs outside of Worcester. Lastly, I must see you again. You still have that ticket voucher from the Chicago trip last year. I suggest you consider coming out here for a few days before it expires in November. We can even go to Martha's Vineyard if you like, but one thing is certain. We have to see each other again, Lynn. I cannot make a permanent lifetime decision otherwise."

V

Likening the luxuries of manmade technology to happiness and content can be an anomaly.

Telephoning a remote place like Boulder, Colorado was a good example. One could get the sensation that the person reached could sound as nearby as the room next door.

Lynn realized this was far from the case, once she closed her office door to place the long distance call to her birth mother.

Normally conversations with Mary Ann Nelson were kept short. Today, Lynn did not care.

The "how-are-you's?" seemed canned. Yes, everyone was all looking forward to getting together for the Fourth, but Mary Ann could tell in an instant that something was wrong. Lynn referring to her as "Mom" was the first tip off. Lynn had made a habit in the past of calling her by her first name, Mary Ann..

"I was thinking I may want to come out to Boulder to see you for a few days," Lynn recited from her practice. "Do you think you and Dad would mind putting up with me?"

"You are always welcome, dear," Mary Ann cradled the receiver closer to her ear and sat down. "Richard had been traveling a lot lately, but I am sure we can check his schedule to make sure he is around. We would love to see you all."

"I was thinking about traveling alone," Lynn stuttered. "Maybe bringing Mag."

Mary Ann discreetly paused.

"Things are a little strained right now between me and Marshall," Lynn confided.

"What's the trouble?" Mary Ann asked.

"It is me," Lynn admitted. "I do not know if I want to stay in this marriage."

"You seemed content when you were both out here last year," Mary Ann proceeded diplomatically. "Has something happened to change that?"

"You could say that," Lynn paused. "There is another man in my life."

"Oh."

"It is so complicated," Lynn tried to reason. "I do not know how it happened, or where this is heading, but I need some time to get my head straight."

"How serious is this Lynn?" Mary Ann scrutinized.

"Pretty serious," Lynn admitted. "I told Marshall everything. He is beside himself. Last night his mother called the house just to say hello. As soon as he got on the phone he fell on his knees in the kitchen and began crying these big tearful sobs. I felt so helpless. He shouts out 'Lynn is cheating on me!' It was awful."

"Who is this person?" Mary Ann wondered. "Is it someone from work?"

"It is a friend I have kept in touch with for years," Lynn shielded her eyes. "He is not here in Duluth. He is married and lives in Boston. I do not know how it happened exactly, but we have grown incredibly close. Last month he came out to see me."

"Oh, my goodness gracious," Mary Ann tried to control her emotion. "Are you in love with this man?"

"Yes," Lynn sniffed. "He reminds me so much of Dad. He is extremely successful in business and just carries himself brimming with this flair of confidence in everything he does. And he loves me. It is like we were meant to be together."

"How old is he?"

"Forty-one."

"Oh."

"I wish you and Richard could meet him," Lynn stammered. "You would understand the anguish I am going through."

"Well, Richard is in San Diego," Mary Ann contained her shock—and anger. "I do not know how he will react to this news."

"Is there any way I can contact him?" Lynn pried. "I really would like to talk with him directly about this."

"Let me give you his cell phone number," Mary Ann hesitated. "He carries it with him all the time. Wait a bit before you try calling. I will need to give him a little heads-up beforehand."

Richard Nelson was a self-made man. He shook the humble surroundings of northern Minnesota shortly after Mary Ann and her parents decided to give Margaret up for adoption.

His first destination point was Panama Beach, Florida—hooking a job as a laborer for a landscaping company. A flamboyant personality, hard ethic for work, and an insatiable fire in the belly to achieve made Richard Nelson a popular figure amongst a customer base of residential retirees.

One such retiree was a fellow named Jack Wholley. Like Nelson, Wholley was an ex-hockey player who migrated from Minnesota to make his fortune in sales. In thirty years time, Wholley built a comfortable existence in the wire and cable business. He sold his distributorship to his son-in-law and moved to Florida.

By the time Wholley made Richard Nelson's acquaintance, the note payments from the son-in-law for the distributorship were six months in arrears. Blowing off a relative as a creditor was one thing. Blowing off the bank was another.

Richard Nelson was directing a landscape crew in front of Wholley's house the day the postman delivered the certified letter. The bank was calling in the son-in-law's loan for nonpayment. Wholley, as a personal guarantor to the loan, was also being notified that he was joint and severally liable. Regardless of liquidating values, Wholley was obligated to the bank one hundred cents on the dollar for the entire sum owed.

It was at that precise moment that Richard Nelson happened to be walking past.

"They say the second happiest day in a businessman's life is the day he sells his company," Wholley wrapped his arm around Richard Nelson's shoulder. "The happiest day is when you buy it back in default."

Richard Nelson was a quick study in wire and cable. Technical knowledge may have been important, but middle managers could be found to fill those roles—a "JAG", Wholley would call them—"Just another guy". Follow through on order commitments and knowing where to get answers to questions you know nothing about? That was what was paramount to success. Ultimately, Richard Nelson learned there is only one component that drives the engine of capital success—sales.

Susan joined Richard once he became settled in Wholley's company. They married and began to raise a family.

The national sales network in wire and cable was a small fraternity. Superstars got pirated from competitors just to garner a major account. Richard Nelson took advantage of the opportunities laid before him. In twenty years time, he leapfrogged to sales positions throughout the warmer states of the country.

Richard Nelson had made a practice of keeping his cell phone on his person despite the significance of certain business meetings. His first reaction in San Diego was to turn off the power after Mary Ann warned him to be on the lookout for Lynn's call. Rising above the hostility, Nelson properly excused himself to the outer sanctum of the manufacturing plant's conference room when the call did arrive.

"I understand you need to talk to me," Richard walked with his head down outside the front entrance door.

"Mary Ann was able to get a hold if you?"

"She told me everything."

"Richard, I don't know what to do," Lynn pleaded. I think I have found my true soul-mate in this lifetime."

"Soul-mate?" Richard balked. "Sounds to me like you have found a conniving dirty old man who better keep his filthy hands off of my daughter."

"Wha-," Lynn started.

"I am very disappointed in you, Lynn," Richard complained. "You are sacrificing not only your marriage to Marshall, but your whole entire family for the sake of some bullshitter."

"It is not like that at all," Lynn reacted. "Peter is special. He reminds me so much of you."

"How dare you compare a two-timing philanderer to me," Richard barked in a constrained voice. He proceeded to the plant parking lot to avoid making a scene. "He is nothing like me from the sound of it."

"I need some advice," Lynn said. "That is why I want to talk to you."

"You want some advice, Lynn?" Richard spun in a circle. "My advice is patch things up with your husband. Put this whole fiasco behind you. It is a mistake."

"Regardless whether this is a mistake," Lynn replied. "I do not know if I want to patch things up with Marshall. I may decide to move on and start a new life."

"I cannot believe this is you talking right now, Lynn. Can you hear yourself?" Richard challenged. "I have a good mind to call my second cousins in Jersey. They know how to handle scumballs like this."

"He is not a scumball," Lynn glowered. "He is anything but a scumball. I am sorry I bothered you."

"Now wait a minute, Lynn," Richard recoiled from his offensive. "I flew off the handle. Forgive me. No, I will not call any cousins in Jersey. Mary Ann told me you wanted to cool your heels for a spell with us. I am all for that if it will help. Let me give you a call later tonight. We can make arrangements and I will buy you a plane ticket to Boulder."

"Forget it, Richard," Lynn deadpanned. "I think I will fly to Boston instead."

VI

The office operator pronounced the four-letter word as vile as it could possibly sound.

"There is a 'Lynn' holding for you, Mr. Collins. She will not give her last name, nor the purpose of her call."

"Put her through please, Stephanie," Peter released his finger from the speaker. Cursed administrative policies, Peter scolded. These buffoons thought they were clearing inquiries to the Pentagon.

"Sorry, Mr. Collins. Seems we have been disconnected."

"Damn." Peter dropped his pencil on the ink blotter. He dialed the Boylston Agency toll free number.

"I hate calling your office," Lynn came on to the line. Her voice reflected her woe. "How come they always have to ask 'the nature of my call?' I should tell them it is your lover calling. That ought to knock them out of their chairs."

"The receptionists are trained to greet callers off of a script," Peter tried to console. "I will check in with the Operations Manager. I know they are supposed to keep a handle on incoming personal calls, but badgering you is uncalled for."

"How am I supposed to reach you Peter—when I need you the most? I feel like you tell those receptionists to block my calls."

The suspicion indicated the depth of Lynn Monroe's anxiety.

"I am sorry," Lynn caught herself. "Things have been going so shitty around here."

"Let me give you my super secret phone number," Peter inspired. "I carry it with me all the time. The number is known only by a select few. That way no one is bothering me with unnecessary things. My partners and I all have our phones on one master account. No one in Accounting is dumb enough to scrutinize those bills."

"What if you do not answer?" Lynn scribbled down the number.

Boy, is she hurting, Peter thought. Lynn has not appeared this insecure since the first day he laid eyes on her at the Brigadier School.

"It has voice mail," Peter assured. "If you leave a message, I will be back to you in no time."

"I was hoping to call you this weekend," Lynn informed. "Will you have your phone?"

"Certainly," Peter stated. "What is the story with this weekend?"

"I am heading out of town—to spend a few days with Monica in Minneapolis. We plan to stuff our faces with junk food and wine. Monica says she will dig out the old Ouiji board we used to tinker with. She thinks it may give us the answers to some of our questions. I have a feeling I may have to call you for some guidance."

"Like what kind of wine to buy?" Peter joked. The idea of channeling Monica's reputed psychic power to a Ouiji board was disconcerting. Their love had taken on a supernatural personality. Visions of Spirit Guides and telepathic messages from Maggie confirmed premonitions in both Lynn and Peter's minds. There was some sort of purpose unbeknownst to them why their paths were crossing.

"It will not be Chardonnay," Lynn tried to join in lightening the conversation. "That wine was disgusting."

"So that is why you scrammed from Bellisio's?" Peter reasoned. "Here I thought you wanted to go to bed with me, but it was the wine."

"Too dry," Lynn revealed. "I like sweeter, fruitier wine."

"How about Lambrusco? Have you ever had Lambrusco?"

"Spell it for me," Lynn grabbed a pad. She relished this temporary escape. The previous day's conversation with her family was too tumultuous. "I will make sure Monica and I pick up a bottle."

The blinking message cursor on the cell phone was shaped like a mock envelope. How could he have missed her call? Peter picked up the gadget from his kitchen counter. He had away been away from his cell phone for only two minutes the entire day. The second he went outside to button down the deck furniture, it rang. The sound of thunder boomed in the sky.

"Hello Mr. Soup-err See-crret! You do not have secrets anymore." It was Monica's voice. "I have kidnapped your soul-mate. She is too nervous to call you, so I am. Actually, she begged me to. Give us a call, and we can discuss a ransom."

Peter jotted down the recorded ten digits. With my luck, I will forget—and accidentally erase the message without writing down the number, Peter mused.

Peter stepped outside to the alcove of the brick faced breezeway. As the telephone picked up in Minneapolis, some unexpected visitors ran to the alcove away from the sheets of rain falling on the driveway.

It was Peter's mother and father. Peter had forgotten that they were back for the season from Florida. He disconnected his phone at the same time he heard the "hello". It was stuffed into his pocket.

"Hey there," Peter's game face welcomed. "What a pleasant surprise!"

"Donaldson Limousine dropped us off an hour ago, but we do not have a morsel to eat at the house. We were going to go out for a bite, but these rains are torrential."

"Well come in, come in and get dry," Peter opened the kitchen door. "Marianne is somewhere inside... Marianne! She'll want you to eat here when she sees you, so plan on sticking around. What's the old saying? We can always add another cup of water to the soup?"

The cell phone rang in Peter's pocket. At first he pretended not to hear it, but the charade was foolhardy. His parents' eyes were riveted to his pants. He pulled out the device at the second ring. The caller ID displayed the 612 Minnesota area code.

"Our workaholic son," Peter's father marveled. "On a Saturday afternoon no less. Never ends, huh?"

Peter pressed the power button—killing the third signal.

"Whoever it is, I am sure it can wait," Peter placed the phone back on the counter. His outside was smiling but his insides were turning upside down. "Let's sit in the other room... Marianne!"

Lynn's face flashed in Peter's mind at each roll of thunder. He and Marianne toasted his parents' return with a bottle of champagne. A crack of lightning caused everyone to flinch in their wicker cane seats on the porch soon after their glasses clinked. Peter joined in the group's lighthearted chuckle at his mother's counsel "Do not be afraid!" He half-listened to the Floridian woe of drought, and Marianne's complaint that the steaks would take another hour to defrost.

"... and all the ponds on the golf course are completely bone dry," Peter's father recounted. "We sure could have used steady rains like this down there, Peter... Peter? Are you listening to me?"

Peter realized he had been caught looking at his wristwatch.

"Dry—bone dry," Peter attempted to pick up where he lost attention. "Is that right?"

"Peter, do you have to be somewhere?" his mother reckoned.

"Um, actually yes. As a matter of fact, I was heading out the door to the pharmacy right when you got here," Peter brainstormed. "I need to pick up a prescription before the store closes at five."

"Well you better get going," his father concurred. "You only have twenty minutes."

"Prescription?" Marianne interrupted. "What did you need a prescription for?"

"My Lipitor," Peter downplayed. "The refill has been sitting there for more than a week. I will be back in a jiffy."

Peter hurriedly exited the porch before his wife could protest. He double-checked that the slip of paper with the telephone number on it was still in his pocket before he jumped in the car and took off.

"I understand you are holding someone very dear to me for ransom," Peter stated in the pharmacy parking lot. Droplets of water fell on the windshield. They were erased intermittently by the occasional swipe of the windshield wiper blades.

"I don't think we can negotiate," Monica nodded her assent to Lynn. Yes, it was indeed Peter. "We are not too impressed with your wine prowess."

Peter could hear the telephone being wrestled from the provocateur's grasp.

"Hi, Sweet Pea!" Lynn bubbled. "I asked Monica to drive to the finest wine store in her suburb to buy Lambrusco. You should have seen the manager's face when we asked him to show us his finest Lambrusco. He said 'Lambrusco? Are you sure?' The only Lambrusco he had has twist off tops! Twist off tops, Mr. Million Dollar Man! My girlfriend, I will have you know, has a different view of you now."

"Did you buy it?"

"We are sipping it as we speak," Lynn laughed. "It is awful!"

"Well, you chilled it, right?" Peter excused. "You have to drink it chilled."

"He says it needs to be chilled," Lynn directed away from the phone. "We already put ice in it, but it still tastes the same."

"It sounds like you are having quite the time for yourself," Peter reclined in the driver's seat. "Did you track down the Ouiji board?"

"Monica can't find it," Lynn said. "She thinks it disappeared the last time she moved."

Peter was disappointed. He had a hunch. From the last time he spoke with

Lynn, he hoped the Monica weekend could evoke some sort of spiritual insight upon the mystery of their affair.

"She has a pendulum instead," Lynn giggled. "You ask it a question and Monica puts her hands on the top of it. If it spins to the left, the answer is yes. If it spins to the right, the answer is no."

"Sounds pretty fool-proof," Peter mocked.

"I thought the same thing too," Lynn exclaimed. "But you should see the answers we have been getting. Monica is dead serious about this stuff. When she places her hands on that pendulum, she is convinced that there is too strong a para-psychological presence to bastardize its intent."

"At first we started out with some simple control questions like 'is the sun hot?'—or 'do salamanders fly?' All of the answers turned out correct. Then we graduated to some more testing questions. Peter, you would not believe the accuracy of the answers we received. It is creepy!"

"Like what?"

"Factual questions—like 'does Lynn love Peter?'—or 'did you and I exist together in a previous life'?"

"What were the answers?"

"Just as you and I suspected," Lynn informed. "Yes."

"I knew it," Peter agreed. "I just knew it."

"We finished moving to the next step right when you called," Lynn reported. "Questioning what will happen in our future."

"And—?"

"Oh, no—those questions were personal," Lynn shielded. "Let's say the answers were of no surprise and will be to your and my liking. That is why we have been trying to call you. Monica wants you to give us some questions. We will ask the pendulum the questions tonight. If you call back later, I can give you the answers."

"Okay—question number one—are, we, soul-mates from the same twig?" Peter blurted enthusiastically—then hesitated. Make sure he speculated—not to ask all 'yes' answered questions. "All right, let me think… question two. Will you and I ever have a baby in this lifetime?"

Good "no" question, Peter figured. Even if Lynn did tell Monica about the vasectomy, chances were too slim.

"Question three," Peter decided to bait Lynn's possible trip to Boston. "Will we physically see each other before the end of this calendar year?"

"Is that it?" Lynn uttered busily writing down the inquisitions word for word.

"Final question," Peter inhaled. "Will we eventually be physically together as a couple in this human lifetime?"

The urge to fall asleep was intense. It was a little past midnight. Eleven o'clock Minnesota time, Peter calculated. He could not call too late.

Marianne rolled over in her sleep. Her breathing was slow and steady. Darn Peter thought. Is she still awake? How can I get to the telephone?

He decided to wait until half past the hour. Regardless of Marianne's state of consciousness, Peter determined he could not call any later than eleven thirty Lynn's time. He did not want her to think in the future that she would have to wait up all night worrying whether he would call. Besides, being caught would not be the worst thing in the world.

Peter slithered from the bed precisely at the appointed time. Marianne's breathing was much deeper. He ventured downstairs and gathered the cell phone from his dashboard mount. He pressed the digits from the slip of paper under the sun visor. He strode to the stoop of the front entrance of the house and sat down on the brick.

"Hi," Peter whispered.

"Hi," Lynn muttered groggily.

"You sound sleepy."

"I was nodding off," Lynn yawned.

"I thought you might still be up kibitzing with Monica."

"She fell asleep a couple of hours ago."

"Where is she?"

"Right here. Lying beside me."

"In the same bed?"

"Uh-huh."

"You are going to sleep together in the same bed?"

"Probably."

"What are you wearing right now?"

"A tee shirt."

"A tee shirt? Is that all?"

"And my panties."

"Jeez Lynn, you are turning me on," Peter flirted. "What color panties?"

"Peter—where are you?"

"Where am I?" Peter viewed the starlit skyline. "I am sitting in front of my house looking at Polaris."

"Where is your wife?"

"Upstairs. Sleeping in bed."

"How do you feel right now?" Lynn questioned. "Sneaking out of your house in the middle of the night to call your mistress?"

"Did something happen there tonight with the pendulum?" Peter was confused by the sudden scrutiny. "Why is Monica asleep so early?"

"We did the pendulum right after we talked with you," Lynn backpedaled. "We rented a movie and it was pretty dull. Monica fell asleep in the middle of it."

"Did the pendulum answer my questions?"

"It did."

"And—?"

"What you thought they would be," Lynn yawned again. "Except for one we could not understand."

"Which one?"

"I cannot remember. I wrote them down somewhere."

"Well, find them."

"They are outside with my cigarettes in my pocketbook on the deck."

"Come on," Peter pleaded. "Please go outside and get them."

"It is freezing out here," Lynn moved outside with the portable. Peter could hear the shiver in her voice. "Let me see… one—yes, two—yes, three—no, four—yes."

"Lynn, I did not write those questions down," Peter could feel a shiver in his spine. Was it because Lynn was cold? "Read the whole question back to me."

Peter could hear Lynn re-close the outside door behind her.

"Number one—are we soul-mates from the same twig—yes. Number two—will you and I have a baby in this lifetime—yes. Number three – will we physically see each other before the end of the calendar year—no. Number four—will we physically be together as a couple in this human lifetime—yes."

"Question three bothers me," Peter pondered. "You did not mention coming to Boston to Monica, did you?"

"Monica does not manipulate the pendulum," Lynn chided. "It is only a tool—not a hundred percent reliable. It is no big deal."

"Well, question three is the one I cannot understand," Peter concluded.

"Question three," Lynn expressed her puzzlement. "What about question two?"

"You never know," Peter reasoned. "If question four is yes, then maybe you will convince me someday to get a reverse vasectomy."

VII

The overhead fan above the griddle was turned on low. Its hum droned the activity around the kitchen, but could not vanquish the aroma of sizzling bacon relishing the small house.

Both had fallen into a routine of unspoken tasks. It was as if they performed these duties without instruction every day for years. Lynn set the table and filled the orange juice glasses. Monica stirred the eggs into the frying pan. Lynn moved to the counter at the sound of the toaster oven. She automatically began buttering the bread—being sure to spread the margarine to each corner without any unmelted gobs—the way she and Monica liked. Both dispersed their allotments to each other's plate. Neither had to ask how much was enough. It was understood to leave a little of everything on the center of the table. Half the fun of breakfast together was to joke about seconds. No, we shouldn't… oh, what the heck.

"Did you sleep okay?" Monica spoke for the first time that day.

"So-so," Lynn peppered her eggs. "I feel tired this morning. My back is sore."

"Your friend coming?" Monica hinted at the code word for that time of the month.

"Suppose so. It has been a few days."

"I overheard your conversation with Peter last night," Monica revealed.

"I kind of figured. You didn't look like you were asleep."

"He really snuck out of his house to call you in the middle of the night?" Monica felt determined to get this pent up frustration off of her chest. "It sounded so pathetic—adolescent even."

"I know," Lynn agreed. She knew her friend. Monica could get very crabby when someone was coming on the wrong way to her closet friend. Coming on too strong was even worse—particularly if Monica was a party to the frivolity—like having the overtures happen under the roof of her own home. "I felt pretty uncomfortable with the whole thing."

"Makes me wonder how much he has actually told his wife," Monica took a sip of her juice. "Men cannot be trusted. They say one thing and do another. Want their cake and eat it, too."

Lynn picked at the eggs on her plate. The prongs of her fork made a dismal clinking sound whenever they touched the dish. It was an irritant to the silence. An affirmation to Monica that Lynn was indeed suspicious.

"This is a puzzling one," Monica shook her head. "The pendulum and my tarot cards both read you are meant to be together—that we cannot question the inevitability of that destiny. But there are so many contradictions."

"How do you mean?"

"Your family situations to begin with," Monica tried to explain. "The responsibilities you have been given as a wife, a mother, a daughter, a vibrant member of your community. That is who you really are. The character incarnated into your body to carry out a life lesson. The thing is, you have evolved into a teacher instead of a student. Your mission is to teach life lessons rather than seek them. Every person in your life is attracted to you because of who you really are. You are their Rock of Gibraltar—their pillar of strength. It seems to be a contradiction—you demonstrating to them the fortunes of deserting their lives in order to seek someone else. Particularly when the other person is sneaking around in the dark in order to talk to you."

The carburetor in Monica's car crapped out on Interstate 35 outside of Sandstone. Lynn had to resort to her cell phone to call for help.

"The part I dread the most is the 'I told you so'," Lynn listened as the connection rang through. "Marshall must have said ten times if he said it once that he did not think your car would make two round trips from Minneapolis to Duluth."

"Marshall? We are broken down on the Interstate," Lynn voiced at the sound of her protector. "Can you come? We need help."

"He figures he can be here in about an hour," Lynn disconnected the line. "If it is the carburetor, he thinks he can get it going to get the car back to the cities. He is going to bring some tools with him."

"Marshall Monroe to the rescue," Monica shouted as she got out of the car. The message hung for a brief moment in the air, then echoed off the adjacent yard of ice fishing shacks stored for the off season near the side of the highway. The women sat on the guardrail bordering the breakdown lane. An occasional motorist would slow in their wake, asking if the attractive females needed assistance.

"No, thanks," the uniform wave became almost an automatic salute. "Help is on the way."

"What do you think Peter would do?" Monica queried, accepting a lit cigarette from her friend. "If you called him because we were broke down?"

"Knowing Peter," Lynn blew out a blue stream of smoke from her mouth. "We would not be waiting an hour on a guardrail. He would have roadside assistance send two transportation substitutes—one for me to drive to Duluth and one for you to get back to Minneapolis. Yours would probably be a big-ass flashing ramp truck to carry your poor sick car to Carburetor Hospital."

"Wow," Monica Chambers rolled her eyes. "He brings out the Calvary, huh? Just like General Custer."

Monica mounted her fist to her lips. She pretended to toot the bugle to charge. A gust of wind blew the blond hair off of her shoulders.

"Sometimes an everyday handyman with a measly pair of jumper cables and a cup of gas primer is all you need instead of a sparkling general," Lynn envisioned Marshall—scurrying around in the garage while they smoked butts on the highway. She did not want to admit that sure, Peter would call roadside assistance, but he would not come.

He would get someone else to fetch the distressed

"I guess Custer learned that at Little Big Horn."

VIII

Sales meetings were held every Monday morning at Peter's insurance agency. The team of twelve producers met in a round table session. They reviewed the prior week's prospecting activities and strategized the best means of follow up. Plans were formulated to pick out the underbelly of opportunity. Who was their accountant? Who was their banker? Who could they use to call in a favor?

By mid-morning the underwriting manager arrived. The team would change its focus—analyzing existing insurance policy forms. Where could coverage be improved? The loss control engineer would deliver her report on each site inspection. In the end, the decisions were made. How strong a case did they have to leverage one of their insurance carriers?

The agency team took seven full years to develop. Each producer had become an expert in a chosen industry field. Each earned well in excess of six figures per year.

One of the few women on the team was Kathleen Leonard. From her first day at the agency, Peter had learned that she preferred "Kathleen" rather than "Kathy" or "Kate". He identified with her choice of formality. He did not particularly care either when people took the liberty of calling him "Pete" in a professional business environment.

Peter and Kathleen had little need for contact with each other during the course of the workweek aside from the Monday meetings. Kathleen's developed area of expertise was non-profit associations, colleges and universities. Worcester, Massachusetts boasts eight colleges making Kathleen's book of business quite lucrative. Her specialty was professional liability. Peter would seek her counsel whenever a technical question arose on Directors and Officers insurance for one of his clients.

Peter and Kathleen had an hour to kill between the sales meeting and a poorly scheduled appointment with the marketing representative from a newly appointed liability carrier. By coincidence, they ran into each other at the coffee station at headquarters' employee cafeteria.

"Care to sit down?" Kathleen motioned to the empty room of tables. "We never get a chance to talk."

Kathleen reported all of her latest goings on. Married without children, Kathleen told Peter about all of her life changes over the past year and a half.

"My husband and I always wanted to live on a lake," Kathleen remarked. The premise sparked Peter's interest. "So for the past two years we surveyed every body of water in the area to find our own piece of heaven. It was a stretch, but we bought the cutest little cottage on Webster Lake. We decided that was where we wanted to be. We sold our old house so fast we were not able to do any work ahead of time before moving in. Originally we planned to tear it down and build a new house. Now, we are perfectly comfortable in our cozy little nest. Our mortgage is a fraction of what it used to be. Rick decided not to bother finding a new job after his last contract consulting stint. Now he is content sticking close to home and puttering around the lake.

"Do you get to enjoy the lake much?" Peter asked. He knew Kathleen committed as many inordinate hours to the job as he did.

"Of course I do," Kathleen boasted. "I am up every morning at four-thirty for my meditation."

"Meditation?" Peter felt flustered. Kathleen immediately covered her mouth.

"I am sorry," she apologized. "I am not supposed to talk about that."

"No Kathleen, don't be sorry," Peter assured. "Please, tell me about your meditation."

"I do not think it is a politically correct topic in an organization owned by a group of devout Irish Catholics," Kathleen worried.

"Try me."

"My brother Mark was the first one to get me involved in it," Kathleen began. "He had a near-death experience in his job as a state cop. After that, he really got into researching things like past life regression, means of getting in touch with your inner self. He and his wife are into it big-time. The meditation I am trying is one of several techniques he has recommended. I am really in the learning stage."

"Your inner self, huh?" Peter hesitated. "Has your brother ever discussed with you the concept of soul-mates?"

"Of course," Kathleen chuckled.

"Is Rick your soul-mate?"

"No. I do not think so," Kathleen confided. Her response was simultaneous. Like she had thought about it before. "Rick is a companion and my dearest friend, but I do not think we fit into the definition of soul-mates. Gee Peter, you seem to know a lot about the topic."

"I have read a few books recently," Peter admitted.

"I have a whole library on para-psychology," Kathleen beamed. "It is not quite like my brother's, but a collection of my favorites nonetheless. What have you read?"

Peter rattled off the names of five different authors. Only a couple could he recall their titles.

"My goodness," Kathleen was surprised. "How did you get involved in it?"

"Do you really want to know?"

Peter devoted the next forty-five minutes to describing his relationship with Lynn—from the first day at the Brigadier School to his present quandary with Marianne.

"You should get in touch with my brother," Kathleen suggested. She could tell Peter was desperate, searching for an answer. "He has so many ideas on how to come to terms with your body, your life and your soul."

"I guess that is why I was so intrigued by your reference to meditation," Peter reflected on his Spirit Guide encounter in Duluth. "I feel I have only scratched the surface of this thing called enlightenment."

"Want to try something neat?" Kathleen offered as she wrote her brother's email address on the back of her business card. "There is an incantation you can use to send your soul-mate your unconditional love and best wishes. Close your eyes and put yourself in a total sense of relaxation. Inhale and call out that person's name as you slowly exhale. Then inhale again and hold your breath for a moment. As you hold your breath, incant your well wishes in your mind… that you send your unconditional love, or any other message you wish to convey. As you chant these thoughts, imagine the host of miles and dimensions your message will have to travel to get to that person. Then exhale that breath with a good, sharp blow—whisking that message away from your soul and onto theirs. Do that eleven consecutive times. You will not believe the sensation you will experience on the eleventh blow."

"What happens?"

"I told you. I am in the learning stage," Kathleen leveled. "My brother keeps telling me it takes some practice."

The revelation was like a newfound genesis. Peter made a beeline to his office after the morning meetings to share his inspiring news. He had to email Lynn.

For the first time he could recall, Lynn had sent an email message ahead of him. The midnight telephone call to Monica's house on Saturday must have had a profound effect, Peter figured.

"No Dot Games, no bulleted questions, no beating around the bush. I do not want to talk to you anymore. Plain and simple. I do not trust you."

IX

Lynn sent the terse message about mid-morning. She was aware that Peter was tied up with meetings each Monday. It would be about noon before he would get to his emails. She figured right.

A frantic phone call would come in as if on cue. An opportune time to be out of the office. Lynn rummaged through her pile of pending homeowners' applications for the odd ball property up in Two Harbors. A nice day to take a drive and snap some pictures, she resolved.

It had become an inadvertent habit—checking the Sent Items window on her computer. The envelope was still closed. Peter must have yet to read her remarks.

Midday traffic was light as Lynn sped along the expressway. She caught herself at a new inadvertent habit—peeking up to the ground level corner room at Best Western Edgewater. The ritual had become automatic. She would look up the concourse every day she drove home from work. Why is it I always think he will be standing there waiting for me?

The drive to Two Harbors took less than twenty-five minutes. Lynn passed the entrance sign to the Superior Shores Resort. The trek that glorious day with Peter seemed to take over an hour. Why does it feel so short now?

I know, Lynn admitted to herself. She adjusted the rear view mirror on the Accord to get a better look at the fading marquee in the distance. I could not wait to be alone with him.

The online Map Quest directions to Congdon Road were right on the money. The majestic dwelling Lynn was looking for spanned the crescent of a hillside overlooking Lake Superior. Lynn got out of her car and grabbed the Polaroid from the back seat. She scrutinized the information taken earlier during her telephone interview and began to wander the grounds seeking the appropriate angle to shoot. The application said the buyers were paying $499,000 for the new home. Who could afford such a price, Lynn thought for a split second? She shook her head to expel the answer that popped into her mind. She refused to look out over the water.

The day's mail was stacked in a heap on her in-basket when she returned to the office. Refusing to acknowledge the presence of her personal computer, she slowly thumbed through the array of envelopes. The mail clerk had developed a routine. Larger envelopes were designated to the bottom to act a foundation for the smaller sizes. The emblematic logo of Peter's agency emblazoned the bottom-most package. A third inadvertent habit… Lynn found herself jettisoning everything around her to slice the parcel open. She pulled out the ten by sixteen color photograph.

"Oh, my God," Lynn covered her mouth. She bit the knuckle of her index finger.

It was a group photograph of businessmen posed in front of a large mantelpiece. Peter was the third person on the right. He looked stunning—like a Hollywood celebrity asked to take a token shot with a host of admirers.

Peter had used a flair pen to inscribe the back of the picture.

"Lynn Dear –

Felt a little uncomfortable knowing you did not have a photograph of me. Thought it would be a nice addition to your manila folder collection. This was taken at an event two nights after I got back from Duluth. You can tell by the smile who was on my mind. I miss you—Peter XO".

Lynn flipped to the visage on the front side. She pressed her lips to Peter's face—and ran her fingertips along the outline of his body. The blue eyes pierced at her. They seemed to penetrate—into her heart.

Why was I so impetuous to send such a rash email, Lynn cursed? She drummed her fingers on her keyboard thinking it would make the computer come to life quicker. Perhaps I can retrieve that email before he reads it. She implored the screens to move. The hourglass icon demanded her to wait.

"Come on, come on," Lynn kept a constant click on her mouse. "Give me my Sent Items window!"

The requested screen flashed at her. The envelope was open.

"Damn it," Lynn cried. "He read it."

Lynn quickly picked up the telephone and pressed the toll free number. After a brief anxious interlude, she placed the receiver back in its cradle.

"I am sorry. Mr. Collins has left the office for the day."

X

It was there, but it was not... a twinge at first, that tapped on the back of an earlobe.

It cannot be, the ego protested. We were not prepared for this. The defenses went up.

The few days later created light flutters. The body rejected the naivete of the psyche.

It began to flourish.

Lynn rose from her desk for her almost mid-morning cigarette. By instinct, she threw on her jacket even though it was balmy outside. Instead of lighting up in the back alley and sitting in the broken metal chair, she found her feet walking purposefully to the Suburban. As if in a trance, she pulled out into traffic and cut across the street to Wal-mart.

She knew why she was in the store, but did not want to recognize the intent. She took possession of an empty shopping carriage and ambled past the drug and cosmetics departments like a farmer tilling a field. It felt like every security camera was on her. She stopped and thumbed through a circular rack of toddlers' garments. The new summer styles were in stock. She selected a couple of outfits for Maggie and laid them daintily onto the bottom of the carriage.

Her face looked back to the drug section. A lone pharmacist was occupied on the telephone. No one was in the aisles. Lynn strolled aimlessly the other way to the Ladies Department. She picked up a package of pantyhose. To the casual observer, it looked like she had to memorize the wording on the cellophane for an exam. After a calculated moment, she tossed a couple of the cardboard jackets into the child seat basket. The cart began to veer towards the medicinal shelves as if drawn by a magnet.

The kit offering was a single standard. No variety of brand names to provoke a semi-educated decision. Lynn buried the box under the garments and paced to the checkout counter.

Lynn centered the package in the middle of the revolving belt. Maggie's new clothes were strategically positioned to act like a wrapping for each side of the box' labels. The cover was enough to calm her quivering fingers. She found herself able to pull the plastic debit card from the sleeve of her coin purse. The elderly woman behind the checkout was more concerned with triggering the register wand on the pantyhose bar codes than bothering with the identity of the purchases. Lynn breathed a sigh of relief.

The back street spot was still available when the Suburban returned. Lynn debated whether to bring the bulky Wal-mart bag into the office. Maybe I can come back out at lunchtime she stalled. Despite the resolve, the white plastic bag swooshed at her side as she entered the building.

The red message light on her telephone console was not blinking. There were no matters of significance to deter her subconscious journey. Lynn took the kit out of the bag and ripped off the box top. A multi-folded set of instructions protected the contents inside like a sphinx holding a riddle. Lynn threw the paper aside. Guidance was not needed in this mission.

She went into the Ladies Room and peed into the plastic cup. Who was it that said you had to wait ten minutes for the test to work? She ignored her pigheadedness not to read the instructions beforehand and set the cup on the back of the toilet. She rearranged her wardrobe and double-checked the lock on the door. Only three minutes has passed, and already the ill-fated ring was forming at the bottom of the jar.

XI

Staring at pregnancy tests did not change their readings.

Lynn defied this fact of scientific nature and stared for the next ten minutes at the fated cup. Even going back to refer to the instructions did not alter its destiny. The directions offered no options on how one could manipulate the inevitable.

A sense of purpose swept over Lynn's being. I have to call him. I have to call him right now. He has to hear this news.

Lynn circled her mouse to call the computer screen back to life. She typed Peter a simple message. "Seems our life is going to change".

A reply came back within minutes.

"How so?"

"I went to Wal-mart this morning to pick up an Early Pregnancy Test," Lynn swallowed as she typed. She could not bring herself to say she already used it. "Ended up spending a hundred bucks on stuff I didn't need. Will you call me when you get a chance?"

The telephone seemed to ring as soon as Lynn pressed the "Send" button.

"You think you are pregnant?" Peter stated. There was no need for identification.

"The ring started forming as soon as I finished peeing."

"Oh, my God, Lynn," Peter exhaled.

Lynn held her breath. What will he say next? I did not think about what his reaction would be.

"So what do you think?" Peter mustered.

"I think I am going to have a baby."

"Do you know what I think?" Peter offered. "I think this is a divine conception. I think this baby is ours."

Lynn smiled. She snuggled the phone receiver to the nape of her neck. They shared the same perception.

"I bet it's a boy," Peter exuded. "You never had a boy before. That's what is in your womb right now. You are growing a little boy."

"It's a girl," Lynn countered. She did not want to raise their hopes too high.

"How do you know?"

"Because I know my body," Lynn confided. "I feel the same way now that I did when I had Maggie. I know it's a girl."

"Peter Collins does not conceive girls," Peter exclaimed. The bravado of the statement caused him to pause. "Lynn, it would be foolish for me to expect, and it is certainly none of my business, but I have to ask you. Have you and Marshall done it at all since I left?"

Lynn closed her eyes. She envisioned the sexual intercourse she had twice over the past eight weeks. One was a glorious night with Peter. One was the not-so-glorious night with Marshall.

"Once," Lynn pronounced. "And only once. It was two days after you left. On the night I told Marshall. I could not help, but crying afterwards. The whole time I was imagining I was making love with you. That's how he found out you know. He could tell."

Peter cringed in his seat. How could he have assumed that Marshall would forsake his duties as a husband? He too had resumed his sexual activity with Marianne. Images of Lynn would bandy about during their rhythmic exercise. It is only natural, isn't it? Peter speculated.

"Peter, I feared this was going to happen the night we were at Superior Shores," Lynn said. "I was at that right time of the month when I was a fertile Myrtle. And you told me you had a vasectomy, but you never did have any of that follow up testing."

Peter leaned his elbows on top of his desk. The doctor who performed the procedure had mentioned there were a couple of different ways to nip the bud. One was foolproof and could only be reversed with future surgery. The other was not. Peter could not remember which procedure was used. Only that he did not follow up as prescribed.

"Chances are if they did a test it would be Marshall's sperm," Peter floated. "But you know what? That would only be a human science test. Doctors can say whatever they want, but I know in my heart of hearts that this is a divine conception. This baby has been conceived in your body at this given point in time for a reason. That is our baby. I know it is."

"Peter, will you do me a favor?" Lynn interrupted.

"Anything."

"Will you go get tested?" Lynn asked. "I do not think I can stand not knowing the answer."

"The call to the doctor's office will be the first thing I do as soon as we get off the phone."

Lynn chuckled.

"What's so funny?" Peter implored.

"I was picturing you—going into the doctor's bathroom in your fancy suit with a specimen jar."

It was a comic relief.

"Don't you worry," Peter replied. "I am bringing my photograph of you with me. There will be some pretty nasty thoughts going on in there."

XII

Requisitioning a follow up vasectomy test did not quite carry that ordinary sense of medical urgency. The blasé attention it received was probably half the reason most people avoided the unpleasantness in the first place. It usually did not accomplish much more, beyond closing out an innocuous file.

Peter came to this realization once he was finally able to get through to the doctor's secretary.

"Yes, I had the procedure... what—I think it was about three years ago," Peter responded. The office could not find his record.

"Well, I suppose you can come to the office anytime, but we are only open Wednesdays until noon," the nurse in authority informed. Peter looked at his desk clock. It was eleven-forty. "And any day next week will be fine."

"I'll be there in five minutes," Peter disconnected the line.

The professional building seemed to be nothing more than a maze of hallways. Peter's first reaction was that the doctor must have relocated his office. He was forced to return to the front foyer to consult the building directory. As it turned out, the office he was looking for was only two doors down on the right. It had not changed. He had charged past it the first time.

The white uniform at the partition recognized the hospital trustee once he entered the empty reception area. The staff took pride in assuring that a blank appointment slate would make for no one remaining in the office by noon on Wednesdays. She casually offered the white paper bag containing the coveted specimen jar.

"You can bring the sample back anytime during office hours," she said in a step ahead. She covered her typewriter anticipating the closing in ten minutes.

"I'd like to leave a sample right now," Peter stated. He refused to be dissuaded by the nurse's abruptness. "Where do I go?"

"Most patients go home," the nurse chastised. "And bring the samples back later."

"Well, why don't we put this one on a rush basis?" Peter suggested.

"We do not do the testing here, Mr. Collins," the receptionist revealed she knew who was speaking with. "The samples have to go down to the lab. Even if your sample was ready right this second, the next lab pick up will not be until tomorrow."

The pads of the blue business suit could not contain the visible slump in Peter's shoulders.

"How long does it take to hear back from the lab?"

"About three days."

Peter turned and walked out of the office—toting the small white paper bag.

Marianne Collins walked out of the next door office at the exact same time Peter entered the hallway.

"Honey," Marianne marveled. "How did you know I had an eye doctor appointment?"

"I didn't," Peter stuttered.

"Are you here to take me to lunch?"

"If you like."

"Great," Marianne bubbled. "What is that white paper bag for?"

Lynn felt compelled to telephone her husband. He had to be paged from the warehouse.

"What's up?" Marshall greeted. It was a rarity for Lynn to bother him at work.

"I'm pregnant," Lynn came right out and said. "I took a home pregnancy test this morning."

"Congratulations."

Lynn ignored the repose of insincerity.

"I called Becky Montagne to set up an appointment to make sure," Lynn continued. "She was so excited. She said she'll see me first thing tomorrow."

"Great."

Lynn pursed her lips and furrowed her brow. Marshall did not have to be so coy.

"It is your baby, Marshall."

"Yeah? How can you be so sure?"

"Because he cannot have children," Lynn snapped. The name Peter Collins was no longer mentioned. The standard reference had become "he", or "him".

"What are you talking about," Marshall balked. "He has two kids."

"That was before," Lynn revealed. "He's been fixed since then."

"Vasectomies don't always work," Marshall doubted.

"Well, he is going to get tested to be sure," Lynn blurted.

"So you are keeping in touch, huh?" Marshall challenged. "You called him before you called me?"

Lynn mashed her teeth at the mindless mistake.

"It doesn't take a rocket scientist to see where your priorities lie."

Marshall hung up the phone.

XIII

The soft stroke of the foam brush against the texture of the window sash gave Lynn a sense of welcomed tranquility. Storm clouds seemed to brew all around her. Marshall was steadfast in his refusal to do any more work around the house. It did not matter if Richard and Mary Ann were flying in the next day from Boulder for the long Fourth of July weekend. It was a rebellion against Lynn's cavalier attitude. Her resolve to hold her head up high. Marshall felt he would be a hypocrite to pretend they were all one big happy family.

Lynn re-dipped the brush into the pan of ivory latex. Was it her fault the lab closed early for the holiday? He was remorseful when he told her they would not have an answer until the following Tuesday. He was as anxious as she was. But then again, how could she explain "his" remorse to her husband?

"I am taking next Tuesday off as a vacation day," Lynn repeated in her head the phone conversation earlier that day with Peter. "No. Don't call me at home if you have any news. I can wait. It will probably be easier to handle after my parents are gone."

Lynn peered outside the window to the open trench in the front yard. An overgrowth of weeds had sprouted between the pallets of untouched landscaping bricks. The walkway to the home had been abandoned since Lynn's admittance of impropriety. She had considered asking one of her contractor clients to come finish the project—more or less as a peace offering—but the notion was fleeting. To Marshall, the disturbance in the front yard was a siren – a symbol of the disarray within their married lives.

Is honesty always the best policy? Lynn pondered, as she edged the corner molding. At this point, she began to doubt it. Her original belief was that her indiscretion with Peter was a one-time only lapse in otherwise good judgement—an isolated incident—a human mistake. Marshall did not see it that way. It did not matter if it was a one-night fling or a four-day sex orgy. The deed was done—and it was unforgivable.

If I knew he was going to be this condemning, Lynn reflected, I probably would not have been such a Puritan the second half of Peter's visit.

XIV

Maggie was the one common link that held the fragile relationship together. Ultimately, it was the joy delivered by a small child that counteracted the unspoken tension—even after Richard and Mary Ann arrived.

Ironically, Richard suggested Enger Tower Park as the perfect spot to view the city's fireworks. Maggie looked warily at her mother upon the mere mention of the fabled landmark. Lynn ignored the daughter's stare. She regarded instead her father and could not help but think of Peter—and both men's affinity to the Ohara Peace Bell. Lynn could sense her daughter's similar perception. She directed a clear-cut signal to the little one—"*Don't say it*!"

Maggie was confused. It was an odd sort of new adult game. A deliberate act—to pretend things were different from what was real—and to say "*Don't say it*!" at what was. From the moment the Nelsons arrived at the house, the playmaking reverberated from everyone.

Daddy held her and stood next to Mommy when Grammy and Grampy got out of the shiny "rent-a-car". Grammy gushed how excited she was. Mommy was going to have another baby. Daddy felt funny—kind of cold. "*Do not say it*!" Daddy said inside. He put her down to get the bags from the car. "*Good excuse to get out of here*" Daddy's head said.

"How is everything, Lynn?" Grammy said to Mommy.

"*Don't say it*!" came out of Grampy's inside. Maggie tilted her head. Grampy was looking at the open hole on the grass but was thinking something else. "Remember what we decided in the car, Mary Ann. We make no mention of anything unless Lynn does. Five days will be long enough."

Not to mention what, Maggie wondered?

Mommy held on to Grammy extra long. She was thinking the same thing as Grammy. "*Don't say it*!"

The play phrase was repeated in the adults' heads throughout supper in the backyard. It became boring. *I know, I know*, Maggie lolled her head. *I am biting my tongue!*

"Is this seafood in the salad?" Grammy asked. It was funny how everyone made up different things to say when they really did not care to think about them ahead of time.

"It is tuna," Mommy said. "I thought it would be a nice added touch."

Maggie could tell the word "tuna" made Mommy think about Peter. He had told Mommy he was going to spend the weekend with his family in a place called Maine. He was going to go fishing with some friends for tuna. Mommy bought the tuna at the grocery store to put in the salad to remember Peter. Maggie decided she wanted to play the game too.

"What is a blue fin, Mommy?" Maggie blurted. The gathering gawked at the odd question.

"*Don't say it*!" Mommy's eyes beamed like a laser. *Mommy was going to get really mad.* Maggie put her head down.

Maggie was not happy again until they all got to Enger Tower Park because the "Don't say it!" game ended. She peered over to the stone bathroom house and the Japanese bell as the clan made its way up the steps to the ledge side gazebo overlooking Duluth's city proper. She knew not to say "*it*" without being told. Just like Mommy and Daddy knew not to say "*he*" or "*him*".

Margaret Ann (Maggie) Monroe had never seen fireworks. It was one of those glorious spectacles that can reacquaint a soul to a new earthen journey. If fireworks were a nuance of a previous life, its memory was swept away. Or was it?

The dazzling reds, greens and purples erupted over the harbor waters. Maggie did not know what was more fun. Watching how happy the adults got when she clapped at the initial burst of light, or her "ooh" when the loud boom came a second later.

The fireworks were a great diversion and Maggie loved the attention. Any mind games were over. She danced around the gazebo and sang out loud at the illustrious show. She knew it would last for only a few short minutes—most fun things do—so she stopped her dancing before anyone told her to so everyone could enjoy. The adults sat quietly. They each looked quietly at the infinite dots of light littering the sky. Maggie got a funny feeling in her stomach. Stars gilded in gold glimmered above the ledge while the manmade colors floated over the harbor. A sequence of purple bursts rose above a fading blue shot while yellowish-white remnants faded below the structured girders of the Aerial Lift Bridge.

Maggie remembered. She remembered what it was like on the other side—in the other realm. She wanted to shout it out, but the others were all too quiet—absorbed in their own thoughts. The Golds were the supreme spirits. Those closest to fulfilling God's will for love and enlightenment. Closer to the Golds were the Purples—the teachers who act outside of "self" for the benefit of creation. The Blues were apprentices within the realm of Pillars—holy and devout and determined to ascend. The Yellowish-whites were all the others on the other side of the Pillars—the ones most loved and cared for.

Did they remember too? Maggie scanned the melancholy faces on her family. Have they been here too long to remember? They clustered together in the other realm, just as they were huddled in the gazebo. Maggie ran up and straddled her mother's lap. She could see the colors of the fireworks radiating a yellowish tinge in the corona around her mother's eyes. She could see her mother's soul, and it was aching. But it was aching for the wrong reasons. The plurality of light in her eyes reminded Maggie of the closeness her mother's soul had to another that was not in the gazebo. Maggie understood who the other light was, but was that her Mommy's lesson? To realize fulfillment only with the companionship of that other? Or is this why they call it Independence Day? To pause and reflect on what was erased before going back to the normal grind of day-to-day life—and game playing?

XV

It had become a summer tradition—Richard's attempt to demonstrate his ability to conquer a golf course. Marshall, Larry and Luke Cloud were treated each year to the tireless effort to exude prowess on the links. It was implied without saying that Richard was determined to bring home a scorecard showing that life pleasures such as winning golf are only afforded to those conscious enough to leave a place like Minnesota for more southern climates. The womenfolk took solace in avoiding the charade. Lynn and Mary Ann diverted Maggie on the annual jaunt to Lake Ely to visit Mary Ann's sister.

The evils of the "Don't say it!" game resurfaced as everyone agreed to meet up later in the day for dinner. The messages made Maggie start to cry. The adults chalked the fussiness up to late nights and humid weather.

Maggie was fortunate to miss the golf. The adult game was stronger than that played on the surface. The men were doomed to a six-hour trudge around a hot sweltering public golf course. One hole was finished only to find a group of three foursomes waiting to tee off on the next. Richard lamented that his chunked chip shots and three putts were due to the slow play. He could not get "in the rhythm". The excuses became too much to bear after the third hour of the odyssey. Luke and Larry had a bellyful on the do's and don'ts of avoiding a slice. And who was Richard to them anyway, other than the slug that put their sister up for adoption?

Marshall seemed to care less about the goings on. His hacks off the tee were half-hearted and his refusal to watch which part of the woods his ball flew into became drudgery for the others. Why did they have to get poison ivy looking for the ball when Marshall was not even bothering to count his strokes?

Richard wanted to approach Marshall at a quiet moment, but there was never an opportunity with the traffic. The question could not come out. "How are things with Lynn?"

"What is it about golf?" Luke professed as he and Larry watched Marshall mimic Richard's rendition of helicoptering a putter. The projectile landed next to a group of beer-bellies indulging a contraband cooler on the back of a cart. The guy with a "Golf is Life" tee shirt scowled. "It is more fun to talk about than it is to play."

"I know," Larry agreed. "And you always forget the vow never to do it again."

Lake Ely was not much better. If it was not for Mary Ann's annual pilgrimage to visit, chances of her sister ever seeing Lynn or Maggie would be slim to none. Rather than taking homage in the chance to be together, Mary Ann's sister was more content with her contrition that Lynn was not the "lets keep in touch—Christmas card type". She took on a special energy to exaggerate in front of her sister the dotting over little Maggie and the news of the coming addition to the family. The "auntie from Ely" was headstrong the entire day to keep the conversation lively and within arm's length of Mary Ann. "See Lynn," Maggie could read from the auntie from Ely. "See what a hot shit I am? You should keep in touch more often." Mommy was playing the game again as she looked at her aunt. "Don't say it!" It was enough to squelch the incessantly burning question that Mary Ann was yearning to ask Lynn. "What is going on?"

Marshall's adherence to game rules broke at the final night's barbecue. The Grandma Cloud rhetoric that incited the schism was harmless in intent—meant to be more generic than obtrusive.

"The two of you must be so happy to be having another baby."

"Yeah," Marshall decided to perturb the sows feasting the last four days at his picnic table. "Too bad we do not know who the father is."

Lynn was preoccupied scooping extra whipped cream on the dessert for Richard, who had been sulking since her husband's sass that golf courses must be easier out west. The proclamation prompted a glob of dairy confection to drop straight off of her ladle. The goo landed on top of her sandal. She could feel the ooze between her toes as Marshall stormed into the house.

"Leave him be," Lynn remarked. She stood helplessly on the deck. The game messages began flying. The garbled static made Maggie cry.

"Hey, Lynn," Richard offered. "You never did get around to showing me how your office looks after the renovations. Why don't we take Maggie for a little ride?"

The idea of an exodus was a temporary comfort. Lynn did not relish any prospect of being around the house in her husband's brood. Besides, she thought as she hosed the cream off her foot, I might have the email news we have been waiting for.

Lynn casually turned on her desk computer while Richard roamed the empty Boylston Agency corridor. Sure enough, Peter's message was there as hoped.

The words caused her to simply shut the system down.

"Only love is real—the seed was not."

XVI

The black duck sat diagonally behind Peter's laptop. Its beady eyes stared blankly back at him. "Fly into the sunset Peter—without a single regret or any guilt. The one duck means you need to do it alone." The words from Lynn's letter not two months before reverberated in Peter's head. Was it prophecy, or bad coincidence?

Peter transmitted the simple electronic message. He wanted to emphasize that "Only love was real" in capital letters and close it out there, but thought better of it. His Spirit Guide assailed to be not afraid, but now he was. Peter was convinced. Between entertaining the family clan over the 4th and anything closely resembling a positive test result, the stress could upset Lynn at what was a critical stage of her pregnancy. The negative connotation "the seed was not" seemed a more stabilizing alternative.

Peter's worry—prophesy or bad coincidence—gelled over the following two weeks. Former co-workers over the span of his business career who eventually got the axe kept coming to mind. Their behaviors mirrored rabbits in a snare. If a right hand turn in order, they would invariably tighten the noose by moving left. In the end, a termination was inevitable. Trapped in that snare, a victim would eventually be the catalyst to its own demise.

Peter felt that rabbit snare closing down upon him. There was no response from Lynn the Wednesday she returned to work. Surely she received the email. The envelope was open. Was it not significant enough to acknowledge?

He resisted the urge to telephone. He did not want to come off as a sniveling whiner—bemoaning a stroke of scientific medical misfortune. And would Lynn consider this fate as a misfortune? Perhaps the pregnancy with Marshall as the father would change her feelings for Peter.

It was Lynn who finally ended the silence after ten long days.

"Are you eating something?" Lynn toyed when Peter answered her call. "You sound like you're eating something."

He melted at the sound of his soul-mate's voice.

"I do not believe the test results, Lynn," Peter stated rhetorically. "I wish in my heart that baby is ours."

"I know," Lynn acknowledged. "I have thought the same thing myself."

"So how did we get here," Peter challenged. "Everything that happened while we were together in Duluth. For Crissakes, even when you did make love with your husband afterward, you told me you were thinking about me. Just imagine the soul up there right now waiting in that celestial sphere planning to incarnate into your baby when it is born. It might be someone we may have experienced in a prior lifetime. He is going to be special."

"You're convinced it's going to be a boy, huh?" Lynn noticed. "I already told you I know my body. I'm carrying another girl."

"Not this time, Lynn dear. It's a boy. Our boy."

XVII

Kathleen Leonard's brother was the motivator who convinced Peter about the inevitability of his fate.

At first Peter was reluctant to take Kathleen up on her offer to contact her brother—particularly after he discovered that she too came from a similar Irish-Catholic background.

"O'Connell," Peter balked at Kathleen's invitation. "Your maiden name is O'Connell?"

"That is nothing," Kathleen laughed. "My brother, Sean is a Massachusetts State trooper, too."

"How did a state trooper get involved in studying the fourth realm," Peter asked.

"Don't you remember I told you he had a near death experience?" Kathleen reminded. "Sean had gone on a white-water kayaking trip several years ago. He tipped over and banged his head during 'flip and recover' practice. Everyone with him, including his instructors, did not realize he had lost consciousness. He experienced everything you read about near death survival—the bright light, the warmth and love as you get closer to it. As it turned out, the instructors got to him in time to resuscitate him, but he did not forget that incredible awareness he felt. He is into soul-searching meditation in a big way now. Both he and his wife Serenity - she legally changed her name to Serenity—teach courses and operate a side business taking nature expeditions. They have traveled to some pretty outlandish parts of the world to experience nature. They say it is the closest way to come in contact with your soul during this earthen journey."

Peter contacted Sean and Serenity O'Connell several times during the month if July after learning the results of the fertility test. He told them his saga with Lynn. He figured that if this couple were indeed free thinkers, then they would be advocates of banning worldly possessions and encourage "going for it".

Sean advised nothing of the sort.

"Do not waste your money on notions like life regression therapy," Sean declared after their initial meeting. "Serenity and I have been through all of that. Believe it or not, we found out we were married to each other in a previous life. That did not prove though the realization we came to that we also are soul-mates. Soul-mates are individuals who know 'who they really are'. That is what your challenge is going to be Peter. For both you and Lynn to find out 'who you really are'."

"I love her so much," Peter confided to Sean. "And she is so far away. I feel like I abandoned her where I left her. To suffer through this pregnancy all by herself."

"Part of the meditative states I told you about is Reiki," Sean conveyed. "It is a high, kind of more advanced state of moving energy. One is actually able to transmit energies like wishes and hope to another no matter how far away. To hope is not to believe that you are already there. Serenity is a lot more proficient at it than me. If you like, I can ask her to wish some energy to Lynn from all of us. It may be a way to assist in finding out who both of you 'really are'."

XVIII

Marshall's mother was distraught by her son's unhappiness. Despite the inherent pride in her gifted psychic ability, she never foresaw such sudden turmoil in her son's marriage. Self-proclaimed psychics abhor elements of surprise. It rubs against their fabric of assuredness in things—and prompts them to behave in ways that make some folks think they are nuts.

Norma Monroe arrived at the split-level without the bother of any advanced warning.

"Marshall, come with me," Norma stood at the sliding deck door like a school marm who just caught a kid smoking. She neither looked at Lynn nor stepped foot in the house. "I will have you home in about four hours. Hopefully that will be enough time for a Sunday dinner to be on the table for you when you get back."

Lynn ignored the parting shot. Maybe I deserve this, she resolved. She looked forlorn as her husband scurried obediently out of the house to his mother.

As much as Marshall resembled a puppy dog when he left, his personality was completely transformed when he returned.

"She took me to some friends of hers," the husband reported. He began eating the serving of spaghetti and meatballs at his place setting in the dining room without taking off his jacket. No mention was made that it was the first time the sauce tasted different from store-bought. "They said they wanted to speak with me under hypnosis."

Lynn squirmed in her chair. If folks were evoking spirits, she sure was getting some odd messages of late.

"What happened?" she asked.

"My Spirit Guide came," Marshall illumined matter-of-factly as if it was commonplace. He paused to regard the glass panes in the frame of the dining room light, and chewed casually on a meatball. The spider's web that had become a permanent fixture between the inside bulbs was missing. The prospect of Lynn scrubbing the inside of the lights would normally have caused some kind of a compliment—but Marshall's thoughts were elsewhere.

"That is my mother's friends' specialty… to call out your Spirit Guide."

"What did she say?" Lynn leaned forward placing her elbows on the table.

"It is not a 'she' or a 'he'," Marshall stabbed another forkful at his plate. "My Spirit Guide is a wolf."

"A wolf?" Lynn puzzled. "I never heard of a Spirit Guide being an animal."

"Well, mine is," Marshall stuck a gob of the macaroni twisted on his fork into his mouth. A straggling string of pasta dangled on the edge of his lip. He sucked it into his mouth staring for the first time directly at his wife. His eyes were cold. They camouflaged any humor in something that would be ordinarily comical—like the stain of spaghetti sauce on the side of Marshall's mouth. "The wolf was not very satisfied with my behavior lately. From now on, I am going to turn over a new leaf."

XIX

The waves of morning sickness became more intense over each passing day. The cramps and persistent nausea caused Lynn to throw up anything she tried to eat. By the middle of the first week back to the office, the vomit bouts extended well into the work- day. She had to be in bed by three o'clock each afternoon. That meant leaving the office early. If not, she would undoubtedly pass out.

If "turning over a new leaf" was indeed Marshall's new resolution, then forfeiting his role as the caretaker was not part of it. Marshall had become a stalwart—cleaning up Lynn's spit up in the bedpan and spoon feeding her broth.

Lynn did not have to worry about Maggie. Marshall made sure his bride was left at peace. He commuted Maggie back and forth to daycare and would have her entertained, bathed and in bed every night without as much as a peep around Mommy.

Something strange happens when one is vulnerable—susceptible to the elements. The caretaker becomes invaluable—like an invisible crutch. The unspoken attention made Lynn remember exactly why she married this man. While the emotional scars of the previous two months kept Marshall buffered at arm's length—Lynn could sense one strong reality. Her family was functioning.

"Marshall, I cannot thank you enough for being such a sweetheart," Lynn decided to say. It had been three consecutive days of nursemaiding.

"Feel strong enough to talk?" Marshall surprised his wife with a deadpan tone.

"Sure," Lynn obliged. She propped the bed pillow behind her head before Marshall did. He pulled the corner chair to the side of the bed. His posture was erect—purposeful.

"Lynn, I have given this a lot of thought, and I am prepared to leave you," Marshall declared. "I have spoken with a lawyer and I have a pretty good idea of my community property rights in Minnesota and with Maggie."

Lynn took a hard swallow.

"Everybody I have consulted has advised the same thing," Marshall stated.

"For me to ask you one question. Your answer will be the basis for my final decision."

"What is it?" Lynn focused.

"Give me two reasons why you think I should stay with you," Marshall leaned forward in his chair. "Two… only two."

Lynn stared for a moment at the "V" formed by Marshall's pointed fingers. The answer flowed from her mouth without hesitation.

"Because I love you, Marshall," Lynn admitted. "Regardless of everything that has happened, the fact is I have never not loved you."

Marshall sat back in the chair to allow the words to sink in.

"That is one," Marshall informed. He folded his arms.

"And secondly," Lynn realized aloud. "I do not think I would ever be able to get over the regret of breaking up this family."

Marshall mellowed at the sight of a lonesome teardrop sloping down Lynn's high cheek.

"We can make this work," Marshall placed his hands on his lap. "You're gonna have to give me some time though, to get over everything that has happened. I've been having a hard time with this 'forgive and forget' thing. I do not think I will ever be able to forget."

"I know," Lynn sniffled.

"I was hoping you come up with two reasons," Marshall stared at his feet. He flicked his right toe as if there was a pebble that needed moving. "And I will stay with you Lynn… on one condition."

She knew what it was. It did not have to be said. The magnitude was even more dramatic once Marshall announced the name—"Peter Collins". It had not been uttered within the house for over two months.

"I want you to promise me—swear to me," Marshall bellowed. "That you will never—ever—have any contact with him whatsoever again."

Lynn lay paralyzed on the bed.

"No more postcards," Marshall stood up. "No more phone calls or cutesy emails… no silly Dot Games—nothing. Not so much as even an intermediary to keep in touch to see how you are doing."

Marshall paced the scale of the room.

"So help me Lynn," Marshall concluded. "If I hear that you have any future contact with Peter Collins I will leave you in the bat of an eye."

Lynn looked down towards the bed comforter. She wanted to wail.

"So? Do I have your promise?"

"There is one thing I have to do first," Lynn pleaded.

"What?"
"You have to let me say goodbye."

XX

Any of Peter's attempts at meditation seemed to go awry. Sean had suggested a variety of approaches to find common ground in finding an answer from within—kundalini yoga, chi, prana. Peter would get stuck on the terminology—asking Sean and Serenity for more detailed definitions on what these sciences were.

"Don't focus on defining things," they would say. "It limits its full potential."

Peter began to rise at four o'clock in the morning. He would slowly walk through the darkened woods behind his house. Each step was purposefully laid like a tiger creeping upon its prey—mindful to touch the ground softly without breaking debris. Sean asked Peter to pick his favorite tree in the area. The one, he recommended, that stood taller than most.

Identifying the right tree had been easy. A century old maple scaled an open field like a sentinel in a posting lookout for its clustered brethren. Peter made a habit of sitting down to get a full frontal view of the tree. His attention focused to the uppermost limbs. Breaking from the sturdy body of hunter green, a few new sprigs of life—leaflets more lime than green—fluttered in chaos at the very top. The slightest breath of a breeze made the leaflets flicker while the rest of its base remained without motion. It seemed to be a miracle in each passing day. Daring new attempts at growth and life—reaching to higher plateau—while staying anchored to its root.

Sean said to empty all thought and inhibition—to reflect on what was happening to the tree.

"See and realize what the tree is doing," Sean's words resounded. "In a couple of short hours, mankind will waken its weary head. They will zoom around without aim—running here, running there—seeking the riches they believe are gained by spinning within day to day life. And there—amidst that hectic pace, will be the top of the tree—reaching in celebration to the heavens. Standing in tribute to the benefit of mankind."

"But does mankind ever stop to take notice of what is happening around them?" Sean challenged. Most often we whiz right past those trees in our cars. We are totally oblivious. Unfortunately for most, they do not recognize the wonder around them until they are just about to see that ominous tunnel of white light. That is why four o'clock in the morning is such a special time for enlightenment. No one is around—just you, and the tree. As you begin to feel as one with the leaf most at struggle, spontaneously snap your focus to the pre-dawn sky just above it. That is when you will see the Supreme Being—'God', as we Irish Catholics monotheists like to say. You will feel your soul. And you will understand what those tiny leaves are exalting."

The O'Connell's guidance was frustrating. Peter acknowledged that expecting miracles at first attempts were foolish. It could take weeks of effort before any kind of answer could come.

"Nothing is happening for me," Peter lamented to his new spiritual mentor. "The uncertainty is just the same for Lynn. Neither one of us have any answers to guide our future."

Sean's response was to step up the effort to "get in touch". He mailed Peter a copy of his favorite meditation tape. It was a steady drone of falling rain with a random sound of sporadic faraway bells.

"Play this into a Walkman while you are at your tree," Sean suggested. "If you do not have any luck, then change your environs. Leave the tree, and find another place. A place you never frequent. Try a mountain, a hiking trail, or if you like, the ocean. Go to the beach. There are just as many opportunities within a sand dune. If you are up to it, come along to one of my expedition journeys. I can't guarantee answers within any given time frame, but you will be amazed at what some of our travelers experience at the most innocuous of times and place."

Peter ditched the tape idea after one half-hearted attempt. He fell back upon what sustained him for the first two scores of his earthen journey—the Holy Rosary.

It was Peter's parents who first acquainted him with the mystery of the Holy Rosary. It is a structured pattern of prayers to the Blessed Virgin Mary that recalls the passion for her Son. In a sequence of five sets, the petitioner recites the Lord's Prayer followed by ten Hail Mary's. A recitation of each step in the Lord's crucifixion and ultimate resurrection is recalled before each new set of prayers. Upon completion, one makes a petition to Mary—whatever request that so moves them.

During the Lenten season of Peter's childhood, the Collins family would gather each night after supper. They would kneel at different sofas and chairs scattered about the living room. Peter's father would be the lead petitioner, reciting the first half of each prayer. The rest of the family would unison the second half. The final petition would vary each night. As children, Peter and his siblings would look forward to hearing the plea of their father. It could be something generic like world peace. Or it could be as specific as expecting a good report card.

Peter's mother took pride in saying the Rosary using holy beads. She would knead the string to mark each set of numbered prayers. Peter preferred his father's finger method—counting the ten Hail Mary's off his right hand, and each introductory Our Father with his left.

After practically two weeks of early morning tree gazing, a bleary-eyed Peter petitioned his first Holy Rosary before falling asleep. No, there will be no lightning-crashing illuminations. I may not get any startling answers or energies, Peter reflected, but it does make me feel good.

"The most innocuous of time and place". Peter dreamt an awkward scenario following his first Rosary. He was driving a car—following behind Lynn and Marshall. They were returning him to the Duluth Airport. Marshall was intentionally forcing Lynn to apply her brakes so that Peter had to slow at their tailgate. Marshall would then lean over the console from the passenger seat. He would make Lynn kiss him—using her patented peck. Peter did not like it. Lynn and Marshall's car veered abruptly up a hill along a residential street bordering the airport. They came to Lynn Cloud's childhood home. Her adoptive parents were crying at the driveway. Their dog Lucky had dropped dead from old age. Its carcass lay on the pavement. Peter watched as Marshall got out of the car. He lifted the dead dog from the ground. He gathered a spade from the garage and began digging a grave in the back corner of the yard. The Cloud clan stood next to their beloved pet as the caretaker ably prepared the final place of rest. Peter noticed how everyone, including Lynn, wrapped their arms around each other's shoulders as Marshall completed the task of filling the hole.

"*Thank God for Marshall,*" Peter could hear Evelyn Cloud say.

Peter looked to the empty passenger seat at his side. The voice of his Spirit Guide returned. It was the first time he heard her since Best Western Edgewater.

"*What does one do with a dead dog?*"

XXI

It was an odd message—particularly from a dream. Peter did not comprehend the riddle.

How do you dispose of a dead dog?

But the premise seemed clear. Marshall was the caretaker. He was the glue to Lynn's family.

Peter's emotion took on a coat of desperation. He felt compelled to relay his intentions in a letter. The significance went far beyond what could be pronounced over the telephone. He assembled his thoughts and wrote a heartfelt note to Lynn.

> Lynn Dear—
>
> It is hard to imagine that next Thursday will mark exactly ninety days to the date since we last said goodbye at the airport.
>
> Do you remember your prediction of where we would be? Either never in touch again with each other, or together permanently—with virtually nothing likely in between?
>
> Who would have imagined at that time what could have evolved over these past three months? Never in a million years could we have envisioned a pregnancy, or the prospect of fertility tests to measure our uncertainty.
>
> There is no doubt that we have come to a crossroad. Not only in our relationship, but for the rest of our lives.
>
> Where do we go from here?
>
> Well… I have given this a lot of thought, and have drawn some pretty definite conclusions:
>
> I love you more than life itself.
>
> While I love my wife and children, I love you even more.
>
> I want you permanently in my life—no matter what the obstacle or consequence.

Whatever you choose, I love you yesterday, today, and a forever of tomorrows.

Your ninety-day prediction is ironic. I can feel the final sands slipping through the hourglass. Please consider this invitation for life—complete with a pillared house. I found myself yesterday scanning the internet for waterfront real estate in Duluth. Lynn, I found it. There is a blue house on Congdon Road that is meant for us.

Love,

Peter XO

Peter sealed the envelope and posted it that morning. It would be three long days through the snail mail he surmised before Lynn would receive the letter. How can I wait this long for an answer?

Peter went to his office and routinely fired up his laptop. By the time he returned with a cup of coffee, Lynn's email was visible on the screen.

"My parents' dog Lucky dropped dead in the driveway yesterday. Without elaborating, it is not the best of times in Minnesota. We have to talk. Please call me."

Peter erased the message on the screen. He de-powered the machine without bothering to walk through its shutdown process. The absence of the standard "XO" at the end of Lynn's email was noticeable, but not devastating.

What was devastating was the news of the dog. No, you do not have to elaborate Peter whispered to himself. I saw the whole thing. You are handcuffed in a web of familial commitment. You cannot, and will not, leave him. Peter called his secretary into the office.

"I need you to cover for a few days," Peter advised his business confidante. "I have got a few things on my plate that I need to take care of. You know how to reach me on the cell if anything worthwhile needs my attention—but take care of it, will you?"

The secretary dutifully nodded. She knew the routine. Appointments with Mr. Tee, or Mr. Green while rare, were normally easy to translate. Poker faced regardless of any situation, Peter's anxiety this time was clearly visible.

"Mr. Collins, is there anything I can do," the secretary frowned. She yearned to hear that Mr. Tee or Mr. Green was waiting at the club, but not this time. "You look so sad."

"Yes," Peter abruptly closed his Day-timer. "Keep this under your hat. You will be doing more than you know."

Peter had always been considered a workaholic by his rivals. His presence midweek at the country club would normally be business related. Showing up unexpectedly at the members' sweeps invoked numerous jokes.

"About time you enjoy yourself."

"Hey, Collins, you can only eat one steak at a time you know."

"Can't bring the money with you."

Peter arranged impromptu golf matches for the next three days. The configuration of retired men-folk, or active business people Peter heretofore just considered lazy by lolling around the golf course, did not seem to mind the sudden availability of a new found companion. In the whole scheme of things Peter figured, these folks would fiddle while Rome burned. Sure they are friendly enough, but in the end when the going gets tough, it is you and you alone who will be standing there.

Lynn received the letter after a mere two days. The content provoked her to cry at her desk.

Monica maintained close email contact with Lynn from Minneapolis. She agreed with Lynn's unconditional promise to Marshall to cease communication with Peter. Staying with Marshall might not be correct, but it was the right thing to do.

"Have you been able to get in touch with him?" Monica typed. She understood Lynn's frustration. It was like Peter had suddenly vanished from the face of the earth.

"I received a letter this morning," Lynn responded. "Peter wants me to be with him. What do I say to him? How do I say it to him? Such simple words on a sheet of paper… but affecting so many lives."

The night was fitful and sleepless. Lynn was exasperated with the inability to get in touch with Peter. She shouted an obscenity at Peter's secretary following the third day's unsuccessful plea for his whereabouts. Lynn waited until after five o'clock eastern standard time to make sure the automated after hours phone system would place her through directly to Peter's extension. She left the same identical message as the one on his cell phone.

"All right Collins, where the hell are you? You cannot send me a letter like this and then start avoiding me. We have to talk."

Peter was driving back from the country club when he heard the animated pleas.

Maybe she wants to tell me her answer is yes, Peter brainstormed. He checked the time on his watch. It was after six o'clock. Lynn would have left her office by now.

Peter detoured his route back to the agency office. He shoved the pile of pre-screened business mail to the far corner of his desk. His gut told him Lynn must have expressed her desires in an email.

His assumption was correct. Amid the dozen or so unread accumulated messages were two sequenced notes labeled with Lynn's web address.

"I received a letter this morning. Peter wants me to be with him. What do I say to him? How do I say it to him? Such simple words on a sheet of paper, but affecting so many lives."

Peter read the rhetorical message a second time. Poor kid, was Peter's initial reaction. How is she going to break the news to Marshall? Peter impudently opened the second message.

"I have been needing to speak with you so bad Peter, but you are not there. I am copying over the message I originally sent yesterday to Monica. I have had such a difficult time trying to come up with the words to say to you. The more I struggled, the more I realized what I said to Monica 'captures it right'. I have had to realize 'who I really am'. And I think the answer is clear. I cannot leave the people in my life. It goes against 'who I really am'."

"Who I really am" sent a shock through Peter's nervous system. Sean's terminology had never been mentioned to Lynn. Where did she get it? Could Serenity's Reiki have played a role?

The suspicion quickly evaporated. It was immaterial. What mattered was the first email message. Peter keyed a series of demands on the laptop. The original email appeared.

My God, Peter's jaw dropped. She is not asking how to tell Marshall. You egotistical arrogant snob, Peter scolded himself. She is talking about me!

XXII

Maggie Monroe wet her bed. The potty training relapsed. It was the first time in half a year since there had been such an episode. The toddler had become close-mouthed about the wet stain on the unprotected mattress.

The daughter refused to acknowledge the discovered puddle. For that matter, she declined to speak at all at the breakfast table. The silence was not noticeably obvious. No one spoke these days at the Monroe breakfast table.

"Magpie, how did that happen?" Lynn approached the subject on the way to the day-care center. "Did you drink too much juice and forget to go potty before bed?"

The little girl stared aimlessly out the rear side window of the GMC Suburban. She did not want to talk.

"Maggie sweetheart, aren't you going to speak to Mommy?"

Lynn had to physically pick up and carry Maggie into the day-care center. She drooped like a dead weight. The burden doubled Lynn's morning cramping.

"She is not quite herself today," Lynn excused as she greeted the center's staff. She set the girl at one of the playmate tables to camouflage the inertness. The staff had become expert in signaling an ailing toddler. Working moms had to take their own sick day if someone looked too peeked. Lynn scurried out of the building. "Please do not hesitate to call me at the office if she gets punky."

The follow up phone by mid-morning was not a surprise.

"Mrs. Monroe—Maggie has had a little accident."

"Accident," Lynn shuddered. "Is she okay?"

"Not that type of an accident," the aide excused. The tone was terse nonetheless. "Maggie did not tell us she needed to use the potty the way she is supposed to."

"I put an extra pair of underpants in her backpack this morning," Lynn offered. "I was worried she might wet herself."

"She did more than that," the aide criticized. "It was not just pee, but number two. She has completely soiled her clothes, Mrs. Monroe."

"Oh," Lynn was taken aback.

"We cannot tolerate this activity with our toddlers, Mrs. Monroe. Maggie is quite aware of the rules."

"Come now," Lynn objected to the apparent crisis. "Certainly a child has an accident from time to time."

"This was not an accident, Mrs. Monroe," the aide warned. "Maggie intentionally went to the bathroom in her pants. She sat in the corner of the room and refused to help out picking up after playtime. When we told her everyone has to help with pick up after playtime, she defiantly stared at me and pushed a bowel movement in her pants."

"I am sorry," Lynn wiped her hand across her brow.

"Mrs. Monroe, are there any problems at home?"

"Excuse me?" Lynn refocused on the unexpected question.

"Deviant behavior is often an adjunct to a deeper causation," the aide counseled. "Maggie has never exhibited this type of defiance. An issue with you and Mr. Monroe, perhaps?"

"Thank you very much for contacting me," Lynn absconded the violation of her privacy. A wave of nausea made her want to vomit. "I will be right over to take my daughter home."

The telephone rang again as Lynn was gathering her belongings.

"This is Lynn," she exhaled the canned response.

"Aah you looking for me?" the Boston accent refrained.

It was Peter. The call was expected, but then again, it was not.

"N-no," Lynn stuttered.

"No?" Peter tried to laugh. "I thought your messages said to call you?"

"No, I mean yes," Lynn bumbled. "I mean 'no'. Not right now, Peter. It is not supposed to be like this. I cannot talk with you right now."

"What's the matter?" Peter hesitated.

"I am really busy," Lynn skirted. "I cannot speak with you here in the office. Let me call you later in the day. Are you going to be in?"

"I was going to go to the gym during my lunch hour," Peter postulated. "I am going to be around all afternoon after that."

"Good." Lynn surmised. "Go to the gym. I will call you when you get back."

It was a half-hearted workout—probably because Lynn had abruptly hung up the phone without so much as saying "goodbye". The unease was confirmed by the voice mail message greeting his return to the office.

"I am at home now." The voice was Lynn's. Peter had never heard her so downtrodden. "Can you please call me here? I will be waiting."

Peter jotted down the number to Lynn's house. The recitation of the home exchange beat like a death knell. Peter had never been asked to call Lynn at her home before.

Peter closed the door to his office. He slowly punched the eleven-digit command.

"Hello?" the voice croaked.

"Lynn?" Peter stumbled. "Is that you?"

"Yes."

"It does not sound like you," Peter attempted to bring some levity to the situation. "You sound different at your house."

"Well, it is me," Lynn's voice returned.

"You left the office early," Peter was content to state the obvious.

"Maggie was not feeling well today," Lynn informed. "I am not feeling well either. I decided we could both use the afternoon off."

"Maggie is with you now?"

"She's sleeping," Lynn tried to whisper. It came out more cracked than intended. "We took a drive so she would nod off in the back of the truck. We went up to Congdon Road."

"Congdon Road?" Peter's eyes widened.

"Yeah," Lynn's smile transmitted over the fifteen hundred miles of phone line. "I wanted to see our blue pillared house."

"Did you find it?"

"It is everything I ever dreamed," Lynn admitted. "I had to see it just once to remember you by."

Peter had to force a breath at the note of finality.

"You made a promise to him, didn't you?" Peter found his whisper was also cracking.

"Yes," Lynn tried to contain. Her eyes began to sparkle green. "I can never talk to you again. He will leave me if I do."

Peter could not respond. His head fell to his knees.

"I have to give this marriage another try," Lynn resolved. "And that means calling it quits with you."

"Marshall must be happy with your decision," Peter stated blankly.

"Not to your standards," Lynn sniffled. "I do not think he will ever be to your standards."

"It is not fair," Peter began to weep. "We belong together—with our little son."

"Stop it!" Lynn scolded. "I cannot think that anymore. I told you it is a girl."

"I feel we are being punished by God," Peter cursed. "I do not know what we may have done in a previous lifetime. I think back to everything bad I have ever done in this life. I honestly do not know why God is doing this to us."

"Please, Peter," Lynn breathed. "Let us be thankful for what we did have. It may have only been for a short time in human terms, but no one can ever take these memories away from us. My love for you will never fade. I cherish the day we will be together again—even though it may not be in this realm."

"I do not think I can bear not having you in my life," Peter moaned. "How will I know how you are?"

"I will be here," Lynn assured. "Thinking good thoughts to you all of the time."

"What about the baby?" Peter grumbled. "How will I even know when you have the baby?"

"I spoke with Monica," Lynn revealed. "She agreed that she will get some kind of word to you. I asked her to promise me to contact you if anything should ever happen."

"Great," Peter sulked.

"I want you to do the same thing for me," Lynn requested. "Could you talk to someone like Kathleen Leonard? Give her my name and phone number? I will weather this so much better if I know she will contact me if anything ever happened to you."

"I will," Peter conceded. He could feel the dignity of life sweeping from his body.

"Wait for me on the other side," Lynn whispered.

"Why do you always assume I am going ahead of you?"

"Because you are my soul-mate," Lynn squeezed the tissue ball against her nose. "I know you will make sure our house has pillars when we get there."

"I love you, Lynn," Peter sobbed.

"I love you, too."

The telephone line disconnected. A wail erupted from Maggie's room as Lynn felt the baby boy within.

Printed in the United States
18635LVS00003B/34-75